THE EMERALD DRESS

THE EMERALD DRESS

VIVIENNE KEARNS

POOLBEG

This book is the work of fiction. References to real people, events, establishments, organisations, or locales are intended only to provide a sense of authencity, and are used fictitiously. All other characters, and all incidents and dialogue, are drawn from the author's imagination and are not to be construed as real.

Published 2019
by Poolbeg Press Ltd.
123 Grange Hill, Baldoyle,
Dublin 13, Ireland
Email: poolbeg@poolbeg.com

A catalogue record for this book is available from the British Library.

ISBN 978178199-757-4

Printed and bound by ScandBook, Sweden.

www.poolbeg.com

About the Author

Vivienne Kearns lives in Dublin. She holds a BA (Hons) in English and Greek & Roman Civilisation from University College Dublin, Ireland. Vivienne's poetry and prose have been published in several anthologies, including the *Fish Anthology 2016*. This is her first novel.

Acknowledgements

A very special thank you to my publisher Paula Campbell for believing in my work, and to Poolbeg Press for publishing this story. I'd also like to thank my editor Gaye Shortland for her patience, support and advice throughout the editorial process. Thanks, Gaye – you are an inspiration. Thanks also to David Prendergast for the beautiful book cover and to the rest of the team at Poolbeg Press for their support.

I'd like to express my sincere thanks to my mother and first reader Monica Treacher Kearns for her endless support and encouragement over the years, and to all of my family and friends who have encouraged my work and read excerpts for me too.

I came across the idea for this story when visiting Rathfarnham Castle several years ago and decided to set the novel in 18th century Dublin after reading Professor Norma Clarke's book *Queen of the Wits: A Life of Laetitia Pilkington*. Laetitia's father was a physician. Laetitia was also a memoirist in Jonathan Swift's circle and Professor Clarke's book brought 18th century Dublin to life for me. After attending a historical-novel writing course given by Tracy Chevalier and Louise Doughty, I was ready to write this story set in Dublin 300 years ago.

I could not have done so without the resources at the National Library of Ireland, Kildare Street, Dublin, and the Dublin City Library & Archives at Pearse Street, Dublin. I'd also like to thank Dr. Séamus Ó Maitiú for his encouragement and advice on the methodology of researching local history in Dublin.

I based the fictional Boden Castle on the architecture of Rathfarnham Castle, Dublin. The Duke and Duchess of Alden have been loosely based on the characters of the Duke and Duchess of Wharton who owned Rathfarnham Castle in 1719.

Finally, just a note to say that the minor role that Jonathan Swift plays in this novel is entirely fictional. Swift's dialogue and actions have been entirely fabricated and all other characters in this novel are fictitious, as is the story. I hope you enjoy it.

For my mother,
Monica Treacher Kearns

Lucy Young hung up the phone.
The Alden diary had been found in Boston.
Its pages were three hundred years old.
She wondered what secrets it might hold.

Los Angeles, Present Day

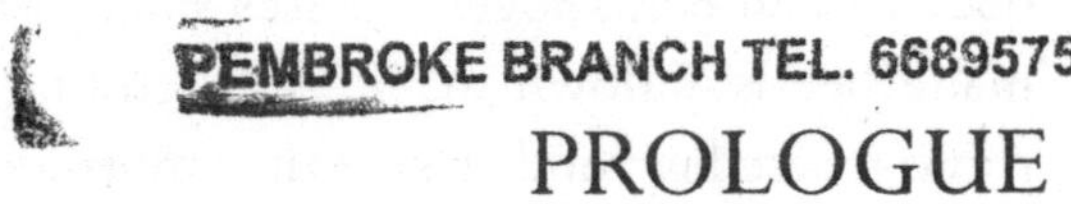

PROLOGUE

When you go to sleep, do you wonder where the darkness takes you? Do you go to a place where worlds collide and only you can see across their thresholds? When I sleep, a door opens in the darkness to reveal her. She is small and sits in the corner of a secret room. Her dress is brocaded with the dust of gold and silver threads, worn and scarce in the cloth. Emeralds hang from her ears. She stares with hollow eyes, her fate marked on lifeless features still. I shut the door on her memory and turn the key in its lock for the last time.

CHAPTER 1

Dublin, 1719

Abigail Harton looked out of the window before dawn and watched her father make his way down the darkened street. She sat in candlelight at her dressing table and opened her sewing box. Inside, threads of various colours were wrapped around ivory. Underneath them lay a wooden needle-case, a white-silk pin cushion, a set of scissors and a small piece of blue poplin embroidered with threads of silver. She touched the birds on the fabric. It was this design that she hoped to sell, though she would first need to create a pattern for the weaver. She brought the poplin to her writing desk and took a sheet of paper from the drawer. As she started to sketch the pattern, she heard movement below. Her mother was awake. She would try to make her eat some breakfast before she started working.

Taking the candle from her desk, she left the room, closing the door behind her. Though she was small, the staircase creaked as she made her way down to the first landing, to her young brother's room where her mother kept the embroidery frame.

Margaret Harton was already there, working by the half-light, stitching a floral pattern onto yellow silk. There were deep circles under her eyes. She had lost weight and her hair had turned grey over the last few months. It had once been auburn like Abigail's own.

'I've almost finished,' Margaret said, moving the yellow stomacher closer to the light of her candle. She examined the piece of cloth that would form the triangular front of a woman's dress. Her work was acceptable. 'How much more do you have to do on the waistcoat panels?'

'Another four hours at least, Mama.' Abigail walked to the bed where her brother Benjamin lay sleeping and felt his forehead with the back of her hand. 'He doesn't have a fever. That's a good sign.'

Margaret looked at her son's face. She feared he slept too much. The paleness of his skin worried her and he hadn't the energy to lift his head from the pillows. The sickness had been with him for three months. But she couldn't think about that any longer.

'Go down and eat while you can, Abigail.'

'Have you had any breakfast, Mama?'

'Not yet.'

'You must eat something.'

'Then bring something up to me. I will continue here a while longer.'

'What did Father say of Benjamin?'

'He says he does much better and will be back to himself in a few weeks. Go on now and tell Brigid to come up to light the fire. I want this room warmed before he wakes.'

Abigail nodded. Taking her candle, she went out onto the landing and down the stairs. Winter was setting in and the house was cold.

She would need to wear her housecoat over her dress to stay warm while she worked.

In the kitchen, sixteen-year-old Brigid was bending over the fireplace, stirring porridge in a pot directly over the flame. Her fair hair had slipped from its ties – she pinned it back as Abigail entered the room.

'Good morning, miss,' she said, her eyes darkened by sleep. 'It's just ready. Will you have some?'

'I'll get it myself, Brigid. Mama asks that you light the fire in Benjamin's room.'

'Yes, miss.' Brigid handed the ladle to Abigail and hesitated before continuing. 'The butcher was asking again about settling the bill. I don't think it'll be long before the others ask too.'

'Don't worry. Everything will soon be as it was before.' Abigail avoided the maid's stare and stirred the oats in the pot.

'Of course.' Brigid hoped that Miss Abigail was right, though she didn't think the chandler would give them any more credit, or the fishmonger for that matter.

When the girl left the room, Abigail scooped a small portion of porridge into a bowl. She poured herself a cup of ale and tried to eat some breakfast, hoping that her father would soon see sense, that somehow in another week or two all would be well. If only Benjamin would get better, it would lift everyone's spirits. She was thankful that they had the embroidery work from Miss Gavin. Without it, she didn't know what would have become of them.

She barely touched her food. Instead she made an ale and tartar brew for Benjamin and took a bowl of porridge up to her mother. The fire was already lighting there, and her brother turned over in his sleep as the burning wood crackled.

Margaret put down her work, grateful for the meal.

'I'll be finished here soon and will help you.'

'Mama, take some rest. I'm sure to have the last waistcoat panel finished by two o'clock and I'll be able to deliver the pieces and return before dark.'

'If you're sure ...'

'I am. You should go back to bed when you're done.'

Margaret didn't know what she would do without such a daughter as Abigail. She just prayed that her husband would return to paying clients soon so that they could sleep soundly in their beds again. Her eyes were not what they used to be and her days of taking in embroidery work were coming to an end.

The morning light seeped through the bedroom window and Benjamin's skin took on a paler hue. Margaret turned away and concentrated on finishing the stomacher. Only then would she rest.

Outside Abigail passed Brigid coming down the stairs.

'I've lit the fire in your room too, miss. There's still plenty of firewood, thank God.'

'Thank you, Brigid.'

Before working on the waistcoat panel, she finished the sketch of her design and made rudimentary calculations. These sample instructions would show a weaver that she had the skill to create a full damask design to enable him to weave her bird pattern directly into the cloth at the loom. She had suggested to Miss Gavin that a dress made from this cloth could then be further embellished by embroidering metal threads onto the stomacher. She checked her calculations again. By the time she had finished, there was enough light to embroider the waistcoat panel.

Abigail prepared the gold thread as her grandfather had taught her to do. She went to the frame by the window and started to work. Not to waste the metal, she laid it carefully on the surface of the cloth and used a couching stitch to secure the golden vines into place. It was best to work slowly to ensure accuracy.

The morning passed quickly. At noon Brigid brought bread and cheese and a little ale to her room. Abigail ate the meal and estimated that it would take another two hours to finish the waistcoat. When she was finally done, no-one would have known that a master had not completed it. Outside the sky had darkened.

She would need to hurry.

She changed into her blue poplin dress, then took the damask-design instructions and went downstairs to collect the yellow stomacher from her mother. She found her sleeping soundly in the chair by her son's bed. Abigail took the piece and quietly left the room. Downstairs, in the old housekeeper's room, she wrapped the embroidered cloths in linen for protection and put them in a basket with her damask design.

The clock chimed in the hall. It was three o'clock, later than she had thought. There would be just enough light to walk to Miss Gavin's house and get back again before darkness fell.

In the hall, she heard footsteps on the stairs.

'Have you returned already, Abigail?'

'No, I am only just leaving, Mama.' Abigail put her cloak on and pulled the hood over her head.

'I'll go instead. It is too late for you to go.'

'I can get back before Father returns.'

Her mother nodded. She opened the hall door and looked outside.

'Keep warm and be careful, daughter. I don't like the look of that sky. Ask Miss Gavin to hail a public cab to bring you home if it gets too late.'

'A little rain won't hurt me.' Abigail kissed her mother on the cheek and left.

Margaret watched anxiously from the door until her daughter turned the corner of Pluncot Street, then locked the door behind her before going back upstairs to watch over her son.

When Abigail walked onto Francis Street, she crossed the road. There were beggars everywhere, some with badges permitting them to ask for alms, but many did not have a badge. It seemed that almost all of the city's people were covered in rags. At least her family had a roof over their heads. If only her father would start working for money again so that they could be secure. She gripped her basket tightly as a group of drunken men walked past and was relieved that they did not pay her much heed. Walking down Engine Alley, she reached Meath Street where she passed a group of people shouting over a cockfight.

Finally, she reached the Gavins' house in Coles Alley. It was still fairly bright but the house already had its shutters up. She was sure today was what they had agreed. She would not go back without trying to deliver the pieces.

She knocked hard on the door. When it opened, Abigail came face to face with the weaver, Hugh Gavin, the man who might buy her design. He was a little older than her and broad-shouldered from his work on the loom. His dark hair was unkempt and for the first time she noticed that his eyes seemed almost black in the fading light.

'I've come to see your sister, Mr. Gavin,' she said and pointed into the basket she had held tightly all the way from home. 'I have pieces to deliver today.'

He moved away from the door to let her pass.

'Come in, Miss Harton.'

Hugh Gavin had seen the girl on several occasions since coming to live with his sister. She was earnest and highly skilled. It was curious – a doctor's daughter working when she should have been more concerned with getting herself wed. It wasn't his business though. The girl walked ahead of him into the kitchen. Seemingly she could design cloth too.

He pulled a chair out at the kitchen table.

'Sit down, Miss Harton. I'll call my sister for you.'

Abigail nodded and looked at her hands. There were scratches on her palms from the basket wicker.

Hugh Gavin went to a door at the other side of the kitchen and called his sister. When she came out from her workshop, he went to sit by the fire.

Miss Mary Gavin was almost as tall as her brother. Her black hair was scraped back from her face and wound into a tight knot at the nape of her neck. Where her brother's eyes were black, Mary's were ice-cold blue. At thirty-two years of age, the severity of her appearance and demeanour made her seem much older.

She sat down at the table and gestured to Abigail to do the same.

'Good afternoon, Miss Harton. I am glad you have come.'

'The work took longer than we thought.'

'You're here now, that's what matters. I hope your little brother is getting better?'

'My father is hopeful he will recover soon.'

'Good, good. Well, let me see the pieces then.'

Abigail took the stomacher and waistcoat panels out and put them on the table, opening the linen cover so that her employer could examine the work.

Mary Gavin picked up the pieces one by one and examined them closely. The waistcoat panels were finished with vines of gold and silver thread on plain white silk. There would be no complaints from her customer when he returned from England and she would get a good price for it when it was stitched together. The stomacher was adequately done. It would do.

'Who stitched the stomacher?'

'The work is good, Miss Gavin. I don't think it can be faulted.'

'No need to get upset, Miss Harton. The waistcoat is of a much higher standard, that is all. It was just a question.'

'I'm sorry.' Abigail chided herself. She couldn't afford to annoy her employer who was currently her family's only source of reliable income. 'The waistcoat is my work and the stomacher my mother's. I thank you for the compliment.'

Mary Gavin noticed the girl's embroidered bluebird on her dress. 'Did you bring the pattern you talked about?'

'It's just an initial sketch.' Abigail took the damask design out of the basket.

Hugh Gavin rose from his chair. He could see the embroidered version of the bluebirds on her dress, but he needed to see if she had the skill to translate her design into a pattern that he could interpret to thread the loom and weave the cloth.

'It is not a copy?' Mary asked.

'No, it's my own design.'

Mary handed her brother the paper showing two bluebirds perched on tangled vines in an original layout.

'It is very good,' he said and glanced at Abigail. 'We may have a commission for a cloth such as this. The fabric needs to be ready soon so that my sister can make a dress for the December ball at Boden Castle, held by the Duke of Alden. How quickly can you prepare a detailed design?'

Abigail nodded. 'I can finish a full design in a couple of days. If you give me the payment for the pieces now, I'll be on my way and can start this evening.'

'That is good news,' he said.

'Wait there,' Mary said.

She stood up and smoothed out the creases in her dress. Then she went into the back room. When she came out again, she handed Abigail the amount they had agreed on.

'Tell your mother there is more work if she needs it.'

'Thank you. I will ask her.'

'Well then, we'll expect to see you with the design in two days.'

'It will be done by then.'

'I will walk back with you,' Hugh said.

'I am grateful, but there is no need. I can make my own way home.' Abigail stood up.

'No, Miss Harton,' Mary said. 'It is not safe to go back alone. It grows dark and I insist that you are accompanied. What would your mother think of us?'

'I'll walk with you to the corner of Pluncot Street.' Hugh was already putting on his cloak. Abigail didn't want to waste money on a public cab as she had been instructed to do, so she waited for him by the door.

'My mother and I are obliged.'

Abigail stepped into the lane, annoyed that she hadn't got away on her own. She should have taken a cab. If anyone saw her walking alone with Mr. Gavin, she didn't know what would be said of her. She hoped to marry to help her parents and would need to marry well. She couldn't afford to ruin her reputation before she had a chance to meet a potential suitor. It was easier for Miss Gavin who was independent with a business of her own and a brother to protect her. Benjamin was little still. Her only chance for a secure life was to marry into one.

'It's a cold evening,' he said after they had been walking in silence for several minutes.

'Yes, it is.' Abigail walked faster. If she could stay ahead of him by several steps, it might look as if they weren't together.

He caught up to walk beside her. 'Your mind is elsewhere, I think.'

'You should go back. I will be all right from here. It's starting to rain again, and I do not wish you to catch cold on my account.'

'And risk my sister's wrath?' He laughed. 'Besides, she is right – it isn't safe.'

At that moment a beggar grabbed at Abigail's skirts and Mr. Gavin pulled her away before releasing her. Abigail looked around – she recognised no-one she knew and was relieved.

'I can take care of myself, sir.'

'I am sorry,' he said, genuinely remorseful for having embarrassed her. He tried to think of something else to say but couldn't find a suitable topic. Miss Harton had managed to gain on him again. For a small person, she certainly showed great strength.

He caught up with her again. They walked in silence until they reached Francis Street. It was raining more heavily now.

'This weather reminds me of being at sea,' he said, trying to catch her attention. 'I'm glad I do not have to sail this winter.'

Abigail looked at him, curious despite herself. 'Have you travelled far?'

'I have been to Paris and London.'

'What is it like in London?' Her father had talked of his visits there and she longed to see it for herself.

'I remember as a boy being scared that if I lost my master in the streets I would never find my way home again.'

'And the clothes, were they very beautiful?' she asked.

'Yes, though clothes are beautiful here too. Your design is as good as any I've seen, and I've been weaving silk since I was a boy.'

Abigail didn't know what to say.

'I'd like to go to London myself one day,' she said then.

'Maybe you will,' he said.

'Maybe.'

If only she could travel. To see everything and do anything that she wanted. She looked up at the man walking beside her. She wanted to ask him more.

She worried again as they got closer to her home that if anyone saw her walking with a stranger, they would be sure to tell her father. They walked in silence until they reached the corner of Pluncot Street where she lived.

'There's no need for you to come any farther – my house is just there,' Abigail said and walked away before he had a chance to answer. She was aware he was watching her and ashamed that she had not been more grateful.

When she reached her front door, Brigid opened it. They had no houseboy and the housekeeper had given her notice months ago. Abigail gave the maid her cloak and went upstairs to find her mother, who was sitting alone in the drawing room.

'Did Miss Gavin pay you?' Margaret asked immediately.

'Yes, here it is.' Abigail handed over the coins. 'She says there is more work for us if we want it. They want to buy my design, Mama. Her brother will weave the damask cloth. My design must be ready in two days' time so that she can make a dress for the Boden Ball in December.'

'Your grandfather taught you well.' Margaret sat back down in her chair, relieved. 'I hope you took a cab to get home?'

'I wanted to save the money. Mr. Gavin walked me home instead.'

Margaret touched her daughter's hands. 'I'm sorry to put you through this, Abigail.'

'It's no matter. It won't be for much longer. How is Benjamin?'

'He is still asleep.'

'I pray his strength will return soon.'

'We shall see ... your father is hopeful. You are a good girl, Abigail. I'll help you with the pattern tomorrow if I can.'

'There is no need.'

'You probably don't want my help anyway.'

'I like the work, Mama.'

'It would hurt your father to think we are doing this behind his back. I'm sure things will change for the better soon with him.'

'I hope so.'

'He is distracted by the new hospital, that is all. But he cannot devote himself to it forever. He realises that, I am sure of it. He is a good man, Abigail.'

'It has been almost a year, Mama, and the embroidery work will not save us for much longer.'

Margaret touched her daughter's face. 'The household payments can wait.' Her wedding ring caught in Abigail's hair and she freed it gently.

'What if Father waits too long?'

'I won't let him. We need to let your father pursue this venture for a little while longer. Let us hope another physician will volunteer and he can return to private practice. Now that we have this payment from the Gavins, we can give him at least until the end of the month.'

'Very well, Mama. I hope you are right.'

'Enough about that now. We go to the theatre tomorrow evening. Don't worry, Sarah and Henry have offered to pay – and I've invited them to join us for supper afterwards.'

Margaret took a tiny cloth rose from her sewing box and placed it in Abigail's hair.

Although her mother had mentioned the possibility of another physician's interest in the hospital before, Abigail wasn't sure whether to believe one existed who would work for nothing.

CHAPTER 2

Abigail was drawing out the full damask pattern on grid paper. She had already made a start on the detailed instructions for the weaver. She went to her bookshelf to look at the illustration of the bluebirds in the book she had taken inspiration from. As she took it down, she was startled when her mother entered the room.

'Abigail, why aren't you dressed yet?'

'I wanted to look at the illustrations more closely.'

'Put the book away for today. I need to dress your hair for this evening.'

'What about Benjamin? Shouldn't someone stay with him?'

'He is a little better. Brigid will sit with him tonight.'

Abigail held the book in her hands. 'I need to copy the birds out again. The full pattern might take me longer than I first thought.'

She searched for the page with the drawing of a princess singing to a bluebird entangled in thorns by a castle window.

Her mother sat down. 'I never thought it would come to this.'

'The Gavins will pay a fair price.'

'Pattern-making is man's work. If your father finds out …'

'What does it matter if he does? We need the income. If I continue with the pattern tonight, I can finish it by tomorrow.'

'Abigail, leave it.'

'Please let me stay at home, Mama.'

'One day will not change Miss Gavin's mind. She will wait, believe me. Now you must get ready.'

'All right – but let me first say goodnight to Benjamin.'

'Very well,' said her mother as she withdrew.

Abigail took the book of fairy tales and went to her brother's room.

'Abigail, is that you?' Benjamin opened his eyes.

'Yes,' she whispered. 'Go back to sleep now.'

'It's not yet dark,' he said as she drew the curtains across.

'You need to rest as much as you can to get better.'

'It makes no difference. I fear I will never be better.'

'Rest will make a difference.' She tucked him inside the covers and sat beside him. 'Brigid will sit with you later.'

'Brigid talks only of cooking mutton.'

Abigail laughed. 'Well, then, I will read to you, but only for a few minutes. Mama says she must dress my hair for the theatre.'

Benjamin turned on his side towards her as she opened the book.

'I wish I could go to the theatre too.'

'You will go when you are better. Where did we finish yesterday?'

'After the Prince started his quest, and he rode into the forest.'

'Ah yes, here it is … Are you ready?'

'Yes.'

'In the dark forest, the Prince looked up and saw lightning flash above him. The rain fell down heavily and he could barely see more than a few feet ahead as nightfall descended. He and his men tried to calm their horses, but the animals did not want to obey. Instead they took their riders into a clearing as if possessed by magic. The Prince's horse reared and, in an

instant, he was on the ground, clutching at his father's sword as if it could help him. Suddenly, a Sorceress appeared, hovering above them, and though it was dark she was illuminated in the sky. The wind howled around her as she floated above them. The Prince saw that her robes were of purple and that she wore a crown of gold. He recognised her garments were from the royal house of his father's enemy. Though she was beautiful, her face was malign as she laughed down at them. Neither the men nor their animals could move as she had put them all in a trance. There was nothing they could do only watch as she drew another lightning bolt from the sky and threw it directly into the Prince's heart, killing him in an instant.'

Benjamin tried to sit up in the bed.

'I still can't believe that she killed him.'

'Rest now. I will read the rest to you tomorrow.'

'Please don't leave.'

'I must, or Mama will never speak to me again.'

Abigail kissed her brother goodnight and got up to go.

'What happens when we die, Abigail?'

'Benjamin, don't ask such a question.' She opened the door.

'Will God keep me in purgatory, do you think?' he asked.

'Hush now. You are not going to die. And stop listening to Brigid.'

'I don't want to be on my own when I die, Abigail.'

'You won't be on your own. You will see Grandfather but that won't be until you are very old. Don't cry now.' She walked back to tuck her brother in again.

'You promise to read the rest of the story tomorrow?'

'I promise to read it until the very end, even though you've heard it many times before.'

'I wish it had a better ending.'

'Maybe when you are better, we will write another ending together.'

'Could you draw the pictures?'

'Of course. And then you can read it to Father and Mama when we are finished.'

'I would like that,' he said and lay back. 'But please read me another little bit.'

'All right – but just a little.'

Abigail continued to read the story without further interruption until all of the Prince's men had been killed by the Sorceress. When she saw that her brother's eyes were closing, she kissed his forehead gently and closed the book. By the time she left the room, Benjamin was asleep.

In her bedroom, she left the book on her dresser. She put on the brocaded dress that Brigid had laid out on the bed. When she was ready, she went downstairs again, this time to her mother's bedroom.

Her parents' room was at the front of the house, beside Benjamin's room. The light was starting to fade, and her mother lit two candles on either side of her dressing table. Then she helped her daughter fasten the last cords of her dress.

'You may catch the eye of a rich gentleman tonight,' she said. 'Come, sit by the looking glass.'

Abigail obeyed and her mother started to brush out her hair.

'It's time you had a husband,' Margaret said.

'But what would you do if I was gone?'

'I would rejoice in the knowledge that you were settled in life.'

'Mama, I won't marry until you and Benjamin are safe.'

'We are safe already.'

Abigail looked at her reflection in the glass and hoped that she would not be introduced to any of the gentlemen her mother was inclined to favour. Her thoughts went back to Mr. Gavin before she dismissed him from her mind. He was not suitable and probably had a woman of his own.

'What are you thinking?' her mother asked.

'Just planning the colours of the design.'

'You are such a strange one, daughter. Though I am sure you will marry well despite it.'

'I am too ordinary for that, Mama.'

'You are pretty enough and have a sensible head. That is a good combination in a wife. A clever man will see it. Just make sure he has the funds to support you.'

'You make it sound like an animal market.'

'It is, daughter,' Margaret said with a laugh.

'How can you think of getting me a husband when Father is not himself?'

'You are not getting any younger.'

'I am twenty years old. I have another year or two yet.'

'I was seventeen when I married – you are becoming an old maid. Besides, the younger you marry, the easier it is to get used to the ways of a husband.'

Margaret concentrated on dressing her daughter's hair into the current high fashion, while Abigail looked at her reflection and wondered what would become of them all.

There was a knock at the door and Brigid came in.

'The doctor is home. He's with Benjamin.'

Margaret put the hairbrush down and Abigail followed her to Benjamin's room.

Inside, Dr. John Harton was sitting by his son's bed, listening to his breathing as he slept.

Abigail noticed how much older her father looked. His grey hair had thinned considerably, and his clothes seemed to hang on his small frame as he leaned over his son.

'How is he?' Margaret asked as Abigail went to her father's side.

'His breathing seems a little easier than earlier. Has he eaten anything today?'

'He took some pottage at noon,' Brigid said.

'That is something at least.'

'Stay here, husband. Brigid will fetch you something to eat.'

'I'm not hungry, my dear. And I must get back to the hospital.' He moved to get up.

'Sarah and Henry are taking us to the theatre. Why must you work tonight?' His wife pressed him back into the chair. 'Surely you deserve to rest for one evening?'

John Harton closed his eyes for several seconds.

'All right,' he said. 'I will go. Just let me sit with Benjamin for a little while first.'

'I am glad,' Margaret replied and led her daughter out onto the landing. 'Abigail, have Brigid finish your hair and be cheerful tonight. Let us not mention the household bills this evening.'

'Yes, Mama.'

Abigail walked up the next flight of stairs to her room. Why did her father want to spend more time with patients who could not pay him than he did with Benjamin? She shut her bedroom door tight and finished her own hair, all the while wondering why her mother couldn't see that their situation was dire? They might have to sell the house and then where would they be? Her sister Sarah and brother-in-law Henry lived in tiny lodgings and they could not move in with them if all went awry. It was impossible.

And why wasn't Benjamin getting better? There was no fever, just weariness. There had to be a way to make him better. Perhaps her mother was right. Perhaps she should find herself a rich husband. At least then she would be in a better position to help her family.

CHAPTER 3

Dr. Harton hired a public cab to take them to Smock Alley. He felt a little easier in himself as he handed his wife and daughter into the small carriage. The Duke of Alden's secretary had not written to him yet, but he was sure that the annuity for the hospital would come through. He had attended the difficult birth of Alden's son at Ashdale House in England earlier in the year and the Duke had been grateful to him for saving the lives of his wife and son. Alden had promised to visit him at his hospital when he was next in Dublin to agree the terms of the annuity. He was sure Alden would not renege on his promise and, when he heard the Duke was back in town, he had sent him an invitation to visit the hospital.

When he got the funds, he would hire another physician at the hospital and spend more time with his family. He sat opposite his wife in the cab. She was as beautiful to him as when he had first met her in Spittlefields in London, the daughter of a French silk designer. This evening he saw worry on her face. Despite his skill as a doctor, all he could do was pray and hope that he was wrong about his son's condition. He couldn't bear to tell his wife yet. It was better that they carry on for as long as they could. What would be, would be.

The jostling of the cab's wheels on cobblestones lulled him to sleep. It had been many hours since he'd been able to close his eyes and he let sleep wash over him as they made their way past Castle Street towards Dame Street.

Abigail woke her father when the cab stopped. Smock Alley was bustling. The theatre had all the newest plays and operas. Torches lit the lane.

John Harton stepped out first and helped his wife and daughter down from the cab.

They were greeted by Abigail's sister Sarah and her husband Henry Wilson. Sarah was two years older than Abigail. She wore a deep-blue dress that matched the colour of her eyes and her black hair had been styled in the latest fashion. Henry was only a few inches taller than his wife. His brown hair was tied back, and his grey eyes were full of admiration as he looked at Sarah.

'Abigail, you look very well,' Sarah said, happy that her sister was out in society. She wished Abigail as much happiness as she herself had found. Henry's law practice was becoming more successful by the month and he was soon to hire an apprentice. And she had news to tell her mother that evening. However, it could wait until supper.

'As do you, sister,' Abigail said. She missed Sarah who been married for almost two years.

'I have not heard of this playwright before,' Henry said.

They looked around and saw a middle-aged man in long grey wig stealing up to the boxes. He wore the clothes of a churchman.

'Is that the Dean?' Margaret asked. She did not want to believe that Jonathan Swift would attend a lowly play about highwaymen and thieves.

'It is he,' Henry said. 'They say he is behind most of the wit in Dublin. He may even have written the play himself.'

Margaret admonished Henry for the comment.

Abigail looked around at the crowd and noticed two young men walking towards them.

'Dr. Harton, I am delighted to see you here this evening,' one of them said.

'It is good to see you too, Dr. Monroe. Allow me to introduce you to my wife and daughter Abigail. This is Dr. William Monroe, who was a student of mine at the College.'

Dr. Monroe proceeded to introduce his friend, Mr. Theodore Palmer.

Abigail looked down to avoid Dr. Monroe's stare. His hair was white-blond and his eyes were of such a clear blue it was as if he could see into her soul. He was not as tall as his dark-haired friend Mr. Palmer, who looked down on them all in the most condescending manner.

'It is lovely to meet you, Miss Harton,' Dr. Monroe said.

Mr. Palmer merely bowed his head towards her.

'And you, sir,' Abigail said, curtseying. She wondered if her mother had set up the meeting.

'We are both up from Cork,' Dr. Monroe said. 'Palmer thought it would be diverting to attend the theatre. Normally I wouldn't have the time. However, he insisted.'

The play was about to start. The seats of the two young men were nearer to the back of the theatre, so the group parted.

Abigail and her family settled themselves in the fifth row from the narrow stage. The boxes above creaked with the weight of the patrons. Abigail looked upwards to see if she could make out Dean Swift above. She could not see him.

The play started and her attention was drawn to the adventurous highwayman who outrageously flirted with the actresses on stage, dressed in nothing except their drawers and stays. Abigail looked at her father who was laughing too hard to notice her. Her time could have been better spent at home.

They met up with the two young men again in the foyer when the play finished, and they all left the theatre together.

As the party stood outside discussing the play, Abigail noticed Miss Gavin and her brother in the street. Seeing her, they started to approach. She did not know where to look. Her mother, distracted and reprimanding her son-in-law for bringing them to such a farce, hadn't noticed.

Abigail moved a small distance towards the Gavins. 'Please do not to talk to me of business here,' she said the moment they reached her.

'We have not come here on business, so why should we talk of it?' Miss Gavin asked.

'I will bring the pattern tomorrow,' Abigail said. 'Please, you'd better go before my father sees …'

'Really, Miss Harton, we will not interfere with your party. Come, brother,' Miss Gavin said and they both walked away.

'She is ashamed of us, I think, sister,' Hugh said as they made their way down Fishamble Street, trying to stop a cab to take them home.

'We cannot blame her. The doctor does not know anything of the work she and her mother have taken from me in the last few months.'

'Really? Then why do they do it? He doesn't seem to be the penny-pinching type, taking his family to the theatre.'

'Brother, there are too many ears around us. I promised Miss Harton discretion.'

Hugh had found it hard to keep his thoughts away from Abigail Harton. He had been trying to push her image from his mind but could not forget her standing at his door in the rain the morning before. He was sure his interest was only curiosity. Why did the Harton women need work with a physician in the family?

He dismissed such thoughts and went home with his sister for supper.

As did the Hartons. But the Hartons had invited two extra guests, Dr. Monroe and his friend Theodore Palmer.

CHAPTER 4

Henry and Sarah took the two young men with them in their public cab to the Harton home. Sarah noticed that Dr. Monroe looked a little shabby, though that was to be expected of a young physician. It took perseverance to build up clients and, with the high rents in the city, it was probably hard for him to keep up a crisp appearance. Mr. Palmer, however, was very fashionably attired. Mrs. Harton had taught her daughters to recognise a wealthy man. The lesson had been lost on Sarah as she had fallen for her husband Henry despite his lack of wealth, and so she was disposed to like Monroe more than his smarter friend.

'Dr. Monroe, have you recently graduated?' she asked.

'It has been two years since I was at the College. I had the honour of receiving your father's instruction in Obstetrics there.'

'Isn't that an occupation for women?' Henry teased, and his wife warned him with her eyes.

'I believe that is why many women die in childbirth. If we physicians do not give our skill to better women's chances, then we do our race no favours.'

'You are, of course, right,' Henry said. 'Please forgive me.'

Monroe noticed that Sarah was regarding him with admiration. A good impression had to be made, if there was to be a chance of Dr. Harton helping him. Word had travelled of how Harton had saved the Duke of Alden's wife and son from a difficult labour and probable death. Harton could introduce him to the best of Dublin society. He had not expected to see his teacher so quickly after returning from Cork. It was only through luck that he and Palmer had met the Hartons at the theatre that night, and luck that Harton still had an unmarried daughter. He tried to decide on the conversation he would raise with Abigail Harton, if he had the good fortune to speak to her directly that evening.

Brigid had done her best to prepare supper with the meagre supplies at her disposal. The dining room was alight with candles gathered from various rooms in the house. The fire had been piled high and gave out plenty of warmth. The ladies and gentlemen of the party walked in from a cold evening to a warm welcome and Brigid took their cloaks and hats to hang in the old housekeeper's room beside the kitchen.

Margaret excused herself and went upstairs to see Benjamin. She checked her son's forehead and found there was no fever and that he slept soundly. On her way down, she called Brigid aside to ask how he had been during the evening.

'He drank some ale but didn't eat much of his supper, Mrs. Harton. I've kept the fire going in his room all evening.'

'Thank you, Brigid.' Margaret whispered a prayer to herself. He had always been a sickly boy and for an instant she wished that Abigail or Sarah had been the weaker ones. She regretted the thought the moment it came to her and chastised herself for being a bad mother.

When she entered the dining room everyone was seated at the table with their glasses raised in a toast.

'Ah there you are, my dear,' her husband said. 'Just in time to praise the rogue of a playwright who gave us much amusement this evening.'

Margaret knew she should be angry about Abigail having been exposed to such crudeness but, such was her worry about Benjamin, she was happy that at least her husband was in good spirits. She sat and took her glass from the table and raised it. She would talk to her husband after service tomorrow about the household income as Abigail wanted her to do. She would ignore their plight no longer.

When the meal was served, Monroe, who had placed himself beside Abigail and opposite Sarah, seized the opportunity to further his cause.

'I am very glad to have met both of Dr. Harton's handsome daughters tonight,' he said as he sipped on his wine. 'You do not know how much you were both admired by the medical faculty at the College.'

'Dr. Monroe, you are too forward by far,' Sarah said. 'However, I accept the compliment on behalf of my sister and myself.'

Monroe was touched by Abigail's shyness.

'I apologise if I have offended you,' he said to her. 'I promise to make it up to you, though I am not sure when. I must return to Cork tomorrow.'

Palmer, sitting on Monroe's other side, overheard the remark and seemed somewhat agitated by the suggestion that Monroe was to depart Dublin.

'You had not told me you were leaving?'

'I must, Palmer. I have several patients who still need my attendance there. I will look for a suitable place in Dublin when I get back.'

'It is lucky then that you chanced upon me this evening,' Dr. Harton said.

'I confess, when I saw you earlier, I hoped that you might know of a position to which I might be suited.'

John Harton admired the young man's candidness.

'You could work with me at the hospital if you like. You would gain good experience and I need someone trustworthy.'

'Is it a charitable position?' Monroe asked, embarrassed to have to bring the necessity of making a living to the dinner conversation – but he needed to be sure.

'When I was in London, the Duke of Alden offered me patronage for my hospital here. I mentioned the need for a paid physician. Now that the Duke is back in Dublin, I have invited him to visit the hospital and hope that an annuity can be arranged within the month. Will you be back from Cork by then?' Dr. Harton was feeling more philanthropic as the conversation wore on. 'In fact, I have been neglecting my private practice of late and could do with some help there too.'

Monroe couldn't believe his luck. 'Well, then, there's nothing left to say. I will start as soon as I return.' He was delighted to see that Abigail had raised her glass with a sweet smile for her father.

With the presence of the two men, Sarah had to leave her good news until she could talk to her parents alone. As they eventually departed, she told them she would see them at the cathedral the next day.

Sarah and Henry dropped the two young men off on High Street near Michael's Court where they said they were staying.

Monroe and Palmer had told a white lie. It was yet early in the night and they wanted to attend a gaming house for a few hours before returning to their separate lodgings elsewhere. Palmer had rented rooms across the river while Monroe had found himself a cheaper establishment, called Brass Inn, on Coles Alley off Meath Street.

CHAPTER 5

Abigail woke with a headache. She was not used to drinking wine so late at night. It was Sunday and she needed to excuse herself from attending service to finish the full damask design for the loom for Mr. Gavin. She put on her housecoat and went down to the dining room where her mother and father were finishing their breakfast.

'Abigail, I was just about to send Brigid up to fetch you.'

'Mama, could I be excused this morning? I'm not feeling very well.'

Abigail ignored the food on the table. She would eat later. She still needed to finish the specific instructions that Mr. Gavin would need to weave the cloth.

'It is not like you to be ill.' John Harton touched his daughter's brow. 'I suppose if you feel unwell you may stay at home. Too much excitement last night, I expect.'

Margaret knew that Abigail was not ill, but the deceit was necessary. When Dr. Monroe joined her husband's practice, she hoped her daughter's days of working with cloth might soon be over.

'When Benjamin wakes, read to him for a little while, will you?' she said. 'He so enjoys those fairy tales.'

'I will, Mama.'

'Now, Mrs. Harton, we must leave if we are not going to be late for Dr. Swift's sermon,' John said. 'Couldn't miss that, could we?'

She laughed. 'No, we could not. Abigail, be sure to eat something. It'll make you feel a little better.'

'I will take something with me to my room.' Abigail placed a piece of bread in a napkin.

'Nonsense. You must eat to get your strength back,' her mother said. 'Sit and have breakfast.

'Very well, Mama, I will.'

'Sarah and Henry will be here this evening. Make sure you are dressed by then. Your father is taking me to see the improvements he has made at his hospital this afternoon, so we will not be home early.'

'Yes, Mama.'

When her parents left, Abigail sipped some ale and went back to her bedroom to finish the bluebird pattern to the size she had embroidered on her own poplin dress. Once that was done, she would make the calculations for the weft and weave of the loom.

Just as she started, her brother came into her room.

'Benjamin, you should be in bed.'

'You promised to read to me.'

'I will later. I have work to do and must finish today.'

'What are you drawing?'

'The birds from the storybook.'

Benjamin looked over her shoulder and saw a repeated pattern of two tiny birds on a simple tree design, that formed the damask pattern his sister had designed for the Gavins.

'Can I stay here with you?' he asked.

Abigail stopped working and looked at her brother in frustration. His face was so forlorn she hadn't the heart to send him back to his room.

'Only if you sit here quietly. I will tell you the story as I work.'

Benjamin smiled and climbed on her bed.

'Start at the beginning, will you?' he asked as he got under the covers.

'All right,' she said and began the tale again, which by now she knew almost by heart.

'A long time ago, in a distant land, there lived a king who was very old. The King's wife had died years before and he had just one son left living. His kingdom had been at war for twenty years and the people of the land had nothing left, not even to eat. The King had no more money to pay his soldiers and so he sent his son to negotiate peace with his enemies, a king and queen who lived in a kingdom that bordered the King's lands to the south.'

'What was the Prince's name?' Benjamin asked.

'The book doesn't give the Prince a name.'

'Can his name be Benjamin?'

'All right, though only if you don't interrupt me again.'

'I won't, I promise.' Benjamin lay back against the pillows and started to hum a tune.

'Good. Prince Benjamin then, and ten soldiers, mounted their horses to make the perilous journey through the mountainous forests to the south, in the hope that they could speak to the king and queen who had declared war on their land twenty years before.'

'Why were they at war?'

'I don't know, the book doesn't say.'

'Why not?' Benjamin said.

Abigail ignored his question. 'They rode every day for seven days, until the seventh night when they were forced to stop after they had crossed into enemy lands. A howling storm savaged the skies with swirling winds and rain and thunder. In the dark forest, the Prince looked up and saw lightning flash above them. The rain fell down hard, and he could barely see more than a few feet ahead as nightfall descended. He and his men tried to calm their horses, but the animals did not want to obey. Instead they took their riders into a clearing as if possessed by magic. The Prince's horse reared and in an instant he was on the ground, clutching at his father's sword as if it could help him. Suddenly, a Sorceress appeared, hovering above them, and though it was dark she shone like a star in the sky. The wind howled around her as she floated above them. The Prince saw that her robes were of purple and that she wore a crown of gold. He recognised her garments were from the royal house of his father's enemy. Though she was beautiful, her face was malign as she laughed down at them. Neither the men nor their animals could move as she had put them all in a trance. There was nothing they could do only watch as she drew another lightning bolt from the sky. She threw it directly into the Prince's heart, killing him in an instant. Then she killed his men, except for one, telling him to take the message to the King that his only son was dead.'

Abigail looked up from her drawing and saw that her brother was no longer awake. She completed her pattern, confident that her workmanship was accurate. When she had finished her calculations, she rolled the paper and secured it with ribbon. Then she carried her sleeping brother back to his bed and kissed him goodbye.

It was noon before she left to visit the Gavins, leaving Brigid to tend to Benjamin. She had forgotten to eat, but there was no time to waste. She would eat dinner when she returned, hopefully with enough money in her pocket to pay the butcher's bill.

Outside the day was calm. The weather was milder than it had been the day before. She made her way through the congested streets towards Coles Alley. People spoke French as they walked past, coming back from the French Chapel at St. Patrick's Cathedral where services were held in their language. She had heard stories of the couturiers in Paris and Lyon from her grandfather. She wondered what it would be like to live that life. When Mr. Gavin had spoken of his visits to Paris and London, she had wanted to ask more. Perhaps she still could.

A crowd on Meath Street caused her to pause for a moment. A speaker was telling the gathering crowd of the evils of slavery in the New World. She moved on as she did not have time to listen.

At the Gavins' house, she knocked on the front door but there was no response. Peeping through the kitchen window, she saw Miss Gavin carrying a large roast goose on a platter to the table.

Abigail continued around to the side gate and stepped into the yard. Mr. Gavin was picking up logs from a pile of wood under the window. He turned on hearing her approach.

'So, you're here to steal our firewood?' he said.

Abigail found herself smiling. 'Yes, but you have caught me.'

'Come – let us go inside.'

He allowed her to pass ahead of him into the kitchen.

Mary Gavin was placing the most delicious-looking roast goose on the table with potatoes and kale and, to her embarrassment, Abigail's stomach rumbled.

'Will you stay for something to eat, Miss Harton?' Hugh asked.

His sister gave him a look.

'I shouldn't stay,' Abigail said, though she was having trouble taking her eyes off the goose. 'I've just brought you the pattern.'

'Miss Harton, please take off your cloak,' Mary said. 'I will not have you leave us on an empty stomach.' She was annoyed with her brother for making the offer – she wouldn't enjoy the meal as much with the young woman looking on – however, she would not be impolite.

Hugh took Abigail's cloak from her shoulders and hung it up.

When they had all sat down, Mary handed a plate to Hugh and instructed him to cut Abigail a large portion of goose to feed her up. She was too skinny for her own good, in her opinion.

'Miss Harton, please have some kale and as many potatoes as you please – here is the sauce. The wine, you will find, is of as good a quality as any you would drink in France.'

Hugh laughed. He noticed Miss Harton blush when she looked at him. He found her pleasing but, at twenty-nine, he was not interested in settling down with anyone yet. Not even a doctor's daughter should she be available. His heart was set on travelling. There were plenty of opportunities to be had overseas. He had travelled more than most and eventually he wanted to see the Americas for himself. All the better if he could persuade his sister to come with him. For a moment he wondered what it would be like if both women at the table were on a ship westward with him and smiled at his fancy.

Abigail was enjoying the meal. She was so hungry she found it difficult to eat as slowly as she ought. She very much enjoyed the banter as Mr. Gavin teased his sister. It was a shame that she could not invite them to her house.

Eventually the conversation turned to weaving.

'Miss Harton, where did you learn pattern-making?' Hugh asked. 'It is generally not a skill one expects a doctor's daughter to have.'

'My grandfather was a silk weaver and designer in London. When he grew old, he came to live with us and taught me to design.'

'Do you like the work?' he asked.

'It passes the time ...' Abigail stopped herself from further explanation. She could not tell him that she hoped she would not have to continue with it. She might need the Gavins for longer than she expected – at least until all was settled with the Alden annuity.

'You do not think it beneath you?' Mary asked.

'Leave her be,' Hugh said.

'We are glad of the work.' Abigail put down her knife and fork. Suddenly she didn't feel hungry anymore but she could not leave yet.

'I apologise,' Mary said, and poured herself a little more wine. 'My tongue is sometimes sharper than I intend. Please, have some more wine.'

Abigail nodded and Mary filled her glass to the brim.

After the meal, Hugh examined the pattern carefully. He was pleased with the accuracy of the directions. He could start preparing the loom and his sister would have the silk ready in time to make the dress for the Boden Ball.

He made Abigail a generous offer for the design, which she accepted.

'I will need some help to complete all of my orders before December,' Mary said. 'If you or your mother can help me with the embroidery, I would appreciate it. You do the best work.'

'I must ask my mother first.' It was wiser not to say no outright, though she hoped they would not have to continue working. Better, in any case, that her mother send word to the dressmaker another day. It would seem less pointed that way.

'You know best.' Mary understood that the girl could not commit to work without her mother's permission.

Abigail refused Hugh's offer to walk home with her. It was early on a Sunday afternoon and she really didn't want to be seen with him a second time. She left the house, wondering if she would ever return.

When Abigail arrived home she had to wait a long time before her knock was answered.

Brigid was crying when the door finally opened. Abigail saw Dr. Monroe walk down the staircase behind her.

'What's the matter, Brigid?' she asked, alarmed.

Dr. Monroe came to her and held both of her hands.

'I met your parents at church this morning and they invited me to dine here today. Abigail, I'm so sorry. There was nothing to be done.'

'What do you mean? What has happened?' She didn't wait for an answer but pulled away from him to run up the stairs.

She went straight to Benjamin's room. The door was open. She stopped in the doorway, appalled by the sight before her. It felt as though the air had been expelled from her body. Her mother, father, sister and brother-in-law encircled the bed where Benjamin lay. His hands were neatly folded across his chest, his skin deathly pale.

She stumbled forward and dropped to her knees by his bed. When she touched his face, he was cold. She buried her head in the blankets.

Her father knelt beside her and held her to him.

'Was he on his own?' she asked. 'Please say that you were at least with him.'

'Yes, Abigail. We were here, all of us. We held his hand before the end. He just could not wait for you.'

Abigail touched Benjamin's face again. In her heart, she had known that this was coming. She knew he was not strong and she had loved him all the more for it.

'It happened quickly, Abigail,' Sarah said and held her sister's hand. 'He was asking for you and then he just fell asleep. We couldn't wake him. There was nothing any of us could do.'

Abigail got up. She could not speak. She left the room and went back downstairs.

Dr. Monroe was still there, standing in the hall. When she started to weep, he held her in his arms.

Monroe knew that the poor boy was never going to live. It was upsetting to see such a young boy die, though there were plenty of children dying on the streets. Miss Harton was soft and warm and nestled in his arms. All he had to do was say the right thing and not let his guard down. There was money in the Harton house, and he wanted some of it. Best to try his hardest at the hospital for as long as he could. Harton was a fastidious man. It was a hand he would be a fool not to play.

'Miss Harton, your brother Benjamin is in a much better place. Rest assured he will find happiness in heaven, as we all will when our days come to an end.' He touched her hair and moved back to look in her face.

'You are very kind, Dr. Monroe.'

'Go back to your mother and father. They have need of you now.'

Abigail started to cry again, and he drew her into his arms once more.

'If only there was something I could do,' he said, patting her back gently.

'There is nothing, Dr. Monroe,' she said.

'Go now,' he said, smiling down on her. 'I will call tomorrow to help your father with the arrangements.'

She pulled herself away from him and went up the stairs quietly. He watched her go as he put on his hat and gloves. She glanced down at him from the landing.

'I am glad that you were here. Thank you,' she said.

'Not at all, Miss Harton. You have my deepest sympathies.'

When she disappeared, he opened the hall door. It was a fresh autumn day. He walked towards Francis Street and home.

Monroe hadn't believed in destiny until now. Life in the past had been what he had made of it. Today, however, had been a turning point. A clear path had been laid out before him. Who knew what fortune lay ahead? Miss Harton was a sweet girl. Innocent. He would be able to handle her with ease. His smile broadened as he made his way back to the inn. Perhaps Olive, the innkeeper's daughter, would be there when he got back.

CHAPTER 6

Monroe wondered if he had made a mistake. He had been working at Dr. Harton's hospital for two weeks without pay and his funds were dangerously low. He didn't know how much longer he could wait, though he wouldn't leave just yet. The possibility of a connection with the Duke of Alden was too tempting to dismiss. He thought too of Miss Harton. A wife was just what he needed. Of his other pursuits, she need never know.

Monroe turned over in his bed in the damp attic and got up for the evening. Palmer was due to call – he knew of a gambling house the aristocracy frequented where he and Palmer were not yet known. Monroe was thankful for his acquaintance with Palmer who in the end had been a godsend. It was a pity though that Palmer knew of his dealings in Cork. He would need to keep him sweet until the future was secure. All was still in the balance.

Though Monroe had not shaven that morning, his blond shadow was imperceptible in candlelight. He checked his attire. He would have to do. He splashed the last of his cologne on his face and rubbed his hands into his hair. At the last minute he decided to wear a wig he had picked up in Cork – it was of the old-fashioned longer sort but would give him an air of respectability.

There was a light tap on the door and Theodore Palmer entered the small attic space. He looked at Monroe with distaste and noticed that he grew shabbier by the week. He was not inclined to help him personally for much longer. He had invested in Monroe's Cork scheme and had lost almost a year's income because of it. He knew he had enough evidence on Monroe to get him to cooperate. He was prepared to blackmail him for a while longer, determined to get his money back. The only trouble was Monroe didn't have a penny.

They walked out into the street.

Monroe was worried that Palmer could destroy any potential professional success in Dublin if he couldn't get him off his back. He hoped that this evening his luck would take a turn for the better.

They walked across the river and onto Abbey street where candlelight from the taverns lit their way.

Palmer turned down a narrow alley, stopping at a back entrance. He removed a large key from his pocket.

'I had to oblige a whore to get this – you'd better not let me down,' he said, opening the door.

Monroe nodded in response and tried to keep his nerve.

'After you,' Palmer said and followed Monroe inside.

The young doctor stepped through a dark hall and into the dim light. They were at the back of a large house. He walked farther down to the kitchen where servants were busy preparing food over a large fire. On the table there were cakes of violet, a tray of tansies and the largest variety of pies he'd ever seen in one place. The smell was intoxicating. Footmen in powdered wigs, wearing silk, brought empty bottles of wine and plates into the kitchen and departed with full vessels again.

Monroe recognised the livery in alarm. It was Alden's. If he was caught, it might jeopardise his chances of a life with Dr. Harton and his daughter. He glanced at Palmer who was following close behind. He had no choice but to carry on.

He opened the door to the gaming room and felt a little bolder. It was full of smoke and candlelight. Gentlemen laughed and drank and peered at the gaming tables. Most were playing cards. The billiards table in the corner was dwarfed by the size of the room. The women laughed and joked with the men, exposing their breasts and legs in advertisement of their business. Monroe did not see the Duke anywhere.

A girl, with pieces of black lace on her face covering her scabs, came up to Palmer and moved her hands over his chest. He looked down and slipped the key and some coins between her breasts. Monroe wondered if Palmer had slept with the girl. He decided not to ask.

'Here is your pot for the night,' Palmer said and handed Monroe a sum of money he could have lived on for six months. 'Make sure you double this or I'll stop paying your rent.'

Palmer steered Monroe to a small table by the window where two men sat.

'Mr. Goulding, Mr. Craig, it is good to see you this evening,' he said.

'Ah! Palmer.' Gilbert Goulding was an older gentleman of considerable girth.

'May I introduce a good friend of mine,' said Palmer. 'Dr. William Monroe, an associate of Dr. John Harton, the Duke of Alden's personal physician in Ireland.'

'That may not be good, Dr. Monroe – I hear Alden does not pay his bills,' Goulding joked. 'Perhaps you mean to take some of my money tonight?'

Palmer laughed and slapped Monroe on the back.

'Sit down with us, sit down!' said Goulding.

Palmer and Monroe sat.

Monroe was surprised at how nervous he felt. It had been a long time since he'd had the money to sit at a table such as this.

Goulding and his companion were playing piquet, a game he himself favoured. There were many coins on the table.

'A doctor, eh?' said Goulding. 'Well, it is good to find one who is recommended. There are so many scoundrels about. I am looking for a physician myself to attend my wife. Harton never seems to be available.'

Goulding's companion tried to look interested. He was having difficulty doing so, having consumed too much brandy and now thinking of consuming more, if only he could find his glass.

Monroe relaxed as he observed that Goulding was almost as drunk as his friend.

'Mr. Goulding, it is very good to meet you,' he said. 'Dr. Harton is indeed busy at his new hospital. I'd be happy to attend your wife tomorrow if you would give me your address. I am free in the morning as it happens and would be delighted to help.'

'I would indeed be greatly obliged,' burped Goulding, 'though you can't tell the good Mrs. Goulding where we met. That wouldn't do at all.'

'We met through mutual acquaintance while out walking this afternoon, did we not?' Monroe winked at Goulding, who patted his new acquaintance on the back a little too heavily for the doctor's liking.

'If you'll excuse me, gentlemen, there's a little tart I'd like to taste in the kitchen,' Palmer said, glancing at Monroe before he left, confident that his friend could double his money. In their condition, Goulding and Craig would not perceive his sleight of hand. They were easy pickings.

Palmer went to see his pretty little friend in the kitchen, sure that as long as he didn't do his business inside her, he would be safe. Except for a short period of illness several years before, he'd been clear of any signs of the disease and had put it down to this safe practice since.

He looked back at the table as he left the main room and saw that

Monroe had already taken charge and was dealing the cards. Hopefully, it would be a good night for them both.

Several hours later, Monroe had tripled Palmer's stake and had managed to hide a third of the winnings before his friend returned to the table. Craig and Goulding decided they'd had enough for one evening. Craig was finding it very difficult to see and tripped over his chair standing up.

Monroe and Palmer helped the two gentlemen outside and found them a cab. Goulding gave Monroe his card through the open cab window.

'Call on the morrow, sir, for I fear I will need your attendance more than my good wife,' he said and fell backwards as the cab pulled away.

The young men watched them leave. When the cab was out of sight, Monroe gave Palmer double his original stake and was rewarded with an extra sovereign.

'You have earned your money this evening, Monroe. We will play this establishment again soon. Buy yourself some new clothes and shave the next time you come out with me, for if you are to hoodwink smart men, you should at least look the part. I'll call on you next week for another try at the game.'

Palmer tipped his hat in adieu and walked a little farther down the street before hailing himself a cab.

Monroe smiled. If Palmer staked him every time and only expected him to double it, he could skim the top and pursue the Harton opportunity for longer. He would also collect the new set of clothes he'd ordered a month ago. He could start to take on private patients himself, starting tomorrow with the Gouldings, a visit he hoped would prove fruitful.

Dawn was breaking. He took the route by the river along Ormond Quay and across the bridge, passing the night watchmen there. Merchants were taking their wares to the ships in the distance. He went down Wine Tavern Street, towards Cock Hill.

There he was seen by Hugh Gavin, who had been at the Custom House at daybreak. In the distance he saw a dishevelled man, wearing an old-fashioned wig, and was surprised to see him throw it down on the street.

'Good morning,' Hugh said as he passed him.

'Good morning,' Monroe replied to the stranger and hurried on.

CHAPTER 7

Monroe slept until noon. He dressed in the clothes he had worn the night before and went down to breakfast. The landlady Mrs. Brass and her two daughters looked on him with suspicion. They did not believe he was a doctor in the first instance. In the second, he was behind on his rent. Now he had a smile on his face and they were cautious.

'Good morning, ladies,' Monroe said and slapped a coin down on the table.

Mrs. Brass took the money, glancing at its denomination before placing it securely between her ample breasts. It was enough to cover his debts and pay for his rent until Christmas.

'It's good to see you this morning, sir,' she said. 'Olive, get three eggs from the cupboard for the gentleman's breakfast. Dr. Monroe, take some ale while you wait. Grace, you'll be late for work if you don't hurry. Get going.'

Mrs. Brass's youngest, Grace, got up from the table and left, taking her sewing box with her.

'Breakfast will not be necessary. I'll bathe when I return and have a good dinner after,' Monroe said and drank from the tankard of ale Olive had handed to him.

Mrs. Brass didn't like his tone. However, reliable paying guests where hard to come by.

'Certainly, doctor, we'll have hot water ready upon your return,' she said.

Monroe smiled at his landlady. Perhaps he'd stay here a little longer.

He walked over to the draper's shop on Hanover Street where he had ordered his suits a month before and hoped they had not been sold on. The linen undershirts had been of a fine quality and a reasonable price.

At the shop, a bell rang as he entered and a slight young man came out from the back to greet him. Monroe made much fuss of paying for his clothes and bought another undershirt, and two pairs of stockings. The young man was delighted and parcelled it all up for him when the cash was produced. With two items to carry, Monroe went to a pawnbroker's down the street and secured himself a pair of plain cufflinks and a plain gold watch. It would not do to buy anything that could be easily recognised by another gentleman who had fallen on hard times.

Monroe made his way back to his lodgings and was very surprised to see Miss Harton walking ahead of him along Francis Street, unaccompanied. He couldn't approach her in his current state of dress. Instead, he followed behind and saw that she went into the dressmaker's shop on Coles Alley. It was a pity he couldn't use the opportunity to speak with her alone. However, he would see her later that evening.

Back at the inn, there was no time to waste. He didn't want to miss the opportunity to visit his new client that afternoon. He would polish his old shoes. They would be respectable enough to wait upon Mr. Goulding and his wife.

There would be time to buy a new wig later in the week.

He bathed, shaved and had dinner, then took his bag and left his lodgings. He caught a cab that brought him past the Phoenix Park to the address on Mr. Goulding's card. The house was nestled in oak and birch trees in a very pleasant situation.

An old servant answered the door, dressed in livery.

'May I help you?' he asked, looking up at the blond man before him.

'Good afternoon, sir. I'm Dr. Monroe. Mr. Goulding is expecting me.'

'Mr. Goulding is not in,' the servant said as he had been instructed to do. 'May I take your card?'

Monroe didn't have a card and realised he would need to order some to gain entry into the more noble of households. At least he had money to invest in a set.

'Do you know when he will be back?'

'He has gone into town, sir. I do not know when he will return.'

Monroe was disappointed. Not because of the fee he might lose, but because of the opportunity to show Dr. Harton that he could secure wealthy clients.

'I will try tomorrow then,' he said and turned away.

Then the sound of a girl's voice made him look back into the hall.

'Who is that, Grogan?' the girl called out from the stairs.

The old servant paused. He couldn't remember the name of the man at the door.

'I am Dr. William Monroe, miss.'

'And I am Miss Elizabeth Goulding, sir.'

'Glad to make your acquaintance.' Monroe bowed deeply.

The girl blushed. She was slightly plump with the wildest red hair piled high on her head, a pure delight to his eyes.

'What do you want with my father?' she asked, noticing how handsome the young doctor was.

'I met Mr. Goulding out walking yesterday. He mentioned your mother was not well and asked me to call today.'

Elizabeth Goulding looked him up and down. She was not sure if she should be talking to a stranger at the door, but she didn't want to let him go.

'Wait there,' she said. 'I believe my father has just returned from town.' She rushed back up the stairs.

Grogan let Monroe into the hallway and observed him. His master had expressly told him to say that he was not at home should anyone call. However, he could not help it if his master's daughter was a numbskull. He did not like the look of the young doctor. There was something odd about his dress. Perhaps it was because he had no wig, or that the doctor's shoes appeared to be older than his own. He didn't meditate on the subject too long before casting his thoughts solely on what he was likely to get for his supper that evening.

Elizabeth Goulding reappeared on the first landing and called down to them.

'Grogan, show Dr. Monroe up to the drawing room.'

She smiled at Monroe as he walked up the stairs behind the old servant who moved at a snail's pace. Dr. Monroe was the first man she had liked the look of since coming up to Dublin and she thought that she might have some fun with him while she was here.

At the top of the stairs, Monroe, carrying his black bag before him, followed the young lady through the first door to the right. It was an extremely pink drawing room decorated in the French style, with gilded edges on almost every piece of furniture. The low afternoon light shone directly into the room and glanced off several looking glasses, almost blinding him.

'There you are, doctor, a little late – but better late than never is what I say.' Gilbert Goulding remained seated in his armchair. He extended his hand to the young man and examined him in the cold light of sobriety.

'I'm sorry I'm later than expected. There was an emergency this morning, a young woman in labour …'

'I had an emergency myself,' Goulding said. 'Forgotten I had an appointment with my lawyer this morning. Just back. It's a good job my Caroline here was not in a very bad way, eh? Please sit down, doctor.'

'Thank you, sir.' Monroe bowed his head and sat directly opposite the couple.

Caroline Goulding affected a cough which shook her enormous frame. There was a large tray of sweet pastries before her and she started to nibble on one as she appraised the young man. Monroe thought that if she was well enough to eat cake, there could not be that much wrong with her. Gilbert Goulding hoped for the same as he adored his wife.

'Elizabeth, send for more hot water for the tea. Or would you like a glass of chocolate, Dr. Monroe?' Goulding asked. He did not care for the sweet mixture as much as his wife did.

'Tea would be most refreshing,' Monroe said, never having tasted the beverage before. He watched Elizabeth Goulding as she left the room.

Goulding regretted inviting the young doctor. It would have been better if his daughter had not answered the door like a common servant. He looked closely at Monroe and was not impressed with his youth.

'And who did you say you worked with?'

'Dr. Harton of Pluncot Street. He taught at the College and has opened a free hospital for the poor in John's Lane. It is there that I have been employed recently. I am not long from Cork myself. I worked there last year but found myself homesick for Dublin and so have returned.'

Goulding relaxed somewhat. Dr. Monroe's working for the poor explained his taste for plain clothing. That the young man had some experience working with Dr. Harton, albeit for the poor, gave him a little more confidence in his medical abilities.

'And how do you know Theodore?' he asked.

'We are old friends from our college days. Theodore studied the law. We met through mutual acquaintances and have been firm friends ever since.' Beads of sweat trickled down Monroe's back inside his new undershirt.

'Good, good. Theodore's father happens to be my own solicitor. The Palmers are a good family … so perhaps it might be safe to leave you alone with my wife?'

Monroe lowered his eyes and did not answer the question.

'How do you like your new doctor?' Goulding asked his wife.

'You are embarrassing the young man,' she said, wiping fresh cream from her rouged lips with her fingers, then licking the pink mixture and swallowing it down with relish.

Monroe did not know where to look until Elizabeth Goulding re-entered the room, supervising the housemaid with the hot water.

'Here is our refreshment,' Goulding said. 'Elizabeth, make the tea for our guest.' He watched as she smiled at the young man and served him tea. He worried that Elizabeth could be flighty. He would have to be careful to safeguard her honour until their return to Galway, where she had several marriage prospects that suited his business interests.

'How goes it at the new hospital? I hear Harton takes great care to attend but does not care enough to raise funds for the establishment. Or so the Palmers tell me at any rate.'

'Dr. Harton has the Duke of Alden's favour. Alden has promised to visit the hospital soon and may give an annuity.'

'Well, that would be prosperous for the Hartons, would it not, Mrs. Goulding?' He nodded to his wife, who was sipping her tea. 'If that's the case, I might be interested in donating to the hospital fund myself. When is this meeting with Alden due to take place, do you know, Dr. Monroe?'

'I'm not sure. It has been hard to pin him down,' Monroe said, whilst noticing how pretty Elizabeth Goulding's hands were, including the large emerald stone on her right-hand ring finger.

Goulding made a note to himself to make enquiries to Dr. Harton and was busy deciding what to do about it when his daughter sat herself down too closely to Monroe for his liking. His wife asked for more cake and, when he turned to hand her a piece, he didn't notice Elizabeth slip a note into the young doctor's medical bag.

Monroe, however, saw the action and acknowledged it with a smile.

'Elizabeth, I thought you were visiting the weaver today. Should you not get going?' her mother enquired.

'Mama, I don't want to go without you,' Elizabeth said and moved herself even closer to Monroe on the sofa.

'Your governess will go with you instead. Go fetch her and have Grogan take out the carriage. You can have it for the afternoon.'

'Oh, Papa. Must I go? I would much rather stay here with you.'

'If you want to go to Boden Castle in a new dress, you had better decide which cloth to buy,' Goulding said.

'Well, if I must.'

Goulding watched his sixteen-year-old daughter pout as she got up from the sofa. She was their youngest child and the only one still at home. Though he loved her very much, he often thought that they had spoiled her, and it had left her head quite empty.

'Mama, I hope you will approve of my choice.'

'I am sure you will choose very well, my love,' her mother said.

Elizabeth kissed her mama on the cheek and smiled coyly at Monroe.

'You will have to excuse my daughter, Dr. Monroe,' Caroline Goulding said when Elizabeth had left the room. 'She is young and silly, though we are determined to indulge her for a few more years yet.'

'I understand, Mrs. Goulding. I have a sister just like her myself,' Monroe said, even though he had no living relatives.

'Yes, yes,' Goulding said, finishing his drink.

'Husband, would you leave us so that the doctor can examine me? It is my chest, I fear. I cannot seem to shift this cough of mine.'

'Of course, my dear, I shall leave you to it.'

Goulding got up as Monroe proceeded to open his bag. He glanced at his dearest wife and hoped that his deepest fears for her health were unfounded.

CHAPTER 8

The month wore on and the weather grew colder.

As was the custom, neither Margaret Harton nor her daughters had attended Benjamin's funeral.

Margaret was awake but chose not to respond when Abigail whispered her name.

'How are you this morning, Mama?' Abigail knelt by the side of the bed, pushing her mother's cap back to see her face.

'Please leave me be.'

'Mama, you must come back to us. Sarah is coming this afternoon with Henry and she will be heartened if you are up and dressed.'

'I cannot, Abigail.' Margaret turned her face back into the bedclothes.

'For Benjamin's sake then. He might not go to meet his grandfather in heaven until he knows that you are well again.'

Her mother moved the bedclothes back.

'Oh, Abigail.' She pushed herself up in the bed. 'I had not thought of such a thing. Hand me my housecoat.'

Abigail fetched the garment and laid it on the bed. 'Brigid is lighting a fire in the drawing room. She will bring you something to drink soon.'

'Where are you going?' Margaret asked, noticing her daughter's cloak.

'I must ask Father for money to pay the butcher. He would not give Brigid more credit yesterday.'

Margaret leaned out of the bed and took her household keys from the drawer of the bedside cabinet. 'There may be coins in your father's desk. In the false drawer.' She felt lightheaded as she handed them to her daughter. 'Be careful not to disturb anything.'

'I will be careful, Mama,' Abigail said as she left the room.

Margaret lay back, pulled the covers up and closed her eyes again.

Abigail went down to her father's office and shut the door behind her. The false drawer opened easily, but when she looked inside there was not even enough money to pay the butcher's bill.

She went back upstairs to give the keys to her mother.

'What's wrong?' Margaret asked, raising herself on an elbow. 'You look unwell.'

'Just a headache, Mama.'

'You found the money?'

'Yes. I have it here with me.'

Margaret lay back in the bed.

'I will get up soon, I promise.'

'It will do you good, Mama. I'll be back before Sarah and Henry come to visit.'

Margaret was sitting up in bed, sipping the ale Brigid had brought up. She watched the girl work with her basket of twigs to start the fire in the grate. She knew had to fight the blackness that threatened to engulf her each time she lost a child. Benjamin had not been the first. He'd had a brother, born before either of her daughters. She let herself remember Edmund, who had passed away at four years of age. Sarah had been three at the time and Abigail one. She closed her eyes and saw the image of both of her boys in her mind's eye.

'Mistress, would you like me to bring you up something to eat?'

'No, Brigid. I'll get up and take something in the drawing room. Bring me some hot water to wash. And Susan and Henry will visit this afternoon so shave some sugar from the cone for baking.'

It was time to start her life again. She would have her household in order by Christmas. Long an acquaintance of Esther Johnson who had influence on Dean Swift, she would request an interview with him through her. The Dean would know what to do.

She pulled on her housecoat and went downstairs to the drawing room. She would write to Miss Johnson. There was no point standing on ceremony any longer. She had at last found the determination to convince her husband to face reality. They had two healthy daughters, with one of them yet to wed. That had to be enough to make her carry on.

CHAPTER 9

Abigail walked to the top of Francis Street, towards the free hospital in John's Lane where her father worked. She tried to remain calm. It was difficult to do when her father's obsession continued to threaten their household. She was determined to talk him around. Her mother either would not or could not do it.

She reached John's Lane. The entrance to the small hospital was crowded by beggars. She hurried past them, her breath clouding around her in the cold, but when she stepped into the foyer she instantly forgot the temperature. The smell of disease and death was overwhelming. Walking up one flight of stairs to her father's office, she tried to ignore the poor and sick on the stairway. There was nothing she could do for them.

On the first floor, she found her father looking through paperwork on his desk.

He didn't look up even as she approached him.

'Papa,' she said and touched his shoulder to get his attention, 'why isn't there a fire in this room? You will catch your death of cold in here.'

'Abigail?' Her father rubbed his eyes. 'Help me find the lease, will you? I am to see the landlord today.'

'I must speak with you about the household first,' Abigail said, determined not to be distracted.

'Please, Abigail, I don't have time for that now.'

'Well, you must take the time.'

He had never known Abigail to argue and looked at her in surprise.

'Do you know there is no money to pay the butcher? And there are several other accounts we must pay or there will be no food in the house.'

'I did not realise …'

'You must realise, Papa, that we cannot continue like this. Something must be done. I am here to ask for your help.'

'The Duke of Alden assured me in Ashdale –'

'You delivered his son in March, over six months ago. How can you still believe he will come through on his promise? Why do you stay here at the expense of your family?'

'My savings – they will help us weather the storm, I am sure of it. I will secure other funding … I will send the Duke a letter tonight. That will jog his memory.'

'Do you have any cash to pay the butcher today?'

'Why don't you put him off for a few weeks, Abigail? We can eat fish until then, can't we? Now help me find the lease, will you?'

Abigail shook her head. He did not understand at all.

'Can Dr. Monroe not see to the lease today?' she asked. 'Susan and Henry are to visit this afternoon. Will you not come home to spend time with your wife? It is so soon after Benjamin's death.'

'I cannot think about Benjamin, Abigail. I stay here to keep my mind at peace. Don't you understand?'

'Father, I am sorry, but –'

'Dr. Monroe is late today. Our landlord visits shortly and there are patients to attend.'

'Can't you ask another to help you? Mama needs your attention this afternoon.'

'Your mother is a strong woman. Do not fret about her so.'

Abigail looked at the peeling plaster and damp walls. 'You must be paid for your work before we become as helpless as the people here.'

'Be patient, daughter. I cannot lose the hospital now. It's my only sanctuary. I will try to come home this afternoon when Dr. Monroe arrives.'

Abigail didn't know what else to say. She looked at the old man before her and knew that she must try to provide for her family until he came around. She had only one option available.

'All right, Papa,' she said, knowing that her appeal had fallen on deaf ears.

'Go home to your mother. When Dr. Monroe comes to relieve me, I promise I shall be home shortly thereafter.'

'Try not to tire yourself too much, Papa,' she said and kissed him goodbye.

She made her way downstairs again and through patients resting in the hallway, wondering if she would have to live like that herself someday.

She did not go home. Instead, she hurried past the Corn Market towards Thomas Street, past the beggars and street traders, and turned onto Meath Street.

The sky had started to clear by the time she reached the Gavin house in Coles Alley. She peered in the front window and could see Mr. Gavin and a young boy, presumably a new apprentice, working green silk at the loom. She went around to the back of the house and looked through the window of the dressmaker's workshop. Miss Gavin was cutting cloth at the large table and a young girl of about fourteen was clearing away the cut-offs.

Abigail knocked on the glass.

Mary Gavin was startled. Then she went to the kitchen to let Abigail in from the yard.

'You gave me an awful fright, Miss Harton, like an apparition appearing, you were,' she said and wiped her hands in her apron. 'Come through to thc workshop.'

'I'm sorry to intrude. Could I have a word with you?' Abigail asked, looking at the young girl who had appeared at the doorway.

'Of course. Grace, bring some wine, will you?'

'Yes, ma'am,' the dark-haired girl replied.

'I was very sorry to hear about your brother, Miss Harton. I'm sure your mother's heart is broken.'

'Thank you.' Abigail had to force herself to speak. 'I'm obliged to you. But I have come for another reason.' She paused for a second before continuing. Looking at the young girl, she hoped she wasn't too late. 'I wondered if you still had work for me?'

'I thought you were not coming back …'

Abigail's tried to focus. 'I'm sorry, Miss Gavin. I shouldn't have come. I can see you already have the help you need.'

'Wait. I didn't say that I don't need you. My brother is working on the green damask you designed. I have that client my brother mentioned coming today and, if she approves, I will make her dress for the Boden Ball. There isn't much time left, and it will need to be embroidered. I need someone with your skill to work quickly. I would be obliged if you could consider helping me with it.'

She waited for a response but, overwhelmed, Abigail could not speak.

'It would be a large piece of work. I could pay you well but you would need to work here with me in the workshop. Would your mother allow it?'

'I am grateful, Miss Gavin. I don't need to ask my mother. I will start tomorrow.'

'That is good news. If the order is confirmed, I will send you a note tonight.'

Suddenly Abigail felt dizzy. 'If I could just sit down for a while?'

'Of course, Miss Harton – sit here in the armchair.' She could see that the girl was close to collapse and shouted in to Grace to hurry up with the wine.

CHAPTER 10

Since Abigail Harton left, Mary Gavin had been anxiously awaiting the Goulding girl who was due to arrive at two. It was now three o'clock.

The second panel of cloth was almost finished on the loom. There was no point in cutting a mantua court dress if Miss Goulding would not pay for it. As well as a petticoat and a stomacher, the outer dress, the 'mantua', needed an extravagant amount of material. She needed to be sure of Miss Goulding's custom. Besides, her brother had received another commission for scarlet silk from their friend, Daniel Long, a master weaver, who had been overburdened with orders that he couldn't fulfil. Mary Gavin wasn't going to let Hugh waste another minute on the green silk if Miss Goulding had changed her mind. If she did, Hugh could sell the green cloth after he completed the scarlet order for Mr. Long.

Mary stood looking out the front window into the street, waiting for the carriage to arrive. The girl would need to approve the green damask before confirming her order for the dress.

Hugh emerged from the kitchen and joined her at the window. He glanced up at the darkening sky. He looked distracted as he often had done when he was a boy in Belfast, working for their uncle as an apprentice. She sensed he had not settled yet into Dublin life but hoped that he would eventually.

A carriage turned into the street.

Hugh went outside. When the carriage pulled up, he opened its door.

Elizabeth Goulding took his proffered hand and alighted, followed by an older woman.

'Miss Goulding, it is good to see you,' said Mary from the front door. 'Please come in.'

'Thank you, madam.'

'I hope your mother is well.'

'She's a little under the weather, though her appetite is good,' the girl said. 'I have brought Miss Mitchell, my governess, with me instead for advice.'

Mary tried to hold her temper. They were past the stage for advice. The cloth had already been started. Either she liked it, or she did not.

'I hope you will be happy with the sample today,' she said.

'Better let me see it then.'

Mary smoothed out her skirts and turned around.

'There is a panel on the loom. Follow me.'

In his workroom, Hugh stepped away from the wooden frame.

'Good morning, Miss Goulding. It's good to see you again,' he said.

Elizabeth Goulding didn't respond – instead she looked at the cloth.

'Is this all there is of it? How will the dress be ready on time?'

'This is the second piece. The rest will be finished in three weeks. That will give my sister plenty of time to make the dress.'

Elizabeth looked at Hugh. He seemed competent enough, but she wasn't going to let a weaver tell her what to think.

'What about the embroidery? And the petticoats? I want more than the stomacher embellished …'

Mary held her breath and stayed silent.

'I rescind my order. I shall engage another dressmaker. You will not have enough time to complete the dress.'

'Miss Goulding, you are quite right,' Mary said. 'If it were just I, then there wouldn't be enough time. However, there is no need to worry. We have employed another embroiderer. A fast and highly skilled one. I promise you that your dress will be ready for the Boden Ball.'

'Who? The child there?' Elizabeth pointed at Grace who was eating a slice of brown soda bread at the doorway. 'She is too dirty and look at her hands. They are full of grease. She could not have the skill required to embroider a dress of mine.'

'Not Grace.' Mary feigned a smile.

'Well, where is this miracle-worker then?' Elizabeth looked around. She was not going to be the laughing stock of the ball. She would prefer not to go than to be seen in a badly stitched dress. She would just have to wear another. However, the cloth on the loom was beautiful. Besides, she had no other dressmaker engaged. It was too late to order another dress. Why did these things always happen to her? Why hadn't her mother come with her? She needed her to tell her what to do. Miss Mitchell could not be counted on to say anything worthwhile at all. In fact, she had been mute since they arrived.

'The embroiderer will start work tomorrow. Is that not so, brother?'

'Yes,' Hugh said. He could not stomach the thought of losing his business on the whim of a spoiled child and turned back to his loom.

'Let me show you an example of the embroiderer's work,' Mary said.

She led the girl into her workshop and took the waistcoat that Abigail had completed from a drawer.

'Isn't it beautiful?'

Elizabeth looked closely at the stitching. It was exquisite and she was relieved. Why had the stupid woman not shown this to her earlier?

'She had better work fast,' she said.

Mary nodded demurely.

'I will commission the dress then. *However*, if it is not ready by the first week of December I will not pay you a penny for it, for it is of no use to me after that.'

'I accept your terms,' Mary said. 'Now that that is settled, will you have a glass of wine while I take your measurements?'

Elizabeth refused hospitality for both herself and her governess, and submitted to having her measurements taken.

When they had finished, Mary escorted the ladies outside to their waiting carriage and was glad to see them gone.

'Well, did you ever come across the likes of that?' she said to her brother when she came back inside. 'She's no lady. I can tell you that for sure.'

Hugh said nothing. His mind was on his work and his new apprentice was not as attentive as he'd hoped. Michael Elgin, a young boy from Usher's Lane, had started two weeks before. The boy was still jumpy and prone to error with the shuttle. Hugh hoped he would improve.

'Hugh?' Mary said sharply.

He looked up. 'It's done now,' he said. 'The order is secured, and when it's finished it will be good advertisement for your business at the ball.'

'You mean our business, don't you?'

'Of course. Young Michael here is testing my patience sorely today, that is all,' he said.

'I shall have dinner ready soon and we can rest a while. Everything always looks better after a hearty meal.'

'What about Miss Harton? Are you sure she'll agree to help you?'

'She already has.'

'She has? I wasn't sure we'd be seeing her again.'

'Well, we shall. She was here this morning looking for work. I will send her a note and dress the frame for the stomacher with a strong linen base this afternoon.'

Hugh's mood improved after his dinner, though his young apprentice's errors worsened as the afternoon wore on.

CHAPTER 11

That evening, Hugh Gavin was weary after he had taken the second panel of damask off the loom. His young apprentice was close to sleep by the time they'd finished.

'Best be off home, Michael. Be back at first light. We need to get this commission completed on time.'

'Yes, sir,' Michael said and got up to go.

At twelve, he was small for his age. He liked working in this warm house. Mr. Gavin was fair too and he was sure he would eventually get the hang of the shuttle. It was a ten-minute walk home, though it usually took him half an hour to get there as he dawdled all the way. Along the river, he could see the outline of ships in the distance. When he was old enough, he would sail away and never come back. If he could succeed in the weaving trade, he could go anywhere.

The door to his house was locked when he got home. That wasn't too much of a surprise. He could hear men shouting close by and tapped on the door again. He waited for a few more minutes but there wasn't any sign of movement inside. He badly needed to relieve himself and went to the side of the house to do it. It was a mistake. His sixteen-year-old brother Joseph was there, rutting himself against a girl.

Michael backed up to get away but fell over a sleeping beggar who called out in protest at the disturbance. The girl with Joseph gawped at him. She was missing most of her front teeth. His brother stopped what he was doing. He grabbed Michael and hit his head hard against the wall. Then everything went dark.

It was light when Michael woke again. He was in his own bed. That was something at least but he was late, and Mr. Gavin would be angry. He tried to sit up, but his vision was blurry. He thought he might be sick. His could feel his face was swollen and one of his eyes wouldn't open properly. He lay on the pallet where he slept with his two older brothers. They were not beside him. His head was heavy, and he ached all over. Joseph must have kicked him when he was down last night. He closed his eyes again.

'*Get up, you lazy runt!*' his father shouted, coming into the room and yanking his son to his feet.

Michael almost passed out again.

'What were you up to last night?'

'I didn't do anything. It was Joseph who hit me.'

'*You good for nothing little brat!*' His father smacked him across the face.

Michael stumbled backwards and fell. As he lay there, he remembered the tall ships on the river the night before.

'Stop telling lies about your brother. If Mr. Gavin lets you go because of this, you'd better be prepared for a right hiding, boy.'

His father went back down the stairs.

Michael decided there and then that he would leave and he wasn't ever coming back. He would try to stowaway on a ship tonight. That way he would have a chance to make his own way in the world. He had seen many boys on ships' riggings at the quays. It scared him but that wasn't going to stop him. It would be better to be dead than to return to his father's house.

CHAPTER 12

Hugh worked long into the night to set up the next panel of silk. He wondered if he should find another lad. The child seemed to constantly be in a world of his own. Mr. Long or some of his fellow weavers might know of a boy or a journeyman who might be available. There would be time to ask after church on Sunday. Young Michael simply wasn't made to work with cloth. He hadn't the attention to detail for it. Mr. Gavin hoped he'd be able to get the boy a position better suited to him.

It was close to three in the morning when he locked up. He brought his candle out to the kitchen. The fire was still smouldering in the hearth and he put a few pieces of wood on it. His cravat felt tight around his throat. He untied it and sat down in the chair. The flames were taking hold and he stared into them.

He had thought that Dublin would feel different, that somehow the work here would be more satisfying because he would be working for himself. Since his sister had left her employment and leased the workshop, he had saved to join her. His Uncle Francis had given him the old loom as a parting gift with no hard feelings and he had sailed with it down from Belfast. Francis had been a hard taskmaster but had trained him well. He was lucky that he and his sister had been taken in by Francis as children when their parents died. And he might have stayed there but for Cousin Sally. Uncle Francis had expected him to marry her. The problem was that he couldn't do it. So, as soon as he was qualified, he had left for Dublin to set up his own business. But he was beginning to feel that it wasn't far enough away. He wanted to travel further, to the Americas, to freedom. For some reason Abigail Harton came into his mind again. She would start working for his sister this morning. His eyes started to close. Exhaustion and the heat of the fire eventually overcame him and he slumped back into the chair and fell asleep.

A note had been sent to Pluncot Street the night before. The bellman, who carried post for a price, had asked that it should be delivered to Miss Harton straight away. Brigid took it to Abigail's room. The message was from Miss Gavin. The stomacher had been cut and was ready to be embroidered. Miss Gavin wanted her to start work at first light. There was no time to be wasted.

After her father left for the hospital the next morning, Abigail went to wake her mother.

She shook her shoulder gently.

Margaret opened her eyes.

'Mama, I am to start work today at Miss Gavin's – she sent a note last night.'

Margaret pushed herself slowly up against the pillows and focused on her daughter's face. The curtains were still drawn in her room.

'Do you need to leave this early?'

'Mama, I must.'

'Have some breakfast first, at least.'

'There is no time. I will eat with the Gavins later.'

'I don't like this at all, Abigail.'

'What else can we do? Go back to sleep. I will be home before dark.'

Abigail kissed her mother goodbye and hurried out of the house with her embroidery tools. Dawn was breaking and Miss Gavin would be waiting for her.

She walked the familiar streets in the early light. Men walking past leered at her. She was alone and conspicuous, her cloak too fine for a servant. It would be better to blend in with the crowd, to be invisible. From tomorrow, she would wear her plainest dress and borrow Brigid's cloak. It would serve a dual purpose. Anyone who knew her might not recognise her in it. She would be out at this hour until the dress was finished. Hopefully she wouldn't need to work after that. She thought of Dr. Monroe. He had called to them every day since Benjamin died. He was such a kind and honest friend. She secretly hoped that he might have the means to save them all.

Mary Gavin hadn't the heart to wake her brother by the fire. It wasn't yet dawn, and she decided to let him sleep for another hour or so. The cloth would not turn out well if he was too tired to work the loom with care.

Grace knocked on the back door and came in. Mary gave the girl some ale and was thankful for her company. Grace had proved herself a quick study and had already started working on the petticoat for the green dress. She had been impressed with the girl's neat stitching. She would make a fine embroiderer and was a good addition to the business. Miss Harton could show Grace how to chalk out an embroidery pattern onto silk while she was with them. There were another two dresses to cut for the ball before Mary could help either of them stitch the dress for Elizabeth Goulding.

She started to prepare breakfast.

'Aren't you going to wake him?' Grace asked as she supped her ale.

'Let him be. Besides, young Michael isn't here yet.'

Grace shrugged and went to wash her hands. 'I'll get started then. I've already had my breakfast.'

Mary hoped that the Harton girl had received her note the night before. Every hour counted at this stage. She went over to the fire with the pot to stir the oats. Her brother was a fine weaver. She hoped that he would receive more commissions soon. There was enough space for a second loom in her workshop. If he took on another weaver in the new year, he might settle better. She was sure they would both get more orders after the Boden Ball in December. They just needed luck on their side until then. She prayed for a sign from God that it would all work out.

She heard a knock on the door and hurried to answer it before any further knocking woke her brother.

To her great relief, it was Abigail Harton.

'Good morning, Miss Harton,' Mary whispered. 'It is good to see you.'

'I am glad to be here,' Abigail answered softly.

'Come in and sit down. Have you eaten?'

'Not yet, but I can wait until noon.'

'Take off your cloak and sit by the table. I have porridge on the fire. I can't have you working on an empty stomach.'

Abigail followed her new mistress into the kitchen and wondered why they were whispering. Then she saw Mr. Gavin sleeping in the chair. He looked younger somehow. His cravat was undone and she could see the broadness of his chest beneath his shirt. She looked away as she took her off her cloak.

'Hang it over there,' Mary said. 'And would you mind stirring the porridge? Please excuse my brother. He had a late night and he did not make it to his bed.'

Mary started to cut the bread.

Abigail walked to the fire. She picked up the ladle to stir the oats and couldn't help but look as the light flickered across Mr. Gavin's face. He was not yet thirty, she thought. His eyelashes flickered and she wondered what his dreams were about. He opened his eyes and caught her staring at him. She quickly looked away.

'Good morning,' he said, and stretched in the chair.

'Good morning,' Abigail said, conscious that her face must be red from the heat of the fire.

'Hugh, you're awake. You'll have something to eat with us.'

'I'll have something later.'

Hugh stood up. The girl's closeness affected him. He wouldn't feel comfortable eating in her company and was conscious of looking dishevelled after sleeping in his clothes.

'I was sorry to hear of your brother, Miss Harton,' he said.

'Thank you.'

'You are good to help my sister at such short notice.'

Abigail nodded.

'Is young Michael here yet?' he asked his sister.

'Not yet.'

Hugh tied this cravat roughly around his neck and swung on his cloak. 'It's best he stays at home, I think. I'll have to find another lad.'

'He is young,' Mary said. 'Would you not give him another chance?'

'He's had too many chances. I'll call in to Mr. Long to see if he can recommend a replacement, but first I will tell the boy and his parents that I can no longer keep him on.'

He nodded goodbye to Abigail and left.

He walked towards the river. In Usher's Lane he came to the boy's house and knocked on the door. There was no answer. He tried the door and it opened. The smell from the dye inside was as bad as he expected. The boy's father was a silk dyer, and he and two of his sons were dyeing thrown silk a deep blue. There was no sign of Michael. A baby screamed upstairs.

Then Mrs. Elgin appeared and walked down the stairs holding a baby in her arms.

All eyes rested on Hugh.

'Good morning,' Hugh said and paused as they all eyed him silently. 'Where is Michael?'

'The boy was late rising this morning,' Mrs. Elgin said, jigging the child on her hip. 'He is almost ready. We beg your patience.'

Michael appeared at the top of the stairs. Hugh watched the boy descend and as he came closer saw that there was a red welt across his face and one of his eyes was closed, black and blue. He seemed smaller somehow. Suddenly his anger at the boy was gone. He could not dismiss him now.

'I'm sorry, sir. I overslept.' Michael thought that if he could just get out and work one last day, he would go to the quays tonight. It would be better to stowaway under the cover of darkness and he would eat well at the Gavins' place today.

'It can't be helped. Come on. It's getting late.'

Hugh led the boy out into the street.

'Wait here,' he told him.

Then he went back inside.

He looked around the small room where Mr. Elgin stood over a bath of silk steeped in alum. Mr. Elgin's two other sons looked at him, their mouths agape.

Michael was a smart lad – perhaps not a natural weaver but he deserved a better chance than this.

'If Michael is to continue as my apprentice,' he stated, 'he needs to live with me.'

'Sir, he is my youngest, and would be a great loss at home in the evenings,' his mother said.

The child on her hip started to cry and she put it to her breast.

Hugh stared at the woman. He would not back down.

'We must have compensation if we are to let him go altogether,' she continued, holding her ground.

'I can easily find another apprentice. His salary remains the same, take it or leave it.'

'Mr. Elgin, have you nothing to say?' the woman said to her husband.

'Let the boy go. He is of no use to me. Mr. Gavin, if you continue to pay me by the week, you have my word that no more will be said on the matter.'

Hugh wondered if he would find it as easy to sell a son if he had one.

'I will pay you his earnings as before. Are we agreed then?'

The mother pretended to cry. 'Oh dear Jesus, what is to become of him?'

'Shut up, woman,' Mr. Elgin said and returned to steeping silk.

'I'll send for his clothes later.'

The woman snorted. 'He doesn't have any other clothes. You'll take him as he is, or not at all,' she said, showing the gap in her teeth.

'I'll take him as he is so,' Hugh said, and left lest he say something that would jeopardise the agreement.

Outside the boy was waiting for him at the corner.

'Michael, from now on you will live with us at Coles Alley. That is, if you work hard and cause no trouble. Do you agree?'

Michael's bruised face lit up. 'Yes, sir.'

'Come then.'

They made their way back to Coles Alley. He noticed that the boy was limping. It was obvious he'd been badly beaten and probably wouldn't be of much use for a few days. He would ask his sister to let Grace help him at the loom while the boy recovered.

When they got back, Mary and Grace were clearing the table. Miss Harton was nowhere to be seen.

'Grace, get Michael some porridge, will you?' Hugh said.

'Yes, Mr. Gavin,' the girl said and fetched a bowl of porridge.

Michael sat and began to eat.

Hugh took off his cloak and sat at the table. 'I have spoken to Michael's parents. They have agreed it would be best if Michael lives with us. That way he can be on time for work.'

Mary sat down at the table. 'I'll be happy to have him here,' she said.

She was glad for the boy and more secure in the knowledge that her brother seemed to be serious about settling in Dublin. If he was taking on an apprentice to live with them, he would be tied here. She looked at the boy and felt sorry for him.

Michael started to choke on his breakfast and Mary patted him on the back. He flinched from her touch. Someone had given him a good beating, that was for sure. His father was the culprit no doubt. Her brother was truly a good man for taking him in.

'It's clear you've had some trouble, Michael,' Hugh said. 'I can assure you that you will not have any trouble like that in this house.'

The young lad bowed his head. He could not look at them.

'You can rest today and tomorrow. After that, we start afresh. Is that acceptable to you, Michael?'

'It is,' the boy whispered. He looked at his master and wished that he was his father instead of the one God had given him. He tried to hide the tears as they streamed down his face. Grace put an arm comfortingly around him while Mary cleared away the dishes.

'I will need Grace to help me with the shuttle today,' Hugh told his sister.

'Of course, brother, but only for today, mind.'

Hugh went to his workshop. He was tired. He passed the back room and could see Miss Harton working inside. He felt as if his world was winding tighter around him. Why hadn't he realised that the boy was being beaten?

He had to get some air. He went out the front door and walked to the end of the alley. He took his time before going back into the house. The boy could sleep in the front room by the loom. He would make up a cot for him in there. Perhaps with some encouragement he would get faster with the shuttle. There was no point in shouting at him, he could see that now. He only hoped that together they could get the green silk finished on time so that he could complete this order and the next of scarlet. He had to meet the deadlines. It was the only way for a newcomer to ensure his business would thrive in Dublin.

Abigail sat working at a small table in the back workshop preparing the vellum. The embroidery frame was too close to the window. Anyone could see her from the back laneway if they chose to peer through the glass. She had hoped that Miss Gavin would have thought to put it somewhere more discreet. There was a space in the corner where the light was good. She would ask Miss Gavin if she could move the frame before she started to work at it. It shouldn't have come to this, to have to hide like this.

Abigail took out the small pieces of vellum she had saved from her sewing box. She would chalk the pattern on the silk tomorrow. First, she must cut the vellum into small strips. She would use them on the stomacher and skirt to raise the trees and branches of her design from the surface of the cloth. After she had cut the shapes, she would wind them with silver thread before sewing them on the cloth. The sooner she could start, the sooner the dress would be complete. She would prepare the metal threads and the purl and cord later. Gold thread would outline the birds. She would attach the vellum bird shapes to the cloth to raise their bodies from the surface as if they were perched on the stomacher itself. It was fine work and would take weeks to complete. When it was finished, the embroidery on the stomacher would match and enhance the damask design in the woven silk beneath.

When the dress was completed, she hoped any embroidery work she did thereafter would only be for pleasure.

Mary joined her in the workroom. Her worktable was set up at the other end of the room. The table was large, and Mary started to tack pieces of white silk together for another order. They worked companionably in silence for the rest of the day.

By the next morning, Michael had recovered enough to work with Hugh again, and Grace joined Mary and Abigail in the workroom. The young girl began working on the oval hoop frame that would be worn under the green dress.

When Grace began to sing, Abigail looked up from her work.

'Girl, you are distracting Miss Harton,' Mary said.

'I'm sorry, miss.'

'I don't mind if you sing,' Abigail said. 'I was just surprised, that was all.'

'Well, the singing bothers me,' Mary said.

Grace stopped singing and Mary continued to work until Hugh called her outside. When she left the room, Grace walked over to where Abigail was attaching the pieces of vellum to the stomacher. As well as the branches and two birds, she had cut out tiny leaves to stitch into place which she would later embellish with threads of deep and pale green.

'It is a pretty design. Mr. Gavin told me it is your own.'

'Yes, it is.'

'How did you think of it?'

'I got the idea from a storybook that I used to read to my brother.'

'He told me about your brother too. I am sorry for your loss, miss.'

Abigail nodded and continued with her work. 'You would have liked him. Benjamin liked to sing too.'

'Thank you, Miss Harton,' the girl said and went back to her work humming.

CHAPTER 13

Present Day, Dublin

In the heart of Trinity College Dublin, Ireland, a continent and ocean away from my home in Los Angeles, I walked across the cobblestone courtyard to the Arts Building to meet Professor Patrick Ralley, a renowned historian and academic in his field.

On the first floor, I found the Professor's office and knocked on the door. It was slightly ajar, so I pushed it open. Inside, a dark-haired man was seated at his desk, facing me. He was younger than I had imagined him to be, forty at most.

'I'm Lucy Young,' I said.

He removed his reading glasses and rose to greet me.

'Ah, Lucy. I'm glad you've come – it's good to finally meet you.'

We shook hands.

'It's really good to meet you too, Professor,' I said, looking up at him. He was over six feet tall.

'Did you have a good flight from Boston?'

'Yes, I did. Thank you.'

He directed me to sit down opposite him at his desk in the small office.

'Would you like a cup of coffee before we start?'

'Perhaps later,' I said and opened my bag.

'Good. I'm looking forward to seeing the diary.'

'Here it is.' I handed him the leather-bound book embossed with floral gilt.

'I can't believe it survived,' he said, examining the cover.

He opened the journal and, putting on his glasses again, looked at the first page where the Duchess of Alden had written her maiden name: *Miss Sophia Lawson*. The entries were dated between 1715 and 1719.

I sat back and watched him scan through the pages with great concentration. Perhaps he was the man who could unlock the diary's secrets.

At length he looked up. 'So it's been in your family since the 1960s?'

'Yes, but as you know my Aunt Jeannie had forgotten about it until last month. It was only when her husband was clearing out their attic that she came across it again. With her recent cancer diagnosis, she asked me to bring it to you.'

'When I spoke to your aunt on the phone last week, she couldn't recall where she had first come across the diary. I didn't want to press her at the time. Has she remembered anything about that in the meantime?'

'Yes I asked her about it when I picked up the diary in Boston last week. She used to tour Europe with her husband every summer and they were always buying old things. They found it in England at an auction at one of those great old houses, though she can't remember which one. She bought it because there are family stories that connect us to a castle in Boden near Dublin. When she saw the diary entries mentioning Boden Castle, she had to have it.'

'So, you might have blue blood in your veins?'

I laughed. I was thirty-four and Chinese American, and hardly likely to even marry into royalty at this stage. The only hint of my Irish ancestry was my green eyes.

'My aunt recently discovered that one of our ancestors, a weaver named Hugh Gavin, emigrated to Boston from Dublin in the early eighteenth century,' I said. 'So it's more likely that we came from peasant stock.'

'I wouldn't be so sure. It's a shame your aunt couldn't make the trip from Boston. It would have been good to talk with her about her research.'

'She was disappointed not to be able to come. She's in the middle of her treatment, so you're stuck with me, I'm afraid.'

The Professor turned the leather-bound book over in his hands. 'The binding seems authentic for the period.'

I watched as he continued to examine the diary.

'My aunt would like to donate it to the university if you think it's of any value for further research.'

'The diary is a significant historical find. We don't have much primary source on the castle from that period. We have practically no information on the Duchess of Alden. And now we have her diary. It's amazing. Did your aunt show it to any other academic?'

'Not that I'm aware of. She has accumulated so many sources over the years that it would take a librarian to sort it all out. She spent a lot of time researching our Chinese history before she had her boys. She even went to visit Xi'an in China, the terminus city of the Silk Road. After her children were born, she lost interest. Now that she's ill, she really wants to find out more about our Irish ancestry. Something to hold on to while she goes through chemotherapy. Her sons aren't interested so she asked me if I'd like to take over. I had a little time on my hands and accepted the challenge.'

'I'm glad that you did. I would be very interested to hear more about your Chinese ancestry too.'

'I'm sorry to say that I don't know anything much about it. I hope that when Jeannie is better she can travel to discuss it further with you.'

'I look forward to that. I hope that she recovers soon.'

The office was very small. I looked around. There were books everywhere.

'I was hoping you might point me in the right direction regarding my Irish genealogical research while I'm here.'

The Professor removed his reading glasses. 'I can collect some sources you could look through today if you'd like.'

'I don't expect you to go to that trouble.'

'It's the least I can do.' He typed something into his computer. 'I believe we have an old journal from Boden Castle in our archives from that period. I've just sent an email to my colleague to find out if you can see it today.'

'I can go over to the library myself if that works better – and leave you to get started on the diary.'

'Not at all, I'm happy to have you here. Have you read all of the diary yourself?'

'I scanned through it on the flight over, but the script is difficult to make out – and I must admit I slept a lot too. So it wasn't a comprehensive study, I'm afraid.'

'Tell me more about your family's connection to Boden Castle.'

'Our Irish ancestor was a man called Hugh Gavin. He was a weaver, who came over to Boston from Dublin on the *Charlotte* in 1720. My grandmother remembered a story told to her by her own mother that someone in Hugh's family had something to do with Boden Castle. Jeannie hasn't been able to find a direct connection to the castle itself as yet but is determined to continue trying. It might just be a wild goose chase though.'

'Perhaps Mr. Gavin himself worked at the castle?'

'Maybe so. I looked for his name as I scanned through the diary but didn't see it.'

'It's unlikely that a weaver would be mentioned in a Duchess's diary.'

'That's true.'

'You could visit the National Library on Kildare Street. They have a genealogical service. You might even be able to match your Mr. Gavin to a street name in the trade lists for 1720 and take it from there.'

'Thanks, I'll definitely check that out. The ship's manifest lists Mr. Gavin as having a wife though we can't make out her name – it's just an initial. It would be good to find out who she was too.'

'I'll help you as much as I can,' the Professor said.

'I'd really appreciate that.'

The Professor received a text and excused himself from the room. He asked that I wait so I remained at the table and started to reread the diary from the beginning.

March 2nd, 1715. I crept out into the blackness. Torches lined the drive and I could see that the carriage was outside and Russo was there. I asked where Alden was and was told to be patient. I hoped he would not trick me. I had no option but to trust him. The carriage drove through the filth of the city and I sipped the gin I had brought for strength. Fleet Street was ablaze with torches on either side of the entrance when we got there. This was where we would marry. Russo opened the carriage door though he was pushed aside by Kilroy whom I have come to despise. Kilroy took my hand and planted a wet kiss on the inside of my palm. His house is where Alden escapes from his father, to meet his friends, to eat, to drink, to gamble. He is only seventeen. Adam Alden, son to one of the richest men in England is going to marry me, the girl his parents hate. There is passion in his eyes and I am satisfied he will go through with it.

The Professor came back into the room with a very large old book and put it down on the desk.

'Her way of expressing herself is remarkably clear,' I said. 'To think that she was only fifteen when this was written. She certainly seemed to know what she wanted.'

'Indeed. But look at this.' He sat down and opened the book.

Then he swivelled it around to face me.

I sneezed. 'Sorry. It's just a reaction to the smell of the old binding.'

'An occupational hazard,' he said with a smile. He pushed a box of tissues over to me.

'Thank you.' I pulled out a tissue.

'OK?'

'Yes, I'm fine.' I looked up at the Professor. 'Tell me – wasn't Sophia too young to marry at fifteen?'

'Not then.'

'What about her parents? Wouldn't they have had to give consent?'

'Yes, they would. However, Alden was the sole heir to a very large fortune. Sophia's father was a mere sea captain. Her parents would have given consent if they'd been asked. His parents, however, might have been a problem. Though her father was a friend of Alden's father. Miss Lawson, it seems, was invited to the Alden residence in Ashdale as a favour to Captain Lawson so that they could help place her as a Maid of Honour at the Royal Court.'

'But she fell in love instead,' I said, 'with their son Adam.'

'You have it,' he said with a grin. 'And she won the jackpot when Adam fell in love with her.'

'Like winning the lottery.' I looked down at the opened book. It seemed to be some kind of ledger. There were columns of items and sums of money, all in copperplate script. 'What's this then?'

'It's an accounts book for Boden Castle for 1719 – from our archives. There are staff names listed too. You might find your ancestor here. It's as good a place to start as any.'

There was a knock on the door. A young redheaded woman peeked inside.

'I wondered if we could have a chat?' she said.

'Yes, come in, Gráinne. I was about to call you. This is Lucy Young.'

The young woman gave me a weak smile. 'Miss Young, if you'll excuse me, I'd like to have a quick word with the Professor.'

'Lucy is not a student, Gráinne.'

'Really, it's no bother,' I said. 'Why don't I wait outside?'

'There's no need,' he said. 'I'll be back in a few minutes.'

He left with Gráinne and I continued to look at the ledger.

On the first page, I could see that the steward of the castle was a man named Charles Radburn. I scanned through the rest of the list of servants' names. I couldn't see Hugh Gavin's name anywhere.

I read on, marvelling at the lists of strange antique items, some of which I had never heard of before like candlesnuffers, rushlight dips and tinderboxes. Before long I found that my jet lag was starting to affect my concentration. I closed the book over. As I did, I heard a cracking sound. I looked at the cover and saw it had a new split towards the top of spine. I couldn't believe it. I had damaged a priceless piece of history. I touched the spine, hoping that somehow it would miraculously repair itself. Then I ran two fingers up along the split, pushing the edges together. Something moved under my fingertips and I saw a piece of metal protruding from the top. I pulled at it and an old key fell out onto the table.

The Professor came back into the room to find me staring at the key.

'What's this?' he asked, eyebrows raised.

I told him what had happened.

'I'm so sorry. I'll pay for the repair.'

'Not at all. I could easily have caused the damage myself. I should thank you really. Now that you've found the key, we'll have to find out what it might open.'

'It was probably a key to the larder,' I said, trying to make myself feel better.

'Please don't concern yourself about it, Lucy. It's really nothing to worry about at all. And, talking of larders, may I take you to lunch? I'd like to chat to you a little more about your aunt and her travels.'

'That's not necessary, Professor. I'm sure you've had enough of me for one day.'

'Not at all. There's a great Italian place around the corner.'

I stood up and buttoned my coat. Though he was attractive, he didn't seem to know it.

'I'd love to,' I said and took my purse up from his desk.

'Great.' He ushered me out of his office. 'We'll go out the Nassau Street entrance.'

We walked out of the Arts building and then out of the campus onto a main road which we crossed, then turned onto a narrow street where the Italian restaurant was located just a little way up from the corner. There he told me about the Duke of Alden's history. I tried to pay attention, all the while hoping that the spine of the accounts book wouldn't cost the university a fortune to be repaired. I wondered what the key from the binding opened. It had to be a room or a drawer at Boden Castle. I hoped that whatever it opened might still be there.

I woke early the next morning and opened the box of papers I had brought with me from Aunt Jeannie's house. At the top of the pile was a copy of the ship's manifest from 1720 when the *Charlotte* had landed in Boston Harbour, carrying silks and poplins from Ireland and with them my ancestor Hugh Gavin, the weaver. Listed beneath his name was another Gavin, his wife. There was an initial beside it, but Jeannie had never been able to decipher it. The photocopy was faded and it was very difficult to make out.

There had been weavers in the family throughout the 18th century and Aunt Jeannie had often wondered if there was a connection with the Huguenots who had settled in Dublin. They were French Protestants, she had told me, who had to flee from religious persecution in France. Jeannie liked to tell a romantic story that Hugh Gavin had married his wife on the ship to America. I, however, hoped that he had married in Dublin as there might be a chance that I could find their marriage records here if he had.

It was getting late, so I showered and had breakfast in the hotel, before making my way to Trinity College to meet the Professor.

He was in his office when I arrived.

'Welcome, Lucy,' he said. 'I hope you're ready for an adventure today.'

'Can't wait,' I said. The damage to the accounts book was still weighing on my mind.

'I've managed to arrange a trip out to Boden Castle to meet one of the guides there. We can take my car.'

'Great.' I had expected to be spending hours in a dusty library. This felt more like a vacation.

Boden was only about two miles from central Dublin. When we reached it, I could see a village across the busy road, with a church spire dominating the skyline.

We parked the car and walked up the drive. The castle stood in a sea of green grass with large oak and slender beech trees at the edge of the grounds, swaying in the distance. It was not as large as I had expected though it was imposing nonetheless. The Professor told me it had been built most likely in the 1580s and had been significantly upgraded in the 18th century. We walked to the front of the building. It was a curious hybrid, neither house nor castle – square, four storeys high, with a flanker tower at each corner. The white rendered walls surprised me – I had been expecting stone.

I gazed up at one of the towers and a movement caught my eye. Someone was looking out of one of the windows. A woman, though I couldn't be sure.

The wind picked up, coming in from the low mountains to the south and I was almost swept away as we made our way to the visitors' entrance at the side of the castle. The Professor caught my arm and steadied me, leading me inside to the ground floor.

We stepped into a porch with large granite tiles on the floor. The original stone was exposed and a stone staircase was embedded into the walls. It was as if the steps were suspended in the air. There was no-one inside.

'Frank told me he'd meet us here,' the Professor said. 'He must be around somewhere.'

There was a dark walnut door at the base of the staircase. The Professor twisted the doorknob, the door opened and I followed him inside.

'I wonder what the parties were like back in the 1700s?' I said.

'Probably wilder than you imagine.'

'If only we could go back in time,' I said.

He laughed. 'If only.'

We found ourselves in one of the castle towers which housed a modern staircase that brought us to the floor above. The Professor explained that the ground-floor area of the tower we were in had previously been used for storage in the early 20th century when Jesuit Priests had resided in the castle.

On the first floor, we emerged into a great hall which lay across the width of the castle and looked like it covered half of the floor space on the first level. The stained-glass windows allowed light to seep onto wooden floorboards, bringing the room to life. For an instant, I was transported back in time and could imagine the glowing chandeliers, and fireplaces further illuminating the room. I imagined people in brocaded dress and powdered wigs laughing as dinner was served to them by many footmen.

A short stocky man approached us from the stairway. The Professor introduced him as Frank, one of the castle guides.

'This is Lucy,' the Professor told him, 'who, as I said, has a great interest in your castle.'

'I'm sorry I wasn't there to greet you, Lucy,' Frank said. 'My colleague Karen took ill and had to leave early. I was just calling for a replacement upstairs. You're very welcome.'

'It's a beautiful setting.'

'Yes, indeed. I have to apologise though. The castle is currently undergoing renovations. I'm afraid I won't be able to give you access to all areas. Some of the rooms aren't safe. There is no-one on site today now except myself and the café staff, so I can't stay with you. Please stay as long as you like. The Professor is as good a guide as any, Lucy.'

'But what about the tower at the other end of this room – do you have workers in there?' I asked.

'No, not at the moment,' he said.

'I saw a woman at one of the windows as we drew near the house. Your colleague, I suppose.'

Frank looked startled. 'You must be mistaken,' he said. 'I saw Karen leave myself earlier and there are no workers on site today.'

'I'm pretty sure someone was there. The top window, I think.'

'When was this?'

'No more than a few minutes ago.' I looked at the Professor for confirmation and he nodded.

'We'd better go check,' Frank said.

He directed us to the main staircase and we emerged on the second floor into a large gallery which he told us was used in the old days for grand balls and parties.

'There's no access to the third floor from here,' he said. 'Follow me.'

We walked to the opposite side of the gallery where Frank opened a door leading to a narrow central staircase.

'This leads to the third floor.'

The Professor and I climbed the stairs after Frank. He hurried on ahead down a narrow corridor, unlocked a door at the other end and disappeared inside.

By the time we caught up, he had reappeared. 'No-one there,' he said and locked the door again.

'It must have been a ghost,' I said and laughed.

Frank didn't look amused.

'Are you sure you saw someone?' the Professor asked. 'Could it have been a trick of the light?'

'Maybe it was our ghost,' Frank said.

'What?' I said.

'Oh, here we go.' The Professor rolled his eyes. 'Not that old story again, Frank.'

Frank ignored him. 'It is said, Lucy, that the Earl of Desmond's daughter, Isobel, lost her heart to one of the castle guards here.'

'They fell in love?'

'They did – and when her father found out he ordered the poor guard to be imprisoned in one of the tower rooms.'

'Oh my God,' I said, feeling shivers run down my spine. 'What happened then?'

'The tale goes that the unfortunate young man was poisoned by Isobel's father.'

'What happened to Isobel?'

'She is said to have gone up to the roof and jumped off, poor thing.'

'So both of their ghosts haunt the castle?'

'I've only ever seen Isobel myself,' Frank said.

'You've actually *seen* her?' I asked.

'It's all hogwash, Lucy,' the Professor said. 'Don't believe Frank for a second.'

'Please, could you show us into that tower room?' I had to see it for myself.

'It's not safe in there.'

'Perhaps we can have a look in from the door?' the Professor asked.

'Well, if you must,' Frank said. 'I haven't met anyone else who has seen her, so I guess I can make an exception for you.'

He unlocked the door again.

'Watch your step. There's scaffolding just inside. Mind your head too.'

He pushed back the door and the hinges creaked.

We stepped inside.

The light was low as I looked around the room. Wooden panelling covered the room and was badly damaged in places. It had been painted white at some stage, though the peeling paint had turned a greyish colour. I could feel a draught seeping in from the old windows.

'What did the ghost look like when your saw her, Frank?' I asked.

'A little lost, I think. It was too dark to see the colour of her hair though I could see that she wore a dress of green or blue. Then she disappeared through the door.'

The Professor shook his head.

'I hate going into this room now,' Frank said.

'Have you thought of inviting a medium to come in?' I asked.

'I did ask the Office of Public Works about it. Emily, my superior, wouldn't listen – doesn't believe in spirits, she says. I never got any further with it.'

'I guess it's a hard thing to believe.'

The Professor walked out into the main room and I followed him.

Frank locked up the room.

It was then I remembered the key we had found in the castle accounts book and wondered what door it had opened here in 1719. I hoped we'd get a chance to find out.

CHAPTER 14

Dublin, 1719

The light had begun to fade as Abigail finished preparing the vellum leaves for the stomacher. She placed her embroidery tools into her sewing box and went into the kitchen where Miss Gavin was preparing to cook a rabbit. She was grinding some cloves, mace and a shallot together with a mortar and pestle.

'I suppose you won't be joining us?' Miss Gavin asked.

'I'd best be going before it gets much darker.'

'It's later than I thought. My brother will walk with you.' Mary went and took a mixing bowl from a cupboard.

'Your brother would prefer not to waste his time with me, I imagine,' Abigail said.

Mary scraped the ground mixture into the bowl and added salt and pepper and a little parsley and sorrel.

'Hugh will not mind much. It's not a long walk. Or I can ask Michael if you'd prefer … He would be happy to get away from the loom for half an hour or so.'

She slid a pile of rabbit meat she'd cut up into a pot and added the contents of the bowl. Then she set the pot to hang over the fire. The butter had melted nicely in a bowl she had left by hearth and she took it to the table.

'I'll take a public cab instead,' Abigail said and tried to smile.

Mary began to beat two egg yolks with a little claret and melted butter. 'Our dinner should be ready in half an hour. Why don't you stay to eat with us and get a cab later?'

'I appreciate your kindness, Miss Gavin, I really do, but my mother expects me home before dark so I would prefer to leave now before she worries. Besides, I don't want to put your brother out every day. I will make sure to leave before it gets dark in future, I promise.'

Mary didn't want to let her go out on her own. She should go outside to make sure that she took a cab, but her dinner would probably burn if she did.

She poured the beaten eggs into the pot and watched it sizzle around the rabbit meat. 'If that's what you want, then off you go. We'll see you here early tomorrow.'

'I hope you have a good evening,' Abigail said and left, taking her sewing box with her.

Outside, Abigail pulled the hood of her cloak up to hide her face. It had begun to rain. She walked from Coles Alley out onto Meath Street. The street traders were closing for the day and no-one paid her much attention until she turned into Engine Alley. A street brawl was in progress on the narrow lane. She stopped, deciding which way to turn. She could go back towards Thomas Street and from there walk to Francis Street which would take her home – or, perhaps, better reach Francis Street by way of Crostick Lane and Garden Lane.

Before she could decide which way to go, she was surrounded by several men and two middle-aged women eyeing up her sewing box.

She turned on her heel to run. Someone caught her arm. She struggled to get away, keeping her box tight to her chest.

'*Miss Harton?*' a man's voice called out. '*Here, let me through. Take your hands off her.*'

Abigail was swiftly pulled away from the crowd. She stumbled backwards and saw that the man who was holding her was Dr. Monroe.

'Are you all right?' he asked, releasing her. 'They have not harmed you?'

'No, I am not hurt. Thank you, Dr. Monroe.'

She despaired at being caught out alone so late in the day.

'Thank God for that.'

'I am much obliged to you, Dr. Monroe.'

'But what are you doing here?' he asked.

Abigail desperately tried to think of what to say. 'I was taking a shortcut.'

'Were you visiting a friend?'

'Yes, a friend. I forgot the time.' Abigail said, admonishing herself for lying. 'We were sewing together.'

'It was lucky that I was passing this way, was it not?'

'Most fortunate indeed.' Abigail clasped the sewing box tightly in her hands.

'Well, no harm has been done. Come along. Your father has invited me for supper this evening and I was on my way there.' Monroe glanced at the dead cock on the street and knew that he had lost his bid. He hoped to make good on the gaming tables tonight, otherwise he would have to answer to Palmer.

'Looks like you won a better prize there, doctor,' a scrawny gentleman called out as they passed by.

'Show some respect for the lady,' Monroe said, and hoped that Miss Harton did not realise that they knew him.

But Abigail's mind was wholly preoccupied by the near miss she had just had.

'Please don't tell my parents about this,' she said.

'Of course not, Miss Harton. There is no need to distress them.'

Abigail nodded, relieved. She must heed Miss Gavin's advice in the future.

Sarah and Henry were drinking wine in the drawing room with Mrs. Harton when Abigail and Monroe arrived at Pluncot Street.

'Where did you get to, Abigail? I've been worried about you,' Margaret said when she saw Dr. Monroe arriving in behind her youngest daughter.

'You really shouldn't be out on your own, Abigail,' Sarah said.

'I strolled through the markets on my way back and lost time. It won't happen again,' she said, standing by the fire.

'Miss Harton took her sewing box with her to visit her friend.' Monroe laughed. 'You ladies so like to talk for hours.'

Monroe was more curious about Abigail than ever. She really had the most admirable high spirits.

'I just happened to meet Miss Harton on my way here,' he said.

The drawing-room door opened and Dr. Harton camc in to sit with thc company.

'Ah, this is where you all are,' he said. 'Good evening, Monroe.'

'Good evening, Dr, Harton.'

Abigail could see that her mother was a little better, though she was still pale against the black dress she wore.

'Now that you are here, I can share my news at last,' Sarah beamed.

'What news?' Abigail asked.

'Isn't it wonderful?' her mother said. 'Sarah is with child.'

The stress of the day had built up and the news was too much for Abigail. She kissed her sister and quickly hugged her brother-in-law in congratulations and tried not to cry.

'I'm so happy for you, Sarah,' she said.

'I'm sorry I didn't tell you sooner. I was afraid to, in case anything should happen, after Benjamin ...' Sarah broke off, dabbing her eyes with her handkerchief.

'It is wonderful news. We should celebrate,' Abigail said.

'That is why we have come to visit,' said Henry. 'To ask you to dine with us tomorrow evening. You too, Dr. Monroe.'

'Mama, you will come?' Sarah asked anxiously.

'I will try,' Margaret said. It was the least she could do for her daughter who was bringing a new life into the family.

Abigail excused herself to summon Brigid to bring some wine. When she returned to the hall, Dr. Monroe was waiting for her there. She hadn't noticed before that he was wearing a new set of clothes.

'Have you recovered?' he asked.

'I was just a little shocked. I shall be all right.'

'You do not need to worry. I shall remember not to tell your parents exactly what transpired on Garden Lane.'

'I appreciate your discretion.'

'Before you thank me, I have a condition,' Monroe said, enjoying the narrowing of the lady's eyes and the flaring of her nostrils. She was a lively girl, that was for sure.

Abigail looked at him carefully.

'What condition?' she asked.

Monroe hesitated a moment before speaking.

'Miss Harton, I can assure you that I have only your family's best interests at heart. If there is anything I can ever do to help you, please let me know.'

'Thank you, Dr. Monroe.'

'I have begun to secure some private patients of my own.'

'Yes?' Abigail didn't understand why he was telling her this.

'I'm sorry, I'm being a fool,' he said. 'What I am trying to say is that I hope to be in a position to secure a household of my own shortly.'

'That is excellent news, Dr. Monroe,' said Abigail. 'But what was your condition?'

'Miss Harton, I would like to ask your father's permission to court you. If that is something you would consider?' He watched her reaction closely.

Abigail had never thought that she would attract such an accomplished man as Dr. Monroe. She found herself astonished at his interest in her after the earlier incident that day.

'I don't know what to say,' she said.

'It's quite sudden, I know. But I want you to know that I have admired your strength these last weeks, especially since poor Benjamin's death. I want to support you with all of my heart. I can't imagine what it must be like to lose such a brother. I pray that you may consider me.'

Abigail looked away. Benjamin was not a month dead. Was it unseemly for Monroe to have asked her so soon? She couldn't quite fathom how she really felt about him.

'I hope I have not spoken out of turn, or insulted you?' Monroe was surprised at how nervous he felt. There was much at stake.

Abigail considered him again. The idea of becoming a wife was overwhelming. She wondered what it would be like to lie beside him at night, to share with him her every fear, her every dream. She felt unsure. She didn't know him well, but he had shown her kindness and was working for her father without recompense.

'I am honoured by your attention, Dr. Monroe.'

'Please call me William,' Monroe said, coming close to her, touching her face.

Abigail looked into his eyes, amazed that she could end this day feeling such relief.

'Dr. Monroe, you may ask my father for his permission,' she said, 'though I would prefer if you would wait until tomorrow. This is the first evening my mother has come down to dinner since Benjamin left us. Let us enjoy Sarah and Henry's news tonight. Tomorrow you may ask my father for his permission to court me, if you are sure.'

'Wouldn't your mother be happy to hear your news right away?' Monroe asked, not believing his luck that Miss Harton, everything he desired in a wife, might be his for the taking.

'I suppose you're right,' Abigail said, pausing as she turned towards the drawing-room door.

'No. Your instinct is better, my dear. There is no rush at all.' He took Abigail's hand and kissed it. 'I shall wait to ask your father's permission.'

Abigail was pleased. He would make a thoughtful husband.

They rejoined the others in the drawing room.

'How well you look in that dress, Abigail,' Sarah said. 'The colour blue quite becomes you. Does is not, Dr. Monroe?'

Abigail looked at the young doctor standing beside her.

'She is the prettiest lady by far, with the exception of course of her mother and sister,' he said and they all laughed.

Margaret glanced at Dr. Monroe and hoped he had an interest in Abigail. It was her dearest wish to have her youngest daughter settled and Dr. Monroe was such a pleasing young man, if a little over-gracious. But she could forgive him that because of the effect he was having on Abigail's too pale complexion.

Abigail thought her father would be proud of her if she could secure such a match. She glanced at her mother. With the prospect of a grandchild on the way, she hoped that her mother might be restored to her usual generous and happy self. She herself needed some time to reflect on the events of the day, to reconsider every nuance of her private conversation with Dr. Monroe. For now, she couldn't help noticing his hands, at how smooth they were and how they had felt against her skin.

John Harton was telling stories of his youth, of his training in Paris, and all listened and asked him questions. Abigail had heard these stories before. She sat close to the fire and felt the warmth of the flames seep into her bones.

When she glanced at Dr. Monroe, he was watching her. She looked into her lap, embarrassed at being caught. As his wife, she would have her own home and children.

'You are too close to the fire,' Sarah warned.

'Sit by Dr. Monroe, Abigail,' Mrs. Harton said. She had been delighted to notice her daughter and the young doctor pass looks between them and wanted to give Abigail every opportunity of success.

Abigail obeyed her mother and sat beside him. She could smell the newness of his clothes and the faint smell of soap from his skin. She tried to distract herself with practical things, sipped her wine and tried to listen attentively to the conversation.

Whatever happened with regard to Dr. Monroe's proposal, she would continue to work on the dress of emerald silk. She had promised Miss Gavin and she would not go back on her word.

CHAPTER 15

Abigail spent a restless night, tossing and turning, her dreams a mixture of Dr. Monroe and the weaver Mr. Gavin. The two men had somehow become confused in her mind.

When she heard her father leave the house, she put on her housecoat and went downstairs to her parents' room.

'Mama, are you awake?'

She saw that her mother was wide awake.

'What is it?' Margaret sat up in her bed.

'Dr. Monroe has asked if he can seek Father's permission to court me.'

'Oh my dear. What was your answer?'

'I told him that he could ask Father's permission today.' Abigail sat on the edge of her mother's bed.

'You seem uncertain, Abigail. Don't you like him?'

'He has been kind ... protective ...'

'I see,' said Margaret.

'It is a good match, Mama. Besides, he is handsome ...'

'Oh Abigail, only agree if you are sure.'

'Were you sure when Papa asked you?'

'I really can't quite remember.'

The two women laughed.

'I am confident that he will be a good match for you,' Margaret said, touching her daughter's hair.

Abigail walked to the window. She had expected to feel differently.

'Your father will most likely bring him to dine this evening.' Margaret got out of her bed. 'You will wear the yellow poplin tonight.'

'Dr. Monroe is not going to notice what dress I wear.'

Abigail helped her mother put on her housecoat.

'I just wish Benjamin could be here,' Margaret said.

'Oh, Mama.' Abigail held her mother close.

'I shall be all right. Come, let us go down and make plans for the evening.'

'I must go to the Gavins. We can talk when I return.'

'Can't you embroider at home? Tell Miss Gavin your good news. She will understand.'

'There is work to be done on the skirt and it is too large to bring home, Mama. I promised her I would finish it on time. Besides, I am to teach her apprentice how to work with metal threads.'

'Can't Miss Gavin teach the girl herself? What if Dr. Monroe finds out you are working there? You cannot risk your future for a dress.'

'Even if Dr. Monroe proposes, we cannot ask him to pay the baker and the butcher.'

Margaret decided to let the matter drop.

'It is clear that he admires you very much.'

'I am not so sure. He may see me as a good business match.'

'Nonsense, child.'

'I must go before I am late.'

'What if Dr. Monroe visits while you are gone?'

'Say that I have gone to see Sarah and Henry.'

Margaret considered her daughter. 'If that's what makes you happy,' she said.

'You know it doesn't make me happy. It's what I must do. I have to get ready.'

Margaret watched her daughter leave. She turned to the book of fairy tales by her bedside and held it to her heart. She would try to let Benjamin's memory go today. She had let one son go before and she could do it again. When she heard her daughter leave the house, she walked upstairs and left the book on Abigail's bed.

Abigail closed the hall door behind her. She was sure that her father would give his permission. The heavy frost had made the cobblestones treacherous and she stumbled on the street. She had to get to the Gavins' house on time. The faster she could finish the dress the less chance there was of anyone knowing about it. Dr. Monroe, she was sure, would be unhappy if he found out. She quickened her step crossing Francis Street. She knew she had to be practical. Miss Gavin had agreed a price and it was enough to keep the household for months if they were careful. If she could finish the dress on time.

CHAPTER 16

Mary Gavin watched Abigail Harton walk into her kitchen. She was impressed when she saw that she had brought stencils to show Grace. If Miss Harton could teach her apprentice to embroider, she would be able to take on more work and build up her business. The Boden Ball might seal her reputation as a dressmaker of the highest quality and, with the help of her brother, she would be able to move her workshop closer to Dublin Castle where business was booming.

'I hope you are well this morning?'

'Thank you, yes,' Abigail said.

'Sit down.' The girl's fingers were blue with the cold. 'You'll have some porridge before you start for the day. You'll work better on a full stomach.' It was in her interests to make sure that she was comfortable.

'You are very kind, Miss Gavin.'

'If you have no food inside you, you cannot concentrate.' She needed the girl to be in the best of health if she was to finish the work in time.

Abigail sat down at the kitchen table and was grateful for the meal.

Grace came in from the backyard, taking off her cloak in a hurry.

'I am sorry I am late, ma'am,' she said. 'Good morning, Miss Harton.'

'Good morning, Grace,' Abigail responded.

'Miss Harton, I have placed the large frame as close to the window as I can. You must tell me if there is enough light, for if there is not we will need to move the frame again before you start. Grace, get the fire lighting in the workroom. And wash your hands when you're finished.'

Grace left to start the fire. Abigail and Mary followed. In the workroom a panel of green silk had been secured on a large frame, ready for embroidering.

'Grace and I will help you with the rest of the dress when the material is cut.'

'Thank you. The silver vines look well against this colour,' Abigail said, trying to focus on the day ahead.

'You can choose coloured threads from this cupboard. Please let me know if you need more and I will replenish them.' Mary looked at Abigail. 'Do you think you can do it?'

Abigail would need to work long hours to finish the stomacher and dress on time. She welcomed it. Here she could forget her brother Benjamin asleep in his grave, her mother's grief, and her father's denial. Of Dr. Monroe's courtship, she was not sure what to think.

'Yes, I can do it,' she said and looked at Miss Gavin. 'I would not have started if I didn't think so.'

'Good.' Mary felt sorry for the girl. If she was to lose her brother, she didn't know what she would do.

'Could I ask a favour?' Abigail asked.

'What is it?'

'Might I move the embroidery frame away from the window?'

'You don't want anyone to see you working here, is that it?'

'If my father was to find out, I might not be able to come back.'

Mary was annoyed that Dr. Harton might stop his daughter working, especially as he himself wasn't able to provide for his family. She could not answer for a moment.

Abigail was in dread of what Miss Gavin might say.

Mary tried to put herself into the Abigail's position and knew that she probably would have asked the same thing.

She turned to Abigail. 'It doesn't matter to me where you work, as long as you have enough light to do it properly and as long as that work gets done.'

'I appreciate your understanding, Miss Gavin.'

Grace finished lighting the fire at the back of the room and Abigail started to work. Mary looked at the two girls in her workshop and thought what an odd pair they were.

Abigail spent the rest of the day at the table preparing more pieces of vellum for the skirt to give the leaves of her design profile on the silk of the dress. She supervised Grace cutting the animal skin. She would start to embroider the bluebirds on the stomacher later. The stitching would help clear her mind and she would be glad of it. Yet her thoughts continued to stray to Dr. Monroe. With him in the family, her family's fortunes would change for the better. She imagined his face again, his blue eyes and the way he had looked at her. She watched Grace and tried to focus on her work.

Mary looked at the clock and wished that her brother would return home soon. He had gone with Mr. Long to collect thrown silk from his suppliers, and young Michael had gone with him. The silk had been ordered by Mr. Long and had been shipped from London. When Hugh arrived home, she would need to talk to him about their Aunt Laetitia in Belfast. She had received a letter from their Uncle Francis saying that she had taken a turn for the worst.

CHAPTER 17

Margaret Harton could not wait any longer. Her daughter's future was at stake. She could not allow her to continue to work at the Gavins. There had been no word from Esther Johnson and she needed to speak with Dean Swift. She would go to the cathedral in the hope that she might find him there. In the looking glass she saw herself clearly. A thin, middle-aged woman, gaunt and grey, dressed in black.

She unlocked the drawer of her dressing table and took out her jewellery box. It contained the only possessions of value she had left – the string of pearls and the emerald earrings she had inherited from her mother. She took out the earrings and wrapped them in a handkerchief, then put them in the pocket of her dress.

She placed a white cap on her head and glanced in the mirror again. She looked matronly enough. It would do.

'It will be good for you to get out, mistress,' Brigid said as she helped her on with her cloak and gloves at the door.

'I am going to the cathedral to say my prayers, that is all.'

'Yes, mistress,' Brigid said and closed the hall door behind her, delighted to have the house to herself.

Margaret made her way to St. Patrick's Street, turning left into St. Patrick's Close. She could hear the young choristers as she approached the cathedral. Evensong was over. People were leaving through the main doors. She made her way against them, pushing through until she was inside.

The Dean was there, talking to a group of men, no doubt on church business. She would wait.

She started to feel nauseous. Looking up at the vaulted ceiling, her head started to spin. Maybe this was a mistake? Then, to her relief, she saw the Dean coming down the aisle towards her. Several people continued to congregate around him – though when he reached her his attention was hers alone.

'Mrs. Harton, I am so happy to see you here,' he said.

'It is good to speak with you again.'

'And your husband? How does he do?'

'He works all hours at the hospital. I fear it will be the end of him.'

'He does God's work.'

'That is why I have come today to see you. Can we talk privately?'

The Dean wondered why so pious a woman wanted a private audience with him without her husband. He was looking forward to his late-afternoon tea, a little daily luxury he allowed himself, and invited her to the Deanery to join him.

Outside the rain forced them to hurry across the road, through the gate and across the narrow garden into the house.

'Let me take your cloak,' Dean Swift said once they were inside.

Margaret gave her cloak to him and then tried to push her straggling hair back under her cap.

She looked as though she was about to be hung, drawn and quartered, the Dean thought and smothered a smile, more curious than ever.

'I have tea in my office. It is where I hide away from the world. Come, join me.'

Margaret followed him into the small room.

'It is a cosy place to hide,' she said, not knowing where to sit.

'It is indeed.' He sat down in his favourite chair by the fire. 'Sit here, and warm yourself.' He pointed to the chair opposite him and pulled a cord by the mantel. Before long his housekeeper Mrs. Brent arrived, and the Dean ordered his tea.

'I do hope you like saffron cake,' he said, when Mrs. Brent had left the room. 'The cook baked it only this morning.'

Margaret burst into tears.

'I am sorry. It was a mistake to come here,' she said.

'Mrs. Harton, I am a man of God. I am here to help you in any way that I can. There is no need to fret for little Benjamin any longer. I assure you that he is already safe in heaven.'

'It is not my son's death that distresses me today.'

The Dean didn't know what to think. He hoped Mrs. Harton's unmarried daughter hadn't got herself into trouble. The saffron cake was losing its appeal.

'Then how may I help you?' he asked.

'It is my husband,' Margaret said, trying to stem her tears. She took the earrings in the handkerchief from her pocket.

'Is Dr. Harton ill? I will pray for him, you have my word.'

'It is not prayer that I ask for but a loan.'

'A loan? Mrs. Harton, does your husband know you have come here?'

'No, and you must promise that you will not tell him.'

'You ask for a loan. I must know first why you need it.'

'I ask only for five pounds. I can repay you, I assure you.' She unfolded the handkerchief to reveal the earrings.

'Mrs. Harton, please put the jewellery away. Please tell me, how has this come to pass? Is your husband gambling?'

'No, he works for nothing at his hospital and the poor cannot pay. He won't attend private patients and has even given up his lectures in the College.' She dried her eyes and continued with her story. 'We have been living on our savings for months but they have almost run out. My daughter has been forced to work for a seamstress without her father's knowledge. She carries the whole household on her shoulders. It is not proper.'

The Dean of St. Patrick's sat back in his seat and listened as Mrs. Harton told of her family's predicament. The tea and saffron cake arrived, and Swift thanked his housekeeper as she set the offering down. He waited until she had left the room before continuing the conversation.

'Mrs. Harton, might I perhaps speak to your husband? A loan will only help you temporarily. You need a permanent solution. Perhaps I can give him counsel on this? I could call to your house this evening and speak to him myself. What do you say?'

'If he knew I was here, it would destroy him. No, I must find a way myself to make him change.'

'Most men don't change unless they desire it themselves.'

'You are wrong. I will make him see sense. I just need more time.' She went to hand him the earrings. 'Please take them.'

'Mrs. Harton, rest assured that I will help you as best as I can. I will loan you the five pounds. You do not need to pay me back until you are able, but you must promise me that you will tell your husband. Your actions today will surely make him see the situation more clearly.'

'Thank you, Dean Swift. I will do that.'

'Good. Now put the earrings away, I have no use for them. Come, please eat some cake.'

Margaret tried to relax. He was trying to make her feel better and she was grateful. He began to talk of other matters, and she managed to eat the slice that he offered her.

He then gave her five pounds, walked her to the door and watched as she passed through the gate of his property. He had loaned many people money over the years and didn't always get it back. With the Hartons, he hoped that he would, for their own sakes. Dr. Harton was a good man with an honourable vocation. Perhaps there was something more he could do himself? He thought of those who could not work, who were sick or mad or fools. There were so many of them but what could be done? He went back to his office to think on it a while and tried to enjoy the rest of his tea.

Walking home, Margaret Harton prayed that her husband would never find out she had borrowed the money. She had no intention of telling him. She would find a way to pay back the Dean on her own. She couldn't risk Dr. Monroe finding out that Abigail worked to support them. With the loan, Abigail would no longer need to work at the Gavins' house. Dr. Monroe might be Abigail's only chance at happiness and it was best that her daughter caught him sooner rather than later. She would worry about how to pay the money back when Abigail's future was secure.

First, she would buy a piece of cream satin to make an embroidered waistcoat for Dr. Monroe. It would show him that he had her approval for the match and she would get it done quickly and give it to him just as soon as it was ready.

CHAPTER 18

'I hope you enjoyed your walk, miss,' Brigid said when Abigail got home.

'Yes, I did, thank you. Is my mother in the drawing room?'

'Mrs. Harton went for a nap an hour ago.'

'Did she have visitors today?' Abigail asked.

'Dr. Monroe was here a short time ago. He said he'd call back in an hour. The mistress spoke to him before she went upstairs.'

Abigail hoped that he had not changed his mind. Perhaps he had reconsidered the incident in Garden Lane. Maybe he thought she should not have been unaccompanied and was a bad choice for a wife. She wouldn't wake her mother yet. It was best that she sleep.

'I'll be up in my room, Brigid. Call me when Dr. Monroe returns,' she said.

Upstairs, she took off her shoes and lay down on her bed. Concentrating on her work for so long had been difficult. She just wanted to close her eyes for a moment. She tried not to think about her circumstances … whether Dr. Monroe had changed his mind or if her father had chosen to reject Dr. Monroe's request.

She felt something beneath her. She pulled a book out and raised it in the air. It was the book of French fairy tales. She hugged it to her and moved into a foetal position. She so missed her little brother and hoped that he was safe in heaven, away from all of the worries of the world.

She went to the last page that she had read to him.

The Good Witch saw the lightning in the forest and heard the cries of dying men. She flew to the sounds to help, but when she arrived the Prince and his men were lying dead on the forest floor. She only had the power to save one.

Abigail's hands traced the tangled vines of the printed forest on the page's illustration.

The witch chanted magic words over the Prince and touched his face. Slowly his body started to disappear and was replaced by the body of a bluebird. For, you see, the Good Witch could not bring the Prince back to his human life. She was only able to turn him into a bird or animal of the forest and she choose a bluebird. When the transformation was complete, the bluebird Prince flew up and away from his saviour towards the lands of his father's enemies.

He flew day and night, through the wind and storm, to reach the high tower of his enemy's castle. There was a window at the very top of the tower where a golden light shone within. The Prince landed on the sill and looked inside. There a young Princess sat at a spinning wheel, spinning silk thread into gold which she wound onto a large spool. There were many spools in the room, half of gold and half of silk. The Prince thought about his promise to his father to end the war. What could he do? He was only a bird. How could he secure peace when all he wanted to do was to comfort the young girl who sat by the window at the spinning wheel? He began to sing a sweet song, and as the Princess looked towards him she did not feel alone.

Abigail fell asleep, dreaming of gold thread and of Hugh Gavin asleep by the fire. When Brigid knocked and called her, for an instant she thought she was in Miss Gavin's kitchen, before realising she was at home. She fixed her clothes and got up to open the door.

'Miss, Dr. Monroe waits for you in your father's office.'

'Thank you, Brigid.'

'He seemed in exceptionally fine spirits, if I may say, miss.'

Abigail tried to smile. 'Is my mother awake?' She glanced into the looking glass.

'She is dressing,' Brigid said as she left.

Abigail put the book under her pillow. She had wanted to place it beside Benjamin in his coffin, but her mother had forbidden it. Abigail was glad now that she had it to remember her brother by.

Monroe was waiting in Dr. Harton's office. It was a charming room, the type a man could relax in at the end of a day. He coveted the space though there was no fire lighting. If he could own a house like this one day, he would order a fire be kept going all day long whether he was there or not. He paced the room, waiting for Abigail to appear. He had been surprised to find that she was out earlier without any chaperone. He would need to speak to her about that. It was not becoming. Today, however, he would simply tell her the good news.

Abigail walked in, looking younger than her twenty years. The veil of sleep had softened her features in the afternoon light and Dr. Harton was moved by her youth. He was an extremely fortunate man.

'Miss Harton,' he said, 'I could not wait to tell you. The answer is yes. Your father has consented to our courtship.'

Abigail turned away from him. Monroe did not know what to make of it.

'Miss Harton, is this not what you wanted?' He turned her around to face him.

'Yes, yes, it is,' she said.

Monroe drew her to him. 'Are you not happy that it is done?'

He tilted Abigail's face to meet his gaze. When she nodded, he gently kissed her on the lips. She was so sweet. He couldn't help himself.

Abigail was not sure that she liked the kiss. There was a taste of wine and pickle when he parted her lips. Nor did she like the musty smell of his clothes. She pulled away. She had imagined something different. She had imagined the smell of wood on the fire, the smell of the weaver.

'What is the matter?' Monroe asked. He did not want to offend. If he could secure her, his situation in the world would be much advanced. To be associated with such an honourable family as the Hartons was something to be cherished. He wouldn't have much longer to wait to secure the home that had eluded him. He smiled and looked at her tenderly. 'I have been too bold. Let me apologise. It is just that I feel deeply.' He was surprised by the esteem in which he held her, the fact that he wanted to do right by her. To marry her properly and forever.

'It is too soon after my brother's death,' she said.

'Of course, I should have thought. Though your mother was exceptionally pleased when I told her earlier.'

'I am glad.'

He went to hold her again, but this time she backed away. He put on his gloves instead.

'Are you not staying to dine with us?' she asked.

'Unfortunately, I have another appointment,' he lied. 'My landlady is in very poor health and I have promised to look in on her this evening. It's just a bad case of gout but I have to keep her happy for fear she will put up my rent.' He laughed.

'I'm sorry you cannot stay,' Abigail said.

'Don't worry. I will not reside there long. With my growing practice, I hope to move to better lodgings soon. I may secure something close to Pluncot Street if I am lucky.'

'I hope I have not offended you?'

'Not at all, Miss Harton,' he said. 'Your honour is what I admire about you most.'

'I bid you good day then.'

It was a dismissal and he was charmed by it. They would have such fun together when everything was in place.

Abigail went back up to her bedroom. It was time to put away childish things. She took the book of fairy tales downstairs and put it on the shelf in her father's office where it belonged.

CHAPTER 19

It was late when Hugh Gavin and young Michael got home. The thrown silk had arrived from London and after collecting it they had gone back to Daniel Long's for supper. Hugh had lingered too long after, talking with his friend. Unlike poplin, a mix of wool and silk, the aristocracy were buying pure silk and he would continue to weave it to try to make a profit. He would ask Miss Harton to design unique damasks for next year too. Most of his cloth from last season lay in a corner in his sister's workroom. The fabric was of good quality. However, it was unfortunate that his original buyer had unexpectedly had a death in the family and had not purchased it, as they had to wear black for months yet. The pattern had gone out of season. So far, the cloth had not caught the eye of any of his sister's clients either.

Mr. Long offered to help offload the old fabric for him. He was inviting merchants and other customers to his house off Weaver's Square tomorrow. He would introduce them to Hugh in the hope that they might buy from him too.

The front door of the workshop was boarded up, so Hugh and the boy went to the side of the house. Hugh hoped that his sister was still awake as he knocked on the side door. At this late hour, his key was useless. In the city, there were too many thieves on the streets at night. All householders had to be vigilant. He heard his sister pulling open the three bolts on the inside of the door.

The weather felt like it was about to take a turn for the worst and he feared that a storm was coming. He thought of the sea and his friend George Thompson who had left for the Americas six months before. What would his life be like if he had gone himself then?

The side door opened and his sister beckoned them inside.

'You both look worn out,' she said. 'Come sit by the fire and I'll pour you some ale.'

'That would be good,' Hugh said.

'There is still some pottage. Sit and I will fetch it.'

'We've eaten already, Mary, at Mr. Long's. Michael, you can go off now to bed.'

'Good night, Mr. Gavin, Miss Gavin,' the boy said and left the room.

'Sleep well, Michael,' said Mary.

Hugh took off his cloak and hung it by the fire, then sat down to take off his boots. He sat back in the easy chair and, enjoying the warmth, closed his eyes.

No, he hadn't gone with George from Belfast. He was here with his sister Mary instead. Aunt Laetitia had paid for his sister Mary's education and had made the connection to place her as an apprentice dressmaker in the noble Brabazon household. Mary had left their employ after ten years and set up as a dressmaker in her own right, leasing this house in Coles Alley. She had offered him the front workshop in the house. She had told him of the business to be had from the merchants and weavers who supplied cloth to the aristocrats who frequented Dublin Castle. The only trouble was that he had seen little of that business. The gentry favoured designs from Paris and Lyon, and what business they did give to local weavers was already tied up. His sister had been like a mother to him since their parents had died and so he had decided to give the venture at least a year. That had been six months ago. He was not so sure that a fortune was to be made in Dublin weaving silk anymore. The mercers and the more established merchants dictated the markets. His sister had a better chance of success here than he did. She had the connections and numerous orders. He was becoming a liability. If he could sell last year's cloth at a good price, and make a profit in the spring, he might be able to buy a passage to Boston.

Hugh was anxious for news of his friend's venture in America. Hugh had given him some capital to invest. He tried not to think of what might happen if his investment there had fallen through. Now that he'd taken charge of the boy, he felt duty bound to stay in Dublin until he could find young Michael a place elsewhere. It would take time, that was all. He thought of Abigail Harton. She was just a girl. He'd see things more clearly in the morning, he was sure of it, after he'd had a good night's rest.

He opened his eyes.

'Mary, did a letter come for me today?'

'And who would be writing to you, brother?'

'George Thompson, that's who. I wrote to him three months ago for news of my investment.'

'That good for nothing? I told you not to give him any money. You can consider it lost.'

'George was a good friend in Belfast and a hard worker. I have no doubt he will do well. Besides, he painted such a picture of America in his last letter that I thought I should like to hear some more about it.'

'Can't you read the newspaper instead? There is better entertainment to be had there.'

Hugh wondered what had got into his sister.

'What did George Thompson ever do to you? Do you not wish him well?'

'Of course I do, brother. It's just that I've had a letter myself.'

'From whom?'

'From Uncle Francis. It's about Aunt Laetitia.'

'Can't that woman leave us alone?'

'Laetitia has taken bad, he says. Our uncle fears she is not long for the world and if we want to see her before she dies, he advises us to travel to Belfast.'

'With the winter upon us? That aunt of ours has nine lives … It's probably a ruse to get us to go back.'

'How can you be so hard, Hugh? Didn't Laetitia help set me up in business and get me started as a dressmaker?'

'And she will never let you forget it, Mary.'

'And what of Uncle Francis? Do you not care to visit him? You let him down over Cousin Sally.'

'Can we not talk of that anymore?'

'Sally would have made you a good wife.'

'She wasn't for me. Can't we leave it at that?'

'You could have had the house in Belfast and Uncle Francis's business too.'

'And listen to the tattle of Aunt Laetitia and Cousin Sally all day long. No, not I. And, Mary, you did not want to be alone in Dublin.'

'Well, there is that, I suppose.' Mary smiled. 'We will do well for ourselves here I am sure … I never did like Cousin Sally much myself.'

Mary sat down by the fire alongside her brother. Hugh was probably right. It was, no doubt, all for the best. Uncle Francis had since taken on a new journeyman who was about the right age for Sally. She was still young and pretty enough to tempt most men. Aunt Laetitia was a temperamental self-appointed martyr. She probably had nothing more than a winter chill.

'Let's hope Aunt Laetitia can wait until January to die,' she said.

Hugh sat back in his chair. His bones felt weary and the anxiety of the last few months weighed heavily on him.

'Mary, I don't mean the woman any harm.'

'I'll write to our uncle tomorrow and ask if there has been any improvement,' she said. 'I can't travel to Belfast until after the Boden Ball myself anyway.'

'Why, have you been invited?' Hugh asked.

'You know very well I haven't.'

'How is your apprentice Grace getting along?'

'She has a good eye, but she is young. I have been fortunate though. Miss Harton is a fast worker. We shall have no trouble completing the order for that Goulding girl, and the Gouldings have always been prompt with their payments.'

'At least Miss Harton is much easier on the eye than Cousin Sally.'

'Hugh, you are a rogue. Abigail Harton is not for the likes of you.'

Hugh laughed. 'I have no interest in the girl.'

'She asked to move the large frame to the back of the workroom,' Mary said.

'Why? The light isn't good there. Are you sure?'

'She doesn't want to be seen in the workroom. If she sits too close to the glass, anyone who cares can look in and then what would she do? She's a proud one all right. I couldn't refuse her for I can't afford for her to go elsewhere.'

'What's the harm then?' Hugh stood up before he fell asleep in the chair. 'I'd best get to bed.'

Mary nodded and locked up the house before she went up to bed herself.

CHAPTER 20

Hugh rose early. He had dreamed of Miss Harton and not for the first time. He rubbed the sleep from his eyes and got dressed. He needed to be at Mr. Long's house before dawn to be ready to meet the silk merchants who were due to visit early that morning. He washed and put on a fresh linen shirt. He tied his hair back and went down to the workroom to wake the boy.

'Come on, lad, get up. There's money to be made today.'

Michael rose from his bed and together they set out for Daniel Long's house with the parcelled cloth. There, Hugh placed his cloth alongside his friend's on a large table for inspection. He was impressed with the amount of silk Mr. Long and his workers could produce and wondered if he would ever be able to build a similar business.

A servant prepared breakfast and the weavers and apprentices sat down together at the table. Mr. Long sat to Hugh's right and young Michael sat to his left. Hugh noticed that the boy's appetite was back and the bruises on his face were healing. He had no doubt that he would improve greatly with care.

'Good morning, Mr. Gavin. How are you this fine morning?' his host asked him.

'Very well, Mr. Long. I want to thank you again for this opportunity.'

'What are good neighbours for?'

Mr. Long worked on commission and never left anything to chance. He couldn't afford to. With weavers to pay, he needed to be assured of a sale and often invited mercers to his house on trading day. He had offered Hugh Gavin the chance to show his cloth in the hope that he could sell to them too. It was the neighbourly thing to do, or so he told himself. Hugh's sister, Mary, was a strong woman. He was only forty and without a wife. His wife had died not three years before and now he had three sons and two daughters to raise. Mary Gavin was just what he was looking for.

'He isn't your neighbour,' young Michael whispered to Hugh.

'He is being neighbourly, that is all,' Hugh whispered back.

'Why?' the boy asked.

'*Shhh*, he is our friend.'

'How is your sister this morning?' Mr. Long asked Hugh as he took a slice of bread and lathered it with butter.

'So that is what he is after,' Michael whispered to himself.

Mr. Long clapped Hugh on the back, and Hugh almost choked on the ale he was drinking.

'My sister is well, Mr. Long. She has many orders to fulfil this winter. It has been a good year overall for her.'

'That is good to know,' Mr. Long said.

The merchants arrived and Mr. Long got up to greet them. He introduced them to Hugh. Unfortunately, they were not impressed with his silk. The patterns were already a season old.

By the end of the morning Mr. Long had sold every yard that he and his weavers had produced.

Hugh was packing up when there was a knock on the door. Mr.

Long answered it. There was a bearded gentleman standing there.

'I hope I have come to the right house,' the man said. He had an American accent.

'If you have come here to buy cloth, then you have, sir,' Mr. Long said and brought the gentleman inside.

'I am looking for a Mr. Hugh Gavin and have been led to believe that he is here.'

'I am he, sir,' Hugh said.

Mr. Long bowed to the gentleman and went back to the large table.

The American approached Hugh.

'I have just called to your house,' he said, 'and your kind sister told me that you would be here.'

Hugh wondered how the man knew his name and dwelling place. 'If it is damask you want, I have many yards to sell,' he said.

'I have this morning arrived from London and I sail home tomorrow to Boston,' the gentleman said.

'I wish you a safe trip, sir. But how may I help you?'

The man smiled.

'Let me introduce myself. I am Tom Fish from Boston, Massachusetts. I am an associate of your friend Mr. George Thompson who now resides in Virginia. He has sent me on an expedition to copy the designs of London and Paris. I promised Mr. Thompson that I would sail to Dublin with a parcel for you before I returned home. I had hoped you would be expecting me. Mr. Thompson was to write.'

Hugh was overcome with relief. 'I did not receive a letter,' he said, shaking the American's hand. 'It is very good to meet you, sir. I have been waiting to hear from Mr. Thompson for months. What news do you have of him?'

'Good news, I'm glad to tell you. He has set up in business and I am to give you this parcel, which I've held safe for many months. He explains all in a letter therein.'

Hugh took the parcel from his new acquaintance.

'I was hoping that Mr. Thompson would return himself.'

'That was his intention, but his plans changed. You see, he married a wealthy man's daughter and has since moved to Virginia to establish a business there. His new father-in-law will not let him out of his sight.' Mr. Fish laughed and slapped Hugh on the back at the same time. 'You know how it is.'

Hugh could well imagine that his friend Thompson had got some girl in trouble and was paying the price for it. He just hoped it wouldn't affect his investment. He looked at the parcel and couldn't wait to open the letter.

'How many yards of cloth have you here?' the American asked.

'Twelve yards of plain silk and nine of the damask, sir.'

'And how much for both?' Mr. Fish asked.

Hugh was surprised. 'You are interested in buying my cloth?'

'It has just occurred to me that it would make a good present for my wife and daughter when I return. I can't go home empty-handed. Well, what say you, man?'

Hugh gave the American a fair price. The amount would more than pay his fare to America.

'Very well. Bring it to the Custom House by three of the clock today.'

'If you pay for it,' Mr. Gavin replied.

'You worry about my honesty?' Mr. Fish said and laughed. 'You are a good businessman I see. I will give you half now and settle the rest when the cloth is safely through customs.'

'What ship do you sail on?' Hugh asked.

'The *Charlotte*. She specialises in shipping cloth from here to America. We sail for Boston tomorrow.' He tipped his hat. 'It's a deal then?'

'Agreed,' Hugh said, shook the American's hand.

'Good day, sir.'

After Mr. Fish left, Hugh placed the cash in a leather purse hung safely around his neck.

There was plenty of time to take the cloth to the Custom House by three, so first he opened George Thompson's letter. He would need to consider its contents carefully when he got home.

CHAPTER 21

Monroe decided to bide his time and woo Miss Harton slowly. He needed to be careful. She must never find out about his past. He would also need to settle his debt with Palmer before he moved further with her. In the meantime, he would try to save and spend his winnings wisely.

He took a cab to his lodgings to avoid the rain. He paid the driver in the alleyway outside the inn and made his way past Mrs. Brass's intoxicated customers, unseen by his landlady. In his attic room he was pleased to notice that the linen on his bed had been changed. How lovely it was to have cash again, even if he had earned most of it by cheating at cards at the clubs rather than from medicine. He eased his feet out of his new shoes and sat down on the bed. It was a pity about Palmer, a real pity he knew so much. There wasn't much he could do about it. He put on his battered old shoes. The new shoes would take weeks to break in.

Monroe opened a wooden box. Inside was a new wig, in the shorter modern style. He took it out, carefully placed it on his head and stood in front of the looking glass. He looked quite the gentleman. Monroe smiled and put the wig back in the box. If he ever got into Alden's society, he would need it. Before going to supper, he opened his doctor's bag to restock and noticed a crumpled piece of paper. How stupid he was to have forgotten it. It was the note Miss Goulding had slipped him when he had attended her mother.

My Dear Sir, I would be delighted to see you at home next Wednesday, 17th. My father is holding a soirée. Say that you have been sent for, and I shall let you in. E.G.

Monroe smiled and then panicked. Today was Wednesday 17th and it was already ten o'clock in the evening. He took out a new shirt and dressed, pushing his feet back into the new shoes. He took out the wig again and placed it on his head. He was halfway down the stairs when he realised he had forgotten his doctor's bag and had to rush back up to get it.

Little Grace Brass passed him on the second landing as she made her way upstairs. She thought her mother's lodger was odd and noticed that the doctor came and went at all hours of the night, smelling mostly of strong spirits. Tonight, he smelled clean and his wig was new.

'Is it an emergency, Dr. Monroe?' Grace asked when the young man passed her by.

'You could say that,' he replied.

Monroe wished Mrs. Brass and her daughters weren't so nosey. He hoped to be in a better class of establishment before too long.

He ran up to High Street to have some chance of catching a cab. Hugh Gavin who was on his way home, tipped his hat at the doctor. Monroe ignored him.

He secured a cab and agreed a reasonable price to the address near the park where the Gouldings lived and hoped the party was not over so that he could still gain entrance. He need not have worried. Old Grogan recognised him and let him in without censure. The party was at full height and young ladies and gentlemen were chasing each other in and out of the downstairs parlour and reception rooms. He had high hopes of seeing Miss Goulding though she did not seem to be downstairs.

He made his way up the stairs, past a group of ladies and gentlemen who had congregated on the landing. The door to the pink drawing room was open. The air was full of smoke, and a shrill voice singing an operatic song in German was at full tilt in the farthest corner of the room.

Mr. and Mrs. Goulding were seated at the other end and Monroe made his way over to them.

Mr. Goulding caught Monroe's eye.

'What are you doing here, doctor?' Goulding said, narrowly avoiding burning the pink silk sofa with his cigar.

'I received a note from Miss Goulding to call urgently,' Dr. Monroe replied, embarrassed by Goulding's tone. 'It said that Mrs. Goulding was feeling extremely ill this evening.'

'Mrs. Goulding, did you call for the doctor? Do you feel unwell?' Goulding asked his wife, annoyed at not being informed by her directly.

'I'm very well, Mr. Goulding, although I did say to Elizabeth earlier that I was feeling a little peaky,' Caroline said, as she finished the Swiss tartlet in her hand. 'I may be ill by the morning though.'

'I am sorry to have taken you out so late tonight,' Goulding said. 'It appears you are not needed.'

'It was no trouble whatsoever. I am only delighted that your wife is in good health,' Monroe replied, casting his eye over to Mrs. Goulding who was now picking on sugared fruit on the table in front of her. 'I'll take my leave, sir, and perhaps call upon you tomorrow?'

'Stay and have a glass of wine for your troubles,' Goulding said. The young man seemed sincere enough.

'I would be honoured, sir,' Monroe replied.

He had just found a chair to sit on when another party entered the room. He watched in amazement as the Duke of Alden himself came in with an entourage of young men, most of whom were clearly intoxicated. The Duke approached Mr. and Mrs. Goulding who sat open-mouthed as he stopped opposite them.

'Your Grace, what a pleasure it is to see you,' Goulding said, standing up to bow. 'I had not dared to hope that you would accept my humble invitation.'

'Not at all, man. My friends and I were out gaming in the park today. I thought you should be good for a bottle of brandy before we return home,' Alden said and flopped down on a chair beside Monroe.

Goulding shouted for a bottle of brandy and Alden's friends dispersed into the room.

'And who are you, sir?' Alden asked Monroe.

'He is my good wife's doctor, Your Grace,' Goulding offered.

'Well, she looks in fine fettle, Goulding. He must be a good one, eh?'

'Very good, sir, very good,' Goulding said graciously.

'Don't you have a tongue in your head, man?' Alden asked Monroe.

'I am Dr. William Monroe, Your Grace. I'm an associate of Dr. John Harton who attended your son's birth earlier this year. It is a pleasure to make your acquaintance.'

'Ah yes, I remember him. And how is Dr. Harton these days?'

'He works hard at his charitable hospital in John's Lane. He may have told you about it?'

'Yes, he did. For the poor, if I recall.'

'Indeed, Your Grace.' Monroe paused. 'Dr. Harton has spoken of you. He tells me you have promised an annuity to support his hospital …' He left his words hang in the air.

Alden looked perplexed. Goulding's face turned puce.

'Do you know, I had forgotten,' Alden said, rising from his chair.

Dr. Harton had saved his wife and son and he was having a very rare attack of conscience. He hoped he would remember to tell his secretary in the morning to do something for Harton.

It was entirely depressing to think of the poor. It was best to ignore them altogether, he found. He was really rather miffed that the miserable-looking pale-faced Monroe had reminded him of his lack of honour in the matter in public. It would be far better to go to the Club in town than to loiter at the Gouldings' any longer. They did not deserve his attention anyway. There were hardly any attractive women for a start, only a miserable set of old fools. The singer, if you could call him that, was completely off key. Alden decided to leave there and then. He wanted to have a good time and he definitely wasn't going to find it here.

'Goulding, I must leave, I do apologise,' he said, and called for his entourage.

'Would you not have a drink before you go?' Goulding asked, trying to keep his honoured guest for longer, without giving further offence as Monroe had done.

'No, sir, it is my stomach that bothers me. It would be best if I go immediately.'

'Let me walk you out then, Your Grace,' Goulding said and had to follow one of the wealthiest men in the British Isles out of his drawing room.

Grogan arrived with a glass of brandy for the Duke. As he was too late, Monroe quickly downed it. He wasn't sure of the impression he had made on Alden. He hoped it had been good though there was nothing that could be done about it now.

Just then he spotted Elizabeth Goulding at the far end of the room wearing an extravagant lilac gown and a large wig.

'Dr. Harton, I see you accepted my invitation. I thought that you might not be coming.' Elizabeth was very impressed by Monroe's physique and his plain clothes. She decided she liked him better than any other man in the room.

'I could not ignore any invitation of yours,' Monroe replied.

'Come with me, will you?' She led him through a side door into an adjacent drawing room. Several candles on the mantel lit the room.

She turned to face Monroe. Giggling, she placed her hand on his chest.

'Doctor, I've been feeling a little unwell and was hoping that you could examine me,' she said.

Monroe could not believe her forthrightness or his luck. She might be useful, though he could not formulate exact plans in his distraction.

'Miss Goulding, Elizabeth, perhaps it might be better if your mother were present ...'

'That would do no good at all,' she said and moved her hands to dust his coat like a good wife would do. She moved even closer.

'Miss Goulding, you put me in a very awkward position,' he said.

Her natural red hair was sticking out from under her wig.

Monroe pulled her to him. It was tantalising, though it would be better to keep her waiting.

'Unfortunately, I have another patient to call on this evening before I retire,' he said, pushing her a little away from his body.

'Don't worry, doctor,' she said, pouting. 'I just wanted a little fun, that was all.'

Now he feared that he had offended her. He needed to keep her sweet.

'I do recommend that you walk every day to keep your constitution strong,' he said.

'And where do you recommend that I walk?' She was smiling again.

'There's a delightful trail in the park not far from here. The trees are quite lovely and private there.' He pushed a strand of her hair under her wig.

'I know it well,' she said. 'Eleven in the morning is the perfect time for one's health, wouldn't you say?'

'Eleven o'clock it is,' Monroe said.

Putting an arm about her waist, he led her back to the pink drawing room, releasing her at the door.

'If it is not raining, I shall endeavour to start tomorrow … walking, that is,' she said over her shoulder as she stepped into the room. 'Until then …'

Monroe saw Mr. Goulding striding down the large room and rapidly retreated.

Goulding went straight to his daughter.

'Where have you been, Elizabeth? You have missed an introduction to the Duke of Alden.'

'What do I care, Father? Alden is married and of no interest to me,' she said, fixing her papa's cravat which had become undone. 'Besides, I hear he is a scoundrel.'

'Don't be such a fool. Think who the Duke could introduce you to, Elizabeth. That is the point. You will need to find a rich husband to live as your mother and I do.'

'I can find my own husband, Father.' She went to sit by her mama before all of the cake was consumed.

Outside, there were no cabs in the streets and Monroe was forced to walk all of the way home. It gave him time to think. On reflection, everything was going remarkably well. He had secured Miss Harton in courtship and Miss Goulding might prove fruitful yet. It would be best not to say a word to Dr. Harton of his encounter with Alden for fear he had lost the hospital's annuity. Alden had not seemed pleased at the reminder of the promise. If he had secured the annuity all the better. He would appear to the Hartons to be the most modest of men.

He kicked a pebble out of his way on the road and wished that his friend Mr. Palmer was dead.

CHAPTER 22

Abigail worked on the silk stretched over the frame in the corner of the workshop. She had made a good start on the vines on the stomacher and was ready to begin embroidering the bluebirds. She pulled away the dustsheet that protected the silk and chose more colours for her design: cobalt blue, burnt orange and red.

Abigail thought that if she worked steadily the dress would be finished within a month and she would be free. Dr. Monroe was becoming more and more attentive. He had told her that his patient list was growing, and he would soon be able to set up a proper household. As a result, he had to spend more time away from her father's hospital, though he continued to help there as best he could. He was a good man and she would have a steady life with him.

Abigail looked at the green silk. The dress would be exquisite when it was finished, and she wondered what it would feel like to wear it to the ball. She ran her hand across the stomacher. The bluebirds were almost identical to the design she had embroidered on her blue poplin day dress.

If only her father could procure private funding for his hospital, if only he would seek Alden out, instead of this constant waiting. Perhaps she could persuade her mother to write to the Duchess to remind her of the promise. She tried not to think about it any further and was lost in her work when Miss Gavin came into the room.

'That's coming on well, Miss Harton.'

'We will finish on time, I believe.'

Mary was impressed. She had never seen such accurate work done so quickly before. The girl looked well too. If she hadn't known any better, she would have thought a young man might be in the picture. The Harton girl was too private. She only talked of the weather and rarely about herself. Besides her need to work, Mary was none the wiser about the girl's life outside of the workshop. The girl didn't seem to trust anyone, and it irritated her.

'Grace will work the sleeves when she has finished the vines on the skirt. She has a steady hand but needs supervision. I trust I can count on you to supervise her?'

'Certainly, Miss Gavin,' Abigail said.

'Good.' Mary lingered for further conversation. When it was not forthcoming, she left the workroom and shut the door behind her.

Abigail was pleased. It was a compliment to be asked to supervise an apprentice. Miss Gavin was a fair employer and for that she was thankful. She wouldn't tell of her courtship with Dr. Monroe yet. She was sure that Miss Gavin would never intentionally betray a confidence, but she didn't want to risk the rest of her life on that assumption. It was best never to give either of the Gavins any news of the courtship until her work with them was finished. It was safer that way.

She continued to stitch bullion knots into the silk to create the impression of feathers. She interweaved her stitches with cobalt-blue French thread and was lost in creating her design. When at last she glanced up, she felt a sense of peace and wished for a moment that she had been born into a family like that of Grace, who could do as she pleased, and whose mother was proud that her daughter had found such a respectable position in the city.

At noon, Abigail covered the silk on the frame and went into the kitchen for refreshment. Mr. Gavin was sitting at the table, hunched over some papers. He covered them as she passed behind him to go to the sideboard.

'Good afternoon,' he said.

'Good afternoon,' she said, turning her head to smile at him.

She poured ale from the jug on the sideboard as he watched her. She was cutting a slice of bread from the loaf when he spoke to her again.

'Miss Harton, have you ever been placed in an impossible situation?'

Startled, she turned around. 'What do you mean, Mr. Gavin?'

'It doesn't matter, it's just that I ...' He turned back to the papers on the table in front of him without finishing the sentence.

'Yes, I have been placed in an impossible position,' she said.

He looked up. The sun shone through the glass, creating a halo of light behind her. Hugh thought she looked like an angel. He knew she could not help him and wondered why he had asked her in the first place.

'My father doesn't know that I work here. He won't take paying patients. We are in debt and I have lost my dear young brother a month ago. I must work here so that there will be food on our table, and I cannot tell my father what it is that I do.' She paused. 'Is that impossible enough?'

Hugh was astonished. He hadn't expected such candour.

'I'm sorry,' he said. 'My trouble is nothing compared to yours. Forgive me for imposing on you.'

He started to fold the papers away but she was curious.

'What impossible situation have you been put in, Mr. Gavin, that you cannot find a way out of it?'

He looked at her again and wondered why he wanted to discuss his future with her. Maybe it was because she worked in his house.

'America is calling me, Miss Harton, but I do not want to leave my sister alone in this city.'

'And what has your sister said?'

'I haven't told her yet,' he said.

'Then she might go with you?'

He smiled, then scraped his chair back on the stone floor and stood up.

'It is clear that you don't know my sister well,' he said, looking at her hair and the way she had swept it away from her face. Her green eyes watched him intently and he found standing close to her difficult. He moved away and leaned against the doorway to the workroom.

'You never know what a person will say until you ask them,' Abigail said.

'Sometimes you do, Miss Harton.'

'Why do you want to leave? You have a good business, a good home.'

'My friend George Thompson went to America six months ago to set up a weaving business in Boston. There is much demand there and great opportunity for newcomers. I invested my savings with him and yesterday he sent me a handsome return on that investment.'

Abigail wondered what it would be like to be a man, to do as one pleased, to work as one pleased, to answer to no-one, to go anywhere one liked.

'Don't you have that opportunity here, Mr. Gavin? To make more money?'

'I would have a better chance to buy and sell cloth in America, to become a merchant and make a better life. Here I am confined at a loom for sunrise to sundown. I don't want that for the rest of my life.'

'I cannot advise you on what you should do, Mr. Gavin.'

'Wouldn't you seize an opportunity like this, Miss Harton?' He wondered why he found it easy to ask her such a question.

'I have never had cause to consider it,' she said, picturing herself on a ship bound for America and wondering what it would be like to go with him. She stopped herself. It was nonsense. She was wasting time.

'You see my dilemma? How can I leave my sister if she refuses to come with me?'

'You must ask her first,' Abigail said and walked to the door where he stood. 'I should get back to work.'

'If you were in my position, Miss Harton, what would you do?' he said, unintentionally blocking her way.

She was standing as close to Mr. Gavin now as when she had kissed Dr. Monroe in her father's office. The skin on her neck flushed and she looked at the floor.

'I don't know,' she said.

He gazed down at her for as long as he dared before stepping out of her way.

After she left, he realised that she had left her bread and ale on the sideboard. He had embarrassed her and for that he was sorry.

He sat back down at the kitchen table and studied George's letter. What he needed was a plan. He pushed the letter into his pocket and went back to the loom.

There was the boy to consider too. Young Michael had come on in leaps and bounds. He couldn't return the boy to his parents. Perhaps he could secure Michael an apprenticeship with Mr. Long in the new year? All he needed to do was to convince his sister that their prospects would be vastly improved if they were to start again in America. At the loom, he pushed hard at the treadles until Michael asked him to slow down. He was going too fast for the boy who had to manually thread the weft.

In the workroom, Abigail leaned her back against the closed door. She wondered why Mr. Gavin had had such an effect on her, more so than Dr. Monroe had when he kissed her. She had been caught off guard, that was all. It meant nothing and she tried to dismiss it.

She was distracted by laughter from the fitting room and realised that the large frame with the stomacher was gone. Miss Gavin must have taken them. She remembered that Miss Goulding was due to visit today – she, of course, had chosen to remain in the background.

She went to the door of the fitting room at the back of the house. It was ajar and she peeked through the opening. A young girl was there with an older woman who Miss Gavin addressed as Miss Mitchell. The girl's name was Elizabeth Goulding and she was the one who would wear the emerald dress.

Elizabeth Goulding was chattering on and Abigail was about to go back to the workroom when she heard Dr. Monroe's name mentioned. She hadn't caught exactly what the girl had said.

She continued to listen at the door.

'Oh, it is lovely, and the colour suits me beautifully,' the young girl said. 'But will it be ready on time?'

'Of course it will,' Miss Gavin said. 'The stomacher is almost finished as you can see. There is ample time yet. You will have the most unique dress of all.'

'Well, you would say that, wouldn't you? Though I think this time you are right. Dr. Monroe will be sure to like it,' Miss Goulding said. 'Oh, it is wonderful to be loved by such a handsome man, don't you think, Miss Mitchell?'

'I'm sure I don't know, Miss Goulding,' Miss Mitchell replied.

'Well, we'd best be getting back. I can't wait to tell my mother.'

'I will send a note when the dress is ready,' Miss Gavin said.

'I shall look forward to it,' Miss Goulding said.

Abigail retreated to the workshop where she paced to and fro. She had definitely heard Dr. Monroe's name. Surely it had to be a different Monroe?

She heard Miss Gavin showing the ladies out to the front door and bidding them adieu.

When Miss Gavin and Grace came back into the workshop, they were carrying the large frame with the stomacher between them.

'Miss Goulding is very pleased with our progress Miss Harton,' said Miss Gavin, smiling.

'I am glad to hear that, Miss Gavin.'

'The stomacher was much admired. Excellent work.'

'Thank you,' Abigail said.

'But that girl is a spoilt brat,' Grace said.

'Be that as it may be, she is a customer, Grace,' said Mary. 'That means we hold our patience and collect her money.'

'Yes, mistress.'

'Now, back to work the pair of you.'

Abigail and Grace applied themselves to the pieces they were embroidering. Grace stitched vines on the skirt while Abigail chose her threads to stitch the birds' feathers.

Miss Goulding's remarks about Dr. Monroe continued to bother her. She decided to ask her mother's advice. She might also ask Dr. Monroe directly. He might know of another Dr. Monroe in the city. It was probably just a coincidence.

CHAPTER 23

The Duke of Alden adjusted his cravat and stood admiring himself in the looking glass. He was not yet twenty-one but had started to put on a little fat of late and was determined to resolve the situation. His friends would come tomorrow for the hunt. In the meantime, he would enjoy his breakfast. He left his rooms on the second floor and went downstairs to his private dining chamber.

Passing by the nursery, he looked in and saw the wet-nurse feeding his son. He was touched at how placid the child was. At least his wife had that one accomplishment. It was a pity that all she wanted to do was to refurbish the ballroom while they were here.

He had travelled back to London during the summer but would have to stay in Ireland now until the ball in early December. He had hoped Dublin would remind him of happier times before he had married. Now that his father was dead and his mother estranged, it didn't feel the same anymore. He couldn't wait to get back to London.

Alden was considering which club he would go to that night

when he remembered his promise to Dr. Harton. He must do something about that before he left.

Suddenly, there was an almighty roar downstairs and he descended the marble staircase in haste. He wondered who his wife was screaming at now. As he reached the bottom stair, his steward Radburn came into the main hall, red-faced, with the Duchess following close behind.

'*What the blazes is going on?*' Alden shouted at both of them.

'Hundreds of pounds wasted, Adam,' his wife said, glaring at Radburn in temper. 'I asked him *personally* to order blue velvet for the ballroom.'

'Your Grace, I pointed out the blue material to the supplier,' the steward said. 'It is they who have got it wrong, I assure you.'

Alden could hear the pleading in Radburn's voice and wondered if either of them would ever get to the point.

'The drapes are jade green. I can't believe I have *jade-green* drapes,' said his wife. 'What are we going to do? The ball will be ruined.'

'What does it matter if the drapes are green or blue?' Alden asked. He couldn't believe the stupidity of the conversation he was engaged in.

'Alden, green is the unluckiest colour in the world. I can't believe you don't know that.'

'For God's sake, woman, you are the luckiest woman in Christendom. I'm sure green curtains will do you no harm. Radburn, get my secretary and tell him to meet me in the dining room.'

'I want that stupid man fired,' the Duchess said and stood firm.

'My dear wife, Radburn has worked for this family for many years, and you've only been in it for four. Order new drapes if you must, but Radburn stays.'

He went into the dining room and began to eat his breakfast in temper. The *Dublin Courant* was delivered to him at the table. He breathed deeply. He would be in London within the month and would call in on the Dean before he left. Swift and Bolingbroke could best advise on his forthcoming attendance at the House of Lords in London when he reached his majority on December 21st.

By the time Edward French came in, he was perusing the newspaper calmly, but the secretary looked as though he had run a mile.

'Your Grace, you sent for me?' he said to his employer.

Alden looked him up and down and motioned for him to sit.

'French, call to my lawyer's office this morning. I have promised an annuity to a Dr. Harton for a hospital. I don't recall the details. Find out where it is and where Dr. Harton resides and settle five hundred pounds on it. Get the lawyers to start legal documents immediately. It must be ready in two weeks. I will present the award to Harton himself before I go back to London. When you return we will go through the estate business.'

'Yes, Your Grace,' Mr. French said, who still had not quite caught his breath.

'Well, what are you waiting for, man?' Alden said.

Mr. French fled the room on his tiny feet. He was perpetually on the move through sheer terror of his employer. Alden watched him go and wondered why his father had ever employed such a scatterbrain.

A footman arrived with a hot plate of bacon, though when it was placed on the table in front of him he didn't have the stomach to eat it.

CHAPTER 24

John Harton went down to his office to consider how he could liquidate the last of his assets. It would buy him more time at the hospital. He refused to let it go yet.

He was searching his bookshelves for some ledgers when, among his personal books, his eyes fell on the book of fairy tales that Benjamin had loved so much. After a moment he could not see at all. Grief racked him for the young boy who had been lost. He sat behind his desk and wept and struggled to control his emotions. There were decisions to be made. His wife had told him of the loan from the Dean. It was humiliating. He acknowledged to himself that he had buried his unhappiness in his work at the hospital. It was time to face the truth.

He unlocked a drawer in his desk and pulled out the unanswered letters that demanded payment of bills, which he had kept hidden from his wife and daughter. He would go back to teach at the College and take on private patients again. The Provost of the College had told him he was welcome to return. The only problem was that the hospital had come to mean almost everything to him. With his remaining savings he would hold his position for another month and then he would shut the hospital down if the annuity didn't come through. He had gone through most of his money to sustain the hospital and prayed that the Duke of Alden would keep his word, and that the hospital would somehow be saved.

He spent some time going through the letters, taking notes, working out how much his remaining savings would cover.

When it was almost time to leave for church, he was shutting his desk drawer when he saw Alden's wax seal on an unopened letter. His hands trembled as he turned the letter over. He broke the seal and took out the letter. His mind couldn't take it in. He forced himself to breathe deeply until his pulse returned to normal and he was able to read the words.

November 9th inst.

Dear Doctor Harton,

Allow me to introduce myself. I am Mr. Jacob Fitzgibbon, counsel to the Duke of Alden, who has instructed me to arrange an annuity for John Lane's Charitable Hospital, Dublin. This is to instruct you to come to my offices next Thursday, November 20th, at noon to detail the particulars so that all can be arranged. The Duke shall present the annuity at a time that is convenient to you both thereafter.

Your servant,
Jacob Fitzgibbon
Solicitor

John put the letter down on his desk, buried his head in his hands and wept again. The date in the letter hadn't yet passed. He could still contact him. He rose from his desk when he was in control of himself again. The hospital would have an independent source of income at last. His prayers had been answered. He promised himself that he would spend more time with his wife and daughters for the time he had left. He could afford to hire physicians for John's Lane now to take his place and would offer a position to Dr. Monroe to secure Abigail's future happiness and safety. It was only a matter of time before he would be back on his feet.

He decided to wait to tell the good news to his wife and Abigail after church. He would accompany them to Evensong this afternoon. He didn't trust himself to speak until afterwards. He needed to impart the news calmly and said a silent prayer in thanks to God for watching over his family.

Abigail assumed that her father had been in his office since he had returned from the hospital that morning, for she had not seen him leave the house again. She came out of her room and saw her mother on the landing below, dressed for church.

'Mama, may I have a word please before you go down?' she called from above.

Her mother looked up. 'It is almost time for church, Abigail. Your father will be waiting for us downstairs.'

'It will take only a few minutes, Mama. There is time.'

'Very well.'

Abigail retreated into her room and stood there waiting.

'Abigail, have you spoken with Miss Gavin yet?' Margaret asked as she entered.

'No, Mama.'

'Abigail, why do you insist on staying there? What is the use of the Dean's loan if you will not quit your employment with that woman? Dr. Monroe cannot see you there.'

'Mama, how are we to repay such a loan? And I will not let Miss Gavin down. The dress is almost ready. I will be careful, I promise.'

Abigail sat down at her dressing table. She was not sure how to proceed. She looked at her mother through the reflection in the mirror.

'Mama, I need to ask your advice about Dr. Monroe.'

'He will take good care of you, daughter.'

'He hasn't proposed yet, Mama.'

'It's too soon for that, Abigail. First you were not sure of him, and now you cannot wait for him to propose? I don't know what's inside your head half the time. Has something happened between you that I should know?'

Abigail turned around to face her mother. 'No … it's just that …'

'You're not sure of him?' Margaret said, seeing the worried look on her daughter's face.

'Please let me speak, Mama. I will marry Dr. Monroe if he proposes and I am sure I will come to love him in time, but …'

'What, Abigail? What is it?'

'I overheard Dr. Monroe's name mentioned in connection with another lady.'

Margaret sat down on the bed and stared at her daughter.

'Where did you hear this?'

'At Miss Gavin's house. The girl who will wear the green dress. She mentioned how a Dr. Monroe would love to see her in it.'

'The idle chatter of a young girl. You'd best pay no heed.'

'She seemed more certain of him than that. She said how wonderful it was to be loved by such a handsome man as he.'

Margaret stood up and began to dress her daughter's hair to keep her agitation at bay. After a pause she asked, 'Who is she?'

'Miss Elizabeth Goulding. She looks young, sixteen perhaps. If you had heard the way she spoke his name, as if they were already lovers.'

'Well, he is courting you, so she is too late.' Margaret snagged a knot in Abigail's hair and her daughter winced. 'I'm sorry, dear.'

'Do you know of her?'

'No. She is probably just a daughter of one of his patients, and has taken an innocent fancy to him, that is all. Do not worry. Dr. Monroe loves you. I have seen it in his face.'

'What if he prefers her money over me?' Abigail said.

'Don't be ridiculous,' her mother said, her patience wearing thin. 'He is making his own way in the world. He is fortunate to be able to choose his own bride and he will choose you.'

Margaret resolved to ask her friends if they had heard of the Gouldings and if Dr. Monroe had an association with them. She would not let her daughter be duped or made an object of scandal by anyone. Miss Goulding was probably just a silly young woman. It was the most likely explanation.

'I will ask Dr. Monroe about it myself,' Abigail said.

'You will not, child. He may not know anything of Miss Goulding's admiration. An inquiry such as that could damage your courtship with him. I will talk to Esther Johnson tomorrow. She will know who to ask about the Gouldings. It is better to say nothing to Dr. Monroe for now.'

Abigail sat back in her dressing chair. She hoped Dr. Monroe was someone she could ask a question of without jeopardising their courtship. If he was to be her husband, it would be better to find that out before she married him.

'I will say no more until you speak with Miss Johnson,' Abigail said, hoping she had nothing to worry about.

Margaret finished her daughter's hair and they went downstairs together as it was time to leave for the cathedral.

CHAPTER 25

Monroe had forgotten it was Sunday. He had got back to the inn at daybreak, still drunk from the night before. He took the bottle of whisky he kept under the bed and quenched his thirst. He had inadvertently said he would meet Dr. Harton for Evensong but had promised to meet Miss Goulding at the Park. It was an easy choice to make. He would rendezvous with Miss Goulding first, and try to make it back to the cathedral on time. Monroe simply could not resist the chance to meet the very young Miss Goulding on her own. After borrowing a basket from his landlady, and taking a very good bottle of wine and some bread and cheese from the kitchen, he covered the lot with a piece of linen he had brought down from his room. He took a cab to the spot in the park where he had suggested Miss Goulding take her daily exercise at precisely eleven o'clock in the morning.

When he entered the gate, he did not see her and sincerely hoped that he would not be disappointed. Perhaps she had walked a little further on. He checked his pocket watch. It was a quarter after eleven and for a moment he thought that she might have gone home. He noticed a girl in a most elaborate hat, fashioned like a sailing ship, and realised it was the lovely Elizabeth Goulding. She was alone. He was surprised that the old governess was not with her.

'Good morning, Miss Goulding,' Monroe said. 'You are looking lovely today.'

'Good morning, Dr. Monroe. You said eleven o'clock. You are not a gentleman, sir, to keep me waiting. I have a good mind to go home.'

'Forgive me, I had –'

'Please don't tell me you had yet another patient to attend to on a Sunday morning? I might begin to believe that you are a liar, sir.'

'Miss Goulding, you are very impatient. I attended early service with Dr. Harton and the preacher went on a little too long,' he lied. 'I left before the service ended so that I might find you. I simply did not factor in how long it would take to get here. Can you forgive me this one time?' He pulled a small cloth-wrapped package from his pocket. 'Please accept these emerald earrings. I bought them especially for you.'

Miss Goulding took the gift and her frown changed slowly to a smile.

'Well, just this one time,' she said, sliding the earrings into her glove for safe keeping.

They walked further into the park.

'There are many more people here than I anticipated at this hour,' she said.

'Where is Miss Mitchell?'

'She felt indisposed as we were leaving and I tired of waiting for her. So I came by myself. She won't be long though – she will hurry here as soon as she realises I am missing.'

'Let's wait in that secluded spot by the trees. We should be safe there until Miss Mitchell arrives. We can see her as she walks through the gate.'

'I prefer to wait for her, sir.'

'It is entirely your choice,' he said.

'What is it you have in the basket?'

'A picnic, just for you, Miss Goulding.'

'You are resourceful, Dr. Monroe. That is what I like about you.'

'Are you not peckish?'

'And you brought the basket to morning service with you?'

'I hurried back to get it. Another reason why I am a little late.'

'How considerate of you. You will make someone a perfect husband one day.'

'You flatter me, Miss Goulding,' he said. 'Not everyone would say so.'

He laughed and wondered if a certain Miss Catherine Sumner would agree – the woman Monroe had married in Cork the year before – a fact Palmer enjoyed hanging over him like a noose.

Palmer had given him an advance to assume the role of a rich young gentleman. It had all been Palmer's fault really. If he had investigated the matter better, the whole mess could have been avoided entirely. Miss Sumner had been ripe for the picking, over thirty, and living with her elderly father in a fine house set in fifty acres of good land by the River Lee just outside the city. The Sumners were new to Cork and it was easy for Monroe to bewitch the lady with his claims of a medical practice in Dublin. He had proposed to her within weeks and her father, the Reverend Sumner, had welcomed the match. Since his retirement, the Reverend had been worried about his daughter's future. Dr. Monroe, a capable and respected member of society, was the perfect answer to his prayers. When the young doctor told him one morning he had to go back to Dublin on urgent business and might not return for several months, the old man panicked. The Reverend himself had married Catherine and Monroe the next afternoon, with Palmer and the Reverend's old housekeeper as the only witnesses.

Monroe's urgent business was quickly forgotten. He stayed in Cork and told Catherine that he had sent his friend Palmer to attend to the matter instead. Monroe had got his new wife with child within the month. He was happy and settled at last, until he discovered that the property in Cork didn't belong to the Sumners after all. It was merely leased. His wife had asked if they could take her father to Dublin when the lease on the house ran out in Cork. Well, that was never going to happen. An old man and a middle-aged woman were not going to scupper his enjoyment of life.

He smiled when he remembered how his friend Palmer had started a rumour that the Sumners were mad and that their family had set them up in Cork away from Dublin to save their relations undue embarrassment. The old housekeeper was let go and was given money to go home to live with her sister's family in Kerry. Monroe stayed in Cork with the Sumners until their lease ran out. He then moved out and denied the marriage had ever taken place.

The Reverend, on realising the deception, had suffered a turn and could no longer speak. Miss Sumner was subsequently ruined by her pregnancy. He had left her in Cork shortly before the baby was due and he hadn't heard from her since. He would deny any claim that the child was his if she ever tracked him down.

When he moved back to Dublin with Palmer, he tried to forget what had happened. He knew there would be better pickings in the capital. It had been heartbreaking really. That the Sumners had led him to believe that they owned their house was unforgivable. He couldn't get over their subterfuge. He had never really thought of Miss Sumner as his wife. She had no charm and had been grown fat by the time he had eventually left. Her stricken demeanour had come to disgust him. Palmer, the only remaining witness to the marriage, also denied it had ever taken place. Miss Sumner had seduced Monroe. Palmer had bandied that fact about in the taverns in Cork. The whole endeavour had been a mistake though he had learned from it. He would not let Miss Sumner ruin his chances elsewhere.

Monroe was ready to take on a new wife. This time he wouldn't take any risks. He had checked the Registry of Deeds in Dublin. Dr. Harton owned the house on Pluncot Street and had already consented to the courtship with his daughter, Abigail. The Gouldings on the other hand, though far wealthier than the Hartons, were not likely to approve a match with their daughter. They could disinherit Elizabeth if they wished.

It was a tricky position to be in and he decided to thoroughly consider it. There was plenty of time to decide which wife to take, depending on how events unfolded, though peculiarly he was quite fond of Miss Harton. A woman had never quite affected him in that way before.

Elizabeth Goulding, however, had the potential to give him so much more.

'Why don't we have our picnic, Miss Goulding?' He took off his cloak, placed it on the grass and sat down on one side of it. He patted the cloak. 'Come, sit beside me.'

Miss Goulding giggled. 'Whatever would Miss Mitchell think?' she said and just then saw her governess approaching.

'*What are you doing, Elizabeth?*' Miss Mitchell called out before she reached them.

'I accidentally bumped into Dr. Monroe,' Elizabeth said.

'I don't believe you for one minute. You know this is not proper. Come away with me this instant.'

Elizabeth turned to Monroe. 'Would you be so kind as to accompany me as far as our door?'

'Of course, Miss Goulding, I should be delighted to,' he said.

Miss Mitchell didn't protest. Instead she turned around and hurried ahead.

By the time they arrived at the house, she had disappeared inside. Grogan was standing at the open door.

'Miss Mitchell makes her apologies and says she is indisposed again, Miss Goulding,' he said. 'She will join you shortly.'

Elizabeth took off her gloves and cloak and handed them to Grogan.

'Would you like to join us for tea, Dr. Monroe?'

'I'd be delighted to, Miss Goulding,' he said. He removed his cloak and handed it to Grogan.

'Grogan, have the footman bring up a tray for tea.'

'Yes, miss,' the servant said, hanging up Monroe's cloak.

'Wait ... are my parents back from church yet?' Elizabeth asked.

'No, miss. They are calling on Mr. and Mrs. Craig after church and are not expected home until this evening.'

'Thank you. We shall be in the drawing room.'

'May I leave this with you?' Dr. Monroe handed his basket to the servant, who reluctantly took it.

'Yes, sir.'

Elizabeth, still wearing the extraordinary hat, led Monroe up the stairs. When they were alone, she sat close beside him on the pink sofa and plucked a blade of grass from his breeches.

'Why did you not go to church with your parents?'

'I told them I was ill. Thank God, for I couldn't stand to be at the Craigs' house all afternoon.'

'Clever girl.'

Elizabeth removed her hat and placed it on a nearby table. Then she moved even closer to him on the sofa.

'What if Miss Mitchell were to come in?' he asked.

'Never mind the governess. I can manage her.'

Monroe needed a drink.

'Do you know, she keeps bottles of port in her room,' she said.

'Who does?'

'Miss Mitchell of course. She thinks no-one knows, but she often wails in the night and I hear her crying. My parents turn a blind eye because she's been with the family so long. She doesn't even bother to dress her hair properly anymore. I really should tell my mother to let her go.'

'But where would she live?'

'She must have relatives somewhere. And, if not, she'd have to find a new position. If she leaves here without a good reference, it's her own fault.'

The drawing-room door opened and Monroe was relieved to see it was a footman bearing a large tray, with hot water, tea things, and plates of pastries.

When the servant left, Elizabeth went to a desk by the window and tried to open a drawer, but it was locked.

'Are you going to write me a love letter, Miss Goulding?' Monroe asked.

'Don't be so silly, Dr. Monroe. My mother must have taken the key to the drawer with her. The tea leaves are inside it, I'm afraid.'

'No matter. Do you have anything stronger?'

'Yes, of course.'

From a side cabinet, she took out two glasses and a bottle of brandy. She brought them to a small table beside the sofa and sat down again.

'We can have this instead.' She removed the cork and poured glasses for them both.

'Miss Goulding, you are an angel, but don't you think it's a little early in the afternoon?' He shifted a little away from her on the seat. He expected Miss Mitchell to arrive at any minute.

'Not at all. My father drinks in the afternoon. This is his favourite tipple. I don't see why I shouldn't drink it too.'

'What about your governess? She might catch you.'

'I'm sure she won't be down again.'

'You can't be sure.'

He gulped down the brandy. What was he doing here? He was jeopardising everything. He should really go home and change before attending Evensong with the Hartons later.

'Very well – I will check,' Elizabeth said and left the room.

Elizabeth went up to the top floor and knocked on Miss Mitchell's bedroom door.

'Miss Mitchell, are you unwell?'

'Please do not come in.' Her governess's voice was muffled through the door.

'*I shall wait until you open up!*' Elizabeth shouted.

After several minutes the older woman came out, looking drawn and pale.

'I am sorry, Miss Elizbeth, but I cannot come down to join you. My stomach is giving me much trouble today and it's getting worse. Please tell me that Dr. Monroe has gone?'

Elizabeth paused. 'He has just left,' she lied.

'Promise me that you will not go out again.'

'I promise, Miss Mitchell. Please do not let me keep you.'

Miss Mitchell's face turned red. She nodded and shut the door on her pupil. Elizabeth hurried back down the stairs, laughing at the poor woman's unfortunate condition.

Monroe was standing by the window. The brandy was very good and he had helped himself to a few pastries. There really was no harm in staying a few more minutes. He was admiring the view when Elizabeth returned.

'Is the governess to join us?'

'Definitely not. She is more indisposed than I thought.' She went to the table and picked up her glass.

'This house has a lovely aspect. I wouldn't mind having a home on this street myself.'

'One day you will, Dr. Monroe. I am sure of it.'

Both were silent for a moment. Monroe looked down at the girl. She was very young. He continued to talk about the view and drank the remainder of his brandy. Elizabeth followed his example and poured them both another.

Within an hour, Elizabeth was posed by the fireplace singing, a second bottle of brandy had been opened and the food consumed. Monroe was sitting back on the sofa enjoying the girl's vivacity. When she reached a crescendo, he laughed out loud.

'*Shhh!* You will disturb Miss Mitchell,' he said.

'Don't worry about that old crone.'

Elizabeth drank deeply from her fourth glass of brandy and approached the sofa, swaying as she walked.

She flopped down beside Monroe, her head lolling on his shoulder.

'I really should go home,' Monroe said, suddenly aware of the dangerous situation he was in. What if the governess or even that butler walked in?

Pushing her back, he stood up to leave, feeling a little unsteady on his feet. He hadn't quite recovered from the night before at the club. He regretted drinking whisky for his breakfast earlier and so much brandy now, and was sorry he'd left the picnic basket with Grogan for he was famished – the pastries hadn't filled the gap. He picked up his hat and walked to the door.

'You cannot go home yet, doctor.' Elizabeth struggled to her feet. 'There is something I have to give you.'

'What could that be, Miss Goulding?' He steadied himself by the door.

'A lock of my hair. Would you like that?'

'Most definitely,' he said.

'Then follow me.'

Elizabeth took him by the hand and led him out and up another flight of stairs and into her bedroom.

She locked the door behind her, fumbling as she did so. 'Just to be safe.' She waved the key in his face. 'I won't let anyone in.'

He knew better than to go along with this but somehow couldn't oppose her. He would only stay a minute, take the lock of her hair and leave.

'I have a scissors here somewhere,' Elizabeth said and sat at her dressing table. When she found the instrument, she cut off a piece of her hair.

Monroe sat down on the bed. Elizabeth sat beside him and gave him the lock of hair which he put in his pocket. She lay back and he lay back beside her. She turned toward him and her arm moved across his chest. Suddenly they were in each other's arms.

'What time is it?' he asked as he kissed her neck.

'Only two o'clock,' she said. 'We have time yet.'

He tried to stop himself. Her father could come home at any minute and kill him. But he couldn't tear himself away.

'Please don't stop,' she said and kissed him again.

It was her first time and when they finished she clung to him. He heard someone on the stairs outside and in an instant he was sober again. If he was found here, there would be hell to pay. He had been stupid. The girl had lured him to her bedroom but he should have had more sense. He sat up and pushed her clinging arms away.

'I'm sleepy, aren't you?' she said and stretched out, smiling.

He looked at her as she lay back.

'Quite the opposite,' he said.

'You will marry me now, won't you?' she said.

'I must get back.' He dressed as quickly as he could.

'When can we meet again?'

'Soon, I hope,' he said and left the room.

He walked cautiously down the stairs. Luck was with him and he encountered no-one. In the hall he grabbed his cloak and made a swift exit.

Out on the street he realised that in his haste to leave he had forgotten the picnic basket – it couldn't be helped.

Elizabeth Goulding had offered herself to him so easily. He was sure that she would most likely offer herself to any man. He couldn't bear the thought. The encounter had cleared his mind on the subject. He couldn't spend his life with a girl who was nothing more than a whore. It was Abigail Harton that he wanted as his wife.

CHAPTER 26

St. Patrick's Cathedral was one of the largest buildings in Dublin. The choir's ethereal voices mingled together in the high vaulted ceilings of the church and Abigail wondered if that was what it sounded like in heaven. She sat beside her parents. Sarah and Henry were on their other side.

When Dean Swift saw the Hartons, he remembered their son Benjamin to the congregation. Abigail looked to see her mother and Sarah wipe tears away and she herself struggled with her grief.

Dr. Harton could not let himself feel anything. When Benjamin's name was mentioned he didn't stir inside. If he did let himself feel, he might crumble and he simply could not let that happen.

After Evensong, Abigail accompanied her parents to speak with Dean Swift and thank him for his kind words of remembrance. Abigail told him how Benjamin had enjoyed fairy tales and through them she would remember him always.

'If only we could all live in such fantastical lands,' she said.

'My dear, they are all about us, if only we had the courage to find them,' he said and smiled. 'Are there not many tiny people and giants amongst us, and horses that have more sense than some of their masters? You have only to look at the fools who administrate the city to know that.'

Abigail thought of all the places that she would never see. She recalled Mr. Gavin's wish to travel to America and secretly envied him his chance to see the world.

'There, I have said too much,' the Dean continued. 'I will see you all next Sunday at service.'

'Yes, we shall be there,' said Dr. Harton and they went on their way.

Outside, Sarah and Henry hailed a cab home. In the distance, Abigail could see Dr. Monroe running towards them, holding his wig on his head in the windy weather.

'I am sorry to have missed Evensong, I was called upon to help an old man this afternoon,' he lied.

'An interesting case, was it?' Dr. Harton asked. He wondered how Monroe had gathered so many private patients in such a short time with hardly any connections.

'Indeed, the gentleman has severe lung sickness. He will be lucky to live three months, poor man.'

John Harton hoped Monroe had been careful. He didn't want him passing anything on to Abigail through contagion. On reflection, his worry was eased when he remembered Monroe's rare visits to the hospital these days and how cautious he had been when treating the patients there. His thoughts turned to getting home and telling his family his good news.

'Brigid will have our supper ready,' he said. 'Dr. Monroe, we would be honoured if you would join us.'

'Thank you, sir. Though, if you don't mind, I would first like to speak with Miss Harton. I promise that we shall be but ten minutes behind.'

John was about to protest but thought better of it when he

remembered what it was like to be young and in love.

'Don't be longer than ten minutes, or our supper will be ruined,' Margaret said.

He and his wife walked on.

Eventually John stopped and turned to her. He could wait no longer to tell her the good news.

'I don't think we should leave them alone,' Margaret said. 'Can we not go back to fetch them?'

'Mrs. Harton, I believe you will be more interested in hearing of our good fortune.' He took Mr. Fitzgibbon's letter from his breast pocket and let her read it.

Margaret didn't know whether to laugh or cry, though she managed to do both before they arrived at their front door on Pluncot Street.

Watching her parents walk on in the distance, Abigail had known she would not be able to keep her promise to her mother. She had to know about Dr. Monroe's connection to the Gouldings.

Monroe wondered what was passing through Miss Harton's mind. He felt she was not herself. He offered her his arm which she took though she did not smile. He hoped she wasn't going to turn into a bore like Miss Sumner.

Abigail noticed that her beau's suit was crumpled and that he smelled of brandy. She looked up at him and saw that he was admiring her. She desperately wanted the security he could bring but had to know the truth.

She stopped and faced him. 'Dr. Monroe … forgive me for bringing this up … but I overheard your name in association with a young lady. A Miss Elizabeth Goulding.'

Monroe tried not to panic.

'What do you mean, Miss Harton?' he stalled, trying to think of a way out.

'I overheard Miss Goulding and an older lady talking to each other as I crossed High Street yesterday,' she said – she dared not mention the Gavins connection. 'The young lady mentioned that Dr. Monroe would be sure to like her new dress.'

Monroe managed a light-hearted laugh, though the blood in his veins began to run cold.

'And what did this young lady look like? I have to say that I am very much flattered I have two young ladies in the city who admire me.'

Abigail thought Dr. Monroe looked a little apprehensive.

'She had red hair and was perhaps sixteen.'

'And she is known to your family?' he asked.

'No ... they walked beside me for several minutes and I overheard her name,' she said, sorry to have to lie. 'I do not know her or her family.'

Monroe was relieved that she was ignorant of the Gouldings. He changed tack.

'You certainly are an excellent eavesdropper, Miss Harton, I'll grant you that.'

'You have not answered my question, sir.'

'I think I can guess at what may have happened, Miss Harton. My cousin Nicholas is newly arrived from London and is staying with friends. Perhaps they are acquainted with these Gouldings? My lodgings are too small for him to stay with me. It so happens that he is a medical doctor too. So, you see, there is another Dr. Monroe in the city as we speak.'

'Why did you not introduce him to my family, or mention him to us?' Abigail asked.

'Because he is only to stay a week more before returning to his obligations in London.'

Abigail thought the explanation didn't make sense. How would Monroe's cousin admire Miss Goulding in her dress at the Boden Ball if he was returning to London the next week?

'Well, that's unfortunate for Miss Goulding as I believe she said that it would be wonderful to be loved by such a handsome man,' she said.

Monroe laughed out loud then. He could see he had Miss Harton hooked and he was enjoying making the story up as he went along.

'My cousin Nicholas is such a scoundrel. He probably told the poor girl he would take her to the ball to get a kiss. In truth, Miss Harton, that is why I was averse to introducing him to you in the first place.'

'So, it was not you she spoke of?'

'Of course not. How would I get an invitation to the Boden Ball at Boden Castle?' He smiled at her. 'In fact, Nicholas has invited me to go back to London with him next week.'

Miss Harton grew pale and he took her hands in his.

'Of course, nothing is settled yet – however, it is an opportunity I cannot dismiss lightly.'

'Do you mean to return to England for good?'

'I have not yet decided, Miss Harton. So much depends on you.'

Monroe liked Abigail's mind. He could almost see its cogs whizzing as she considered the situation. She would be an asset as a wife, especially if she inherited the house on Pluncot Street. Miss Goulding, on the other hand, would probably move on to another lover when she realised how poor he was, though he had keenly enjoyed the tumble with the trollop earlier. She was light in the head and her parents would never approve of him. Miss Harton, however, was for the taking, and he was more than happy to settle for that. She would do quite nicely.

Abigail did not know what to make of Dr. Monroe. Did he really mean to leave for London?

'Miss Harton, I have come to love you very much,' Dr. Monroe faltered. The time was right to ask her.

Abigail immediately stopped walking.

'Please let me ask you a question,' he said, looking around for somewhere more private to speak with her. 'Follow me.'

Monroe guided Abigail into a coffee house and asked the host for a private room.

'No, that is not proper,' Abigail protested.

'Please, I beg of you – I need to speak to you in private for a few minutes – I will not detain you any longer than that.'

She allowed herself to be manouevered into a small room.

'Did you want coffee with that, sir?' the host asked, looking Abigail up and down in a whimsical manner.

'Yes, two coffees, please.'

Monroe shut the door for privacy and turned to Abigail.

'Miss Harton, I cannot wait any longer to ask you to be my wife. I worried that I would not be in a position to ask you for a long while yet. Now I have happy news. I have come into a small inheritance from my uncle, Nicholas's father. That is one of the reasons Nicholas is visiting here. I did not wish to mention my good fortune to you until it was safely in my hands.'

Before Abigail could answer him, Monroe cut her off.

'I haven't asked your father's permission yet … but I wanted to be sure of your feelings on the matter before I spoke to him.'

He knelt before her.

'Please do me the honour of becoming my wife.'

Abigail sat down at the table in the room. It was all very sudden. One minute he talked of going to London and the next of marriage. She should have felt at her happiest, but somehow she didn't. He was a man she hoped to trust. Someone who could support her family. Yet she found herself unable to speak.

'Miss Harton? I hope I haven't offended you. If you are unsure …'

'It's just that you have surprised me, Dr. Monroe, that is all.'

'We needn't tell anyone if that is what you'd prefer. Just please let me know that you will be mine?'

She didn't respond.

Monroe rose to his feet. He was perplexed. He had expected her to jump at the chance of marrying him, of marrying anybody.

'Miss Harton?' he asked.

'It is too sudden,' she said.

He took her hand and kissed it.

'You are right as always. I am content to wait for your answer.'

He touched her face, incredulous that he might secure such an honest girl. She would say yes when the time was right, he was sure of it. What other prospects did she have? He would spare her heart as much as possible, for he could never change his ways. He promised himself he would be careful with her.

She blushed and he realised he wouldn't be able to resist for much longer.

Fortunately for Abigail, they were interrupted by the arrival of their coffees.

Abigail and Monroe returned to Pluncot Street and when supper was over Dr. Harton shared the news of the hospital annuity with the family. Monroe looked at the happy scene. He was satisfied to be part of it and wondered what it would be like to live in a house like this one and have Miss Harton and their children around him. He would be a happy man indeed. He was somewhat surprised by his own hankering for family life.

When Dr. Harton coughed, Monroe had an idea. Perhaps he wouldn't have to wait too much longer to secure domesticity.

CHAPTER 27

The Duke of Alden had made arrangements for the annuity to be paid to Dr. Harton of John's Lane Hospital before he left for London. This morning he would make the presentation to the doctor and after go to the Dargan Club to eat.

He left his bedchamber to get dressed. When he looked at his wife, he was not surprised to see that she was still asleep. She was consumed with the frivolities of the forthcoming ball and had not retired until almost three in the morning. She was beautiful still. Perhaps when they returned to London he would rekindle their romance. He wanted as many male children as she could produce to secure his bloodline. He decided he would shower her with gifts when they returned to England and all would be right again. There were several other ladies already expecting his offspring, but he needed legitimate sons.

He did not take breakfast after he dressed. Instead he went straight to the awaiting carriage which took him into town. His first stop was at the offices of his lawyers in Capel Street, the honourable

Messrs. Fitzgibbon and Cole. The building was dark and damp but, apart from that and the fact that Mr. Jacob Fizgibbon needed a new suit of clothes, all seemed in order.

Alden reviewed the documents he'd requested be drawn up and was happy to sign two copies, one for Dr. Harton's records and one for his own.

'Well, that is settled then. Now to the hospital,' Alden said, exasperated by the old gentleman who was taking his time fixing his wig and putting on his cloak.

'I am very pleased to accompany you, Your Grace,' Mr. Fitzgibbon said.

'Don't forget the papers, sir.'

Alden went out onto the landing to wait for the gentleman. The damp smell in the room was unsettling.

Mr. Fitzgibbon was uncharacteristically nervous. Whilst dealing with his wealthiest client, he almost forgot his own name, never mind the documents. He stepped out onto the landing, drawing breath.

Alden was gracious in allowing the old gentleman to descend the rickety and dim staircase before him. Then he remembered something.

'Did you bring the cash?' he asked.

The little man turned around.

'Yes, the first year's annuity, as you asked,' he said, checking his pockets though he knew he'd put the cash in with the papers in his satchel.

'Good, I shall feel better giving it to Harton myself before I leave because of the delay. My little boy is eight months old next week.' He clapped the old man on the back as they reached the pavement outside.

'Indeed, Your Grace,' the solicitor replied, happy that his client would soon be returning to London.

When they got into the carriage, Fitzgibbon fished in his head for something polite to say.

'It a pity that the Duchess could not come with you today.'

'You are right, Fitzgibbon. However, she finds herself too busy with the preparations for the ball. She is also arranging our departure to London immediately afterwards.'

'Indeed,' Fitzgibbon replied. He could not think of another topic and the rest of their journey was endured in silence.

It was close to midday when the Alden carriage stopped outside the small hospital in John's Lane. The driver stepped down and opened the door before the Duke alighted from the vehicle with an air of distaste for his surroundings. He had not realised the place was quite so wretched and for a second pondered on whether he should get back into the carriage and go straight home. Before he could make up his mind, Dr. Harton came out to greet him in full periwig and stockings.

Alden despaired when he saw that the doctor had brought his entire family with him for the occasion.

'How very good of you to come, Your Grace,' Dr. Harton said. 'Please let me introduce my –'

'Yes, yes, let's do it inside, man, it's freezing out here,' Alden said and walked into the hospital foyer ahead of the rest of the group. It was remarkably desolate inside and Alden found himself with an itch that he was desperate to scratch.

John Harton followed Alden, his family and associates following behind.

Abigail was there. Though the dress was not yet finished, Miss Gavin had allowed her the day off so that Dr. Harton would not know of her enterprise. She watched as her father, mother and Dr. Monroe went into the hospital ahead of her. She lingered for a second to try to talk with Sarah on the steps, but Henry turned back for his wife and ushered her into the building. Abigail had no choice but to wait to ask for her sister's advice later. She went inside.

Dr. Harton had introduced everyone to the Duke of Alden in the foyer, leaving Dr. Monroe until last.

'Ah yes, I remember Dr. Monroe from that night at Goulding's soirée,' Alden said. 'Dr. Harton has you to thank for reminding me of my promise. Dr. Monroe.'

Abigail wondered if he was smiling or sneering at Dr. Monroe as he said it.

Monroe bowed deeply and Dr. Harton looked at him with renewed respect. He hadn't been well of late and Monroe had proven himself invaluable in the last couple of weeks.

Mr. Fitzgibbon started the proceedings and showed Dr. Harton the deed of annuity for the hospital, giving him one copy after he had signed both. Fitzgibbon would lodge a copy in his office for safe keeping.

Dr. Harton thanked both Mr. Fitzgibbon and the Duke profusely.

'And to start you on your way, here is the first year's annuity in cash,' Alden said.

He handed the money over, took the glass of wine offered him and swigged the whole thing down in less than five seconds, said his goodbyes and left with Mr. Fitzgibbon shortly thereafter.

Everyone was relieved when they had gone.

'Dr. Monroe, how can I thank you enough for your words to the Duke,' Dr. Harton said, placing a hand on his protégé's shoulder.

Monroe could not have been more delighted.

'There is no need, sir. I had only your family's welfare at heart,' he said.

'Well, I am very thankful, as is Abigail. Your position is secure here, Monroe. I can finally offer you a good living.'

'Thank you, sir. I look forward to our many years of working together.'

'You are almost like a son to me,' Dr. Harton continued, feeling particularly sentimental now that his ambition had been achieved.

'You honour me too much, Dr. Harton.'

'Now if I could just get rid of this indigestion, all would be right with the world.'

'And how might I ask is your stomach?'

'Better of late, thanks to those powders you mixed. They have certainly helped.'

'I am glad. It is a mixture my good father created.'

'You must show me the measures, Dr. Monroe.'

'Of course, all in good time. Rest is what you need now. That alone will do the trick.' Monroe patted his employer warmly on the back.

'I hope you are right, Dr. Monroe.'

'As do I, Dr. Harton, as do I.'

CHAPTER 28

Dublin, Present Day

I called to see the Professor at his office. When I arrived, however, his colleague Gráinne told me that he was running late and let me into his office to wait there. Sitting down at his desk across from his chair, I noticed that the Duchess's diary was open.

I swivelled it around and began to read.

3rd March 1715: I have sent word to my father that I am safe. That I am married. Alden lies beside me. I suspect he has married me to hurt his father as cruelly as he can.

We are still in Kilroy's house and the party continues downstairs. There is laughter below, most likely at my expense, but I have had the last laugh. I am daughter-in-law to the Marquis of Alden, the wealthiest and most important Whig in England.

I have opened the drapes. The light of the moon seeps in to find us and Alden breathes softly in his sleep.

There is a commotion downstairs—

There was an indentation in the paper, a deep dash. The writer had pushed down hard with her pen after the last word. The ink was blotted too. Sophia had closed the pages before the liquid had dried. I turned the page to read on.

I shook my husband awake. There were men in our room. These people are barbarians.

I saw Alden's father, the Marquis, standing at the front of the crowd.

'Is this how you treat me?' he shouted.

Alden got up, naked for all to see. The Marquis came towards him, holding a note in his hand. It was the note that he had written to his papa.

'Is this how I am to find out you've married? And to this whore?'

'She is my wife,' Alden said and winked at me.

'You've had enough whores already, and you had to marry this one?'

I thought the Marquis would have a fit in front of us. Alden got on his knees, holding on to his father's stockings, mocking him.

'Father, forgive me this one dalliance?' he said, laughing and playing to the crowd. 'It was the only way I could have her!'

The Marquis seemed to inflate, so much so that he couldn't speak.

'I am in love with little Sophia here. Can't you find it in your heart to forgive me?' He laughed again and pretended to grovel.

'I will not have it! Put some clothes on this instant. You are leaving with me.' He pulled my husband up by his hair.

'You cannot be serious?'

'Do you want to lose everything?'

'This is ridiculous.'

'I'll leave it all to your sisters, do you hear me? I will disown you if you defy me in this.'

The crowd's laughter turned to sniggering.

Now Adam's face was white. He didn't look at me again, stumbling to put on his drawers, his stockings, his breeches, his shirt, his coat.

I held the bedclothes to my face, so that only my eyes were showing.

My own father stepped forward from the crowd. I had not noticed him until then.

Adam glanced my way. 'I'll send word to you, my dear,' he said and winked at me.

The crowd laughed as he took his wig from the bedpost and left.

Has my plan failed?

My father told me to get dressed. I was naked underneath the sheets.

'Get out! Get out!' I screamed, until they were all gone.

I turned the pages forward. I couldn't wait to read what happened next. The Professor had helped me to work out the old script, how an 'S' looked like an 'F' and other variations and I was finally able to read the text fluently.

15th September 1718: Alden has returned from the continent. I have told him that I am with child. To my surprise, he grows more attentive. He no longer denies me the dressmakers I have brought from Paris. I pray that I may live to be the mother of many children if I can keep him happy this way.

I scanned the pages until I came to the point where Sophia gave birth.

30th March 1719: I thought I was going to die until the doctor came to Ashdale House yesterday. Thank God he was up from London and in Ashdale when my time came. The midwife did not know her trade as she ought. It is thanks to the good Doctor Harton that my son was born safely, though he had to move my baby around in my body before it would come out. It was such an ugly business. I am surprised by Alden's continued tenderness.

I was curious to see how many children Sophia had given birth to and logged onto the National Library Database to see if I could find more information on her. Perhaps the Aldens had descendants still living. I wondered again if there was a connection with my family. Maybe Aunt Jeannie had been right all along and blue blood was running through my American veins.

I turned the pages until I came across a reference for Boden Castle.

15th September 1719: The ship smells worse than a sewer. I am convinced it will sink. I am sick to my stomach and cannot write further. Why should my husband travel and not I? He visits his friends in Ireland and I will surprise him there.

18th September 1719: I have arrived at Boden Castle. It is a miserable place. The steward Radburn is a sullen man, though he runs the household efficiently and minds his own business well. The castle is situated two or so miles from the city and I have ordered new fabrics to hang on the walls, and Italian paper for the bedrooms. Alden spends much of his time with his friends in town. The child keeps me occupied and I believe his father is happy with his presence here. I will try to conceive again before he tires of me.

Perhaps the Irish air will improve my chances. I am determined to have another child inside me soon.

I wondered what it would be like to have been a woman in the 18th century. It seemed perilous. Even if you were lucky to have been born into a wealthy family, you still needed to marry to secure your future. I didn't want to think about it.

I looked about the Professor's office and felt claustrophobic. The office was so small. After waiting over an hour, I took out my laptop and ordered a biography on Adam Alden's life on the National Library's database. Hopefully I could find out what had happened to his wife Sophia. The library was located on Kildare Street close by, so I left the College and took my time wandering up Nassau Street, wading through people who were mainly heading in the opposite direction.

The National Library was housed in an imposing structure on Kildare Street. At first I thought I was in the wrong location. The centre of the building was guarded by police. There was another side gate and I was relieved to find directions to the library there and followed them. Inside was a circular foyer lit by coloured glass designed with figures of famous artists and writers, Shakespeare and Da Vinci included. After I had inspected them all, a security guard at the base of the stairs directed me to the genealogy section on the first floor. However, when I arrived all of the researchers were occupied. I went up to the second floor where the Professor had said the reading room was located. There, the bookcases were carved perfectly to fit the round walls behind them. Above, a large skylight dominated the room, spilling light over the opulent wooden desks and green art deco reading lamps. I felt like I'd gone back in time to the 1930s.

I checked in at the reference counter to collect my order of the Alden biography and was asked to take a seat at one of the wooden desks. Within minutes, a librarian delivered the book and I thanked her. I texted the Professor to let him know where I was.

When my cell phone rang I left the reading room to take his call.

'Lucy, how are you?'

'I'm good. I'm sorry I didn't wait at your office for you.'

'It's no problem. Gráinne told me you'd dropped by. Do you want to catch up later on?'

'That would be great. I've been meaning to ask your advice on my Hugh Gavin research. I don't really know where to start.'

'No problem at all. I'll see if I can find anything for you here today.'

'Thanks, Professor. I really appreciate it. I'm reading a little more on the Aldens in the meantime.'

'They were an interesting family. Do you know that Alden's father reputedly kept a mistress in a tower for years?'

'Why doesn't that surprise me?'

The Professor laughed. 'Why don't you call up to my office on your way home? I'm free tonight and can cook you dinner if you like.'

'I'd love that,' I said. 'I'll walk down to you when I'm through here.'

'OK, great. See you later then.'

I hung up. The Professor was cooking me dinner. That was a surprise. I was more than curious to see where he lived.

I went back into the reading room and started to read the book. It was full of gossip, but not that enlightening on Alden's wife, Sophia.

I had scanned her diary into my laptop and looked through the pages to see if I could find anything about a servant or a weaver that might give me a connection to Hugh Gavin. I couldn't find anything. In Sophia's diary her domestic situation seemed to be her main concern. Her husband, she feared, was straying from their marriage bed.

29th September, 1719: Little Tom is six months old and Alden grows less attentive. I suspect he keeps a lover. He still comes to my bed and I do my utmost to make him happy but he attends engagements on his own. He plans to go to London to arrange how he will be presented in Westminster in December. I will go with him but am determined to make my mark on his Irish friends before we leave. We will host a Winter Ball at Boden Castle in early December. I shall meet everyone that way.

Such beautiful cloths of embroidered silk have been brought from Lyon and Paris. I can hardly decide which ones to wear.

I went back to the biography to read more on the Duke who purportedly had been quite a rake. It made for fascinating and somewhat lurid reading.

I checked my watch when I had finished the fourth chapter. It was getting late and I'd had enough research for one day. I returned the biography to the reading desk and went back to Trinity College, to the Professor.

On Nassau Street, my cell phone rang. It was my sister in Los Angeles. I took the call.

'Hi, Becca, are you still checking up on me?' I said, smiling.

'Just calling to see if you were OK, Lucy,' she said.

'I'm fine, sis. Thanks for asking.'

'Are you? It was to be your wedding day today. Do you need to talk?'

'Haven't been thinking about it really,' I said. 'How's Mom?'

'She's still coping with the fallout.'

'I'm sorry you had to deal with it all.'

'What are sisters for? When are you coming home?'

'I might stay in Ireland a few days longer.'

'OK, but talk to Mom, will you? She'd be heartbroken if she lost you over the whole thing.'

'Tell her I love her, OK?'

'I'll tell her that,' she said and hung up.

CHAPTER 29

The Professor was ready to leave when I arrived. We walked back to his car together and talked about the contents of Sophia Alden's diary.

It was a short drive to his house, a downtown mews in Donnybrook, on the south side of the city. The house was surrounded by plants on all sides. He parked to the rear of the building and we walked through the back garden with apple and pear trees and flowers of every colour. There was a small side door. The Professor took out his keys and unlocked it.

I stepped into his kitchen. Though the house looked Victorian from outside, inside the décor was sleek and modern. Light poured in from the sliding doors that made up most of the back wall. From here the gardens looked even more glorious.

'It's like the Tardis,' I said.

'I'll take that as a compliment. Let me take your coat.'

I handed it over and he hung it on a coat-stand by the door.

'How long have you lived here?' I asked.

'About ten years and I'll be working for another twenty at least to pay for it.'

'It's worth it though, right?'

'I guess,' he said.

The Professor seemed distracted. I hoped I hadn't said the wrong thing.

'What's for dinner?' I asked.

'Spaghetti bolognese. Sorry, I forgot to check if you were a vegetarian. It's the only thing I can cook.'

'It's a good job I eat meat then. That's perfect,' I said and sat down at the kitchen table.

'Can I offer you a glass of wine? I have a Pinot Grigio, I think.'

'Pino Grigio it is,' I said.

He poured me a glass and started cooking dinner. His skills needed some attention, I noticed. When the pasta eventually started to stick to the pot I had to look away as it would have been impolite to intervene.

I looked out to the garden full of wildflowers. It had started to rain and suddenly there was a trousered behind reversing out of the tall grasses. A man stood and ran bent-double towards a shed at the back wall. I watched as he emerged again wearing a hooded windcheater.

'Who is that?' I asked and pointed in exaggerated horror.

'Oh, that's Tommy, the gardener. He's out in all weathers.'

'Will he be joining us?'

'God no. He'll be finished soon.'

'Good.'

We both laughed.

'Once we've eaten, I'll go through what I found out about the mysterious Mr. Gavin this afternoon.'

'Was there anything new?'

'A few things. First though, let's eat. Have another glass of wine.'

I accepted. The gardener, a portly gentleman well into his sixties, came in and happily accepted a glass too. He toasted to our health and took his drink outside to admire his handiwork in the pouring rain.

'Tommy certainly seems content out there,' I said, taking a sip of the white liquid.

'He's a godsend really. There's a lot of maintenance in that garden and, while I love to look at it, I'd much prefer to be reading a book.'

'He's doing a great job. The garden is beautiful.'

'I agree.' The Professor turned his attention back to the cooker while I sat back at the table to enjoy the view.

This was supposed to have been my wedding day. I smiled, thinking I was spending it instead with a professor who was humming as he stirred the sauce, adding tomatoes from a can to the bubbling pot. I wondered why he was single. Maybe he wasn't. But there were no photos and there hadn't been any mention of a girlfriend. What did I care anyway? I pushed the thought away when he came over to plate up at the table.

He served up a very large portion of pasta and the sauce turned out to be quite tasty. I was hungry and had no trouble finishing it all off.

As I sat at the table sipping my wine, the Professor made coffee. It was a very pleasant way to spend the evening. I hadn't expected to be enjoying my vacation so much.

'How long are you staying in Dublin, Lucy?'

'My sister called to ask me the same thing today, would you believe? I haven't decided yet though I hope to stay long enough to find some answers for Aunt Jeannie. I really appreciate you helping me too and for the meal of course,' I said and tipped that last drop of wine from the glass.

'The university can't thank you enough for your family's donation of the diary. I'm looking forward to researching it further. Why don't we go through to the study with our coffee? I have some photocopies for you on Hugh Gavin.'

'Great, I can't wait to see what you've found.'

The Professor's office was at the front of the house. It wasn't what I expected. The desk was large and modern, with an ergonomic office chair, complete with swivel and wheels. Like my own house in California, there were books everywhere, for reference on his desk and stacked in corners on the floor. I immediately felt at home.

'It took me a while but I found Mr. Hugh Gavin and his sister a Miss Mary Gavin, who was a dressmaker and embroiderer in Belfast.'

'Wow. And it's the same Hugh Gavin?'

'I'm pretty certain it is. Mary Gavin died in 1752. Her will was recorded in the Betham list. There's a small abstract here, which states her profession as a dressmaker and that she left nearly everything to a daughter who was still living when she died. She did, however, bequeath her brother a small gift and his address in America is on the will. It matches nicely with your Aunt Jeannie's research.'

'Belfast though? Aunt Jeannie thought that Hugh Gavin lived in Dublin.'

'On the registers it shows that his sister moved from Dublin to Belfast in 1735. There may have been a family connection there.'

'Are there any records in Belfast for Hugh Gavin?'

'There was no will in the Betham list for him, which makes sense if Mr. Gavin left Dublin for America in 1720. He would have been in America when his sister died thirty-two years later.'

'I wonder if he was still living then himself?'

'You'd need to search for that in the States, I'm afraid.'

'Are there any Dublin records for him?'

'Unfortunately, most of the Irish birth, death and marriage records were destroyed in the Irish Civil War in 1922. It'll take some digging but I'll keep looking for you, Lucy. There's a digital record of church registers online. I can send you the link and you can take a look yourself, though I don't hold out much hope.'

I typed the web address into my smartphone, suddenly aware of how close the Professor's chair was to mine.

'I hope I can find out more about the mysterious Hugh Gavin before I go home.'

'The fact we've found his sister is a great leap forward. I'll continue searching for documents on her first. She's our best bet for now.'

'Can I do anything to help?'

'You could check through the archives database. We have very few records of Dublin dressmakers of that period, though Mary Gavin may be mentioned in one of them. If she is, we may even get an address for her. If she was unmarried at the time, she may well have lived with her brother in Dublin before he left for America.'

'Professor, I can't thank you enough.'

'It's no problem at all. I'm enjoying doing it for you,' he said and got up from his chair.

I stood. 'Thanks for dinner. I can't tell you how much I appreciated getting a home-cooked meal so far away from home. I'd better get going though. It's getting late.'

The Professor looked awkward standing by the door. It was as if he couldn't make up his mind about something.

'I'll call you a cab so,' he said eventually. 'I shouldn't have had that second glass of wine. I could have given you a lift back.'

'That's no problem, Professor.'

'We can have a coffee while you wait for the taxi.'

'That'd be great,' I said and followed him into the kitchen.

We sat at the table and I asked him about his research on Jonathan Swift who had lived in Dublin three hundred years before. The Professor was able to bring the old city to life. I could almost imagine how it might have been to live then. But the cab arrived just as we'd finished coffee and I had to go.

'I'll see you tomorrow afternoon then?' he said.

'I'll look forward to it.'

I took the taxi back to my hotel and wondered about the Professor's life. Surely there was a mystery there. Perhaps he'd lost the love of his life and that's why he always looked so forlorn. Maybe I'd never know but I hoped I'd find out before I went home.

Looking out of the cab window, I tried to imagine what it must have been like for Hugh Gavin and his sister Mary three hundred years before. It was incredible to think that they might have lived in Dublin at the same time Sophia Alden visited Boden, and when Johnathan Swift had preached in St. Patrick's Cathedral. Could they have met each other? Had Mary Gavin made any of the dresses for the Aldens' December ball there in 1719? I wondered if I would ever really know.

CHAPTER 30

The next afternoon I called into the Professor's office to search the archives database as he had suggested. He smiled and got up from his desk when he saw me and asked me to take a seat. I noticed his hair was tousled as if he hadn't combed it. I smiled back.

'I hoped you slept well, Lucy.'

'I did, thanks. And how are you, Professor?'

'I'm grand. You'll be glad to know I have an update for you on Mary Gavin.'

'Really?'

The Professor turned his computer towards me so that I could see the documents he was reading. I tried to pay attention to the screen.

'I've found two Dublin connections for her.'

'That's great, Professor. Who did you find?'

'Well, the first reference lists her as a dressmaker in *Watson's 1729 Almanack of Dublin*. It had a list of street names and who lived on them.'

'It makes sense that Mary was a dressmaker. Dressmaking is mentioned in old family letters from our ancestors later in the 19th century as a family tradition. So where did Miss Gavin live?'

'At Number 8, Coles Alley. It's now called Meath Place. It was located in the Liberties, close to High Street, and not far from Christ Church Cathedral. Here, let me show you.'

The Professor unrolled an old map of Dublin city.

I sat forward to pore over it with him.

'Is that Trinity College?' I pointed to a group of buildings listed only as 'The College'.

'Yes, it is. And you can see Dame Street here. The most direct route from the College then to High Street was by Castle Street. That's Dublin Castle there, see? It was the seat of power at the time. The English King's representative in Ireland, the Viceroy, lived there. Today of course the parliament is housed in Leinster House on Kildare Street where you were yesterday.'

'In the same building as the National Library?'

'Correct, though the library is housed in a wing built onto Leinster house in the late 19th Century. The library structure didn't exist in the 18th century.'

'When does this map date from?'

'This is Charles Brooking's 1728 map of Dublin. You can see Coles Alley there in the Liberties. It's not far from Weaver's Square. It might be that Mary Gavin lived there with her brother. It's likely, as he was listed as a weaver on the *Charlotte* manifest. Hugh Gavin may have leased the house in Dublin. His sister might have taken over the lease when he left for America. Unfortunately, there's no real way of finding out. Unless you've access to a time machine.'

'A Tardis. Wouldn't it be great if someone invented a real one?'

'It would indeed,' he laughed.

'You said you'd found two connections for Mary Gavin in Dublin?'

'We have a series of letters referencing Boden Castle. They are in storage in the archives here. The name *Mary Gavin* is showing up in the search string associated with them. I'm afraid we'll have to wait another couple of days before they are available. A lot of staff are on leave in the summer so they're a little short-staffed at the moment. But I can tell you that the letters are addressed to the Duchess of Alden and are dated from December 1719 to the end of February 1720.'

'Oh my goodness. That's the connection. It was Mary Gavin, not her brother, who was connected to Boden Castle. She may have made the Duchess's dress for the ball. Aunt Jeannie was right. I shouldn't have doubted her. Do you mean the letters were written by Mary Gavin to the Duchess?'

'Just a second.' The Professor looked at his screen again. 'It just says here that they reference the name *Mary Gavin*. The search references another woman, a Mrs. Goulding, who could have been a friend of hers. Maybe she recommended Mary Gavin to the Duchess on her arrival in Ireland.'

'The letters stopped early in 1720, did you say?'

'The Aldens' son, Christian, died shortly before his first birthday in London in February 1720. To my knowledge there is no record of Sophia returning to Ireland after that, so maybe that would explain why her correspondence with Mrs. Goulding ended. We can take a closer look when we've got access to the letters in a few days.

'How did little Christian die?'

'It seems that the Duke had told his wife to keep their son safe in their country house at Ashdale as there was an outbreak of smallpox in London at the time. The Duchess didn't listen to her husband. She may have been worried he was having too much fun in London without her, but he had been telling the truth about the smallpox epidemic. She brought her son to London and he died shortly thereafter. The Duke never forgave her and they had no children after that, I'm afraid.'

'Oh, that's so sad,' I said.

Suddenly, I wanted to go home to see my sister Becca and her boys.

CHAPTER 31

Dublin 1719

Someone was shaking Abigail.

'Wake up, for God's sake!'

Her mother was hovering over her, holding a candle aloft.

'Hurry, Abigail!'

Abigail got out of bed and followed her mother down to the first landing.

'What is wrong, Mama?'

The clock on the landing showed a quarter to three. She entered her parents' bedroom door. Her mother had placed the candle by the bedside. The damped-down fire added further light to the room.

'You father is delirious. I cannot wake him.'

'Let me see, Mama.' Abigail felt for her father's pulse as he had taught her to do. His skin was hot to the touch.

'How long has he been like this?'

'He was complaining of stomach pains last night. He went out to eat with Dr. Monroe.'

'Where did they go?'

'To a chop shop on Wine Tavern Street.'

Abigail took a cloth from the nightstand and poured water from the jug into the ceramic bowl beneath it. She hoped the cause of her father's illness was bad meat. If it was the ague, they would have to pray.

'Has he been vomiting?'

'No, he just grips his stomach in agony.'

Abigail wiped her father's forehead and the coolness of the water seemed to revive him.

'Daughter?'

'How are you, Papa?'

'The pain is too great … I need opium. The Apothecary Smyth … he will know what to prescribe.'

Her father seized his stomach again and curled up small in the bed.

'I will fetch him, Papa.'

'Castle Street is not safe at this hour,' her mother said. 'The Viceroy holds a ball in the Castle tonight. I'll wake Brigid instead.'

'Brigid is too young to go, Mama.'

Margaret wondered how much more suffering she could take. She prayed that her husband would survive as she gave her daughter the house keys.

'I can't lose him, Abigail,' she said and went back to her husband's side. 'Please God, let him live,' she prayed.

'I will be back as fast as I can.'

Abigail got dressed. She woke Brigid from her sleep.

'My father is ill and I must get help. Lock the door after me. Then go and build the fire up in my parents' room. I will return within the hour. Listen out for me.'

'Yes, miss.'

'May I borrow your cloak? It would be better.'

'Of course, miss.'

Brigid got up and followed Abigail out to the hallway where she was putting her pattens on over her shoes. She bolted the door after Abigail left.

Out on the street, no-one was around. Mr. Smyth's shop was not ten minutes away if she hurried. The moon was full, and Abigail could see the poor who slept in doorways on her route to Castle Street, which was busy with carriages leaving Dublin Castle through the main gate. It was after three o'clock in the morning and the lords and ladies were only then going home.

She reached the apothecary's door and knocked on it until she heard movement inside.

'Who is it at this hour?'

'It is Abigail Harton, Dr. Harton's daughter. My father is very ill.'

Abigail could hear the bolts being pulled back inside.

'Why didn't you say so?' Mr. Smyth said and ushered her in.

In the main shop, shelves were lined with medicines in blue and white ceramic jars. Mr. Smyth stood patiently beside the counter.

'Well, what are his symptoms, Miss Harton?'

Abigail described her father's condition and his visit to the chop shop. She looked at the labels on the jars. '*Ambergris*', '*Dragon's Blood*', '*Jesuit's Bark*'. Then she saw it: '*Opium*.'

'He will need opium for the pain.'

'I have opium pills already made up. Let me give you something else for his digestion. He will need it if a chop shop is to blame.'

Mr. Smyth set to work. He brought a piece of Peruvian Bark to the large table in the centre of the room and began to grind it with a pestle and mortar.

'It will not take long, Miss Harton. Bring the cacao powder down from the top shelf, will you? You can make him a chocolate paste that might help settle him too. Add in a little cinnamon spice. It's on the counter below you. Don't use the Indian powder. It would be too hot for his stomach.'

'How much of the cacao powder do I use?' she asked.

'Eight ounces should be enough for a few draughts,' he said.

Abigail took the cacao powder down. The jar sat between a human skull and a jar of boiled woodlice. She shivered as she measured out the ingredients on the shop scales.

Mr. Smyth stopped for a moment. 'Miss Harton …'

'Have I used too much sugar?'

'No, that's not it. It's just … No, I shouldn't bring it up with you now.'

Abigail stopped to look at him. 'What is it, Mr. Smyth?'

'Your father promised payment last week. I have given him credit at the hospital. I'm afraid it cannot go on much longer. Tonight has to be an exception.' He poured the ground bark onto paper and sealed it.

Abigail was taken aback. Her father had given her money for the household from the annuity to pay the outstanding household bills. Why hadn't he paid the apothecary? Who else had not been paid?

'I am sorry, Mr. Smyth. I will talk to my father when I return.'

'He told me that Dr. Monroe would drop in the money. He's your father's right-hand man these days, I believe? Perhaps it would be better to talk to Dr. Monroe about it? I don't want to upset Dr. Harton as he lies ill. However, as you can see, I am not a wealthy man.'

Abigail didn't know what to think. Why had Dr. Monroe not paid the apothecary's bill? She would talk to him as soon as she could. There had to be a reasonable explanation.

She finished the chocolate paste and Mr. Smyth handed her a parcel of the other medicines he'd prepared. He took seven opium tablets from a drawer, wrapped them in paper and pushed them into her glove to carry home.

'Be careful with these – they are not to be taken all at once. And Miss Harton, I would be obliged if payment could be made in the next day or so. I will not be able to supply you or the hospital again until I receive it.'

'Thank you, Mr. Smyth. I will make sure that you are paid.'

'Goodnight and be careful. I would walk home with you, but my own wife is ill and needs attending,' he said.

When she had left, Mr. Smyth locked the door behind her.

He was getting too old for this business. In his earlier days he had been much shrewder. Now he felt sorry for everyone, even to the extent of putting himself out of pocket. That is what he had admired in Dr. Harton, his willingness to help the poor. However, he had promised himself that he would give no more credit to his friend until he had been paid. Though he couldn't turn his daughter away. He admonished himself for being an old fool. The sooner his son finished his studies to take over the apothecary business, the better.

He climbed the steps to his bedchamber, where his wife paced the floor.

'Who are you?' she asked, confused. 'I cannot find my mother.'

'I am your husband, my dear. Remember? Why don't you come to bed? It's too cold to be standing there in your shift.'

'Are we at home?'

'Yes, we are on Castle Street and all is well. Now, come to bed.'

'It's just that I forget sometimes.'

'It is no wonder – you are very tired. All you need is rest.'

She got into her bed. Her husband was a good man. He would take care of her. She nestled into him and he put his arm around her in the draughty room.

'It will be all right, Mr. Smyth, won't it?'

'Of course, my dear. Go to sleep if you can.' He regretted that they had not had any daughters that might keep her company. If only he had the money to have a woman sit with her. As he drifted off to sleep, he hoped that Abigail Harton would arrange to pay her father's debts.

Abigail walked along Castle Street. Surely it had been an oversight? Dr. Monroe had been so busy that perhaps the payment had slipped his mind.

Carriages passed her by on the street. She slipped in horse dung as she crossed to the other side and steadied herself against a wall to wipe the manure off her pattens against the cobbles of the street, glad she was wearing them as her shoes would have been ruined.

'*How much for your services, madam?*' a man's voice called out from a passing carriage.

Abigail had to turn back and walked towards the Castle, in the opposite direction of home, to get away from the vehicle. She peered into the Castle courtyard. There were servants standing by with lamps who helped the ladies and gentlemen climb the steps of their carriages, many of which were marked with the coats of arms of the highest-ranking families in the city.

She was about to turn back when she saw a young man in fine clothes stumbling into a public cab. It was Mr. Palmer. He looked in her direction and she was sure that he recognised her. Another man climbed into the cab behind him though she didn't see who it was. Might she ask for a lift home? The cab was on the move and coming in her direction. She was sure that Mr. Palmer would oblige her and waved her hand to stop the cab, but it didn't stop. Perhaps it hadn't been Mr. Palmer after all.

'That was a bloody close call,' Palmer said to Monroe in the cab. 'What the hell was Abigail Harton doing at the Castle?'

Monroe laughed. 'I have no idea, Palmer. No idea at all.'

'I hope you know what you're getting involved in there, Monroe. Is she respectable?'

'I hope so though she has the habit of turning up in the most unusual of places. I cannot wait to marry her.'

'Let's hope she didn't see you.'

'It was too dark and she was too far away.' He had seen the Apothecary Smyth's upstairs light go out as the carriage passed the shop and calculated that Miss Harton was quite respectable after all.

Brigid waited by the window until she saw Miss Abigail coming up the street. It was raining hard. She opened the door just as Abigail reached it.

'Oh, miss, you are soaked through. Let me help you.' Brigid took the sodden cloak away.

'How is my father?' Abigail asked.

'The same. Your mother is asking for hot water to mix with brandy for your father. I will take it up when it has boiled. I have brought her up some ale in the meantime.'

Abigail removed her filthy pattens in the hall and brought the medicines upstairs to her parents' room.

'What did Mr. Smyth say?' her mother asked.

'He had given me Peruvian Bark and some spearmint for his stomach.'

'What about the opium?'

'I have that too. Help me, will you?' she said before turning to the bed. 'Father, can you sit up a little?'

John Harton was perspiring heavily. Helped by his wife, he managed to prop himself up in the bed.

Abigail brought a cup of ale to his lips and placed an opium tablet on his tongue.

'Try to swallow this,' she said.

Her father gulped at the liquid until he swallowed the pill. Then he eased himself back down into the bed.

By the time Brigid arrived with the hot water, John Harton had visibly relaxed.

Abigail mixed half of the Peruvian Bark and chocolate paste into the water and managed to get her father to drink half a cup before he fell asleep again. She felt his pulse. It was slower than before, but it wasn't normal. Her mother sat in a chair on the other side of the bed with her head in her hands. Brigid looked like she was about to cry.

'Brigid, you have been very good. Why don't you go back to bed?' Abigail said. 'Dr. Harton is quieter now. I think the medicines are working.'

'Thank you, miss,' the girl said, and left the room.

'Mama, I must get ready for work.'

'Abigail, you cannot go today. You must stay with me and pray that your father will come through this. What are we to do if he dies? God, please help us.'

'Hush now, Mama. God will take care of us as he always has. We must wait for the medicines to do their work. I will be home by early afternoon.'

'Why can't you stay here?'

'I will go to Sarah and Henry's lodgings and ask Henry to fetch Dr. Monroe. After that I must help finish the dress for Miss Gavin.'

'Abigail, you must come back directly. I don't want to be alone with him.'

'You will not be alone. Brigid is here and Henry will bring Dr. Monroe.'

'Dr. Monroe will wonder where you are.'

'Then say that I am visiting Sarah. The dress is almost finished, Mama. Then you will have me back again.'

'What if your father is gone by the time you get home? What if you miss him as you did Benjamin?'

Abigail did not respond and left her parents' room. She couldn't stay in the house and wait for her father to die. She took the key from her mother, went down to the office and checked the drawer in the desk where the cash was kept. There were only a few coins there. The bulk of the money from Alden was at the hospital but there should have been a certain amount here for household expenses. Surely it hadn't been spent already?

She would call to her brother-in-law and sister before going to the Gavins' home. It was out of her way, but she had to let Sarah and Henry know what had happened.

Monroe had visited the club in the early hours of the morning. Luck had generally been on his side since he had returned to Dublin. His opponents were usually fools. But when he'd placed his remaining cash on the last pot with Mr. Craig, he'd lost it all. Craig must have been cheating too. Monroe stormed out into the street.

He remembered that Dr. Harton kept a good bottle of claret in his office at the hospital so he made his way to John's Lane. It had begun to rain and he cursed the misery of his life in general. Palmer was ill and threatened to write to Catherine Sumner if Monroe could not pay him back in full within the month. It was out of the question that his 'wife' should know his address in Dublin. It simply could not happen.

He arrived at the hospital soaked through and went up to Harton's office to which he had a key. He found the claret and settled into Harton's chair. After drinking half the bottle, he fell asleep, only to be awakened by a scream at dawn. The smell inside the dark building was foul. Monroe got up to see what was going on. Dr. Harton had hired two graduates from the College, Doctor Klinton and Doctor Simons. They hadn't much experience tending to the sick, but then neither had he. Dr. Harton had tasked him instead with the administration of the wards. The attendants were supposed to keep the place in order, so why should he?

In the ward across from Harton's office, he didn't see much evidence of order. Flea-infested sheets were strewn about and unemptied chamber pots added to the odours that wafted from the patients themselves. There weren't enough beds and most of them shared the same pallets with at least one other patient. He would need to check that none of them had turned to corpses in the middle of the night.

Monroe promised himself he would cease working at the hospital once the business with Palmer was done. He would prefer to go back to England than to endure the sick and the poor of Dublin any longer. There was no money in it.

He went downstairs and into a small side ward where Simons and Klinton were preparing a patient for amputation. Dr. Simons was twisting the tourniquet. The patient started to strain against the ties that held him down.

'What happened here?' Monroe asked.

'A cart tipped over and crushed his lower leg this morning.'

'Do you know what you're doing, man?' Monroe asked.

'Yes, I know what I'm doing. My father is a surgeon and I assist him when I can. Now can I please get on? We are trying to save this man's life.' Klinton started to cut through the flesh and forced the saw through bone. He needed to concentrate for the patient's sake.

'Where's Dr. Harton?' Monroe asked and saw that the man's right leg had been crushed right up to the knee. He thanked God that he wasn't the one on the receiving end.

'Harton didn't come in this morning. Stand out of my light, will you?'

Monroe stood back. He wondered what had possessed him to study medicine. Law would have been more palatable, with easier access to funds.

'You're doing a good job, Klinton. I have my own patients to see this morning. I'll be back in the afternoon.'

Dr. Klinton didn't bother to respond. The tourniquet had slipped and the amputee was bleeding out.

Dr. Simons managed to stem the blood flow and hoped that it wasn't too late. He felt for a pulse.

Monroe went back upstairs to have another drink. The whole place disgusted him.

By the time Dr. Klinton had finished, the patient was dead.

Abigail made her way to Sarah and Henry's home on Dame Street. There was a candle lighting in the upstairs room. She knocked on the door and waited until Henry answered the door.

'Abigail? Why are you here? What's wrong?'

'It's my father. He is very ill.'

'Come inside. Sarah is awake.'

Abigail went upstairs to the second floor of the building where they lived in one large room. In the corner, their bed was already made and all around was clean and tidy. Sarah was standing by the hearth making breakfast.

'What has happened?' she asked, alarmed, hanging the ladle by the fire.

'Papa is unwell. His stomach is giving him much trouble. He is sleeping now but I am worried. I have been to Mr. Smyth who has given me medicines that have helped settle him.'

'I will get ready,' Sarah said.

'Must Sarah go back with you?' Henry asked, afraid for his pregnant wife.

'It may not be safe for you, Sarah. I have really come to ask for your help, Henry.'

'What can Henry do that I cannot?' Sarah asked.

Abigail noticed that her sister was beginning to show she was with child. She should have spoken to Henry at the door.

'Will you fetch Dr. Monroe at the hospital for my father, Henry?'

'Of course, I will go with you.'

'I am sorry but you must go alone. There is another errand I have to make.'

'What errand is that, Abigail?' Sarah asked, frowning in puzzlement.

Abigail ignored her sister's question.

'Henry, you are managing the annuity for my father, are you not?'

'Yes, I have instructed Mr. Fitzgibbon to disperse funds as per your father's discretion.'

'The Apothecary Smyth tells me he has not been paid, that he is still owed a considerable sum.'

'I was not aware of that. We must speak to Dr. Monroe about it. Your father has given him some of the administrative tasks at the hospital. Perhaps it was an oversight.'

'Mr. Smyth tells me Papa promised to pay him last week.'

'I will ask Monroe this morning,' Henry said. 'He said he noticed that your father might be getting forgetful.'

'He is grieving for Benjamin,' Sarah said. 'Our father has a sharp mind. He is not doting yet.'

'What if this is something new?' Abigail asked her sister.

'I don't believe it. I must go to Pluncot Street this morning and talk to him myself,' Sarah said.

'Please don't, Sarah,' Abigail said. 'You must not risk harming the baby. Please wait until the illness has passed.'

'She is right, my love,' Henry said. 'And your father would not wish it.'

'I will stay then ... though only for the baby's sake.' Sarah moved the pot away from the fire. The breakfast was ready, but she hadn't the stomach to eat it.

'I'll go fetch Dr. Monroe at once, Abigail,' Henry said.

'Thank you, Henry.'

Henry escorted Abigail downstairs and went back up to his wife. He wanted to extract a promise from Sarah that she would not visit her father while he was gone.

Upstairs in Dr. Harton's office, Monroe was seated in the doctor's chair, gulping a glass of claret. The room was a mess, with papers and books spilling out over the desk.

He remembered that Harton stored cash in a strongbox in the large cabinet. Harton had given him keys to both which he wore around his neck. He knew there was a lot of money in the box and he started to sweat. Harton kept a ledger detailing every amount paid from the fund. Maybe he would take just a few guineas. He took the keys from his neck and opened the cabinet, and then the box. He sat looking at the money until the screaming started outside again. This time a woman was howling in pain. Couldn't they let him be? He couldn't take his eyes off the cash. Before he knew it, he was stuffing all of it deep into his pockets.

He left the box and cabinet open and opened all of the desk drawers haphazardly to make it look as if a thief had made the mess. After he'd thrown a few books on the floor, he went out leaving the door open behind him, and went down the stairs. He stopped halfway down as it occurred to him that he might make the money back again at the gaming tables and return it before anyone found out. He was thinking of going back up to tidy the office when he saw Henry was standing in the foyer. What the hell was he doing there?

Henry saw him. 'Thank God you are here, sir.'

'What has happened, Henry?' Monroe asked.

'It's Dr. Harton. Abigail has asked me to fetch you. He's extremely ill – his stomach, I believe.'

'I am sorry to hear that. We wondered where he was this morning.'

'Can you fetch your bag and come with me, please? I have a cab waiting.'

'I cannot come immediately, Henry. I must assist with the amputation of a leg. You go on ahead and tell Dr. Harton I'll be there as soon as I can.'

'Please hurry,' Henry said. 'From what Abigail says, he urgently needs attention.' The thought of the doctor's work made his blood run cold and he couldn't wait to get out of the hospital.

When Henry left, Monroe went back into the side ward and saw Klinton covering the amputee with a sheet. An attendant picked the leg up from the ground and laid it beside the corpse. With luck the City would collect the body that day.

Abigail felt lightheaded, though it had passed by the time she reached High Street on her way to the Gavins' home. She would finish the stomacher this week. Grace had finished embroidering the silver threads onto the skirt and was adding shades of pink to effect flowers on the vines. The girl was skilled enough to continue to work without her supervision. She would miss the Gavins. Sometimes she felt more at home there than at Pluncot Street.

As she hurried up Coles Alley, she was surprised to see her employer walking towards her with Grace by her side. Miss Gavin was carrying a large basket and looked as if the whole world had come down around her.

'Miss Harton, you are late. I thought you could be relied upon.'

'My father has been ill. I could not get away any earlier,' Abigail said, feeling it was unfair for Miss Gavin to be so unkind.

'Then I thank you for coming today,' Miss Gavin responded, obviously trying to hold her temper. 'Grace and I are going to the shoemaker with silk to make the shoes. We have fittings to take on Drogheda Street afterwards and should be home before you leave. I would be most obliged if you made good progress today.'

'I promised that I would finish the work on time, and I will.'

'Good,' Miss Gavin said and walked away with Grace in tow.

What was wrong with that woman? She was pleasant one minute and severe the next. Abigail couldn't understand her.

She made her way down the alley to the Gavins' house. The door to Mr. Gavin's workshop was open. He was humming a melody as he wound the warp with new scarlet threads at the loom. The kitchen was warm and she took off her cloak and hung it by the fire.

She went into the back workshop and looked at the stomacher. It could be finished by the end of the week if she hurried, though her eyes were sore through lack of sleep. As she threaded a needle with blue silk, she recalled the fairy tale that had inspired her design. The bluebird had come every day to sing to the Princess in the tower and the Princess had only felt at peace when she heard his song.

Hugh Gavin was enjoying the peace of the morning. He had heard Miss Harton arrive and had stopped himself from calling out to her. Instead, he worked steadily, trying to keep her out of his thoughts.

At noon, he and Michael went into the kitchen, where his sister had left pottage warming by the fire.

'Put another log on the flames, Michael.'

'Yes, sir.'

Michael liked his new master. There had been no beatings, not even an unkind word. Miss Gavin was a bit sour, but he believed most women were like that, though he liked Grace. She was always tousling his hair and teasing him about his ears. They stuck out too much, she said.

'Go and ask Miss Harton to eat with us,' Hugh said. 'I'll set the table.'

The boy went to call her. Hugh had forgotten his cravat. He would go to fetch it before Miss Harton joined them. Then he checked himself. What was he so concerned about? He was in his own home and the damned cravat strangled him. Abigail Harton wouldn't notice anyway. He went over to the fire and stirred the pottage until it started to bubble in the pot. It smelled good and he fetched a large bowl from the table. There was a clatter from the workshop room. What was the boy up to back there?

'*Mr. Gavin!*' Michael called out, '*Sir, please hurry!*'

Hugh put the bowl down and went into the back room.

Abigail was lying on the floor.

'My God – what happened?' he asked, bending over her.

'She was finishing a stitch, so I waited. Then she just keeled over. I didn't go near her, I swear.'

'She has fainted – Michael, go fetch a glass of the sweet wine.'

The boy hurried away.

The embroidery frame was lying on the floor alongside the girl. He moved it out of the way and touched her face. She felt cold and her skin was very white.

'Miss Harton,' he whispered, 'Abigail …' There was no movement. He needed to get her off the floor. He pulled her up, sliding an arm under her legs, and carried her into the kitchen, setting her down in the large chair by the hearth.

He knelt beside her. 'Miss Harton, wake up.'

Abigail stirred, then opened her eyes and saw him.

'Rest a while. You are unwell.'

Michael came over with the wine, spilling some of it on the floor in his haste.

Hugh took the glass from the boy and held it to Abigail's lips.

'Take a sip. It will revive you.'

'I was threading a needle …'

'Please drink.'

'Really, I don't need anything. I feel much better now,' she said, trying to compose herself.

'Drink – and you should eat something too. I will take you home afterwards.'

Abigail sat back in the chair and took a sip of the wine. She was not in a position to argue. Her head was spinning and she was afraid that if she stood she would fall down.

Hugh looked at the girl and moved a stray strand of hair from her face as she sipped her drink. He took his hand away. What was he doing?

He got to his feet. 'Michael, get Miss Harton a bowl of the pottage.' He went to put on his cravat. She needed rest. That was all. She had been working too hard. He would take her home himself. The dress could wait a day or two.

Young Michael came over with the pottage. Abigail put her glass on the floor and took the bowl and spoon from him. She raised a spoon of the broth to her lips.

Her thoughts were beginning to settle. She would be ready to embroider again in a little while.

When Mr. Gavin came back into the room, she glanced up.

'You look a little better,' he said. 'I'll take you home when you are ready.'

'I must get back to work.'

'You are not well enough, Miss Harton.' He could see that she was upset. 'Is there something troubling you?'

'I must finish my work here by the end of the week.'

'Why? There is plenty of time. Miss Harton, please don't be stubborn. You should not work today. What if you faint again?' He sat down opposite her.

'My father is very ill. I didn't sleep last night. That is all.'

'You should have sent us word.'

'I didn't want to let your sister down.'

'You won't – you work quickly and there is time. I'll take you home when you're feeling a little better. Try to eat some more first.'

She knew that he was right and so she finished her meal by the fire. Michael and Hugh ate at the kitchen table.

When Abigail had finished, Hugh came over and took the bowl from her.

'I'll take you home now,' he said.

'I don't want to trouble you any further.'

'I cannot in all conscience let you go alone.'

She stood up. She was still very pale.

'Please let me go. I will get a public cab.'

Hugh stood back from her and waited for a moment before he spoke again.

'If that is what you wish, Miss Harton. I will fetch one for you.'

He went out to the street and hailed a cab. There was no pleasing the young woman. All he was trying to do was help. When the cab stopped, he went back inside to get her.

She followed him out and saw a figure walking up the street.

It was Dr. Monroe.

In her confusion, she stepped back into the house and waited for him to pass by.

Hugh followed her in. 'Are you unwell again?'

'I thought I saw an associate of my father.'

Hugh looked out and saw the dishevelled man he had met on the street before, entering Mrs. Brass's inn. There was no one else about. It was starting to wear thin, this hiding of hers.

'The way is clear,' he said. 'We hope to see you tomorrow. I will tell my sister what has happened. She will understand.' He handed her into the cab and watched her go.

When the vehicle moved away, Abigail did not look back.

Monroe had decided to go back to tidy Harton's office and lock the door. Now that he had a big pot to play, he could cheat at the gaming table tonight and return the money before his employer noticed that it was gone.

Now, as he walked up the alley towards Mrs. Brass's inn he noticed there was a cab outside the dressmaker's place and he saw a young woman step out of the house and then quickly retreat. For a moment he could have sworn it was Miss Harton – but that was absurd. She was no doubt at home this minute attending to her poor father like the good daughter she was.

He slept for an hour, then washed his face and hands and changed his clothes. He made sure to put most of the money he had stolen from the hospital under the floorboards before he left for Pluncot Street.

When Abigail's cab stopped outside her home, the driver refused to take payment. Mr. Gavin had paid her fare in advance, he said. Now she would have to pay him back. She should have been grateful, but she didn't want to be beholden to anyone, especially him.

Brigid opened the front door for her.

'Oh Miss Abigail, I am so happy that you are home.'

'How is my father, Brigid?'

'He is doing much better.'

'That is good news.'

'Your mother is still with him, and Dr. Monroe has sent word that he is on his way.'

'Dr, Monroe has not arrived yet?' Abigail was surprised. 'What could have delayed him?'

'I don't know, miss.' Brigid bit her lip.

Abigail went upstairs to her parents' room. Her father was sitting up in bed, her mother helping him sip a bowl of broth. She took the broth and spoon from her mother and sent her away to rest. She sat and helped her father eat. She would stay with him until Dr. Monroe arrived. She wanted to know what had delayed him for so long – and why Mr. Smyth the apothecary had not been paid.

CHAPTER 32

In a house on Drogheda Street, Mary Gavin was thinking she had never come across such a silly group of girls. Even Grace had more sense than the three of them put together. Their dressmaker had run off with the butler and they hadn't a stitch to wear to the Boden Ball. An invitation from the Duchess had been received and they were all determined to wear something new. Their mother had ordered many different floral damask cloths and the girls couldn't make up their minds which to choose. Each wanted to see what the others would wear before deciding. In the end Mary chose for them – there was no time to squander if their dresses were to be ready on time. The emerald dress that Miss Harton was working on was almost ready. She and Grace would have enough time to make up three unadorned dresses for these girls in time. Thank God the previous dressmaker had made the girls new petticoats, hoops and stays before she had deserted them.

At last, decisions made and measurements taken, Mary thankfully started the long traipse home with Grace.

When they arrived in Coles Alley, Hugh was in foul humour and Daniel Long was sitting at the kitchen table, with a platter of bread and cheese before him and a cup of ale. He immediately stood up when Mary entered the room and smiled at her.

'Lord help us,' Mary muttered under her breath. 'When will this day end?'

'Good evening, Miss Gavin,' the visitor said.

'Good evening, Mr. Long.' She took off her cloak. 'Grace, go and see how Miss Harton is getting on.'

'She is not here,' her brother said. 'I sent her home earlier.'

'Why? What has happened now?'

'She was not well.'

'The Master had to carry her to the fire,' young Michael said, his mouth full of bread and cheese. 'She fainted out cold on the floor this morning.'

'For God's sake.'

Mary went to the back workshop to check progress on the stomacher. It remained almost as it had been the night before.

'She has made no progress at all,' she said when she returned to the kitchen.

'Mary, she was ill,' Hugh said.

'Did you call a doctor for her?'

'Her father's a doctor. She will fare better at home.'

Mr. Long had the good sense to remain mute. Miss Gavin was a handsome woman and he wanted to stay on her side in this argument.

'There's a doctor at the inn,' Grace said, 'though I don't think he's very good.'

Hugh was curious. Miss Harton had mentioned seeing an associate of her father in the street. 'What's this doctor's name?'

'Dr. Monroe. He comes in very late most nights and clearly intoxicated in my opinion.'

'And who asked you for your opinion, Grace?'

'No-one, begging your pardon, Miss Gavin.'

'Well, Miss Harton better be back tomorrow,' Mary said.

Her brother had had enough. He bade farewell to Daniel Long and left the kitchen.

Sitting at the loom, he thought about the associate of her father's that Miss Harton had claimed to see that morning. The name Monroe was familiar to him. He was sure he'd noticed it in the *Dublin Courant*. The paper was in the kitchen. He would wait until later to read it. He had wasted too much time already.

Young Michael came scurrying in to join his master. He had never seen Mr. Gavin so close to temper and didn't want to tempt fate.

Daniel Long was in two minds about what to do next.

'I see you are very busy, Miss Gavin. I'd best be getting home,' he said.

'Please do not hurry yourself, Mr. Long,' Mary said, 'I could do with some company. Let me get you more ale – or, I am about to have some sweet wine if you would care to join me? There is almond cake I baked yesterday too.'

Daniel Long smiled. Mary Gavin would be a noble addition to his household if she would have him.

Abigail watched from her parents' bedroom window for Dr. Monroe. At last he appeared and she went down to the hallway to greet him.

'We thought you would be here earlier,' she said.

'I came as soon as I could.'

'Did Henry not tell you this morning that my father needed you?' Perhaps her brother-in-law hadn't expressed how ill her father was.

Monroe looked at her. She didn't usually interrogate him in this way. He remembered the woman at the dressmaker's place near the inn that morning. It must have been her after all. She must have seen him. What had she been doing there?

'We had to amputate a patient's leg at the hospital this morning. There was so much blood that I went back to my lodgings to change my clothes. I'm here now. That is what's important.'

Abigail was chastened by being reminding of the heavy burden a doctor had to bear.

'Now tell me, how is your father this evening?'

'He is much better. Mr. Smyth supplied medicines and they seem to have made a difference.'

'Good news indeed. I'd best go up to him.'

'Yes, of course. This way.'

He followed Abigail up to her parents' bedroom.

Dr. Harton was sitting up in bed, his wife hovering over him.

'How is the patient?' Monroe asked.

'Ah, there you are, Monroe. I'm much restored, I'm glad to say. It must have been the meat at that chop shop. I hope you did not suffer the same consequences?'

Monroe laughed. He liked the good Dr. Harton. 'I am fine,' he said. 'I'm lucky to have the constitution of an ox.'

Monroe checked the warmth of his employer's skin and the rapidity of his pulse.

'All seems to be well again though it might be best to take a little spearmint for your stomach this evening. Most likely you'll be well by morning.'

'What if he is ill again in the night?' Margaret asked.

'Madam, I am confident that all danger has passed,' Monroe replied.

'There – you see, my dear, I shall be fine. Thank you for coming, Monroe.'

Margaret bent her head and started to cry.

Monroe closed his bag. 'I will call again tomorrow,' he said.

Abigail ushered him out onto the landing.

'Dr. Monroe …' She paused. 'There is a small matter I would like to discuss with you before you leave.'

Monroe could see that the girl was upset. He needed to be patient with her.

'Miss Harton, pray tell me what troubles you.'

'Please come downstairs with me. We can talk in private there.'

'Lead the way,' he said.

In the drawing room Abigail waited for him to sit. She did not join him.

'I am sorry to raise this matter with you,' she said.

'I hope I have not offended you in any way. I assure you that is the last thing I intend.'

'It is nothing of that sort, Dr. Monroe,' she said, pacing the room as he watched from his seat. She swung around to face him. 'I fear that my father may be becoming forgetful.'

Monroe was surprised. 'What makes you say such a thing? I have not seen it.'

'This morning Mr. Smyth informed me that our bill was not paid and that Papa had asked you to pay it on his behalf. But I know that you could not have forgotten such an important payment.'

The colour drained from Monroe's face. He had not expected the apothecary to bring up such business with Miss Harton. Her father had given him the cash to pay Mr. Smyth – however, he had gambled it all.

'Dr. Monroe, did my father give you the money for the apothecary?'

'What? No ... he must be confused ... I am sure it is all a misunderstanding. Try not to worry – I will go to see the apothecary myself tomorrow and will pay him myself if necessary.' He stood up and kissed her on the forehead. 'You've been under a lot of strain. When you consent to be my wife, we can share these troubles. It will be easier for you then. Can I ask you again to consider me as a husband? I long to call you my own.'

Abigail bowed her head. The family needed someone like him to help them. She needed someone. Why couldn't it be him?

'I will marry you, sir,' she said. It was best to make the decision now.

Monroe couldn't believe it. 'Only if you are sure, my dear.'

Abigail looked directly at him. 'I will not go back on my word.'

Monroe drew her into his arms. What a treasure she was. So resolute. 'I will ask your father's permission tomorrow when he is feeling better.'

She pulled away. 'Yes, Dr. Monroe, that would be best.'

She wanted to get back to her mother and father upstairs and opened the drawing-room door to show him out. Monroe followed her down the stairs to the hall.

As he opened the front door, he turned to her. 'Do you know how happy you have made me?'

'As you have made me, Dr. Monroe. I will see you tomorrow,' Abigail said, hugging her arms for warmth as the cold air invaded the hallway.

'You must call me William from this day forth.'

'When my father gives his permission, Dr. Monroe.' She managed to smile.

'Tomorrow then.' He stole a kiss before leaving her.

Abigail closed the door as Brigid walked up from the kitchen. She hoped the maidservant hadn't seen Dr. Monroe kiss her, though she was sure Brigid wouldn't say anything to her mother if she had.

She had expected to feel differently about the proposal. She felt only relief. Maybe it was because her father was so ill. She was worried about him, that was all. When her father was better, she would feel happy in the knowledge that they would all be safe in the world.

She had only to work to the end of the week for the Gavins. She would get there early tomorrow to make sure that the stomacher was finished by then.

Monroe could hardly contain himself. The day had gone so much better than he could have anticipated. He was at the point of being downright joyous. He had got the pretty Miss Harton. All he had to do was walk her down the aisle. He wondered again why she had been at dressmaker's shop on Coles Alley that morning. With her father ill, what had she been doing there? There was so much more to find out about Abigail Harton and he would enjoy doing that very much indeed.

He decided to go straight back to the inn. It was too early to go to the Dargan Club and he needed to plan a proper strategy before he gambled with most of the hospital's money.

CHAPTER 33

From early the next morning, Hugh worked steadily at the loom, moving the heavy reed back and forth as Michael pushed the shuttle across the loom to weave the cloth. It was strenuous work. And though the air had grown cold, he worked in his shirtsleeves.

Reading the *Courant* the night before, he had come across Dr. Monroe's name in an article stating that Dr. Harton, Abigail's father, had secured an annuity from the Duke of Alden and that Dr. Monroe had been appointed to a position at her father's hospital the previous month. What surprised him was that Miss Harton hadn't told him or his sister any of this.

Mary was dismayed when she had heard the news. She feared that she would lose Miss Harton immediately because of it. Hugh had asked her not to say anything and she had reluctantly agreed.

He stopped the loom and wiped his brow. He really didn't know what to think of the girl anymore.

When the workshop door opened and Abigail came in, he immediately stopped working.

'Good morning, Mr. Gavin, I don't want to disturb you. I just wanted to thank you for your help yesterday.'

'It was no trouble, Miss Harton. I hope you are feeling better.'

'I am, thank you.'

'And your father?'

'He is much improved too,' she said and stretched her hand out. There were two coins in it. 'I wanted to give you this for the cab fare that you so generously paid yesterday. There was no need.'

Hugh was astounded. 'You do not need to pay me back. I would have done the same for anyone.' He turned back to the loom. 'I'd be much obliged if you would keep it.'

'I do not mean to offend you, sir,' she said and drew her hand back.

He started the machine again. 'Was there anything else?'

'No, Mr. Gavin.' Abigail turned away and left the room, closing the door behind her.

She bumped into Miss Gavin out in the hallway.

'Miss Harton, you look like you've seen a ghost. Please tell me you are not indisposed again? I hope you are not going home already?'

'I am not going home, Miss Gavin. I will complete my work as I have promised. Grace has already finished the silver vines on the dress and I am sure she will complete the flowers on the skirt by the end of next week. She does not need my supervision anymore.'

'If that is what you say, Miss Harton, I will take your word for it. Time is not on our side.' She paused. 'I must say that I was surprised when my brother told me that your father has been funded by Alden at last.'

Abigail did not know what to say.

'He read it last night in the newspaper. I promised I would keep silent on it, but I find I cannot keep that promise. I am shocked, Miss Harton, that you did not tell us any of this before now. I had thought you were an honest girl. But please do not let me take you from your work any longer.'

Abigail didn't respond. Hugh Gavin and his sister had been offended by her silence, though her father's hospital wasn't any of their business. There were only a few more days left to work.

She made her way to the workroom. She just needed to keep calm and finish the thorns surrounding the birds with silver thread. She should not have handed Hugh back the money and was sorry for it. There was nothing to be done about that now. She took out the thread and continued to embroider the top of the stomacher. Before the week was out, her work would be complete.

Hugh worked late and didn't see Miss Harton leave. The boy had fallen asleep on his pallet by the loom and his sister was baking a pie for their supper. He went to sit by the fire.

'You've been quiet today.' Mary chopped a shallot and spread the pieces with some herbs on a slice of beef.

'I'm tired, that is all.'

'So Miss Harton will be gone by the end of the week.' She rolled the beef tight and secured it with tape.

Hugh didn't respond.

'She will need some of the scarlet thread tomorrow,' Mary said.

'I will wind a bobbin later.'

'I wonder what she will do next? She is pretty enough to catch a husband without a dowry, don't you think?' Mary placed the meat into water to boil over the fire, then added claret for good measure.

Hugh got up abruptly and put on his cloak.

'Brother, where are you going?'

'Out,' he said. 'For some fresh air.'

'At this time of night?'

'When else am I going to get it?' He left, shutting the kitchen door behind him.

Miss Gavin watched her brother through the window as he crossed the yard. She hoped he wasn't sweet on Miss Harton. He wasn't that much of a fool, was he?

She went back to the table to mix flour and lard for the pastry. She would need to find another embroiderer as soon as possible. Maybe Mr. Long might be able to direct her on it.

When Hugh made his way down Coles Alley, all was quiet. November had truly arrived. He walked towards Meath Street and couldn't get Abigail Harton out of his head. He made his way down Engine Alley and turned onto Francis Street. Before long, he realised he had walked to Pluncot Street and almost to the Hartons' front door. When the door opened, he immediately turned back before he was seen. What was he doing?

Tomorrow he must check the *Almanack* for the earliest passage to Boston. He would meet Mr. Fish there and then travel on to Virginia to his friend George Thompson.

He made his way towards the river, to where the ships swayed in the darkness. Sailors stumbled up gangplanks on their way back from any pleasures they could afford.

On the quays, a woman offered herself to him for a penny. Her teeth were black and her clothes threadbare. She beckoned him to follow her to a building behind. Children were huddled in a doorway close by. He knew nothing of true suffering. He handed the woman a shilling and went home. He would feel sorry for himself no longer.

It was almost midnight by the time he got back to Coles Alley. Two men were being thrown out onto the street as he passed by the inn. Grace's mother, Mrs. Brass, followed them out with a kitchen knife.

'*And don't come back until you can pay for your pots!*' Then she spotted him. 'Oh, Mr. Gavin, is that you?'

'Yes, Mrs. Brass, it is.'

'What are you doing out at this time of the night?'

'Needed to get some fresh air,' he said.

'Is that all you were getting?' Mrs. Brass winked at him. 'Come on in for a free pot. It's on the house. It'll do you good, a man of your size.' She looked him up and down with a grin on her face. He was a handsome one at that.

'I'd best be off to my bed,' he said.

'What a lonely bed it must be,' she muttered under her breath and went back into her paying guests. She couldn't remember the last time a man had refused a free pot of ale. There was something wrong with the Gavins. They were too uptight for their own good. And her Grace was beginning to get airs and graces about herself too. She would have a word with the girl in the morning. Maybe it was time for Grace to work at the inn with her sister Olive. That would spite Miss Gavin and her uppity brother altogether.

CHAPTER 34

When Mary came down the next day, Hugh was already up. They hadn't spoken further the night before. Mary had known not to agitate him when he was in such a foul humour.

'You must have been up before dawn,' she said.

'I had a lot of catching up to do.'

'Sit down and get some heat into you,' she said and cut him a slice of yesterday's bread.

Hugh put a log on the fire and sat down, putting the bread on a fork to toast it.

'You were out late last night,' she said, gauging his reaction as she measured out flour to bake fresh bread.

He would delay telling her no longer. He pulled the stale bread off the fork, threw it into the fire and stood up.

'There is nothing for it but to tell you.'

'Tell me what?' she asked.

'Mary, I have tried to make it work here, but I cannot. I have decided to leave for America in the new year.'

Mary sat down abruptly. She watched as her brother took George Thompson's letter out of his pocket and put it down on the table in front of her.

'George writes to say that he has established a business in Virginia and invites me to join him there. I am going to take him up on his offer.'

'Why? You have the start of a good business here, Hugh.'

'I mean to do well in life, Mary, and there is more opportunity there to expand.'

'But you can do that here. You are much better off here. Please consider this further before you settle on it.'

'I'm sorry, Mary. Please understand that I have been thinking on this for some time.'

'Family matters most, Hugh. You will have no-one there.'

'I can't spend the rest of my life in that front room. I know that you are disappointed …'

'What about the boy? I cannot afford to keep him. What is to happen to him?'

'I will speak to Mr. Long about taking him on. I know you had great plans for us in this city, but I have thought long and hard about this.'

'You could lose everything there, Hugh.' Mary stood up. 'The trouble is that you don't know what it is that you seek and, because of that, you'll never be happy anywhere.'

'Please let's not argue. Perhaps you might consider coming with me?'

'I don't want to go to America. You know that. I have a good business in Dublin and respectable customers. Think on this further, I beg you. You could marry and have your own family here. Perhaps a master weaver's daughter who will inherit her father's business.'

'Mary, I am resolved to go.'

Hugh walked out of the kitchen and left her there looking after him in dismay. He couldn't go until the spring, not until the scarlet order was complete. There was plenty of time to change his mind. Mr. Long might have the answer. She would speak to him. Maybe he would let her brother share his business.

Margaret stayed in the bedroom while Dr. Monroe examined her husband. The young man looked as if he'd been out half the night – most likely tending to the sick at the hospital. She hoped that it would not be long before he asked for Abigail's hand.

'Your husband fares much better today I see, Mrs. Harton,' he said at last. 'He'll be up and about in no time.'

She closed her eyes. 'Thank God.'

'Though he should stay in bed for another few days. Do you hear that, Dr. Harton? No work, not even downstairs in your office.'

'I have no objection,' said Dr. Harton, smiling.

'I will make sure he stays in bed,' said his wife.

'I'm sure you will,' Monroe said. 'Mrs. Harton, I had hoped to speak with Miss Harton this morning. Perhaps you could ask her to meet me in the drawing room?'

'Oh, Dr. Monroe, she is visiting her sister this morning. We had not expected you so early today.'

'Tell her I am sorry to have missed her.'

'I will, Dr. Monroe.'

'In that case, Mrs. Harton, may I have a short while alone with your husband? I have some business to discuss with him before I go.'

'Of course,' she said, happy to leave her husband in such safe hands.

Monroe smiled at the woman he hoped would become his mother-in-law before he braced himself to ask Dr. Harton for his daughter Abigail's hand in marriage.

Mrs. Harton went out to the landing. Passing by the looking glass, she noticed that her eyes had dark circles beneath them and her skin was very pale. Though she had not yet reached her forty-sixth year, she looked almost as old as her husband who was close to sixty.

She walked downstairs to her husband's office and took from the bookshelf the book of fairy tales that Benjamin had loved.

She could see her son's face clearly in her mind. Why couldn't he have lived? The gilded cover of the book was beautiful. Her husband had bought it in France, sure that his children would appreciate it one day. Now, two of those children were dead. She opened the story of the Princess and the bluebird.

She smiled as she touched the hand-painted picture. It showed the bird on the window ledge of a high tower, encased by vines of thorn, singing to a Princess who was spinning threads of gold. She turned the page and read on …

The Princess looked forward to hearing the birdsong each day. Her father, the King, had been so long at war that the she had forgotten his face. Her mother, the Queen, had died so long ago that she had no memories of her at all. When the King had remarried and gone to war, the Princess thought that her stepmother would be kind. Only too late did she discover that the new Queen was an evil Sorceress in disguise, when she locked her in the castle tower from morning until night. The Sorceress had no intention of freeing the girl, for with her magic she could ensure that the Princess would spin gold until her dying day. The bluebird was the only creature who gave the Princess some moments of happiness each day as he sang to her.

She closed the book. She could read no more and hoped that her daughter would not have to embroider gold threads until her dying day. She wished that Abigail's life would be a happy one.

'Mistress?' It was Brigid at the door.

'Come in.'

'I'm sorry to disturb you, mistress. Dr. Monroe and the Master have asked that you join them.'

'I'll be up shortly,' she said and Brigid departed.

Margaret put the book back on the shelf and went upstairs to her bedroom on the first floor.

'My dear, I couldn't wait to tell you,' John Harton said.

Her husband's colour was back and her heart lifted. 'What is it, my dear?'

'Dr. Monroe has asked for Abigail's hand in marriage. She has already accepted him.'

'Oh, I am so very glad.' Her prayers had been answered. 'We are very happy to welcome you to our family, Dr. Monroe.'

'I am beyond happiness myself.'

'Abigail will be home by supper. Let us celebrate then.'

'That would be most welcome.' Monroe turned to Dr. Harton. 'I shall see you then, sir.'

'I look forward to it.'

Margaret led him out of the room. She was relieved that Abigail had secured him. The sooner the engagement was announced, the sooner her daughter would be safe. She hoped her husband would return to good health, if that was what God willed. She had lost Benjamin and might still lose the man she loved but she must accept that.

After she had shown Dr. Monroe out, she went back to her bedroom. Her husband had fallen asleep.

She went to her dressing table and took out her jewellery box from the top drawer. She saw dismayed to see that she had left the key in the box – she was becoming forgetful. She opened it up. Its contents had reduced over time. The pearls lay inside the pale-blue silk-inlayed box. Her mother had given them to her on her wedding day. Sarah had preferred the jade necklace and had taken that. The pearls were meant for Abigail's wedding day. She couldn't see her mother's emerald earrings in the box so she searched the drawer, to no avail. She frowned. Surely she hadn't left them at Dean Swift's house? If she had, he would be too discreet to bring them back to her. She would have to approach him and ask him. How embarrassing if she hadn't left them there after all. She could even have lost them on the way back. She was deeply saddened at the thought of such a loss. But she might have simply misplaced them.

She must do a thorough search but she had no time to do it now.

She took the last of her coins out of the box and locked it again, removing the key this time. If she hurried she could place the engagement announcement in the *Courant* at once. Once it was printed, there would be no going back.

She put on her cloak, left the house and walked towards the river. She thought about the tale of the Princess and the bluebird. She couldn't remember how it had ended. Whether the King had saved his daughter, or if the Prince had been transformed into human form again.

CHAPTER 35

Mr. Edward French wasn't feeling very well. As Alden's secretary, he wasn't up to the job and he knew it. Every waking hour was filled with trepidation. The Duchess had decided to supervise his efforts on a daily basis when her husband was absent. As a result, his nerves had worsened. He should have been free to run the estate with only his master's direction. Alden had gone out riding this morning towards the forests of Montpelier Hill and would be gone until dusk. By right Edward should have been back in his London office, with a glass of port, looking through his business papers, feeling at ease. Instead, he had been compelled to visit Irish tenants to put the fear of God into them, which did not come naturally to him. He suspected they merely laughed at him. He set out for Boden Castle again.

Reaching it he dismounted, led his horse to the stables, handed it over one of the grooms, and hurried into the castle. There was much work to be done, to say nothing of doing the final invitations for the December ball.

The Duchess was in his office when he returned. Could a man not work and report to his master without having to report to his master's wife too? He took off his gloves and tried to be civil.

She was standing at the window in a yellow gown with her back to him.

'Good morning, Duchess. I hope you have had a good morning.'

'I have added several more names to the invitation list,' she said, turning around.

'I will make sure that they are delivered.'

'Have you sent out the last batch yet? Those I gave you yesterday?'

'I had more pressing business this morning, Your Grace.'

The Duchess of Alden walked towards him.

'There is no more pressing business than this, French.'

'There is time yet, I can assure you.'

'Are you contradicting me?'

'Of course not.'

'Here are the additional names. See they are all delivered today.'

'Yes, Your Grace.'

'Get on with it, French,' she said, standing over him at his desk.

He took out a quill. His fingers started to shake and he almost sent the inkpot flying. Why didn't she write them herself or have one of her ladies do it?

'Your Grace, you will have to excuse me. I work faster on my own.'

'I doubt that very much indeed,' she said and left the room.

At Pluncot Street, the footman couldn't quite believe he had been asked to deliver an invitation to such a lowly place. A maid, whose attire was well worn, opened the door.

'Is this the residence of Dr. and Mrs. Harton?' he asked.

'Yes, it is,' Brigid said, assessing the lofty gentleman in a grey powdered wig and velvet livery. He had a sweet smell and she wondered how he had managed it.

'Well then, be sure they receive this,' the footman said, handing the invitation to her carefully so that she did not touch his hand.

The Duke was an odd fish, he thought, socialising with anything and anyone. The girl was pretty enough on closer inspection, though not quite to his usual standards. He could do much better at the castle, or in London if he could persuade Radburn to let him go back with the Aldens to Ashdale.

He bowed deeply to the maid and went back to the waiting carriage.

In Coles Alley, Abigail clipped the last thread on the stomacher. The bluebirds were encased in a web of tangled thorns made up of gold and silver thread on the emerald background. The branches were thin and faded towards the bottom of the stomacher so that the design blended into the delicate damask and embroidery of the skirt.

Mary and Grace had already arranged the finished dress over the hooped frame and petticoat that were already on the mannequin in the corner of the workshop room. All they needed to complete the dress was the stomacher.

She looked at the two women now intent on one of the other commissions and realised that she would miss working with them after today. Gathering her tools, she placed them carefully in her sewing box. There was some scarlet thread on the bobbin still. By right she should give it back to Miss Gavin, but she couldn't quite make herself do so. Instead, she would sew red roses onto her white poplin dress at home with it. Her mother would help, and they could sit and talk as they had done before.

There was a shift in the light outside. The days were getting shorter and their greyness starker. She closed the sewing box. There would be no daydreaming of another life anymore. She was bound to her parents and to Dr. Monroe. All was settled and she had made her choice. She would have children of her own, God willing. Her fiancé was a true and honest man who helped the most vulnerable of the city. It was enough.

'I have finished,' she said.

'And with over a week to spare,' said Mary, looking up from her work. 'Thank you, Miss Harton.'

Abigail took the stomacher to the mannequin and Grace helped her fasten it in place.

Miss Elizabeth Goulding would be one of the finest ladies at the ball.

'It is perfect,' Grace said.

Mary Gavin rose to examine the finished garment.

Abigail stood back to admire the craftsmanship of the dress's construction. She would probably never see it on Miss Goulding who was to wear it to the ball which would take place the following week.

'As I've always said, Miss Harton, you do the finest work,' Mary said.

'I am glad that I have been able to help you. But now I must take my leave.'

'I would offer you a glass of wine, but Grace and I have only a few days to finish the other dresses on time,' Mary said.

'There is no need but thank you.'

'We are due to deliver the dress to Miss Goulding next Wednesday. I will have your payment after that. Perhaps you could stop by on Thursday?'

'I would be much obliged, Miss Gavin.' Abigail was pleased to be leaving on such pleasant terms.

She looked around the workshop once more, took her sewing box and bade them farewell.

Mary nodded a goodbye. She would need to find a replacement for Miss Harton soon if she was to build her business, especially if her brother followed through on his plan to seek adventure in America.

In the kitchen Abigail put on her cloak. The fire blazed in the hearth and the room was homely. A pie was baking by the fire and for a moment she wanted to stay. She looked towards Mr. Gavin's workshop door. It was closed. She could hear the loom working and held her breath. Should she say goodbye to him and the boy? It was too hard to do so now. She would say goodbye when she returned next week for her payment.

There was sleet in the air and daylight faded as she hurried along the streets with her box hidden beneath her cloak.

Brigid welcomed her home and she wondered why she was feeling ill at ease. She no longer needed to lie to her father or her future husband about her work.

'Dr. Monroe is here. There is news,' Brigid said.

Abigail gave the sewing box to Brigid. What news could there be? She made her way to the drawing room, where her fiancé and parents waited. She kissed her father and mother and went to sit beside Dr. Monroe. She shivered despite the warmth of the room.

Monroe looked at her, thinking that the fresh air suited her complexion.

'Your father and I have received an invitation today to the Boden Ball,' her mother said. 'From the Duchess of Alden, no less.'

'We will hire a carriage like the old days,' her husband said.

Abigail was delighted that her father had received the recognition he deserved. He could now re-establish himself as a private physician. Dr. Monroe would run the hospital. The annuity was enough to pay the salary for her father, her fiancé and the two new physicians already employed.

She noticed that Dr. Monroe was looking at her curiously. She hated to deceive him and resolved to tell him about her work for the Gavins before they were married.

'That is wonderful news,' she said. 'What will you wear, Mama?'

They all laughed. Everything was coming right again.

Hugh decided he would leave when the weather was a little warmer and the crossing safer in the spring. He had already spoken to Daniel

Long, who had offered to take on the boy, though he hadn't told young Michael of his plans yet. In the meantime, he had sworn Mr. Long to secrecy. Michael would have to be handled gently. He didn't want the boy running back to his parents before he'd had a chance to get to know Mr. Long's sons. They were good boys, around his own age, and he would do well in the Long household. Hugh would take Michael to visit there tomorrow.

He went into the kitchen to wash his hands before supper. Mary was frying chicken meat and sweetmeats over the fire. She looked up, and he could see her mood had not improved. He poured himself a cup of ale and sat down.

'So Miss Harton has left us,' she said, regarding her brother.

Hugh put his cup down on the table. 'I didn't see her go,' he said.

'Didn't she call in to you to say goodbye?' She could see from her brother's expression that she had not. 'I thought the girl had better manners than that.'

Mary brought the pan over to the table and divided its contents between three plates that had been set out there. 'I'm sure she'll say goodbye to you and wee Michael when she calls for her last payment next week.'

Hugh did not care to answer his sister. His voice might betray his feelings if he did.

Young Michael came out from the workshop and sat down at the table. Mary noticed that the boy had put on some weight. He was looking healthy again. How could her brother think of leaving him behind? She tousled the boy's hair affectionately.

'Are you happy here?' she asked, all the while looking at her brother.

'Yes, mistress, I am,' he said.

Hugh pushed his chair away from the table and stood up. Taking his cloak, he walked out into the night.

'Never mind my brother, Michael. He has a lot on his mind these days. Besides, I made apple tart today and when we are finished our supper we shall each have a slice and I have some fresh milk to have with it too.'

Young Michael smiled and continued to eat his meal. He wished that Miss Gavin was his mother instead of the one that had been given him.

Hugh walked along Coles Alley and set out to Mr. Long's house near Weaver's Square where he might find better company. But there was some light left so he continued on to Tenterfields, where woven cloth was set out to dry, and before long he was out into open country, leaving Mr. Long's house far behind him.

Did Miss Harton think so little of him that she could walk away without a word? Did she not consider him a friend? He walked a little further on before stopping to look up at the sky.

There was a full moon but soon the clouds obscured it. He wondered what America would be like. Would he feel at home there? In truth, he had never really felt at home anywhere. His aunt and uncle had made him feel like an outsider. He had felt he could only secure their loyalty by marrying their daughter. It might have worked well, but Sally had a sharp tongue and the bossy nature of her mother. What was the point of living if there was no joy in it? Miss Harton had shown him what a woman could be like, a woman he could marry.

He saw a carriage coming towards him, heading towards the city. It was travelling fast, and he stepped closer to the thicket for safety. The carriage passed by as the clouds cleared the moon and he could see it was the Alden party, with several mounts following behind, their riders already drunk, on their way no doubt to spend the night gaming in the city. The way these young men wasted their time and money astounded him. If he had been born to a life of such grace, he would do so much to make life better for those he loved. But to think about that was just a waste of time. He was leaving this island and spring seemed a long way away. It could be endured. He would say his goodbyes to Miss Harton when she returned for her payment.

He turned and walked back towards the city and home.

When he at last arrived, he was hoping that his sister would be in bed, but she was still up, waiting for him.

'I've kept your supper warm, Hugh,' she said.

She took a bowl to the fire, filled it to the brim and brought it over to him.

'I am sorry,' she said. 'I should not have told you about Miss Harton leaving us in front of Michael.'

'What did that matter?'

She sat down opposite him. 'Are you still determined to go to America?'

Hugh looked at her. She was strong. She would survive him leaving.

'Yes, Mary. It will not be immediately but I will not be changing my mind.'

'There's nothing else to be said so. I'd best get some sleep before dawn.'

She rose to her feet, took a candle and went upstairs.

Hugh knew that his sister was a good woman. She was sharp with her words sometimes, that was all. He had no doubt but that Mr. Long would look out for her when he was gone. He finished his supper and took his bowl over to the sideboard. The fire was dying down so he threw on a log and sat with his ale to finish it there. He would not sleep yet. His mind was too busy.

He picked up the *Courant* his sister had brought home earlier and began to read the news. There were several personal announcements. A missing person, and a lady selling linen shirts on Essex Street at ten per cent discount if you mentioned her name.

The name Harton was in an article at the end of the sheet. He held the paper closer to the fire to see. He was astonished as he read the words. The paper crumpled in his hand. Mr. and Mrs. Harton had announced the engagement of their daughter Miss Abigail Harton to Dr. William Monroe, the physician at the hospital her father had founded.

He stood and put on his cloak and hat. This time he went straight to the inn. A harder drink was what he needed.

CHAPTER 36

Hugh swung the axe until his arms ached. He brought it down again on another log and another. He couldn't stop.

It was Thursday and he should have been working but young Michael's father had asked he be allowed home to see an uncle who had returned from England.

Miss Harton was bound to another man. He had to accept things the way they were. It was clear that she had no interest in him, and in any case he was resolved on leaving the country in a few months, most likely never to return. He put the axe down as the back gate opened.

When he turned around Miss Harton was there, in the yard, with him. It was as if he'd conjured her up.

'Good morning, Mr. Gavin.'

'Good morning, Miss Harton … my sister is not here.'

'Do you expect her soon?'

'She went to visit a client and should be back within the hour.'

He turned away to pick up an armful of wood.

When he straightened up she was just standing there watching him, looking ill at ease.

'You'd better come inside before you freeze,' he said.

Abigail followed him into the familiar kitchen. Hugh started to build the fire high and she wanted to move closer to the flames, to warm her hands, but she stayed where she was.

'Please sit down, Miss Harton,' he said.

Abigail did not move.

'I should call back this afternoon,' she said.

'If that is what you'd prefer, but I'm sure Mary won't be much longer.'

She hesitated, then nodded and sat down at the table.

Hugh tried to remember what he was doing.

'Can I offer you something to drink?'

'No, Mr. Gavin. Thank you.'

He poured himself a cup of ale and tried to think of something polite to say.

Abigail shifted in her seat, uncomfortable in the silence.

'Have you decided if you will go to America?' she asked.

'Yes. I've decided to go, perhaps in the spring.'

'Did you ask your sister if she would travel with you?'

'I did, but Mary will stay here. She's made herself a home in Dublin and has a good business here. She will not sail with me.'

'I am sorry. I am sure she will miss you.'

'And you, Miss Harton? What will you do?' he said, curious to see if she would tell him her news.

Abigail hesitated again. She had nothing to hide.

'I am to be married, Mr. Gavin, to Dr. Monroe. He has been kind to my family.'

'I read of your engagement in the *Courant*. I offer you my congratulations.'

'The *Courant*?' she said, startled. 'I didn't know there was an announcement … I thought to tell you both personally but …' She couldn't finish the sentence.

He could bear it no longer. 'I will leave you to wait for my sister.'

'I wish you a safe journey, Mr. Gavin.'

'I wish you a happy life, Miss Harton.' Abandoning his ale, he strode out into the yard.

The *Dublin Courant* was on the table. She searched to find the announcement. There it was. Her name was printed clearly alongside Dr. William Monroe's. It was as if it was happening to another person and not to her. She clutched the newspaper. Her parents had not told her about the announcement. She was sorry that the Gavins had found out this way.

Hugh stood outside, feeling he had been rude to make such a sudden exit. But it was difficult to stay close to her.

His sister came through the yard door.

'Looks like we have enough wood to last us the winter,' she said.

'Miss Harton is inside.'

'I don't have her money yet. I'll have to explain.'

'She doesn't quite seem herself.'

Mary only half listened to what her brother was saying and battled her way past the firewood to the back door.

Abigail stood up as she entered the kitchen.

'Good morning, Miss Gavin.'

Mary thought the girl might faint again she looked so pale.

'Good morning, Miss Harton,' Mary said as she took her cloak off and put it on a chair. 'I'm sorry but I have to disappoint you. I haven't collected the money yet. There's been a delay. I am to deliver the dress to Elizabeth Goulding tomorrow. I forgot to send you a note about it. You'll have to come back the day after, I'm afraid.'

'Of course. I'll call again then. Thank you.'

'Why don't you have some wine and tell us your news, Miss Harton?' Mary stood with her hands on her hips.

'I won't stay.' Abigail paused. 'I have just told your brother … about my engagement.'

'We already learned of it. We saw the announcement in the *Courant*. We were most surprised.' Mary could not understand the girl. Why hadn't she told them before now?

'I didn't know my parents had made it public – as I was just saying to your brother, I intended to tell you personally.'

'No matter. I wish you well. Grace can deliver the payment to your house if you wish. There is no need to come back here. She will be discreet.'

'I am much obliged to you,' Abigail said.

Mary nodded. 'If you ever need employment again, you know where I am,' she said.

'Thank you, Miss Gavin. I don't think that will be necessary.'

'Very well. Let me see you out.'

Abigail moved towards the hall, not wanting to encounter Mr. Gavin again, and Mary followed.

'Good day to you, Miss Harton,' Mary said as she held the door open.

'Good day, Miss Gavin.'

The dressmaker watched Abigail walk down the alley. She was astonished that the girl had worked in her house for almost three months but had not taken her into her confidence about the engagement.

Back in the kitchen, she began to noisily take the crockery out to set the table for a dinner of cold pie and ale.

Hugh came in the back door and walked through to his workshop without a word. He looked around the room. There was nothing left here for him anymore. He would write to George Thompson tomorrow to let him know of his intention to join him. He would speak to Mr. Long about selling the loom too. His sister had proven she was more than capable of making her own living and she would have a good friend in Mr. Long, and more if she wanted. It was time to make his own life, his own decisions, and there was nothing in Dublin that warranted him staying for longer than his current obligations demanded.

CHAPTER 37

It was Friday and the day of the Boden Ball.

Margaret Harton touched her husband's forehead. He had relapsed during the night. The medicine Monroe had prescribed didn't seem to be working.

Monroe had left more medicine for her husband when he awoke. Margaret took the powders and went down to the kitchen where she found Brigid sleeping. She left her be and took a jug of ale from the larder and poured it into a cup. Then she mixed in the powders with a spoon. It tasted of salt and she prayed that her husband could keep it down.

In the hallway, a draught almost put out her candle. She hoped it wasn't a bad omen as she went quietly back up the stairs.

Her husband would not be well enough to attend the Boden Ball that evening and she would not go without him. She had already asked Dr. Monroe last night to take Abigail instead. They were engaged and it would be proper that she attend with Dr. Monroe on behalf of the family. She regretted the fact that she could not give

Abigail the emerald earrings to wear to the ball. Further searches in her bedroom and the house at large had not located them. She could have left them at the Dean's or, God forbid, she could have lost them.

Ordinarily she would have been deeply upset about the matter but it paled into insignificance compared to her fears for her husband.

He called for her and she went to attend him.

The house was still quiet when Abigail awoke. Just when she thought everything was taking a turn for the better, her father had become ill again. She got out of bed and touched the white material of the dress she would wear to Boden that evening. She and her mother had embroidered red rosebuds over the white silk base with the scarlet thread she had taken from the Gavins.

Abigail drew back the curtains and saw that it was going to be another cold day. She regretted that she had finished working for Miss Gavin. It had helped to focus her mind and helped her forget her worry about her parents. She thought too of the journey to America that Mr. Gavin would take. In her heart, she knew that some part of her wanted to go with him, though she pushed the thought away and reminded herself that she was safe here, safer than she had ever been before. She would marry Dr. Monroe and her future would be secure. It was the best for her mother and her father and best for her.

She touched the silk of the only evening gown she possessed and imagined herself sailing on a great ship across the ocean. What would it feel like to have the sun on her face and the wind on her body as she stood on deck to watch the sun cross the skies? To have that much freedom. To escape.

She put on her blue day dress and housecoat and went downstairs to help Brigid prepare breakfast.

The sun was high in the sky and Mary wondered where Grace had got to. The emerald dress needed packing before it was transported to the Goulding residence across the river. It needed to be there by early afternoon. That would give them just enough time to make any minor adjustments.

Mary went into the workshop and unfolded the linen in which to wrap the dress. The Gouldings were sending a private carriage to pick them up at noon and it was almost ten o'clock now. She looked at the exquisite work that Miss Harton had done. It was a pity to lose such a talent, she thought yet again. After the Gouldings, she and Grace would take a cab to Drogheda Street. She had delivered the three dresses there yesterday but had been asked to attend later this afternoon in case the ladies should require her services before leaving for the ball. It was going to be a long day. Hopefully she and Grace would be back home before dark, that was if the girl ever showed up. It was getting cold and the sky was a clear blue. She hoped the roads wouldn't ice over for they would have a treacherous journey home if it did.

Then she heard Grace call her from the kitchen. She went to see what had taken her so long.

'Please, Miss Gavin, you must fetch your brother,' the girl gasped.

'What's wrong, Grace? Sit down and catch your breath.'

'There's no time, mistress – we need to find Dr. Monroe.'

'Is your mother ill?' Mary asked.

Hugh came out from his workshop.

'A man came to the inn in the early hours this morning looking for Dr. Monroe,' said Grace. 'He's dying and wants his friend, Dr. Monroe, to help him.'

'Have you sent word to the hospital?' Hugh asked.

'Yes, my sister Olive went to fetch him but Dr. Monroe is not expected there until two o'clock this afternoon. His friend grows weaker by the minute. My mother does not want a stranger dying in her house. It'll be very bad for business, she says.'

'Dr. Monroe might be at the Hartons',' Miss Gavin said, pouring the girl a small glass of ale.

'I'm sorry, mistress, I don't mean to be a gossip, but Dr. Monroe goes to a gentleman's club every night and doesn't come home until all hours. The man told us that he might be at a place called the Dargan Club. I was hoping, Mr. Gavin, that you might go to see if he is still there.'

Hugh was shocked. Did Miss Harton know the type of man she was marrying?

'Of course, Grace. What is his friend's name so that I may tell him?'

'Theodore Palmer,' Grace said and gulped on her drink. 'I don't think he is long for this world.'

'I will do my best to find the doctor.' Hugh grabbed his cloak and hat and left.

It took him fifteen minutes to run to the Dargan Club. He banged on the door for entry. After he banged and shouted repeatedly, a jaded young footman finally opened the door, looking the worst for wear with his wig askew and rouge staining his lips.

'What do you want, man?' the young fellow asked.

'Dr. Monroe, is he in there?'

'He is not to be disturbed. It's a very important game.'

'His friend is dying and needs his help.' Hugh pushed his way past the servant and strode along a hall. Hearing the sound of voices and laughter, he threw open a door to reveal a group of richly dressed men, with women on their laps, playing cards and drinking around a table by the fire.

He recognised the Duke of Alden among them, having seen him on a previous occasion.

He walked up to the table and doffed his hat.

'Who are you, sir?' the Duke asked and kissed the pretty young thing on his knee.

The others laughed and continued their game.

'I am sorry to disturb you, sir. A man is dying and I have been asked to fetch Dr. Monroe.'

'Ah, Dr. Monroe, you have been found out and must do your duty,' the Duke said to one of the card-players.

Hugh looked across the table and recognised the man who had passed him by several times near Coles Alley. He had no woman about him. For that Hugh was grateful.

'Your friend Theodore Palmer is at your lodgings, sir. He needs your help.'

Monroe was annoyed to have to leave when such a pot was at stake. He had done well overnight and wanted to fleece these gentlemen for more. He had finally been asked to play at the same table as the Duke and was establishing a camaraderie that would prove useful. However, he would have to leave. There would be another opportunity tomorrow night.

He rose to his feet. 'Gentlemen, you must excuse me,' he said, looking suitably solemn, and followed Hugh out of the room.

'Please hurry,' Hugh said and strode on ahead.

The young footman was asleep on a stool by the main door. Hugh let himself and Monroe out.

'And Palmer is at the inn, you say?' Monroe asked.

'Grace said he asked for you specifically.'

'And who are you, sir?'

'My name is Hugh Gavin. Grace works for my sister, Miss Mary Gavin, the dressmaker in Coles Alley.'

'I see.'

Hugh stopped a public cab, and they soon reached the inn.

Olive led them into the kitchen where Palmer lay on the floor with a pillow beneath his head, coughing blood and choking as he tried to speak.

Palmer's eyes darted fearfully between Mrs. Brass and Hugh, and he gasped when he saw Monroe beside him.

'It's all right, Palmer, I'm here now. Mrs. Brass, move that chair to the fire. You, sir,' he said to Hugh, 'help me put him up on it. The cold floor does him no good.'

'Dr. Monroe,' said Mrs. Brass, 'I'm not having a man die in my kitchen. I've got the dinners to start. You'll need to take him out of here quick.'

'Of course, Mrs. Brass. Let me examine him first. It will only take a minute. Then we can take him home.'

'I'll get a cab,' Hugh said and left, not waiting for an answer.

'Why is he being so helpful?' Monroe asked his landlady.

'He's a good man. There's not many of them around here these days.' She went out to get a mop and a bucket to clean the blood off her kitchen floor.

'Monroe, I will forgive your debts if you can save me,' Palmer pleaded.

'Try not to worry, man. You'll live yet. How long has this been happening?' He had noticed small syphilitic sores around his friend's nose and ears in the last few weeks. If an internal one had perforated, there was nothing he could do. Palmer would be dead within the hour if the bleeding did not stop. He took a blanket from the back of a kitchen chair and put it around Palmer's shoulders. All he could do was wait.

Hugh was back within five minutes. Palmer had passed out. Together they took the dying man out into the cab and got him back to his more illustrious lodgings across the river.

An old woman led them up to the room and hovered at the doorway.

'Is there anything else I can do, doctor?' Hugh asked, when they had settled Palmer into bed.

'No, you can go, man. I'm much obliged for the help.'

'If you're sure?'

'I'm sure.'

Hugh reluctantly left the room.

Palmer's bleeding had not stopped and his skin was very white. There was nothing to be done. He had lost too much blood. Monroe would stay and watch Palmer die. It was the least that he could do to clear his debt.

Palmer's eyes opened and he stared at Monroe.

'I did not write to your wife – you've had my loyalty,' he said, choking on his own blood.

'Thank you, Theodore,' Monroe said before Palmer passed out again.

Monroe decided he would send word to the Hartons that he would call later than expected. That way he could keep his options open. He checked his bag to make sure he still had the documents that Dr. Harton had signed for him.

There was a light tap on the door and Palmer's landlady came in.

'I have something for you to eat downstairs, doctor, if you so wish,' the old woman said. She gazed on Palmer who was bleeding all over her best linen.

'Thank you,' Monroe said and followed her out onto the landing.

'Does he have long?' she asked.

'Let's hope not, for his own sake,' he replied.

The old woman walked down the stairs in front of him, wondering if it was too soon to ask the gentleman if by chance he needed to rent a room.

Grace helped her employer fold the emerald dress carefully for transport. When it was ready they still had some time to wait.

'Have you had anything to eat since morning, Grace?' Mary herself had had a bite and sup a while earlier.

'No, Miss Gavin.'

Mary cut some bread and cheese and treated Grace to a glass of milk that she had bought in the market. It was fresh and full of cream. She poured herself a mug of ale and joined Grace at the table.

But Grace couldn't eat or drink anything.

'What's up with you, girl? Haven't you ever seen a dying man before?'

'It's not that, miss. It's what the dying man said in the night.'

'And what did he say in the night?' Mary asked and took a long draught of ale. 'Let me see your hands – are they still clean? Have you packed the sewing box?'

'It's by the door and ready.'

'So what did this Mr. Palmer say then?'

'It affects Miss Harton. I don't know if I should say.'

'Spell it out, child. I'll not tell anyone.'

'Mr. Palmer said that Dr. Monroe was already married to another and wasn't to be trusted.'

'What? What did you say?' Mary asked, astonished.

'Mr. Palmer said that Dr. Monroe had married a woman in Cork and that he believed the woman was still alive.'

'Nonsense.' Mary shook her head. 'That's just the ramblings of a dying man.'

'What if it's true? Shouldn't we tell Miss Harton?'

'It couldn't be true. Dr. Monroe will have us for libel. Grace, promise me that you won't say another word about it to anyone.'

'If you think that's best, miss.'

'I'll tell Mr. Gavin about it myself. He will know what's best to do.'

Grace was relieved. Mr. Gavin would warn Miss Harton. She felt lighter now that the burden of knowledge wasn't upon her anymore. She managed to drink her milk and eat a little bread and cheese.

After Grace had finished, Mary put the crockery in the basin to wash later. She noticed a stain on her skirt. She couldn't go into a home of the quality in a dirty dress. She went upstairs to change and tried to dismiss Grace's story from her head.

She would stay out of all dealings with the Hartons, she decided, as she pulled on a new overdress. It was best her brother knew nothing. She didn't want him interfering in Miss Harton's life, getting them into trouble that they could ill afford.

CHAPTER 38

Elizabeth Goulding had missed her cycle two months in a row and knew she was with child as she had three older sisters who had discussed the condition freely with their mother in her presence. She was unsure what to do, but she was happy when she thought that her parents would have to let her marry Dr. Monroe now.

The dressmaker, Miss Gavin, would be here after noon with the dress that she would wear to the ball that night. She had been looking forward so much to it and, ever since Dr. Monroe had told her he'd been invited too, it had been even better. She turned to face the mirror and looked at her profile. There was no real change in her shape as yet and she hoped the dress would fit properly. If not, she would simply have to tighten her stays.

She put on her dressing gown and went into her mother's dressing room.

Nancy, their maid, was attending to Mrs. Goulding's hair at the dressing table.

'Elizabeth, you are up at last,' her mother said. 'I thought you would never wake. Have you washed yet? Your dress will be here soon.'

'Mama, I washed yesterday.' Elizabeth said, taking a French pastry from the dressing table. She slumped down on the bed, wondering whether she should tell her mama about her predicament.

'What ails you, child? Are you not excited at the prospect of meeting all the gentlemen at the Castle tonight?' Caroline applied white powder to her cheeks, wondering if a touch more rouge would be too much.

'Nancy, leave us please,' Elizabeth said.

Mrs. Goulding turned to give her daughter her full attention.

Nancy withdrew, closing out the door behind her but leaving it a little ajar.

Elizabeth sat on her mother's footstool. 'Mama, can you keep a secret from Papa?'

'What is it, dear?' Caroline was a little worried at the seriousness of her very frivolous daughter's tone.

'You must promise first, Mama.'

'Of course, Elizabeth. Just tell me what it is.'

'There is a very good reason why I am not that excited at the thought of meeting new gentlemen. I have already met a young man, whom I should like to marry, and whom I am sure would like to marry me.' She watched as her mother's face puffed up like a fish.

'Who is this man?' Caroline asked, hoping it was just another silly notion her daughter had dreamt up.

'It is Dr. Monroe, your physician, Mama.'

Caroline couldn't speak. Monroe was a common toad, angling his way into nooks and crannies where he didn't belong.

'Forget him, Elizabeth. Dr. Monroe is engaged to a physician's daughter and has no money. You must really look above your station for a partner in life. Otherwise you will never be happy.'

'But, Mama, he loves me. He will cast off Miss Harton when he wins Papa's approval, and besides ...' Elizabeth stopped, astonished when her mother jumped to her feet and stood over her with a hairbrush raised above her head.

'What are you talking about?' Caroline said, so full of temper that she hit her daughter smack on the top of her head with the wooden brush. 'You are never to speak of this again, do you hear me? And as for Dr. Monroe, I will have your father banish him from this household. I knew there was something fishy about him. A man that good-looking cannot be pure of heart.'

'Mama, you do not understand,' Elizabeth said, shocked at her mother's reaction.

'*Nancy!*' Caroline shouted.

Nancy, who had been standing outside taking everything in, waited a few seconds before re-entering.

'Nancy, tell Mr. Goulding to attend me here *at once*. I shall send for you later when I am ready to finish dressing.'

'Yes, ma'am,' Nancy said, sorry that she would not hear the rest of the argument.

Caroline sat back down on her dressing stool. Sweat beaded on her forehead as she looked at her daughter who was crying at her feet.

'Did he make advances to you?' she asked.

'What do you mean?'

'You know very well what I mean, young lady.' She was breathless from the exertion. She looked her daughter square in the eye. 'Did he kiss you?'

Elizabeth giggled. 'He loves me, Mama and I will marry him.'

'You didn't answer me, Elizabeth.'

'Yes, he kissed me, Mama.'

'And then he has asked you to marry him?'

'He hasn't yet. But I am sure he will once he knows.'

Caroline grew more nervous. 'Once he knows? Once he knows what?'

'That is what I wanted to tell you, Mama. But you must first promise not to tell Papa.'

'I will promise no such thing.'

'You will have to like him, Mama, for I am with child and have to marry him, no matter what you say.' Elizabeth rubbed her head where it was sore. 'Now go ahead and tell Papa. I don't care anymore.'

The dressing-room door opened.

'Tell me what?' Gilbert Goulding asked.

Caroline felt ill. She wondered how this could have happened right under her nose. She had successfully married off three older daughters, and to fail with the last one was too much to bear. She was determined not to let her youngest daughter be the prey of such a conniving man. She would find a woman to get her daughter right if that was what she had to do.

'It's all your fault,' she said to her husband. 'If you hadn't invited him it might never have happened.'

'Invited whom where? What has happened?' Mr. Goulding didn't know what was going on. The last time his wife had been this animated was when he had agreed to take her to London.

'*Dr. Monroe! That scoundrel has given your daughter a full belly!*' Caroline shouted and threw the hairbrush at her husband, hitting him full in the face.

He didn't feel a thing. His world stopped and he had to sit down on the chaise longue.

'What did you say?' He looked at his wife and daughter, both of whom were crying.

'Mr. Goulding, your daughter is with child, and it is your friend Dr. Monroe who has fathered it.'

Gilbert surprised himself when he started to cry too.

'Papa, it is not a bad thing. Dr. Monroe will marry me, I am sure of it. I am sure he loves me.' Elizabeth turned to her mother. 'Mama, it doesn't matter that he is poor. You and Papa can help us. I am sure he will become a great physician one day.'

Caroline grew quiet. 'Elizabeth, there is one thing I know – I will not leave you to be devoured by that wolf for our money. That, I can assure you, is all he is after.'

'Mama, he will be at the ball this evening. You can talk to him then and see that he is a good man. We *cannot* be parted.'

'You will not go to the ball, young lady. We leave for Galway at the end of the week and that will be an end to it.'

'I will run away. You cannot keep me against my will.'

'She is right, my love,' Gilbert said to his wife. 'Elizabeth, you will stay at home this evening. Your mother and I will talk to your young man tonight.'

'I want to be there. Can I not go too?' Elizabeth asked.

'If you want to marry Dr. Monroe, your mama and I must speak with him alone. You must stay here. Are we agreed?'

Elizabeth knew she should follow her father's instructions, so she crossed her fingers behind her back. 'Yes, Father,' she said and got up to kiss him on the cheek. 'I knew you would understand.' She looked coldly at her mother.

Nancy came back to announce that the dressmaker had arrived.

'Go downstairs and make sure you are happy with the dress, Elizabeth,' said her father. 'We have paid for it, so you may as well have it for another ball. Hurry up now, and don't say any more on this. Do you promise?'

'Yes, Father, I promise.' Elizabeth wondered why she had been worried about telling her father. He was the one who had agreed with her in the end.

She went downstairs and wrote a little note to Dr. Monroe and sealed it. Her mother and father must not know that she had sent it. She hurried out to Grogan and asked him to deliver it personally to her beloved Monroe.

Caroline waited until their daughter had left the room to chastise her husband.

'You cannot be serious, Mr. Goulding,' she said.

'Of course I'm not serious. We shall tell her tomorrow that the doctor denied the child was his, and she'll be back in Galway before she knows it. It's best to be gentle with her, don't you think?'

She was relieved that he had a sensible plan. 'I am sorry, Mr. Goulding – I had no idea that this was going on.'

'I know, my love. We will sort it out. We will see Monroe this evening at Boden and tell him that his plan has not worked.'

'What if he tells everyone of her condition? Who will marry her then?'

'If we give him enough money, he'll keep his mouth shut, I am sure of it.'

'What of her future?'

'Elizabeth can have her child in Rochester. My sister will take her in, and no one will be the wiser upon her return. I would prefer that she marry one of my tenants than that good-for-nothing Monroe.'

'You are too good a husband. I am blessed to have you, my dear Mr. Goulding.' She went over to sit by him. 'I am sorry to have thrown the brush at you.'

'It is I who have been blessed, my dear. I only wish for you to feel better about this, and for Elizabeth to be settled with a good man. That, I am determined to accomplish.'

He embraced his wife whom he truly loved and only wished he had paid better attention to the society he had invited into his home.

CHAPTER 39

Monroe was running late. He had slept a few hours after returning to the inn and felt quite refreshed. Now that Palmer was dead, he didn't need to be continually looking over his shoulder.

Dr. Harton hadn't recovered from his stomach ailment. The powders he had given him were doing the trick. Now he had to be sure that Harton wasn't well enough to attend the ball that evening. If the old man died, it would be the icing on the cake.

He walked up the stairs to the solicitor's office on Capel Street. He wasn't doing anything wrong, he assured himself. After all, he was about to marry Miss Harton and was entitled to have some financial reassurances. Harton had taken him into his confidence, asking him to review the new lease for the hospital. He had done so and made some valuable corrections.

He had been honoured to take on the task of delivering the papers to Alden's legal counsel, but that was not all he was delivering to Fitzgibbon.

He found the doorway that led to the solicitor's offices on the first floor of the building. The building reeked of the chop shop that occupied the rooms below. He knocked on the office door.

'Come in!' Fitzgibbon called out.

Monroe entered.

'Mr. Fitzgibbon, you are keeping well, I hope?'

'Yes, yes. You'll have to excuse me – I am extremely busy.' He stood up to greet Monroe, reminded unpleasantly of his instant dislike of the man. 'Please tell me what I can do for you?'

'I come on business for Dr. Harton,' Monroe responded, treading carefully. 'I will not keep you long.'

'On what business?' Fitzgibbon was fast losing patience. The construction noises from the street had given him a headache. He had an urgent matter to attend to and needed to complete it before the Aldens returned to England.

'Dr. Harton would like to negotiate further on the lease for the hospital in John's Lane,' Monroe said. 'I have the papers here.'

Fitzgibbon was surprised. Dr. Harton's son-in-law Henry had been appointed to deal with the Harton family's legal concerns. He had presumed he would be dealing with Henry on all Harton's legal matters. It was curious. He took the papers from Monroe.

'Dr. Harton has given me a new set of instructions to deliver to you regarding the price he is willing to pay,' Monroe said. 'He has also made some revisions to other papers of a legal nature, here included.'

'Why hasn't Dr. Harton or Henry delivered these to me personally?' Fitzgibbon asked.

'Dr. Harton has been feeling under the weather of late and asked me to drop them in to you,' Monroe said, looking Fitzgibbon directly in the eye.

Fitzgibbon held the stare. He was used to larger men trying to intimidate him and didn't appreciate it.

'I will take the instructions. You may tell Dr. Harton I shall call on him next week when I've had a chance to look at these in detail.'

'I shall see him this evening. I am to go in his place to Boden Castle Ball tonight,' Monroe said.

Fitzgibbon was surprised but he had wasted enough time on chitchat.

'That is neither here nor there, Dr. Monroe. Good day to you, sir.'

'I'll relay your message to Dr. Harton,' Monroe said, and tried to hide the smirk on his face as he left the room. 'I bid you good day.'

Fitzgibbon sat back down and put the Harton papers aside without opening them.

But, as the day wore on, the matter niggled at him. It was distinctly odd. It was late afternoon before his curiosity got the better of him. He opened Harton's instructions and was astonished by what he read.

CHAPTER 40

Brigid was having difficulty arranging Abigail's hair. The styles were getting higher and she had already failed at several attempts to pile the hair high enough over the little cushion that sat on top of Abigail's her head. It was supposed to be hidden beneath the creation, but Brigid couldn't keep it steady enough to conceal it.

'Let it be, Brigid,' Abigail said at last. 'I will wear the wig instead. It is much more the fashion these days anyway.'

'Oh miss, I am sorry,' Brigid said.

She curtsied and left the room, in truth relieved to abandon her attempts. At least she had not had to apply the pomade. The smell was foul. She could not understand how the latest high styles were considered beautiful.

Abigail looked at herself in the glass. Her natural hair was her most attractive feature. She was disappointed to have to cover it. At least the wig would match the white of her dress. She was brushing out her hair when she heard her mother call out and ran down the stairs to the first-floor landing.

'Abigail, your father grows worse. When is Dr. Monroe due?'

'Not for at least an hour,' Abigail said. 'Oh, Mama, perhaps I shouldn't go to Boden tonight? I am sure Dr. Monroe would prefer to stay here too.'

'We cannot slight Alden. He might not renew the annuity and then where would we be?'

'Alden will hardly know if we were there or not. So many will have been invited.'

'Abigail, we cannot risk insulting him. I am only sorry that your father will not get to meet the Duchess again. I'm sure she must be quite fond of him. After all, without him she and her child would most likely not be here.'

'I can't leave you on your own with Father.'

'Don't worry. Brigid will help me. And perhaps Dr. Monroe can try another remedy.'

'I will stay at home,' Abigail said.

'Nonsense. Your father will be over this in a few days and I will not have you miss Alden's invitation. It is a great honour and someone from the family has to go.'

'I hope you are right.'

'Go down and ask Brigid to bring up some ale. It might do your father some good.'

Abigail quickly went downstairs. She hoped Dr. Monroe would be able to help her father to settle before they left for the evening.

Monroe made his way from the solicitor's to the inn. All was in place. At Boden Castle he might find further favour with the elite of Dublin society and widen his sphere of influence. And who knew, he thought to himself, it might lead to connections in London society where he and Miss Harton might be able to eventually settle. But he was getting ahead of himself. It was growing late and he needed to get moving.

Reaching the inn, he went into the kitchen where pottage was bubbling on the fire. There would be food at Boden but he was hungry and needed something to sustain himself in the meantime. He burnt his hand removing the lid. It smelled good and he helped himself to a bowl of the broth, spooning sweetmeat, lamb's tongue and cabbage into his bowl. He poured a tankard of ale from a jug on the table which was warm from the heat of the fire and tasted rich with the food.

Soon this part of his life would be over. He would move into better rooms closer to the Harton residence. Eventually he and Abigail would inherit the house on Pluncot Street. When Dr. Harton died, he would let Mrs. Harton live with them for as long as it was tolerable. Abigail's mother was a sensible woman and would be a good companion for his wife while he pursued other interests. There would be children running around and he laughed when he realised how happy that would make him. To have a legitimate son of his own. He thought of Miss Sumner and wondered whether she'd had a boy. He would make enquiries in the new year.

The medicines he had been giving Dr. Harton for his indigestion were harsh on the stomach. He smiled to himself, knowing that there was no rush. He had learned patience since the business in Cork. He was beginning to realise that it was a very admirable virtue.

Mrs. Brass came into the kitchen with her eldest daughter Olive.

'How would I know how much the old fart is worth?' the mother said to the daughter.

'There's no point in me pursuing him if he isn't worth a toss, Ma,' Olive said.

'Dr. Monroe, I didn't see you there,' Mrs. Brass said and stared as she saw that he had taken some of her supper from the pot.

'Hope you don't mind,' Monroe said and smiled sweetly at the old woman. 'I've a big night tonight, Mrs. Brass. I wanted to make sure I can endure it.'

'She doesn't mind a bit,' Olive said and sat down beside him.

He'd been generous with them of late and she wanted to milk him for all the loose change she could get.

Mrs. Brass, on the other hand, suspected Monroe was a good-for-nothing. She had never known a respectable doctor to come home late with rouge on his lips and grass on his breeches. But his money was good, and she couldn't ask for better than that.

'Should we be expecting you home tonight? I've a mind to lock up at eleven of the clock.'

'Don't worry, Mrs. Brass – I shall be out until dawn – of that I have no doubt. I might not even come back.' Monroe laughed and drained the last drop of ale from the tankard. He got up from the table and belched.

'Dr. Monroe, your room is safe here for you as long as you need it. I can't say it any straighter than that,' Mrs. Brass said.

'You always were a very straight woman,' Monroe said, eyeing her figure, 'although I'm sure you have your softer edges.'

The innkeeper was astounded. She was well past the age of luring anyone into her bed. Did the young doctor think her stupid? She wasn't about to let any man get the better of her. To think the young scoundrel was trying to pay her a compliment. She almost laughed in his face but managed to smile serenely and said nothing.

'Well, I must go and dress. My fiancée will be anxious,' he said.

He climbed the back-staircase to his attic room and began to prepare for the ball and all that it offered. He stripped himself down and admired his physique. He had walked everywhere to save money and it had done his figure good. He had never been a broad man – his slender frame gave him an air of elegance that many a wealthier gentleman coveted. Lifting his arms, he found he smelled a little pungent. He washed himself for the second time that week with water from the jug by his bed and put on his best linen undershirt before donning his newest suit. All was plain until he remembered the waistcoat that Mrs. Harton had embroidered for him. He had not taken it out of its wrapping yet and hoped it would pass. He couldn't believe his eyes. The garment was exquisite, with vines of yellow thread winding around the fresh flowers in bright colours as if they had been freshly plucked from a meadow. The silk was an enchanting shade of cream. He put it on under his coat and admired his reflection in the looking glass. He no longer looked plain. He was the gentlemen he always should have been.

He put on his wig and admired himself again before going downstairs.

He was about to exit the inn when he heard Olive call him. He turned back to see her bustling up to him.

'Yes, Olive, what is it?' he asked, irritated at the delay.

'I'm so sorry, Dr. Monroe. I almost forgot. A message came for you this afternoon.' She took a piece of paper out from the top of her dress. 'I've been keeping it safe for you here.' She winked and moved closer to him.

'Thank you, Olive, but I must dash.' He put the paper in his pocket and left. He didn't want to know what the message said. No doubt it was from a patient demanding a visit – the last thing he needed now.

He had reached the Watch Tower before his curiosity overcame him and he pulled the message out to read it.

If anyone on the street had seen him reading they would have seen a happy man transformed in an instant to a stricken one. His discomfort, however, was fleeting. It seemed that Miss Elizabeth Goulding had told her parents that she was with child and she demanded that he call off his engagement with Miss Harton immediately. It was a pity that she hadn't told him she was with child. He could have done something about that. Mr. Goulding had forbidden his daughter from attending the ball. The note declared that she would come alone without her parents' knowledge and that they should run away together.

He walked on in the direction of the Harton house and thought it would be folly to take Miss Harton to Boden now. Elizabeth needed to be contained. She was too much of a wild card and he could not jeopardise his position with the Hartons. He intended to marry Abigail, to have the illusion of a respectable life and all that could command. The thought of kowtowing to the Gouldings did not appeal. They would never accept him. He would be forever required to lick at their boots for bringing their daughter so low. They might even disown her. It was too late to redeem himself there and he consoled himself that he would by far prefer the elegant Miss Abigail Harton to Elizabeth Goulding. He must contrive to keep Miss Harton at home this evening. It was such a disappointment. He had been longing to get her on his own. It was such a long drive out to the Castle and back. Who knew where the night might have ended?

By the time Monroe arrived at the Harton house, he had devised a way to leave his fiancée behind. It had to be done delicately but he was confident it would work.

However, he was unaware of the note that Mr. Fitzgibbon had sent to Dr. Harton's son-in-law Henry that afternoon, where he expressed serious concern with the contents of Dr. Harton's new instructions, received from Dr. Monroe earlier that afternoon.

CHAPTER 41

When Mary Gavin had finished dressing the three girls in Drogheda Street, she gathered her tools and told Grace to do the same. The night of the Boden Ball had arrived and all of her commissions had been delivered. She would give the girl tomorrow off and intended to stay at home with a bottle of claret herself.

On the street, she and her apprentice climbed into a waiting cab. The long December evenings had set in and it was very cold. She noticed that Grace's dress was too thin for the winter weather. She would make her a warmer one before she left for Belfast to visit her Aunt Laetitia.

The streets were full of people. As the cab passed the corner of Arran Street, a shoe boy touted for business, and two young boys ran from a baker's shop as an older gentleman tried to catch them. The river smelled to high heaven and there were beggars everywhere. She closed the cab window and saw that Grace was already asleep. The girl had a second job at her mother's inn, fetching and carrying for the clientele. It was no wonder that she was exhausted. Grace had a good eye and steady hands and could sew a seam as straight as any tailor in the city but it was a shame that Miss Harton was gone. She was as excellent an embroiderer as Mary had ever come across in her career and she would be hard pressed to replace her.

She looked out as the cab made its way through the streets of the city. Her life was happy here. She had done well for herself. She didn't own the house or the workshop yet, but she had a long-term lease that would secure the premises for her lifetime.

She took the letters she had received from her Uncle Francis from her pocket and read them again. She had convinced her brother to accompany her to Belfast before the month was out. It would be good to celebrate the days of Christmas in the city where they had been born, with the only living relatives they had left in the world.

As she drew near home, Mary saw a scuffle in the alley. She instructed the cab driver to stop in the laneway at the side of the house and ushered Grace into the yard to avoid the drunks, shutting the yard gate behind them.

Hugh opened the kitchen door.

'What's happening up the alley?' Mary asked, following Hugh inside.

'Just the usual blackguards being tossed out of the inn, I expect.'

'Grace, would you like to have something to eat before you go home?' Mary asked.

'Mrs. Brass wants Grace back before six,' her brother said.

'It's not yet five o'clock.'

'She needs Grace's help with the cooking,' Hugh said. 'Come, Grace, and I'll walk you back.'

'That's all right, Mr. Gavin. I can go myself.'

'Mr. Gavin will walk you home,' said Mary. 'God knows what's going out there.'

When Hugh and Grace had left, Miss Gavin helped herself to a glass of claret.

Hugh left with Grace by the front door and walked up Coles Alley.

'Do you and Miss Gavin still plan to visit your aunt and uncle for Christmas?' Grace asked.

'Yes – my sister is most anxious to see our aunt who is poorly.'

'You will come back, won't you?' Grace was worried that she would have to work for her mother again.

Hugh could see the concern on her face. 'Of course we will. My sister likes Dublin better, for all of its noise.' He smiled kindly at the girl.

'And are you going to America?'

'Yes, Grace, but my sister will stay here. Your position with her is safe.'

'And what of Miss Harton?'

'She is to be married. There's no need for you to worry about her.'

'Is she still to marry *him*?'

'Him? Dr. Monroe?' he asked, puzzled. 'Of course, yes, she is.'

'Is it wise though after what Mr. Palmer said about him?'

'What Mr. Palmer said?'

'Don't you think it matters?' she asked.

'What are you talking about, Grace?'

'Don't you know?' Grace was amazed. 'Miss Gavin said she would tell you.'

'Tell me *what*?' he asked and stopped, turning to face her.

'Tell you about what Mr. Palmer said Dr. Monroe did in Cork.'

'What he did in Cork? Grace, for God's sake, tell me the whole story. My sister has told me none of this.'

'Oh, Mr. Gavin, she told me she would – otherwise I'd have told you myself. Mr. Palmer said that Dr. Monroe was already married to a woman in Cork, and that he spent her money and her father's money. And then he said that Dr. Monroe had denied the marriage had ever taken place, and the young woman was left with child, destitute and disgraced.'

Hugh couldn't believe what he was hearing.

'Are you sure, Grace? Did you hear this yourself?'

'I did, sir, with my own ears. And Mr. Palmer said that Dr. Monroe owed him a great deal of money and that the doctor would be sure to come to his aid that night.'

'And is Monroe's first wife still alive?'

'Mr. Palmer spoke as if she was. Mr. Gavin, I am worried about Miss Harton. I told your sister that she should warn her. But maybe she has already?'

'I don't believe she has,' said Hugh, his face darkening.

'Oh, Mr. Gavin, if you do not tell her I fear that she may never know. What if she is to suffer the same fate? No one deserves that.'

'Did Palmer mention Monroe's wife's name?'

'Catherine Sumner. I memorised it so that I could tell Miss Gavin. It's such a pretty name, don't you think?'

'Come,' he said and walked ahead of her towards the inn.

Grace had to run to keep up with him.

'Will you tell her? Miss Harton, I mean?'

'Yes, I will, Grace. Thank you for confiding in me. Go on now.'

He watched until the girl was safely inside her home.

Hugh turned and wondered why his sister had concealed this from him. Miss Harton might be a cut above them, but that didn't signify that they should leave a lamb to the slaughter if Palmer had been telling the truth. He passed his house and kept walking. His sister would try to convince him to mind his own business and he didn't want to hear that. There was no time to waste. With Palmer dead he had no way to verify whether it was a lie or not. He had to tell Miss Harton.

'Yes, miss.' Nancy handed the stomacher to the silliest young lady she had ever known.

Elizabeth held it to her chest and Nancy fixed it in place at the back with the linen ties that had been sewn on each side of the garment.

Nancy needed Elizabeth's help lifting the main part of the dress, the mantua, over her head as it was so large.

When it was on, the maid stood back to view the final effect. It was the first time she had seen the completed dress on her young mistress, as she had not been present for the final fitting earlier that day. She thought that Elizabeth did indeed look pretty and her hair complemented the colour of the dress. It was a pity that it had fallen flat and would have to be powdered white.

'My hair is not high enough anymore. You will have to fix it,' Elizabeth said.

Nancy was dismayed. 'I would have to do it all over again and don't you have to hurry, miss? It's a long way to the castle.'

'You are useless at dressing hair anyway.' Elizabeth got up from the dressing-table stool and promptly sat back down again under the weight of her dress. 'Fetch my newest wig – it will have to do. And tell Grogan to get a cab.'

Nancy, looking forward to a night without having to serve a Goulding woman, happily ran down the stairs to find Grogan, who was eating a boiled-beef pie in the kitchen.

'Grogan, Miss Elizabeth is going to the castle after all. You are to fetch her a cab immediately.'

'What? Mr. and Mrs. Goulding have already left. She's not going on her own, is she?'

'You had better go with her then,' Nancy said and ran back up the stairs to her mistress's dressing room. She took the largest wig she could find to bring to the young lady in her boudoir.

'I had thought you had gone to make the wig yourself,' Elizabeth said when she returned.

Nancy ignored the girl. It was better to say nothing, as anything she did say would be ignored or twisted against her. She was tired of being a maid and had been thinking of joining the theatre instead. Actresses were paid better than maids and could mix in the best circles. Maybe she would find herself a husband among them. She decided there and then that she would not return to Galway with the Goulding family. Instead, she would take the chance tomorrow to meet with her sister and convince her to go to Smock Alley to see if they could be taken on at the theatre there. Lord knows, she had plenty of practice acting at the Goulding residence.

'Nancy, you are pulling my hair. Put the wig on properly.'

'I'm sorry, miss – it is a little tricky.' In the glass, Nancy could see that the powdered white wig made Elizabeth look washed out. Nancy felt a little bad for not at least attempting to dress Elizabeth's own hair properly, though Elizabeth was right – she had made a mess of it. Nancy helped the girl put on her shoes which were covered in the emerald damask and matched the dress.

Elizabeth attempted to flounce out of the room but had to shuffle out sideways as the dress was so wide, all the while trying not to fall over its hem.

Nancy followed with Elizabeth's black silk cloak.

Elizabeth started to descend the stairs. She had to make her way down them sideways, biting her lip as she held onto the bannisters.

Nancy had intended to help her but got into a fit of giggling and had to go back into the dressing room to contain herself.

'Miss Goulding, the cab waits for you outside,' Grogan said. He had put his cloak and gloves on and was holding the hall door open. 'I shall come with you.'

'You will do no such thing. I am more than capable of going on my own.'

'It is not proper, miss,' he said, not knowing quite what to do. He did not want to get into trouble with Mr. Goulding for letting a girl of sixteen go out on her own.

'My parents will be at the castle when I arrive. They expect me. You do not need to worry.'

Nancy came down to help Elizabeth put on her pattens to protect her silk shoes from the mud on the streets.

'Now, both of you must help me lift my skirts off the ground.

One of you on each side.'

Nancy and Grogan complied.

Grogan knew he should go with her, but what could he do? She was headstrong and accustomed to having her own way. Besides, his arms ached. He had bad rheumatism and the cold winter's night air would not help the pain. And so he decided to err on the side of his own comfort and let his master's youngest daughter go to the castle on her own.

With their young mistress safely inside the cab, the two servants retreated to the house.

Nancy happily disappeared upstairs, and Grogan went to warm his hands by the kitchen fire, thereafter finishing his beef supper without thinking of the girl again.

It was a long drive to the castle. Half an hour into the journey, Elizabeth started to wonder if she had been right to come alone. After all, what did it matter if Dr. Monroe did not see her in the dress? He had seen a lot more of her than most. She held her stomach tenderly. She couldn't wait to marry him. When he knew about the baby, he was bound to honour her with a proposal. But what if he disapproved of her travelling on her own to the ball? She dismissed the thought. Why shouldn't she have as much fun as him or any man? Alden's parties were infamous and she wanted to see one at first hand. She would be a woman of the world, and not the naïve girl everyone thought her to be. Her independence would convince her parents that she could make decisions for herself.

Another half hour outside the city brought total darkness. They were in the middle of the countryside and she grew more apprehensive. The castle had to be close by. She crossed her legs and wished that she had not had that last glass of wine as she was not sure her bladder would hold out for much longer on the bumpy road.

When at last they arrived at the castle, she paid the driver and went inside. She handed her cloak to a footman and continued to the entrance hall on the first floor. Everyone stared at her and she smiled serenely back at the crowd, sensing that they admired her beauty and the sophistication of her dress and manner. She followed other guests to the main staircase and emerged at the second-floor anteroom which led to the main ballroom. She could not see Monroe anywhere, so she had made her way to the other end of the expansive room.

She had reached the end when she saw her parents emerging from a room on the other side. She turned around and walked up a narrow staircase to the next landing. She was sure they hadn't seen her. After several tries at locked doors, she found a small bedroom and hid in it. Thankfully there was an empty chamber pot under the bed and she relieved herself with difficulty, hampered by the dress. Peering out of the third-floor window, she had a good view of the carriages coming and going and tried to think of a way to alert Dr. Monroe whom she hoped had already arrived.

CHAPTER 42

The cab Monroe had hired for the evening stopped outside the Harton house. He left the driver to wait and wondered if his plan would work.

He walked up the granite steps to the hall door and knocked. Waiting, he turned and looked up the street and thought what a pleasant place it was.

The door opened.

'They're all upstairs, Dr. Monroe,' Brigid said.

'Bring some wine up directly,' he told her.

'Yes, sir.'

Monroe held his case tight to his chest as he ascended the stairs.

Margaret was relieved to see the young doctor. Her husband had been ill all day.

'Doctor Monroe, I fear your medicine is not helping my husband anymore.'

'Try not to worry, Mrs. Harton. I will do my best to set him right for the evening.' He went to his patient's bedside.

'I cannot seem to keep anything down,' Dr. Harton said.

His complexion was pale and waxy, and he was bathed in cold sweat. Monroe reckoned that the powders he'd given him were working their way through his body. He would give the old man another dose to ensure he remained unwell for the evening.

It was all working out for the best. With Dr. Harton so ill, he would be able to convince Abigail to stay at home with her parents.

'Do you have any pain?' Monroe asked.

'My stomach still ails me,' Dr. Harton said. 'And my head is so clouded I cannot think straight.'

Monroe smiled.

'I can give you a little of the medicine now. There is nothing more you can do but rest after that. Mrs. Harton, please give your husband another dose of this medicine should he have another attack later.'

'Thank you, Dr. Monroe,' Margaret said. 'I shall make sure that he takes it.'

'I wonder if it is best –' Monroe stopped speaking as Abigail came in. She was looking lovely in a white dress with scarlet rosebuds on it, her hair dressed in the most becoming fashion. The white dress suited her skin well. It was such a shame that he would not be taking her anywhere this evening in it.

'Dr. Monroe, it is good to see you,' she said.

'I came to check on your father before we left.'

'Here is Brigid with the wine,' said Margaret.

Brigid set the tray down on the dressing table and withdrew.

'Let me mix this into wine to help you sleep a little,' Monroe said, taking a small amount of powder wrapped in paper from his bag. He had mixed it with spearmint and ginger.

'I appreciate your attention, though I feel your medicine is making no difference to my ailing belly,' Dr. Harton said.

'Nonsense, man, you'll be up and about before you know it.' Monroe carefully stirred the powder into the liquid. 'Now sit up and see if you can take a few mouthfuls.'

'Thank you, Monroe.'

With Monroe's help, he sat up against the pillows and took a few sips of the liquid, grimacing at the taste.

'If you two ladies would kindly leave us alone,' Monroe said, 'I will examine Dr. Harton further before we leave.'

'Very well, doctor,' Margaret said.

She and Abigail withdrew.

'I will feel better knowing that you have this in you before we go,' Monroe said, holding the cup as Dr. Harton sipped.

'I hope I can keep it down,' Dr. Harton said, coughing as the fluid went against his throat.

'Your colour has come back a little already, sir,' Monroe lied.

Dr. Harton downed several more mouthfuls.

'Hopefully, it will do the trick,' said Monroe, 'and Miss Harton and I can safely go to the Boden Ball knowing that you are on the mend.'

'It is kind of you to take my place this evening, sir. I'm sure Abigail will enjoy the spectacle very well. Be sure to look after her, won't you? For you know how some of those gentlemen are.'

'I know it well.' He held the cup to Dr. Harton's mouth again. 'Drink, doctor – please – you need to get it down.'

Dr. Harton managed a few more swallows and then, with effort, drained the cup.

'Good. Now rest,' Monroe said.

Dr. Harton lay back against the pillows, exhausted. 'I am all right now, Monroe,' he said after a minute. 'You can go and join the ladies. And I hope you and Abigail have an enjoyable night.'

'I will call up again before we go.'

Monroe left the old man looking even more waxy, his eyes closed.

The women rose from their seats when he entered the drawing room below.

'How is he?' Abigail asked, approaching him.

'Please sit, ladies.' Monroe led her back and they sat with her mother. 'He looks a little better, though I fear the sickness hasn't left him yet.'

'Did he drink your mixture?' Margaret asked.

'Yes, he did. It is better he has something to expunge from his system rather than retching on an empty stomach. I fear that he may have another attack tonight. I would prefer to stay with him and I wonder, Miss Harton, if you would mind if we didn't go to Boden after all?'

'I would much prefer not to go,' Abigail said, relieved at his suggestion.

'But what of Alden's invitation?' Margaret asked.

'Of course, Mrs. Harton, there is that to consider too. Perhaps we should wait and decide in an hour. If he has settled by then, Miss Harton and I will go. If not ...'

'Yes, that is best,' Margaret said. 'I will go sit with him now. I will ask Brigid to bring you some wine.'

'Have you seen a case like this before?' Abigail asked Monroe after her mother had left the room.

'Many times,' he answered, admiring the aspect of the room, which was charming in candlelight.

'And the outcome?'

He forced himself to concentrate. He must do this properly.

'My dear, in some cases the outcome has been very good indeed. In only one case such as this have I seen a deterioration.' He moved his chair closer to Abigail, taking her hands in his own. 'You should try not to worry. If the necessary care and attention are given, the outcome should be positive.'

Abigail was somewhat reassured.

Then she heard her mother call her from upstairs. She hurried out of the room, Monroe following her.

Her mother was on the landing, looking distressed.

'He has got sick all over his nightshirt, Abigail. We will have to change it. Ask Brigid to bring up a fresh one.'

'Let us see how he is first,' she said.

They hurried upstairs and entered the bedroom.

Dr. Harton looked like a ghost against the white pillows, his eyes closed, his nightshirt stained with some of the medicine.

Monroe hurried to his side and felt his brow.

Abigail went to the other side of the bed. 'Father,' she whispered.

He didn't respond so she shook him gently. When he opened his eyes, the look in them frightened her. Then he jolted upright and threw up again over her dress.

'Abigail, go and mix half water with half wine,' Monroe said. 'If you have lavender or camomile, please add it. Add some sugar too – it will be easier to drink that way.' His powders had worked again. The old man looked so ill he was sure that Abigail would want to stay behind. If he could get some fluids into him, he would be safe enough for the night.

Abigail ran down to the kitchen.

'My father had been sick. We will need new bedsheets and a new nightshirt,' she told Brigid.

'Yes, miss.'

Abigail added water and wine to a cup. Brigid kept sprigs of lavender in the kitchen and she added some of their flowers to the liquid. She shaved some sugar from the cone and added it too.

'Bring your dress down and I will soak it for you before it dries out and stains,' Brigid said.

Abigail looked down. Her dress was ruined.

She and Brigid climbed the stairs. On the landing she gave the cup to Brigid to take to Monroe and went on up to her own bedroom. There she took off her dress. Her bluebird poplin day dress was still on her bed. She put it on and took the ruined dress down to the kitchen. Then she hurried back up to her parents' bedroom.

Her father was wearing a fresh nightshirt and Brigid was spreading a new cover on the bed.

Dr. Monroe was trying to get her father to sip from the cup but the pale liquid was trickling from his mouth. He wiped it away before it stained her father's nightshirt.

'I think the worst of it has come up,' he said. He put the cup of water and wine on the dressing table beside him.

Abigail placed her hand on Monroe's arm.

'You were right – we had best not go this evening,' she said.

'Indeed, my dear, it would be best. We shall stay … and just hope that Alden will not be unduly insulted.'

There was a pause then Margaret tentatively asked, 'Do you think it would be safe if you went on our behalf, Dr. Monroe? For if you were there to explain what has happened, the Duke would know the truth first hand.'

'That might be wise,' he answered, relieved that she had taken the bait.

'But what of Father, Mama?' Abigail said. 'What if he deteriorates again?'

'The Apothecary Smyth is close by and can be called upon for advice if necessary,' Margaret said. 'Is that not so, Dr. Monroe?'

'Yes, indeed,' Monroe replied.

'Then, it is settled. Abigail, you will stay, and Dr. Monroe will go.'

Monroe nodded in as serious a fashion as he could muster.

'You have such an excellent family, Mrs. Harton. I am indeed honoured to be joining it. I shall leave now so that I may return all the earlier. I will call back in to check on your husband on my way home.'

Monroe touched Harton's forehead once more and was sure that the old man would survive the night.

'Make him drink as much as you can,' he said before leaving.

Abigail followed him onto the landing.

He kissed her on the forehead. 'I shall not be too long, my dear, though it is a long drive out.'

'Would you not stay? The Duke of Alden will hardly notice that we do not attend.'

'It could make a serious difference to our futures, and indeed the hospital annuity, if the Duke takes offence. I must go as your mother suggests, though I swear I will not stay long. I will be back later tonight. Please trust me on this.'

She nodded and he bid her goodbye.

As Abigail went back into her parents' room, Monroe walked down the stairs with a smirk on his face. He did not notice Brigid on the landing above him as he turned to go down the last stairway and out into his waiting cab.

Margaret tended to her husband for another hour. When he grew weaker, she ordered Brigid fetch the apothecary. She watched Abigail pray by her father's side and hoped to God that he would live so that their whole world would not fall apart again. It had been a mistake to ask Dr. Monroe to go.

CHAPTER 43

Hugh arrived at the Hartons' home. He knocked on the door and waited for an answer.

Abigail, assuming the apothecary had at last arrived, ran downstairs to open the door.

'Mr. Gavin,' she said, surprised.

'Miss Harton.'

'Please come in.'

He stepped into the hall.

Abigail shut the front door and looked at him expectantly. She presumed he must have brought the payment from Miss Gavin.

'I'm sorry to disturb you, Miss Harton, but I must speak with you.' He tried not to take her in, the blue dress, her auburn hair around her shoulders. He could barely look at her without feeling the pain of knowing that she could never be his.

'Have you brought the payment from your sister?' she asked.

'That is not that I have come about, Miss Harton.'

'What brings you here? You must pardon my haste but my father is gravely ill and I have to get back to him.'

'Forgive me but I urgently need to speak to you about a certain matter.'

'What could be more urgent than my father's condition, Mr. Gavin?'

'I assure you that it is important.'

'Very well, Mr. Gavin – but please be brief. We are expecting the apothecary any moment.'

'Miss Harton, I must tell you something that Grace heard at the inn about Dr. Monroe. I fear you do not know who you are engaged to.'

Abigail stared at him, astonished. 'I do not care to hear vulgar gossip, Mr. Gavin. And I am surprised you should come here with it. Please, I don't have time for this.'

She went to open the hall door, but he stood directly in her way.

'You must listen to me, Miss Harton. Please listen carefully. Dr. Monroe's friend Theodore Palmer confessed things to Grace as he lay dying.'

'Please, Mr. Gavin, just leave.'

'Mr. Palmer told Grace that Dr. Monroe is already married to another woman, a Miss Sumner, who lives in Cork.'

Abigail couldn't believe what she was hearing.

'You have no right to spread these tales. Now please leave.'

'I am not spreading gossip. It is a dying man's confession which Grace confided in me. I am here because I am concerned about you. I only urge you to take care.'

Abigail couldn't bear to listen to him anymore.

'Mr. Gavin, I am sure you think you are doing the right thing. However, I can assure you that what you have heard is untrue. Dr. Monroe is a respectable physician.'

'Grace has no reason to lie, Miss Harton. Please say that you'll at least consider this.'

'I will. Now please leave. I must go to my father.'

There was a knock on the front door and he stood aside to allow her to answer it.

Abigail was relieved to see the apothecary and Brigid on the doorstep.

'Mr. Smyth, thank God you are here,' she said.

They stepped inside and Brigid took Mr. Smyth's cloak and hat.

The apothecary nodded at Hugh.

'Good evening, sir,' he said.

'Mr. Smyth. This is Mr. Gavin, an acquaintance of my mother's,' said Abigail. 'Mr. Gavin, this is the Apothecary Smyth.'

'It is good to meet you, sir,' Hugh said.

'And you, sir.'

'Mr. Gavin,' Abigail said, 'please wait a moment while I take Mr. Smyth up to my father.'

He nodded gravely.

As Abigail and the apothecary reached the landing outside the bedroom there was a loud thud and a cry. Alarmed, she threw open the door.

Her father lay on the floor, her mother kneeling by his side.

'Father!'

'What happened, Mrs. Harton?' Mr. Smyth asked.

'He fell. He said he was feeling better and wanted to sit by the window, but when he tried to stand out he fell.'

Mr. Smyth went out to the landing and called down the stairs. '*Mr. Gavin! Please come up, sir! Your assistance is needed!*'

Hugh ran up the stairs.

'Please help me with him, sir,' Mr. Smyth said to him.

Together, they carried Dr. Harton back to his bed. Mr. Smyth checked him for injuries and found none, so they settled him beneath the covers.

Margaret knelt by her husband's bedside and held his hand. 'Dr. Monroe's powders seemed to help at first, Mr. Smyth, but since he took some earlier he has been worse than ever.'

'He has taken some water and wine since, with a little lavender and sugar, on Dr. Monroe's instructions,' Abigail said.

'I'm afraid Dr. Monroe must be called,' Mr. Smyth said, feeling Dr. Harton's brow. 'His fever is high and his pulse is racing. I need to know what medicine he has taken before I can give him another remedy.' He looked at Abigail. 'Your maidservant told me Dr. Monroe has gone out to Boden?'

'Yes, sir, he has,' said Abigail. 'We were all invited to the ball tonight by the Duke of Alden so Dr. Monroe went to represent us and offer our apologies.'

'Dr. Monroe must be contacted,' Mr. Smyth said. 'I must know how he made up those powders. To give Dr. Harton anything else now might do more harm than good. Could you send a manservant to fetch Dr. Monroe back? It is better I consult with him in person.'

'There is no manservant to go,' Margaret said.

'I will go to Boden,' Abigail said. 'I will try to get a public cab to take me there.'

'You will not go, Abigail,' her mother said. 'Brigid will call Henry and he can fetch Dr. Monroe. It is too dangerous for you to go there alone.'

'I will fetch Dr. Monroe,' Hugh said. 'There is no time to waste going to contact your son-in-law.'

'I'm sure, Mr. Gavin, you have your own business to take care of,' Margaret said, 'and it is better a member of the family goes.'

'Mama, Mr. Gavin is right. Sarah and Henry live in the other direction. It will take too long to get there and back. Henry may not even be at home. I will go with Mr. Gavin instead.' Abigail left the room before her mother could object, beckoning to Hugh to follow her.

Downstairs, she put on her pattens and cloak, pulling the hood up over her head.

'I will get a cab,' Hugh said and opened the door.

'Please hurry.' Abigail followed him outside.

It had started to snow though the flakes weren't sticking on the ground. Hugh had run ahead of her down Pluncot Street. She hurried after him but the iron rings of her pattens were heavy and slowed her down.

On Francis Street, Hugh secured a cab and helped her into it, before directing the driver to Boden Castle.

The driver was surprised by the destination and asked for payment upfront, considering the distance and the weather. But his cab wheels were robust and he was happy to make a week's pay despite the falling snow. It would be an adventure after all.

Inside the cab, Hugh sat close to Abigail. She pulled her cloak tight around her. It was freezing but she tried to move away from him in the small cab. She stared out of the window. The news of Dr. Monroe's marriage could not be true. It wasn't that she didn't believe Grace. She was sure that Grace had overheard something of the sort from Mr. Palmer, but Dr. Monroe had hinted to her that his friend was a scoundrel and not to be trusted. She felt angry that Mr. Gavin should confront her about something so personal. But she should not blame him. Clearly he was doing what he considered his duty in the circumstances.

'I am sure this business with Palmer is a misunderstanding,' she said at last.

'You must tell your mother tomorrow. She will want to investigate, even if you choose to ignore it.'

Hugh was upset. He had never done anything to make her question his honesty. He was trying his best to help her and despaired to think that she thought so little of him that she would wantonly ignore his advice.

'My father may not be with us tomorrow. I will not trouble my mother with this matter until he is better. Besides, it is Mr. Palmer who was not to be trusted, not Dr. Monroe.'

'Grace was with him as he lay dying. Why would he lie?'

'Grace must have misheard him.'

Abigail did not know what to think. Mr. Palmer had dined with them occasionally over the last several months. She had never much liked his manner. But why had Dr. Monroe not told her that his friend was sick? How could he not?

'He has not told you of his friend's death, has he?'

'My father has been ill, and Dr. Monroe most likely did not think to ...' Abigail stopped herself. It made no sense that her fiancé had not told her of Palmer's death. 'It's all been so sudden.'

The roads were not even as they left the city. The cab jolted and they had to hold on to the side panels to stay upright.

'Grace tells me Dr. Monroe sleeps late, rising most days after noon,' Hugh ventured to say.

'He is a doctor. You cannot judge him by the hours he keeps.'

'He was in the Dargan Club with Alden's men the night I fetched him to help Mr. Palmer.'

'I am sure he was invited there legitimately.'

'Miss Harton, I beg you to examine your conscience. If not for yourself, then for your family's sake. Do not make a hasty decision on this. It is for your sake that I tell you. If the marriage in Cork exists, you will be ruined.'

He stopped and said no more. He had said enough. If her father survived this illness, he would appeal to him directly to take care for his daughter's sake.

Abigail looked out of the cab window. They were well into the countryside.

It couldn't be true. How could Dr. Monroe deceive a woman in marriage? But what had Mr. Palmer to gain by telling this fiction? She stared out at the woods around them, seeing nothing. Then she remembered how Elizabeth Goulding had spoken of a Dr. Monroe at the Gavins' house when she had visited there. Dr. Monroe had told Abigail that Miss Goulding had been referring to his cousin Nicholas Monroe, visiting from England. But when she had asked after his cousin last week, he seemed to have forgotten about the man's presence in Dublin. She suddenly felt nauseous.

Abigail became aware of the man sitting next to her. She knew from her own first-hand experience that Mr. Gavin was honest and true. He worked hard and respected his sister. He had saved young Michael and taken him into his home, offering the boy a future. He had taken care of her when she had been ill. He was with her now. Who should she trust? She could not think about this. She first had to find out what exactly Dr. Monroe had given her father. She had to bring Dr. Monroe home with her.

She considered the fact that her father had grown worse after Dr. Monroe had attended him. She dismissed the thought. He was young and inexperienced, that was all. He was a good man, she was sure of it. It had to be a misunderstanding.

Hugh could see that Miss Harton was considering his words. He hoped he had not hurt her too much. He wanted to tell her that everything would be all right, that he would take care of her, that she needn't worry about anything ever again. But he couldn't. She was engaged to another. He had to stay silent on that at least. He had to hope that she would make the right decision, that she would see what a scoundrel Monroe was, and that perhaps one day he might have a chance.

The cab slowed down as it entered the castle grounds and made its way along the gravel drive which was lit with torches to show the way. The castle's stone structure was formidable as they drew nearer.

There were many carriages and drivers waiting outside, despite the falling snow. Abigail was taken aback. How would she find Dr. Monroe with this many people about? She caught Mr. Gavin looking at her.

'You must allow me to talk to him alone,' she said. 'You cannot mention this business about Mr. Palmer. I must persuade him to return with us.'

'You think he will need to be persuaded?' Hugh asked.

'That is not what I meant,' she said. 'I do not want you to say anything to him about this Miss Sumner. I will talk to him tomorrow about that. Tonight, he needs only to help my father. Do you understand?'

'You have my word, Miss Harton.'

The cab stopped a little way down the drive. Hugh opened the door to help her down and walked with her to the castle entrance. The snow was falling thick and fast and he hoped they would find the doctor quickly. The roads would be impassable before long if it continued to fall.

They made their way to the main entrance and into the entrance hall. At the door Abigail explained to the porter that they were in urgent search of Dr. Monroe, her father's doctor, and he allowed them to enter.

They made their way to the staircase and emerged in the anteroom on the second floor, conscious of people staring at them because of their unsuitable attire as they entered the ballroom.

Eventually Hugh spotted Monroe hovering about a gaming table at the far end of the room talking to an elderly couple, and pointed him out to Abigail.

They made their way through the crowd towards him.

CHAPTER 44

When Monroe had arrived two hours previously, he couldn't believe his eyes. The splendour of Boden Castle was almost too much to take in. He adjusted his wig and went through the entrance hall. No one asked for his invitation at the entrance, though he held it plain to see.

He went up the stairs and passed through the anteroom on the second floor. The scene took his breath away. The ballroom was full of people and all of the Viceregal court seemed to be there, under gleaming crystal chandeliers, in all their finery. He went in to find the gaming tables. There would be a wealth of new friends to establish and he could kill two birds with the one stone by taking as much money from them as possible.

The room glimmered in golden light despite the lateness of the hour. There was gold inlay on the ceilings and the walls were papered with patterns of greens and reds and blues.

And the people. They were everywhere. Monroe hadn't ever seen so many packed this tightly in one place before. The men were dandified in couture and the women had the widest dresses and highest hair that he had ever seen. There was a small orchestra in one corner of the room and ladies and gentlemen were standing in groups, laughing and talking over the noise of the others around them.

Monroe spent an hour at the gaming tables before he spotted the Duke and Duchess of Alden, with a group of men Monroe recognised from the Dargan Club. He approached Alden's cluster and tapped one gentleman on the shoulder.

'What do you want?' the man asked and looked Monroe straight in the face in derision.

'Sir, I am sorry to interrupt. I came with a message for the Duke which I must deliver personally.'

'Is that you, Dr. Monroe?' Alden asked, assessing the blond gentleman before him.

'Dr. Harton had to send his apologies. He cannot attend this evening's festivities due to ill health.'

'I am sorry to hear it. Give the good doctor my best wishes when next you see him,' Alden said, then turned his head, dismissing Monroe. He'd had enough of the cheat from the night before.

Monroe bowed his head. He would wait until the Duke was drunk before trying to sit at his table. He had an hour or two to kill yet. He moved away towards one of the nearby tower rooms where some of the gentlemen had retreated to drink and play. They welcomed his company, and he spent a lucrative hour or so with these new acquaintances.

When he at last ventured back out into the ballroom, he at once found himself face to face with Mr. and Mrs. Goulding. Their daughter was nowhere in sight and for that he was grateful.

'You have a nerve to show yourself here,' Mr. Goulding said.

'What do you mean, sir?'

'After what you did to our daughter?' Mrs. Goulding whispered, seething.

'Mrs. Goulding,' said Monroe, 'surely there is no need for your husband to speak in such an ungentlemanly manner?'

It was too much for Gilbert Goulding. He pushed Monroe against the wall, but the doctor side-stepped out of the way.

'Mr. Goulding, please,' said his wife, grabbing her husband's arm. 'I beg of you – this is a private matter.'

'What is going on here?' Alden approached, attracted by the commotion.

'It is nothing, Your Grace, just a misunderstanding,' Monroe said.

Mr. Goulding couldn't control his temper. '*Nothing? You are nothing but a scoundrel! I let you into my house and this is how you repay me?*'

'Mr. Goulding, please stop. Everyone will hear,' Caroline Goulding begged, noticing the crowd growing around them.

'What the devil is this all about, Monroe?' Alden asked.

The men at the nearby gaming tables forgot their cards and turned to look at the unfolding drama before them.

'His daughter has accused me of getting her with child, Your Grace,' Monroe said, 'and I suspect that I'm only one of her many lovers.'

The Duke laughed.

Mr. and Mrs. Goulding had never encountered such disrespect in front of their peers before this.

In the distance, Monroe saw Miss Harton looking about the room with the weaver following close behind. He couldn't believe his bad luck.

Alden recognised the young lady approaching. It was Dr. Harton's daughter.

'Is this not your fiancée, Monroe?' Alden asked. 'It seems you've got yourself into a bit of a mess tonight.'

Abigail approached the group. All eyes were on her in anticipation of what would happen next.

'Dr. Monroe, I am sorry to disturb you. My father needs you

immediately,' she said, trying to ignore the men who seemed to be laughing at her at a nearby card table.

'Does Miss Harton know of your antics?' Caroline Goulding asked Monroe. 'Miss Harton, I am sorry to have to tell you that your fiancé is untrue to you.'

Abigail looked at her while Alden clapped Monroe on the back.

'It seems Monroe's been diddling another, Miss Harton,' Alden said to a chorus of jeers. 'Miss Goulding is already with child, and I've no doubt there are a few others in that particular condition too. I only hope that you have remained chaste, my dear?'

'I beg of you, Your Grace, say no more,' Mr. Goulding said. His wife had started to weep.

Abigail looked at Dr. Monroe for answers. Could it be that Mr. Gavin had been right?

'Do you have a wife in Cork, sir?' Abigail asked an astonished Monroe.

'*She is asking if he already has a wife in Cork!*' Alden shouted to the company at large. 'In truth, I have not had a better entertainment in months. My dear fellow, you are welcome to sit and play cards with us after all.'

Goulding lunged at Monroe who fell against Abigail. She was thrown against one of the gentlemen at the gaming table who tried to pull her onto his knee. She managed to pull herself away.

Hugh rushed to her side. 'Please, Miss Harton, let us leave. We can ask another of your father's colleagues to attend him.'

Abigail did not respond.

Meanwhile some gentlemen had restrained Gilbert Goulding.

'Come, my dear,' he said to his wife when they released him. 'We will get no justice tonight.'

Monroe watched as the Gouldings left the ballroom. That was something at least. He turned to his fiancée. He doubted he could persuade her to stay. However, it was still possible to ingratiate himself with Alden and his friends. What could she do anyway? She was publicly engaged to him and would find it difficult to get another man to take her on if she broke her promise. Still, it was best to be kind.

'Abigail, you have my word that this is all a fabrication to do my character harm in your presence. Please let us talk somewhere privately.' He tried to take her hand.

She stepped away from him.

'Mr. Smyth wants to know which medicines you have given my father.'

'It is mostly chalk with spearmint and ginger to help his stomach,' he lied. 'Smyth will know what to do.' He gestured towards Hugh. 'Let this fellow go back with the news. Please, let us talk.'

'Mr. Smyth asked that I bring you back. He would prefer to consult with you in person.'

'Some spearmint should be sufficient and rest, as I prescribed earlier.'

'Spearmint? That is all you have to offer? When my father might be dying?'

'Monroe, bring your lady and sit at the table with us, I want to hear all,' Alden interrupted. This whole diversion was most entertaining.

'Come, let me talk to you alone without witnesses,' Monroe said to Abigail.

'Mr. Gavin, could you leave us, please? I will join you outside presently.'

Hugh didn't want to leave her with the scoundrel, but he did not want her to be embarrassed any further.

'I will wait for you at the entrance door,' he said and went out, intending to get the waiting cab to come up close to the door.

'Why don't you stay with me, Abigail,' Monroe said. 'Your father will be back to himself by the morning.'

'How can you not come when I ask you? Can you not see how

urgent this is that I should come all the way here? Is my father's life not important to you?'

Monroe caught her by the arm and drew her to one side, away from Alden and his cronies.

'You father is well enough. It is just a stomach disorder and Mr. Smyth is as capable an apothecary as I have ever come across. Abigail, I urge you to think of who we can meet here tonight. Think of how my business will increase. I may even be able to secure a better annuity for your father's hospital. How can you ask me to pass up this opportunity? It is only for us that I ask you to stay.' Spittle had formed at the corners of Monroe's lips and he wiped it away.

Abigail could not believe that she had attached herself to such a man. How could she have been so blinded by him?

'I cannot stay with you,' Abigail said and turned to leave.

Monroe grabbed at her arm again. She broke away from him and hurried to the closest door. Her world changed from hope to unhappiness in an instant. He had lied about Elizabeth Goulding. There never was a cousin Nicholas, it had always been him. He had got the girl with child. And what if he really had a wife in Cork? She felt sick. She could never marry him and she might never marry another having been associated with one so low. It was clear that he wanted to mingle with Alden's group for connections. He did not care a whit for her father's safety. How could he be this cruel? She knew here was no point in trying to convince him to return with her. He had told her the medicine he had given her father and hopefully that would have to be enough for the apothecary.

Monroe watched as Abigail Harton left the room. He was surprised at how disappointed he felt. He had great affection for her still. Maybe there was time to call her back. He was about to follow her out when Alden stopped him.

'Come now, Monroe, let her stew a while – I want to know how you managed to get the Goulding girl with child under old Goulding's nose,' Alden said, and the men at the table laughed again.

'I must make Miss Harton understand. I cannot let her leave like this.'

Alden called his steward Radburn to the table.

'Radburn,' Alden said and winked at Monroe, 'there's a young lady just left, wearing a blue dress ... what was that peculiar pattern, Monroe?'

'Bluebirds,' Monroe said. 'But let me follow her myself.' Abigail Harton and her family were his bread and butter and he should not have alienated the only tolerable girl he had ever met.

'Nonsense, man. Radburn, go after the bluebird lady and detain her in the north-west tower room. The third-floor room. You know the one. Monroe, you can join her there shortly. Come sit with us a while. I mean to be entertained.'

Radburn was gone in an instant to catch the bird lady in the blue dress before he lost his job. Bluebirds or a blue dress, something like that.

'There is no need to detain her,' Monroe said, thinking that such tactics would anger Abigail beyond remedy.

'Nonsense, man. Radburn will keep her for you and you can sit with us awhile, and then take her home,' Alden said, taking some snuff. He couldn't wait to leave for London to get away from the tedium of his friends here. However, he intended to have as much entertainment as possible this evening.

Monroe found he had no choice but to sit and find favour with some of the wealthiest men in the country instead of rescuing his fiancée. Abigail's father would live another day. He would only stay a while with them. He turned to joking and telling his secrets to Alden and his friends.

As Abigail made her way out, she was blocked by a group of young men who were grabbing at every woman who passed them by. There was a door to her immediate left so she went through it and found that it led to the servants' stairway. She descended two flights and emerged in the kitchens. The servants was busy at work and only some turned to look at her as she made her way through the bustling room. She moved quickly, guessing the direction she must take to reach the main entrance. She went through the doorway on the other side, and through a cavernlike room before reaching another corridor beyond. It was very cold. She walked down the corridor, hoping that it might lead her back to the main entrance.

She came to a large door with a brass hoop. She pulled it open. Inside there was a narrow tunnel lit by torches in wall sconces. The torches were few and far between and she was afraid to venture further. However, she thought it was likely to lead her out of the castle, perhaps to stables or kitchen gardens. She walked on. It was freezing. She was beginning to think she should turn back when another door appeared with a small blackened handle. She opened it gently, half afraid of what she might find inside.

Her instinct had been true. She found herself in a crypt with new and ancient coffins stacked on shelves against its dampened walls. The smell of death pervaded the air. She quickly retreated and pulled the door shut behind her.

She followed the corridor back and continued blindly until she began to hear the faint sounds of voices and laughter.

She came to a door which was suddenly flung open and a startled young maid stood before her.

'I'm sorry, madam, I didn't expect you to be there,' she said and curtseyed.

'I would be much obliged if you could show me the way out,' Abigail gasped.

'Of course, madam,' the girl said. 'Please follow me.'

At the castle entrance, Hugh was anxiously waiting for her.

'Miss Harton, thank God. I was just about to come back to find you.' He looked behind her. 'Where is Dr. Monroe?'

Abigail quickly found her pattens in the entrance hall and put them on.

'He has given me the information Smyth needs. We can leave now.'

'Isn't he coming with us?'

'No, he cannot come,' Abigail said.

She strode back to the waiting cab. How could she have been so naïve? She should have seen it clearly all along. Dr. Monroe didn't care for her or her family. Or rather, he did only when it would be of benefit to him. He was more concerned with climbing the social ladder, blind to the fact that he could never succeed. Alden and his friends would never accept a doctor into their fold. And all the while her father lay sick in his bed. Dr. Monroe would never have the kind of money required to mix with the likes of those in Alden's circle. He could never be their equal. He was merely their pet. A person to entertain them until the next fool came along.

She reached the cab and had to stop to catch her breath.

Mr. Gavin caught up to her.

'Ms. Harton, wait. I can try to convince Dr. Monroe to come. Please stay here.'

'He will not come, Mr. Gavin. I thank you kindly for your efforts but we are wasting time. He has told me the medicines he administered. Let us leave?'

Hugh realised that she had finally witnessed Monroe's true character and he thanked God for that.

Their driver pulled up and Hugh helped her into the cab and followed her inside. He tapped on the outside door to let the driver know they were ready to set off for the city.

Elizabeth had been waiting upstairs for over an hour. She looked out the window and saw an elderly couple leaving in haste. She realised they were her parents and they looked in bad temper.

She waited until she could no longer see her family's carriage in the distance, until they were well and truly gone, before she descended the staircase in regal fashion. She touched the two bluebirds on silver and golden vines on the stomacher of her gown and could see that she was being greatly admired as she came down the stairs to re-enter the ballroom.

She adjusted the emerald earrings the doctor had given her the week before as a present. They were beautiful and she thought that he must be richer than he appeared, to be able to afford them for her. It was also a sign that he loved her.

She was unaware that she had narrowly missed Abigail Harton who had left seconds before. When she reached the bottom of the stairs, she was accosted by a rather large servant of some sort or other.

Radburn, the steward, saw the two birds on the girl's dress. The gown may have been green or blue. He really couldn't tell the difference but she had to be the right one. He grabbed her firmly by the arm. Some of these flighty young women could twist themselves away, he found, and he wasn't going to take any chances. His job was on the line. He couldn't wait for Alden and the Duchess to go back to England. The Duke's playacting was too much to bear and the Duchess was the most distasteful woman he had ever met. Even tonight she had already gone to bed in a huff.

The girl tried to pull away from him. Her hand hit off the staircase and Radburn saw the stone from her emerald ring fall down the stairs. She had not noticed. He would have a servant search for it later. It probably was some cheap trinket.

'What are you doing, sir? Don't you know who I am?' she said, trying to break free from the buffoon who had gripped her fast.

'Madam, I must ask that you wait upstairs awhile,' Radburn said and, without waiting for an answer, he manhandled the girl with the birds on her dress back up the staircase. There were certainly bluebirds on her dress. She was definitely the right one.

'I beg your pardon, sir. I have every right to go into that

ballroom tonight. I do not need to wait upstairs. My parents have already left.'

'The Duke has asked that you wait upstairs for your friend,' Radburn said.

'What friend?' Elizabeth asked, wondering what the man was talking about. She reached the top of the stairs and began to think that the servant was a little mad.

'You are to wait for Dr. Monroe in here.' Radburn walked her down a narrow corridor to the north-west tower room. 'He will not be long.'

'Why didn't you say that to begin with?'

Radburn had almost lost his job the month before, ordering 'jade green' drapes for the Duchess instead of blue ones or so she said. He wasn't about to lose his livelihood for the upstart in front of him.

'I am sorry, madam. Please follow me.' He took a candle from a window ledge along the corridor and guided the girl into the tower room. Then he left and locked the door, relieved to have succeeded in completing his master's request.

Elizabeth sat for an hour in the oppressive room with its carved oak panelling that covered the walls from ceiling to floor. She decided that she had waited long enough. The emerald stone from her ring was missing and it was nowhere in the room. She had to find it. But when she tried to open the tower-room door, it was locked. Why had the servant locked the door? And where was Dr. Monroe anyway? Why hadn't he come for her? She went to the window and saw that more guests were arriving. She was missing out on the festivities. She paced back and forth in frustration. Part of the panelling was hanging loose near the corner of the room and, as she passed it, she noticed that there was a hidden door behind it. Maybe she could get out that way. But when she tried to open the door, it wouldn't budge. She noticed a keyhole in it. There had to be a key for it somewhere in the tower-room. She had to find it. The tower room was compact and simple. There was a dressing table, a bed and two chairs by the window. She searched everything in the room, including the fireplace, but couldn't find a key anywhere. She shouted out in frustration and sat down on a chair by the window to think. What if Dr. Monroe didn't know where she was? She leaned down to place her candle on the ground and that was when she saw it: a small gleam of metal under the stone window ledge. She moved her candle closer. It was a key, lodged in a crack in the stone. She teased it out. This had to be the one. Maybe she could get out after all. Leaning through the gap in the panelling, she turned the key in the lock of the door. When it creaked open, she could see nothing but darkness, so she took her candle and managed to manoeuvre herself inside. To her dismay, she found only a small dark space with no windows or other doorways. The room was empty but for a wooden chair. She lifted her candle and examined the rough walls to be sure. But there was no other way out.

She turned to leave but, as she did, her wide skirt caught the door and swung it shut. The draught as it closed blew out her candle and she suddenly was in darkness. She ran the flat of her hand all over the surface of the door but found no handle or knob to pull it open. There was no lever or catch around its outline either. There was nothing. She tried to scream for help but the dust in the room began to choke her. So she stopped crying out.

She had to hope that Dr. Monroe would be up to see her soon. She tried not to panic. She would just have to wait. There was no point in screaming if there wasn't anyone outside. She remembered the chair. She would sit close to the door and listen for footsteps. But when she turned around, she stood on the hem at the back of her dress and tripped. She fell back, hitting her head hard against the stone wall before she reached the ground. For a moment she stared upwards into the darkness and wondered where she was. Then all went black around her.

CHAPTER 45

In Pluncot Street, Mr. Smyth had finished bleeding his patient. It had not improved Dr. Harton's condition but he was sure he would rally soon. He had ordered Mrs. Harton make up a hot spearmint drink for her husband to drink. The beverage seemed to have settled his patient's stomach. There was not much else he could do until Miss Harton returned with Dr. Monroe.

He heard the hall door open. He left Mrs. Harton to attend to her husband and went out onto the landing to see who had come in. It was Dr. Harton's daughter Sarah with her husband Henry so he went back to his patient.

Downstairs in the hallway, Brigid helped Sarah take off her cloak. From the looks of things, she guessed it would be late spring before Sarah's baby was born. Henry handed Brigid his cloak and looked up the stairs.

'How is Dr. Harton?' he asked Brigid.

'He does a little better. He is not in as much pain as earlier.' Brigid hung up the cloaks.

'Mr. Smyth is upstairs with Dr. and Mrs. Harton.'

'Mr. Smyth, the apothecary?' Henry asked.

'He knows his medicines better than any doctor to my mind,' Brigid said a little smartly.

'Is Dr. Monroe not here?' Henry asked.

'No, Miss Abigail has gone to fetch him back from Boden with Mr. Gavin,' she said.

'Boden? Monroe went to Boden? Even though Dr. Harton is extremely ill?' Henry was incredulous.

'I saw him as he left and he seemed happy to go, as far as I could see,' Brigid said. 'He was smiling.' She had never liked Monroe. 'Please tell the mistress I will bring more wood to build up the fire shortly.'

'Thank you, Brigid. I don't know what they'd do without you,' Sarah said.

Brigid bobbed a curtsey. She had always liked Sarah and Henry.

'Who is this Mr. Gavin by the way?' Henry asked.

'You had best ask Mrs. Harton,' Brigid said, 'for I do not know myself.'

Mr. Smyth was closing his bag when the young couple entered the bedroom.

It was getting late and he was worried about leaving his wife at home on her own for so long. Her memory grew worse and he did not want her to fret. His patient was sleeping soundly and he doubted the doctor would wake before morning. He wished Monroe would arrive soon. He couldn't clearly remember whether he had safely secured the door to his shop and hoped his wife could not get out before he reached home.

'Sarah, Henry, I am so glad you are here,' Margaret said.

Sarah went to her mother's side. 'I couldn't stay away any longer, Mama,' she said.

'How is he, Mr. Smyth?' Henry asked. He was shocked at the

paleness of his father-in-law's face.

'His pulse has settled and his temperature has lowered. I believe the worst is past.'

'What of his colour?'

'It's usual after bleeding. That should be set to rights in an hour or so.'

'Only for Mr. Smyth here, I don't know what I would have done,' Margaret said.

Sarah took her mother's hand.

'Henry, you must tell her,' she said, 'I think it's best that my mother knows what's happened before Dr. Monroe arrives.'

'Better to talk in private,' Henry said, looking at Mr. Smyth.

'Tell me what?' Margaret asked.

'Come down to the drawing room with us,' Henry said. 'Please excuse us, Mr. Smyth.'

They left the apothecary with his patient and Sarah linked her mother's arm as they went down the stairs to the drawing room.

'Who is Mr. Gavin, Mama?' Sarah asked when they were all seated in the drawing room. 'Brigid said something about him accompanying Abigail to Boden Castle.'

'Mr. Gavin is the brother of Miss Gavin, the dressmaker.'

'Are they your friends? You have not told me of them.'

The strain was too great and Margaret couldn't shoulder Abigail's secret alone any longer.

'Before we got the Alden annuity, our savings were gone,' she said. 'Your father used most of our funds for his charitable hospital. He wouldn't listen to me. He refused paying work and Abigail and I had to take work from Miss Gavin. Remember all of those walks Abigail took? She was all the while at Miss Gavin's, embroidering a dress for the Boden Ball. Mr. Gavin called this evening and offered to accompany Abigail to Boden to fetch Dr. Monroe when your father deteriorated.'

Sarah knew things in the house had been a little shabby, but she would never have guessed her father had put the family in such a precarious situation.

'You should have told us, Mama. We could have helped you,' she said.

'You must not tell your father or Dr. Monroe any of this. Neither of them need to know, especially now that Abigail is engaged to Dr. Monroe. I don't want him to think any the less of her. Your father has promised to spend less time at the hospital now that that annuity has come through and we shall soon be all right again.'

'Oh, Mama,' Sarah said and wrapped her arms around her mother to comfort her.

'If your father could only recover, I would be happy again.'

Henry looked out the front window and saw a cab stop outside. His sister-in-law stepped out of it with a gentleman.

'Here's Abigail now. It that Mr. Gavin with her?' he asked.

Margaret got up from the sofa and looked out the window. She nodded as she watched how Mr. Gavin sheltered Abigail from the falling snow. There was no sign of Dr. Monroe.

'I'd best get her in out of that weather,' Henry said and went to fetch her.

Hugh had sat close to Miss Harton in the small cab as they made their way back to the city.

'I am sorry the doctor didn't return with you,' he said.

'It is not your fault, Mr. Gavin.'

'What reason did he give?' he asked.

'He gave me the names of the medicines that Mr. Smyth needs. It is enough,' she said.

'I can't believe he stayed behind.'

'It seems you were right, Mr. Gavin. Dr. Monroe has proven himself false. Can't we leave it at that?'

'And what of your father's health?'

'Mr. Smyth will know what to do.'

'Is there another doctor we should fetch?'

'Mr. Smyth is a skilled apothecary. I trust his judgement best.'

'I only wish I could have helped in a better way.'

Abigail looked at the man who sat beside her and wondered if, had they met in other circumstances, she would have considered him. It was too late for that. For if what he said was true, and if Dr. Monroe was already married to another woman, who would want to marry her now? Even Mr. Gavin would have nothing to do with her then.

'I am the one who should be sorry,' she said. 'I should have believed you earlier.'

She looked out of the window. They were approaching Pluncot Street.

'There is no need to apologise, Miss Harton. I am only concerned for your future. What are you going to do?'

'What can I do?' Abigail did not want his pity. 'I must continue to help my family. I will continue to work as an embroiderer. I will ask your sister for work until my father regains his health.' She could not speak of it any further, and silently prayed that her father would get better.

Hugh held his counsel. He would speak to his sister to ensure she would give Miss Harton work should she request it again.

'You must tell your parents of Monroe's character, so that they understand. It will be hard for you, I know.'

'When my father recovers, I will tell them,' Abigail said.

The cab stopped outside her house and he helped her out.

'What will you do when Dr. Monroe returns?'

'That is between Dr. Monroe and myself.'

'I don't mean to intrude, Miss Harton, but perhaps I should stay. You will need to be careful with him.'

'Thank you, Mr. Gavin. I can manage.'

'Let me see you inside at least,' he said, and knocked on the door. 'I must let you know that my sister and I leave for Belfast next week. Our aunt has requested we visit her there.'

The thought of Mr. Gavin being gone from the city saddened her.

'When will you return?' she asked.

'Early in the new year, please God,' he said. It was getting colder and he stood close to shield her from the snow that was falling heavily around them.

Henry opened the door and Abigail was relieved to get into the warmth of the house.

'Dr. Monroe is not with you?' Henry asked.

'No. He would not come away from his friends,' Abigail said. 'How is my father?'

'He fares much better. Mr. Smyth is with him now. Mr. Gavin, I am much obliged to you for taking care of Abigail. My mother-in-law has told us of how you and your sister have helped the family.'

Abigail looked questioningly at Henry who nodded and smiled at her.

She turned to Hugh. 'Thank you again. Though you may not think it, I am very grateful,' she said.

He bowed his head. He might never see her again and he couldn't bring himself to say goodbye.

'Sir, may I ask for your further assistance before you leave?' Henry said. 'I will explain upstairs.'

'I am only too happy to help,' he replied, relieved to delay the moment of departure.

'Then dismiss your cab and come inside.'

'Henry, what is it?' Abigail asked.

'We'd best speak upstairs. There is something I need to tell you and your mother about Dr. Monroe. It will not be easy, Abigail, but I can see that you have already ascertained the manner of the man you have promised to marry. I am sorry to be blunt, but it's for the best. Come along.'

Abigail couldn't bear to hear more. It was bad enough that Mr. Gavin had told her of Dr. Monroe's infidelity, without having to hear it from her own brother-in-law the same evening.

Hugh came into the hall from outside and closed the door behind him.

'There you are, Mr. Gavin,' Henry said. 'Please follow us to the drawing room upstairs.'

'I will go on ahead,' Abigail said. 'I must first tell Mr. Smyth what medicine Dr. Monroe was giving my father.'

She went to her parents' room and informed Mr. Smyth of Dr. Monroe's message. That the medicine he had administered was merely a mix of chalk, ginger and spearmint.

'It must mostly be chalk for I can't smell or taste anything from it,' Mr. Smyth said, not knowing what to think of Monroe. 'If that is all that was given, then when your father wakes have him take some of the Peruvian bark and cordial water if he is feeling better. He may have toast if he asks for it. That should settle his stomach. There is nothing more to do here for the moment. I must get back to my wife and will call again early in the morning.'

'Thank you, Mr. Smyth. We are very much obliged.' Abigail looked at her father. He seemed to be sleeping peacefully, so she went down the stairs with Mr. Smyth to see him out. As they passed the drawing room, Henry called both of them inside.

Mr. Smyth told them that Dr. Harton was out of danger, but that they should not give him anything heavy to eat or drink, other than what was prescribed, until he returned.

'You should not let Dr. Monroe prescribe anything else for my father-in-law, Mr. Smyth,' Henry said.

'What do you mean, sir?'

'Why would you say such a thing?' Margaret asked.

'I fear Dr. Monroe is not of good character,' Henry said. 'When did Dr. Harton first become sick, Mrs. Harton?'

'Several weeks ago. Dr. Monroe gave him his own remedy, though the powders didn't seem to agree with him.'

'That may be what Monroe intended,' Henry said.

'*What?*' Abigail said. 'What makes you say this, Henry?'

'I have had news from Fitzgibbon, Alden's solicitor. He tells me that Monroe lodged your father's will along with a new lease on the building. The will has been signed by your father and it leaves everything to Monroe. Fitzgibbon believes that the will is false, and that Monroe is up to no good here.'

'That is shocking. I cannot believe it, sir,' Mr. Smyth said.

Margaret cried out and began to pace the room. Abigail sat down on the chair behind her, stunned.

'There is something else you should know,' Hugh said. 'Dr. Monroe may be married already to a woman in Cork.'

'Where did you hear this?' Margaret's world had started to crumble.

'From his friend Mr. Palmer. When I heard about it, I had to tell Miss Harton directly and that is why I came here earlier.'

'Oh, sister,' Sarah said, putting her arm around Abigail.

Margaret sat down and buried her head in her hands. She tried to breathe. The tightness in her chest would pass. She just needed to sit still and draw in as much air into her lungs as she could. She wished everyone in the room would leave. There didn't seem to be an escape and she believed it all to be true. She just wished that she had never laid eyes on Dr. Monroe and hoped that she would never see him again.

'I will talk to the Constable in the morning,' Henry said. 'We cannot let Dr. Monroe get away with this. Just pray your father continues well throughout the night.'

'I must go home,' Mr. Smyth said. 'I will return as early as I can tomorrow morning. I cannot leave my wife alone any longer. Dr. Harton is much settled and I believe he is over the worst. All we can do now is pray that he recovers.'

'Dr. Monroe said that he will return here on his way home tonight,' Abigail said.

'It is already the early hours of the morning. I doubt he will be here before dawn,' Henry responded.

'But what if he is on his way here now?' Sarah asked. 'We cannot let him near my father.'

'I am worried about that too, Sarah,' Henry said. 'We will stay here tonight. Mr. Gavin, that is why I called you up. Can you stay too? The night watchmen are not far should we need them.'

'Of course, I am happy to assist,' Hugh said, and sat by the window to keep watch in case Monroe returned sooner than expected. He wanted to kill the man for what he'd done to the Harton family, though he would settle with protecting them for the night.

Sarah saw how tired her sister looked. She could only imagine how difficult it must be when Abigail's fiancé was the subject of such derision and scorn.

'Abigail, why don't you go and rest? I will sit with Mother and Father for a few hours,' Sarah said.

Abigail was grateful to her sister. All eyes seemed to be on her. She couldn't bear to see the pity on their faces. She kissed her mother goodnight and thanked Mr. Gavin again before excusing herself, though he followed her out to the landing.

'I hope you sleep well, Miss Harton. Please try not to worry. All will be resolved, I am sure of it,' he said.

'Thank you for assisting us tonight.' She tried to smile at him.

Then she climbed the stairs and did not look back.

Upstairs, she undressed and got into bed. She shut her eyes and knew sleep would not come, and lay there, trying to forget her pain if only for a few hours.

CHAPTER 46

It was after four in the morning when Radburn saw the last guests to their sleeping quarters. His master had long since passed out in the library where he had been drinking heavily with Bolton and his political allies. Radburn had managed to clear the last of those out an hour before by offering them the Duke's carriage to take them home to the city.

He made one final sweep through the castle to make sure there were no malingerers hiding anywhere before he retired for the evening. He went through the ballroom to the gaming room where footmen were still collecting discarded glasses from the tables and food from the floor. He checked the tower rooms and anteroom one last time on the second floor and went downstairs to the dining room and salon which were clear. He would have to wait until the rooms were relatively respectable before catching a few hours' sleep and decided to make notes for the following day's tasks in his daybook.

In the kitchen the staff were still washing dishes and crystal from the party.

'Thanks be to God that's over for another year,' the housekeeper Miss Wright said. She often wondered what Radburn did in his spare time but was afraid to ask in case he had her dismissed.

'I quite agree, Miss Wright.' Radburn was feeling convivial which was a rare sensation for him.

'Would you like to join us for a glass of wine before you go up?' she asked, hoping for some gossip on the night's proceedings.

'It's a bit early for wine at this hour of the morning, don't you think, Miss Wright?' he said to frighten her.

Miss Wright grew pale. She was furious with herself for being too familiar with him. He was a very odd kind of fellow. She had to remember to be careful in future.

'I'm sorry, Mr. Radburn, I wasn't thinking,' she said and turned back to help the kitchen staff.

'Well, you'd want to be thinking,' Radburn said, smug in the knowledge that he had such power over her.

His office was close to the kitchen and no sooner had he put his foot across its threshold when he remembered that he hadn't checked the north-west tower room where he had left the girl. He hoped the young lady and gentleman had gone home but he didn't want to be surprised by them in the morning.

He stumbled against the old carpet and managed not to fall by grabbing on to the edge of his desk. Outside, he could see that there were several hours of work left for staff in the kitchen. Thankfully most of the other guests were asleep or had gone home.

He took a candle and made his way to the third floor. When he got to the north-west tower room, he paused outside. All seemed quiet, so he proceeded to venture inside without announcement. The lady and gentleman were nowhere to be seen.

But, as he turned to leave, he heard a sound in the corner of the room where the old priest's hiding hole was located within the wall itself. It was strange. He looked behind the loose panel, whose hidden mechanism had been damaged, and saw that the key was in the lock of the door. He heard the sound again, as if someone was moaning inside, so he opened the door. When he peered in, it took several seconds for his eyes to make out the shapes before him.

Then he saw her lying on the floor and stepped into the secret room. She lay motionless and stared up at him in the most horrible way. He put the candle closer to her face. Another moan escaped from her lips.

He had to get her outside. He would put her on the bed and she could sleep until the morning. He placed the candle outside the door and lifted her up from the ground. But the dress was so heavy and cumbersome that he couldn't manoeuvre her out the little doorway. He put her down on the chair, leaning her back against it while he caught his breath. Only then did he notice that the back of her head was covered in blood. The strength from his legs left him and he found himself kneeling before her. He did not even know her name. Her head rolled against the back of the chair and then fell forward. When her head dropped, he thought that she was dead.

He got out of the room as fast as he could. His hands were covered in blood. He needed time to think, to decide what to do. If he was accused of her murder he would hang for it. He put the candle down and wiped his hands dry on his linen handkerchief. When he started to pull the secret room door to close it, the girl raised her head. He knelt at the doorway, watching her. She stared at him, but she did not move. He thought he heard her whisper something but could not be sure. He couldn't risk his future. She was dying and he wasn't going to hang for anyone. He closed the door as she watched him. Then he turned the key in the lock and got up from the floor.

He left the tower room and locked it. He was crossing over to the servants' staircase when he remembered his candlestick and had to go back to retrieve it. Out in the corridor again, he made his way to his own room without being seen. The other servants would not get to their beds for hours yet. In his bedroom he changed his clothes entirely. He couldn't afford for anyone to find her, not until he'd decided what to do, so he pushed the key into the binding of his daybook. No one would find it there. Not even the Duke. He went back to lock the outer tower-room door. Only then did he go back down to the kitchen to finish his work for the night. He had a bottle of whiskey in his office. He would think a while before deciding what to do.

CHAPTER 47

It was seven o'clock in the morning by the time Monroe returned to the city. He was pleased with himself, having departed with £100 of the Duke's cash. It was enough to rent a proper house for himself and Abigail when they were wed. He would talk her around, he knew he could. He would also convince Mrs. Harton that Theodore Palmer had been envious of his good fortune and that was why he had told such abhorrent stories and lies about him having a wife in Cork.

Monroe directed his cab to John's Lane Hospital and asked the driver to wait for him. As he walked up to Harton's office, he reflected on the fact that Miss Harton was worthy of his affections though he had lost her trust. The only way to win her back was to ensure that both she and her mother needed him.

For a moment he asked himself was he doing the right thing, for he truly liked Dr. Harton, but there was no other way. He opened the door to the supply cabinet and calculated how much arsenic he would need to kill the old man. With the forged will he had deposited in Mr. Fitzgibbon's office, he would inherit the house on Pluncot Street when Abigail's father died. Perhaps then she would find it easier to change her mind about him when he offered them comfort and shelter. Of course, her mother Mrs. Harton could stay with them too for he was fond of her. It was such a shame that Abigail had not stayed at home. There was really no need for this at all, but his hand had been forced.

Monroe went back to the cab and told the driver to take him to Pluncot Street. As he approached the house, he could see candlelight in Dr. and Mrs. Harton's bedroom. They were up, so he adopted a mournful air before knocking on the hall door. He didn't have to wait long.

The maid looked nervous and ushered him in politely.

'Is Mrs. Harton up yet?' Monroe asked.

'Yes, sir. I am to take you up to the drawing room,' she said.

Monroe followed the girl upstairs. In the room, he was surprised to find a large group of people waiting for him. Mrs. Harton looked furious which he had expected, and Henry, Sarah, Abigail and Mr. Smyth all stood up as he moved towards them. He became aware of another man standing behind him. It was the weaver from Coles Alley, Mr. Gavin, who had accompanied Abigail to the castle. The situation might be trickier than he had first anticipated though he knew he could talk his way out of anything. He settled in to enjoy the scene.

Mrs. Harton was so angry that she dared not speak. She had promised Henry that she would only listen.

'Dr. Monroe, please be seated,' Henry said and pointed to the chair by the fire.

'Am I not allowed first to see my patient?' Monroe asked.

'My father is much better this morning. We must talk first,' Abigail said.

'My dear, is that not what I tried to tell you last night, that he would mend and be better by morning?'

'You could not have known that,' Margaret interjected, before turning to the window. She could no longer bear the sight of him.

'How could I not? Am I not the doctor here? Did you not just say that Dr. Harton is better this morning?'

'My father-in-law is better only through the efforts and expertise of Mr. Smyth the apothecary,' Henry said.

'Dr. Monroe ... it is not only that. Why didn't you tell us Mr. Palmer was dead?' Abigail asked.

'My dear, Abigail, I did not want to worry you.'

'And what of Elizabeth Goulding?' Abigail asked though it pained her to do so.

'She is a liar. It was my cousin who got her with child as I told you.'

'And her parents, why did they accuse you?'

'It was just a misunderstanding, that is all. My cousin Nicholas is the philanderer, not I. He always tries to blame everyone except himself.'

Monroe moved away from the fireplace.

'Do you not love me, Abigail? Do you not believe that I am true? That all I do is to secure our future as man and wife?'

'And what of your wife in Cork, a Miss Sumner?' Hugh asked.

'Miss Sumner was Palmer's wife in Cork, not mine.'

'It is you who are the liar, sir,' Henry said.

'I think it best I come back tomorrow when all of your nerves have settled down. It is understandable as Dr. Harton was so ill. Perhaps you will be able to hear the truth tomorrow. I give you my leave until then.'

'Stay where you are, sir. You have gone too far this time,' Henry said.

'How could you have cheated my husband so?' Margaret said. She could no longer remain silent.

'Mrs. Harton, it is natural that you are upset, that the Gouldings are upset. They are good people, but their daughter is a trollop who thinks that she can blame me for her condition. Well, she will not get away with it.' He went to Abigail. 'Please believe me, my dear.'

Abigail withdrew from him. 'Elizabeth Goulding is sixteen. I heard her parents accuse you themselves. It is you who lie.'

'If only that were all,' Henry said.

'Oh, come now, Henry. What other lies have you been told?' Monroe said, trying to think of a way to get the poison into Dr. Harton, who was upstairs, before he left.

'It has been brought to my attention that you have falsified legal documents including my father-in-law's will.' Henry took a document from the mantel and waved it in his face. 'Did you really think you could get away with it?'

Monroe couldn't see his way out of it, but he could still get the house. He just needed to get upstairs.

'I have falsified nothing, sir, and before you slander me further, I wish to see my patient before I leave so that he may explain that document to you.'

He walked to the door but Henry blocked his way.

'You will not touch him now or ever,' Henry said. 'Dr. Harton told us himself that he did not fashion any new will naming you as his heir.'

'This is all a misunderstanding.' Monroe went for the door again. 'I bid you all goodnight.'

'Not quite yet,' Henry said. 'I have instructed Mr. Fitzgibbon to go for the Constable. You will wait here until he returns.'

Monroe looked around. He could not afford to be taken by any constable with so many witnesses. Henry was a slight young man and the only one between himself and the door. He made a run for it, boxing Henry to the floor before making his escape. Hugh was fast on his heels as Monroe ran down the stairs and out the front door.

Monroe made his way down New Row and through the back alleys past Wormwood Gate. He kept running and hid in a doorway until Hugh Gavin passed by. There was no-one else following him. When it was clear, he doubled backed to the inn, packed everything he owned into a sack and slung it over his shoulder.

As dawn broke, he caught a cab to go to the river. He couldn't stay in the city any longer. He hadn't any friends he could trust and he certainly couldn't go back to Cork. He was sincerely disappointed to be leaving Dublin when he had almost secured a wife and a home of his own. But it could not be helped. It was best to try to get away before the Constable came knocking on his door.

Hugh was a bigger man than Monroe and didn't have his speed. After leaving Pluncot Street he lost Monroe in the back alleyways close to the Dargan Club. He thought that Monroe might seek help there. It was imperative that he find him quickly. At the club, he pushed through the footmen to gain entrance and searched every room in the house. Most gentlemen slept where they sat. The working women were long gone. It was clear Monroe was not there and that he probably wouldn't find him now. He would have to tell the Hartons that Monroe had escaped, though he would scour the streets of Dublin to try to find him later.

Miss Harton had been living under much strain, he thought, as he made his way back. She had borne it well in the months she had worked for his sister and he loved her the more for it. He would make his way home to let Mary know that he was safe and what had happened, before he returned to Pluncot Street to assist Henry should Monroe return there.

All was quiet on Coles Alley. Neither his sister nor the boy were up yet. He left a note for Mary and then went outside again and looked towards the inn. Perhaps Monroe had returned there? He was making his way up the street when he saw Monroe step out of Mrs. Brass's establishment and hail a cab that was passing by. He saw Monroe step into it and he tried to wave the driver down as the cab went by him, but it did not stop. He ran behind as it made its way in the direction of Thomas Street. He just about managed to keep it in his sights. He noticed that most of the cabs were travelling in the opposite direction. A riot was erupting on Skinners Row ahead of him, spilling out onto Fishamble Street. He slowed down and stayed on the edges of the crowd. Monroe's cab had managed to get through.

As he escaped, Monroe looked back over the city he had called his home. The streets were full of beggars and fools. The cab made it down the quays as the morning sun glinted on the river. He sat back in his seat and left the riot behind him. He could make a better start in England, or the Americas where no-one knew him. He would be smarter this time. Unhindered too. No-one would know of his wife in Cork. There would be no Palmer breathing down his neck. He would set up as an Apothecary Surgeon this time. That way he would always have what he needed on hand to progress his business and his life efficiently. It was a pity Abigail Harton would not be by his side, though he was sure that there were a thousand Abigail Hartons out there for him to find. He smiled as the cab approached the Custom House Quay. The world was ripe for the taking. After he paid the driver, he climbed the nearest gangplank only to be stopped by the captain of the ship.

'This is a trade ship for Liverpool, sir. We take no passengers,' he said.

'Would you take five pounds, Captain?' Monroe asked.

'For that, I'll take you there and back.' The man laughed and pocketed the money.

'Then show me to my cabin,' Monroe said and the captain happily obliged him.

'You are lucky, sir, for the tide is high and we are just about to sail.'

'I've always had a little luck on my side.' Monroe clapped his new friend on the back.

The gangplank was raised almost immediately and the ship began to make its way down the river towards open water. Below deck, Monroe felt safer. They would never find him here. And he had enough money in his pockets to start afresh anywhere. He sat down and accepted an offer of wine from the captain's own supply.

As Monroe drank he decided he would travel on to London. It was where he had always wanted to go. There were sure to be plenty of rich ladies for the picking and gaming houses for the taking. He had made a connection with Alden too. He would find a good wife and keep her ignorant of it all. A double life. It appealed greatly. When the captain returned to deck, Monroe settled down in his bunk and slept soundly despite a rough voyage across the Irish Sea.

Hugh had spotted Monroe's cab on Custom House Quay. He saw Monroe alight from the vehicle in the distance before stepping aboard a vessel. By the time he reached the river, the ship was at least five hundred yards down the river. He asked around until he found out where the ship was bound. It was sailing to Liverpool. He hoped very much that Monroe would never return.

He raised his collar about his neck to keep warm and went back to Pluncot Street. The Hartons were safe at least. Life went on about him as usual with horses and carts and people crowding the streets. He walked down the quays to Bridge Street to avoid Skinners Row. At Pluncot Street all was quiet again.

Henry answered the door.

'Did you find him?'

'I followed him to the quays. He got ahead of me and is on a ship bound for Liverpool. I could not get there in time to stop him.'

Henry listened intently. 'That is good news, is it not?'

'I believe so. I doubt he'll come back here again.'

'There is no need to contact the Constable now. The less said on this the better.'

'I agree. Please tell me, how is everyone upstairs?'

'Dr. Harton is awake and feeling better. The ladies are resting still. I will give them the news later.' Henry shook Hugh's hand. 'I thank you again for your help last night. Will you come in and have some breakfast?'

'No, though I would like to see Miss Harton before I go, if I may?'

'Of course.'

Hugh removed his hat and stepped into the hall.

'Have something to eat while you wait,' Henry said. 'You look exhausted, man. I'll ask Brigid to fetch her down. Come with me, and I'll pour you some coffee.'

Henry called Brigid from the kitchen and she went up to Abigail's bedroom. Brigid had heard most of what had happened the previous night from Henry and was shocked that Dr. Monroe had turned out to be such a scoundrel. When she peeked inside the bedroom, Abigail was sleeping. She didn't want to disturb her. Mrs. Harton would know what best to do. She went down to the main bedroom and paused by the door.

Her mistress was sitting by her husband's bedside.

'How could I have been so stupid?' Dr. Harton was saying to his wife. 'I believed everything he said. I thought he was the best choice for Abigail and for the hospital.'

'You are a good man, husband. How were you to know? Be content that he cannot fool us anymore. We will face it all together when you are well enough. Rest now.'

'I have let you down badly, my dear.'

'It is I who have let you down. I was too eager to see that all was right with him. But I only wanted what was best for the family.'

'I do not want to contemplate what a narrow miss our daughter had.' Dr. Harton leaned back against the pillows, closing his eyes.

Brigid knocked lightly on the door to let them know she was there.

'Come in, child,' Mrs. Harton said. 'Has Mr. Smyth returned?'

'Not yet, mistress. It is Mr. Gavin. He is downstairs with Henry in the dining room. He would like to see Miss Abigail before he goes. But she is still asleep. Shall I wake her?'

'And what of Dr. Monroe? Did Mr. Gavin catch him?'

'I do not know, mistress. Mr. Gavin returned on his own. Should I ask him?'

'No, Brigid. I will see the gentlemen myself. Leave Abigail be. Sit here with Dr. Harton until I return.'

'Yes, mistress,' the girl said.

Margaret was worried that Mr. Gavin had witnessed their worst hour and that his sister would soon know their whole business. She hoped that he would be discreet. She wanted to thank him for protecting her daughter and for chasing the scoundrel Monroe out of their house. She sincerely did want to thank him for that. She wondered if he had taken Monroe to the Constable.

As she descended the stairs, she worried about Abigail. She wanted the world to go away, to leave her alone, to leave her family alone. But she would face Mr. Gavin first. He was waiting patiently in the dining room with Henry and rose when she entered.

'Good news, Mrs. Harton,' Henry said when he saw her. 'Mr. Gavin followed Monroe to the quays. He is bound for Liverpool as we speak.'

Hugh assisted her to a chair.

'Oh, I cannot tell you how that relieves me,' she said. 'Are you sure it was him?'

'Very sure,' Hugh said. 'You should have nothing further to fear from him. I suspect he will never return.'

'And the Constable?'

'There is no need to call him, I think,' Henry said, 'if you and Mr. Harton are content to leave it at that. When Dr. Harton is feeling better, Mr. Fitzgibbon will destroy the will on his instruction, and all shall be right again.'

'And what of Miss Harton?' Hugh asked.

'She is a strong girl. She will bear it well,' Henry said.

'Mr. Gavin, how can we ever repay you?' Margaret said.

'It was my pleasure to be of assistance. Now I must take my leave – but, as I said, I would like to speak with Miss Harton before I go.'

'She is sleeping still,' Margaret said.

'Then I will call on her tomorrow.'

'Abigail tells me you sail to Belfast soon to visit your aunt. Please wait until you return. It will be less painful for her to talk by that time.'

'I hadn't thought of that. If there is anything else I can do for you before I go, you have only to send for me.'

'We are most grateful,' Henry said.

'My sister and I will be gone until late January. Grace will bring Miss Harton's payment tomorrow.'

'Thank you, Mr. Gavin. I am very much obliged to you,' Margaret said. 'Come, I will show you out.'

In the hall she stopped and turned to him. 'Mr. Gavin, I would ask you not to discuss this business with anyone, especially for Abigail's sake.'

'No-one will hear it from me,' he said.

'Thank you. I hope you and your sister will have a safe trip to Belfast.'

Margaret opened the door and he stepped out. Turning, he bowed then departed.

She closed the door and went back upstairs to her bed and lay down beside her sleeping husband. She knew she would not sleep until he was fully recovered.

CHAPTER 48

February 1720

Hugh and Mary Gavin were at last bound for Dublin. Hugh was on deck while Mary stayed below, safe from the sharp winds of the bay.

There was snow in the air and he pulled his cloak around him. It was good to be on the move again. They had stayed longer than expected in Belfast. His sister had wanted to help nurse their aunt back to health but that was not to be. She had passed away and their ties to Belfast had been considerably weakened because of it.

He had told his uncle of his plans to travel to America and they had said their final goodbyes. His cousin Sally wished him well and he was glad that they had reconciled.

He looked back towards the city of his birth and tried to imprint the image on his mind, knowing it was probably the last time he would visit. He did not regret his decision to leave his cousin behind. She had married a journeyman weaver who worked for his uncle. His aunt's bitterness towards him had dissipated before the end. He was free of his Belfast connections at last. The only person who tied him to Ireland was Mary and he hoped that he could leave her with a clear conscience. He was confident that Daniel Long would express his interest in her before he left. He hoped she would accept him. Daniel was a worthy match.

Hugh decided he would stay in Dublin until summer. It would be better to sail to America when the weather was more settled. February was not a good month to set out on a journey across the Atlantic Ocean. He didn't acknowledge to himself the real reason he did not want to leave so soon.

As he walked the deck, the ship moved out to sea and he watched the men work the sails out. He wondered how he would feel when he left Ireland for good, almost certain never to return. The enthusiasm he expected to feel had deserted him these last months. Somehow the adventure did not capture his spirit as it had before.

He went below deck and tried not to think of Abigail Harton. She came into his thoughts when he least expected. He hoped to control that in time. Miss Harton, he was sure, would not consider him as a match. He assumed that she was ashamed of the association. He would travel to America alone and wished her well. As he joined his sister below deck, the snow turned to hail.

CHAPTER 49

Abigail Harton was gazing out the window of the drawing room on Pluncot Street, wondering if she would ever see the Gavins again. Neither the weaver nor his sister had returned to Dublin and it was now late in February. When she had enquired at the inn the previous week, Grace told her she had received a letter from Miss Gavin saying their aunt had died but that Mary had not mentioned when they would return.

'Come away from the window and sit by me,' Margaret said.

'Yes, Mama. In a minute.' Abigail did not move.

'Henry called in while you out walking. He and Sarah have accepted my invitation to move here.'

'And what did Father say?'

'He said yes of course. They are to move in next week. Henry has been generous to us over these past few months, helping with the household. It's the least we can do until they can buy a house of their own. Sarah will be glad of our company when the baby arrives. It will be a happy house again, just wait and see, Abigail.' She studied her daughter. 'Why aren't you pleased?'

'Oh Mama, of course I am. But how can I be happy?'

'Hush now, and be patient. The whole Dr. Monroe affair will soon be forgotten.'

'That is easy for you to say.'

'Dr. Klinton visited your father yesterday morning. He is a good man and has his own money. He is unmarried, I believe.'

'Please try not to peddle me off to Dr. Klinton, Mama.' She turned to face her mother.

'If he is not to your liking, I am sure you will find another. It may take time but we will find someone for you.'

Abigail went over and kissed her mother. They both knew it was unlikely a respectable man would have anything to do with her after her engagement to Dr. Monroe, after an article had appeared in the *Courant* accusing him of absconding with most of the hospital's annuity fund. When Dr. Klinton had reported the robbery to the Constable, the incident had leaked out and was now circulating in pamphlet form.

'I have told Henry and Sarah that they can have your room,' Margaret said.

'What? Why didn't you ask me first?'

'With the baby coming, Benjamin's room is too small, Abigail. It's no bigger than a closet. It's best they have your room. You can take the housekeeper's room if you'd prefer it. It's warmer down there by the kitchen.'

Abigail went back to the window. Was she really to be relegated to the housekeeper's room? She had to get some air. The thought of sitting in for the whole afternoon was unbearable. It was as if she had already ceased to exist, and now the sanctuary of her own room was to be taken from her for God knows how long. If she had been a man, she could have made her own way in the world.

'I have an errand to run,' she said and left without waiting to hear her mother's reply. In the hall, she put on her cloak, stepped out of the house and pulled her hood up.

She would walk to the cathedral but it was not far enough. She needed to stretch her legs further. She made her way to Francis Street and headed towards the river but a band of men was loitering on the corner of New Row and, being unaccompanied, she decided it was safer to go back. Before long she found herself walking along Engine Alley. She wished she was still working for Miss Gavin. If only she had the sanctuary of that place now. Her work there had kept her mind occupied. She needed to be busy again, for when she thought of her future it held no happiness. She would likely raise her sister's children rather than her own. She passed Mrs. Brass's inn on Coles Alley and was standing outside the Gavins' home before she knew it.

She peered in through the glass of the front workroom and was surprised to see Mr. Gavin inside. He looked up and saw her. She stumbled backwards into the street and waited for the door to open.

Then he was standing in front of her.

'Miss Harton, you are welcome to come inside,' he said.

'I'm sorry to disturb you. I didn't know you were home.' She hardly knew what to say.

He gently caught her arm.

'Please come in.'

'Is your sister home?'

'She is working on a commission near Stephen's Green. Come in and tell me your news.'

He ushered her into the hallway and through to the kitchen.

'Come and sit by the fire,' he said.

She sat down, determined not to cry.

He poured her a glass of wine and hoped that it would bring the colour back to her face.

He handed her the glass and sat on the other side of the fire empty-handed.

'We came home only a few days ago. I was going call on you.'

'I was very sorry to hear about your aunt,' she said.

'Thank you, Miss Harton. I am glad that we travelled to Belfast to see her before she left us.'

'I hope that your sister is well,' she said.

'She is very well, thank you. She is glad to be back in Dublin.'

She sipped her wine.

'And you have taken on another commission, I see.'

'Yes, Mr. Long has given me some work.'

He stood up, poured himself a cup of ale and returned to sit opposite her again.

'Does this mean that you have changed your mind about going to America?' she asked.

'No, no, but I will delay until summer to give Mary more time to adjust. Besides, it will be more comfortable to sail in warmer weather. And I am hoping that my sister and Mr. Long will come to an understanding by then. But please forgive me, I have not asked you about your mother and father. I hope that they are both well?'

'My mother is very well, and my father is almost back to himself.'

'I am glad to hear it.'

'And Sarah and Henry?'

'They are coming to live with us on Pluncot Street. Their baby will be born soon.'

'That is good news. You will enjoy their company too, I hope?'

'Yes. It will be lovely to have a baby in the house.'

There was a pause and Abigail looked into the flames.

'And Monroe. May I ask if there has been any news as to his whereabouts?' he asked.

'We have not heard from him. Henry believes that he will never return and I pray that he is right.'

She got up from the fire and placed her glass on the kitchen table.

'I thank you for the refreshment, Mr. Gavin. I won't delay you any longer.'

'Will you not wait for my sister's return? She would be glad to see you, I am sure.'

'No. I must get back, but I would be honoured if you and your sister would drop in to see us some afternoon next week. You could let me know when – perhaps send Michael with a message?'

'It would be our pleasure, Miss Harton,' he said, much pleased. 'I hope you will allow me to escort you home?'

'Thank you. I would be obliged.'

They walked along the streets together slowly. How different this was to last year, when she had tried to hide her association with him, walking so fast and hoping he would fall behind. How stupid she had been not to value his care for her then. Why had she chosen to value others over his honesty? What a fool she had been.

'If you forgive me, you do not seem yourself, Miss Harton.'

'I am envious of you, Mr. Gavin, that is all.'

'Why? In what way?'

'I wish I had your freedom. You can travel the world as you please while I am confined to live with my family.' She turned to face him. 'Thank you, this is far enough. I don't want to keep you away from your work any longer.'

'Miss Harton, we are not so unalike. I know what it is like to be tied to a place by family. It is the reason I came to Dublin in the first place and why I went back to Belfast. To try to make my sister happy.'

'Yet you can leave her if you please.'

'When she comes to an understanding with Mr. Long I can go with a clear conscience.'

'Do you expect that to happen soon?'

'The subject has not been broached yet though I fully expect it will.'

'But Miss Gavin is your only family.'

'I will make a new one,' he said.

Abigail looked away. She was aware of how close he was to her.

She remembered how he had made her feel in the kitchen that day. Of how he was making her feel. She didn't know what to do.

'I must go,' she said and crossed to the corner of Pluncot Street.

He let her walk away. This would not be the last time he would see her. He did not plan to leave for several months. He would see her again next week. There was still time.

When he got back to his workshop, he opened the drawer of his desk and took out the damask design for the emerald dress. It was exquisite. The instructions for the loom were as accurate as any he had seen before. It was a shame she could not travel as she wanted to just because she was a woman. Maybe she would get a chance to travel yet.

CHAPTER 50

Abigail was at the window when the clock struck three. The Gavins were due to drop in at four o'clock.

'Are you quite well?' her mother asked. 'You seem a little preoccupied. There is no need to be. It is only Mary Gavin and her brother who visit after all.'

'I am fine, Mama. Where is Father?'

'He is pottering about in his office downstairs. Best to leave him there for now. When they arrive, he can join us then. By the way, your father proposes giving Benjamin's book of fairy tales to Sarah for her baby. Is that all right with you?'

Abigail could not answer.

'Abigail, have you heard what I have said?'

'I am happy for Sarah to have the book, Mama. It is unlikely that I will have children to read these tales to.'

'Oh Abigail, you must not say that. Henry has promised that he will find someone suitable for you. His business becomes more and more prosperous. You must have hope.'

'People will not forget, Mama.'

'We must put our faith in Henry, that is all.'

Abigail wanted to shout out at the injustice of her fate, though she could not. What a fool she had been.

She excused herself and went up to her room to embroider some of the christening gown for Sarah's baby for a while. But instead she found herself taking the storybook from her bookshelf.

Opening it, she read the page where the Princess had listened to the bluebird sing in the tower and how the bird had inspired her to hope again. Abigail brushed her hand over the illustrations on each page. The Evil Sorceress had been painted a dark blue as she hovered outside the tower. The bird, the colour of the sky, sang to the Princess, his long tail feathers showing hints of red. The Princess, dressed in silken robes, sat at the spinning wheel.

Abigail turned the page and read how the Princess had been enchanted by the bird. How she had worked less and less at the spinning wheel until the day came when she refused to spin any more gold for her stepmother, the evil Sorceress. In a fit of rage, her stepmother tried to kill her, but the Good Witch intervened and saved the Princess's life by changing her into a bluebird, as she had done for the Prince in the forest.

Abigail looked at the last page. There the Princess flew away from the tower with the Prince and they made a happy life together in the lands that bordered both of their fathers' kingdoms. In sorrow at the loss of their children, the kings declared peace though they never saw their children again. The Sorceress was cast out by her husband. In greed, she took the gold that the Princess had spun in the tower as it was the source of her magic. As she sailed from the harbour to another land, the weight of the gold sank the ship in which she sailed. When she tried to save her riches, she was drowned and was never seen again.

A tear fell on the page as Abigail remembered Benjamin's reaction at how the story had ended, of how he had wanted the

Prince and Princess to return to human form. Perhaps they had.

She closed the book and, picking up the christening robe, started to embroider. After a short while she could not concentrate and went down to sit with her mother again.

'Have they arrived?' Margaret asked when Abigail entered the room.

'Not yet, Mama – it is early yet.'

There was a knock on the door and shortly thereafter Brigid came into the room.

'Excuse me, Miss Abigail. Mr. Gavin is downstairs.'

'And his sister?' Abigail asked.

'It's just Mr. Gavin, miss.'

'Why is he on his own?' Margaret asked.

'I don't know, mistress.'

'Please send him up,' Abigail said, 'and tell Dr. Harton he has arrived.'

'Abigail, please don't keep Mr. Gavin here too long. It is bad enough that he knows all of our business.'

'We must be polite, Mama. I have invited him here.'

'He was to bring his sister. That would have been different. I really don't have anything to say to him anymore.'

'Mama, don't you remember how he helped us the night Father almost died? How can you dismiss him so lightly?'

'I am sorry, Abigail. I do not like to recall that night. We have to look to the future.'

'Should he suffer because of that? Father wants to thank him for his courage. We should be thankful to have the opportunity to do so.'

'Your father was ashamed when he found out that you worked for the Gavins. I want him to be left in peace.'

'Mr. Gavin is a true friend. It will do Father good to speak with him. Can you not see that?'

The door opened and Brigid let Hugh in.

'Good afternoon,' Hugh said. He carried a roll of paper in his hand.

'Mr. Gavin, you are very welcome,' Abigail said. 'Please sit down.'

'Thank you, Miss Harton.' He sat on the sofa.

'Please accept our sincerest condolences, Mr. Gavin,' said Margaret. 'Abigail has told me that your aunt in Belfast has sadly passed away.'

'She has gone to a better place, Mrs. Harton.'

'Brigid, where is Dr. Harton?' Margaret asked.

'He is asleep in the chair in his office, mistress. Shall I wake him?'

Margaret hoped her husband would remain downstairs until Mr. Gavin had gone.

'Please do,' Abigail said.

'Yes, miss.'

Abigail sat across from Hugh. He smiled at her when she glanced up at his face.

'Where is your sister?' Margaret asked.

'She was indisposed and sends her apologies.' He could not tell them that his sister had refused to accompany him. She was busy catching up on her commissions and had not budged in her decision to stay at home.

'I see,' Margaret said.

'What is that you have, Mr. Gavin?' Abigail asked

Hugh unrolled the paper he had brought with him.

'I found this at home and thought that you might like to have it.' He held out the first sketch she had made of the damask design of bluebirds on silver vines.

'I cannot take this back,' she said. 'It is yours now.'

Hugh kept the drawing in his hands. He was glad not to let it go. He sat back in his chair and rolled the paper back up.

There was a pause.

Margaret was staring blankly at Hugh and Abigail was fidgeting in her seat.

'I hope Dr. Harton has fully recovered?' he asked then.

'My husband is almost back to full health, thank you,' Margaret said. 'He had a lengthy road to recovery.'

It had been a mistake to come, Hugh thought. Mrs. Harton's expression was not as welcoming as he had expected.

'Have you made any further plans for America?' Abigail asked.

'I leave next month,' he said. 'My sister has become engaged to my friend, Mr. Long, and I can leave in good conscience.'

'Oh, that is good news,' Abigail said, though the expression on her face belied her words.

Margaret did not like the way Mr. Gavin was looking at her daughter or she at him.

'I wish you every success in America,' she said. 'Where do you travel to?'

'To Boston first, to meet the merchants my friend Mr. Thompson sells his silk to. From there I will travel to Virginia, where they venture to raise silkworms.'

The door opened and Dr. Harton came in, his hair tousled by sleep.

'It was good of you to call, Mr. Gavin,' he said. 'I must apologise for my delay.'

'Not at all, Dr. Harton. I am glad to see you so well,' Hugh said, getting to his feet.

'I can never express fully how thankful we were to have your assistance that night,' Dr. Harton said. His eyes watered as he shook the young man's hand.

'Not at all. I was glad to be of assistance.'

Dr. Harton sat on the sofa and Hugh sat back down beside him.

Brigid returned to serve them drinks and they spent a pleasant couple of hours in each other's company. When the clock struck five Mr. Gavin got up to take his leave of them.

Abigail rose to her feet. 'Thank you for visiting this afternoon,

Mr. Gavin. I hope that we will see you before you go.'

'I hope so too, Miss Harton. Perhaps I could call on you tomorrow?' He had to see her once more.

'Why don't you join us for supper? With your sister if she is better? We eat at seven,' Dr. Harton said. 'Sarah and Henry will be here. I am sure they would appreciate the opportunity to thank you once again for your help.'

Hugh accepted the invitation promptly before Mrs. Harton could take it away, and then he was gone, passing Brigid on the stairs and giving her a big smile.

The next evening, Abigail wore her blue day dress. It reminded her of her brother Benjamin and it gave her hope. Mr. Gavin had awakened something in her that she thought she had lost. A desire to be noticed.

Sarah and Henry arrived precisely at seven in the evening and Abigail grew agitated with each passing minute thereafter. There was no sign of Mr. Gavin. Why was he late? What if he had changed his mind?

'I think we should tell Brigid to serve,' said Henry after more time had passed. He was hungry and wanted his supper.

'It would be rude to start without our guest,' Abigail said. 'I am sure he will be here shortly.'

Sarah and Margaret looked at each other. Normally Abigail was the first to admonish tardiness.

'Let's just hope our supper hasn't got cold,' Henry said. 'I shall blame him if it is ruined.'

Dr. Harton laughed. 'I have never known you not to eat because of that,' he said.

Hugh hurried down the street. He cursed himself that he had forgotten the time. He'd had work to complete and was late because of it. He needed to finish his last commission before he dismantled the loom to move it to Mr. Long's premises. Mr. Long had already hired it out to another weaver. Hugh had to keep reminding young Michael that he wouldn't be taking him to America. It would be difficult to leave him, though he was sure that the boy would thank him for it when he was older. It was best that Michael remain in the same city where his family lived. Besides, Mr. Long had offered him an apprenticeship and his sister had agreed the boy would continue to live with them after she and Mr. Long married. With Mr. Long, she would have protection. His friend had been a persistent fellow and it had worked. Hugh smiled to himself as he turned onto Pluncot Street.

He saw Henry looking down at him from the window and waved hello, but the fellow turned away as if he had not seen him. He had expected to be welcomed tonight and hoped that he had not been mistaken.

Brigid greeted Hugh at the door and led him up to the dining room.

'Mr. Gavin, it is good to see you so soon again.' Dr. Harton rose from his chair to greet the young man.

'Sir, I am happy to meet you in more pleasant circumstances,' Henry said and shook Hugh's hand.

'As am I, sir,' Hugh replied.

The men sat back down at the table.

Henry poured Hugh a glass of wine and as Hugh took the first sip, he glanced at Miss Harton. Was he imagining it, or was she avoiding his gaze?

'I hope your sister is better?' Margaret asked.

'She is a little better today, thank you.' He had failed to budge her on her decision to stay at home.

'Dr. Harton tells me you plan to leave for America soon?' Henry said.

'I have yet to secure my passage. There is much to organise.'

'And you will not change your mind and stay?' Sarah asked.

'It is too late for that. I have sold my loom. Mr. Long takes it before the end of the week. My friend George Thompson is eager for me to join him in Virginia. They plan to raise silkworms there and hope that their business will prosper.'

'And you will raise these worms?' Sarah asked, almost choking on her meat at the thought.

'No, not at all. I don't have the skill for it. I plan to weave cloth and, when I understand the country, I may try my hand at merchandising. I have seen how mercers profit here. The population grows in America and George tells me there is much opportunity there.'

Abigail listened to Mr. Gavin as he spoke with enthusiasm about his new adventure and was disappointed that he seemed so eager to go. She sipped on her wine and tried to smile at the company about her.

By the time supper was over, Dr. Harton had thanked Mr. Gavin several times more for accompanying Abigail to the castle that night and for enlightening them as to the true nature of Dr. Monroe. Eventually the ladies left the dining room while the gentlemen took their brandy.

The men's conversation centred on speculation about Monroe's whereabouts. However, there was nothing to report from any of them. It seemed that Monroe had simply chosen to disappear.

The ladies joined them for the rest of the evening. Hugh looked at the Harton family and wished that he could be part of their family too. They were good people.

He did not want to outstay his welcome, so before it grew too late he rose to leave and the company offered him a warm goodbye.

He was thankful when Abigail offered to walk down to the hall with him.

As they descended, he knew he might not have an opportunity to speak with her before he left Dublin.

'I hope you will visit us again before you leave?' she said when they reached the hall.

Brigid emerged from the kitchen and passed them with a smile, carrying a tray of pastries upstairs.

They watched her until she turned the bend of the stairs.

'May I speak with you alone?' Hugh said.

'Of course, Mr. Gavin.' Abigail led him into her father's office on the ground floor.

'Miss Harton, this may be the last time we meet … and … I wanted to say …'

Abigail watched as he tried to find his words. Mr. Gavin has been a good friend to her. She had not appreciated his friendship at the beginning of their association and perhaps this is what held him back now. How could he know how much she had come to admire him?

'Mr. Gavin, I want to apologise to you if I have ever seemed ungrateful.'

'Ungrateful? There is no need for you to be grateful. I only wanted your safety, your happiness. I am sorry that Dr. Monroe was not who he made himself out to be, for your sake.'

'You cannot help that. That is for me to live with.'

'What will you do now?'

'I will stay here with my family When my sister and brother-in-law move in, I will help with the child.'

'You are worth much more than that.'

He looked at her closely. Why shouldn't she find happiness? He searched her face for a sign. Could he ask her to come with him? How presumptuous that would be? He had better leave and say no more … but he found that he could not.

'Miss Harton, I have thought of you often these last few months and it is difficult for me to think that I may never see you again.'

Abigail waited as he stood awkwardly before her.

'Yes, Mr. Gavin,' she said when he didn't continue. 'It is difficult for me too. You have become a good friend.'

'Yes, it is difficult to say goodbye … that is, to part with you …'

'I had better get back upstairs to my family,' she said. It was too painful to listen to his goodbye any longer. 'They will be wondering what is keeping me ...'

'Please wait. Just another moment. I ...'

'Yes, Mr. Gavin? Please ... What is it you wish to say?'

'Miss Harton, I want to ask if you would consider becoming my wife?'

He watched as every emotion seemed to pass over her face. Now that he had said it, he could not take it back.

'I don't know what to say,' she said, trying to compose herself. She felt happiness and joy and realised that she loved him. She began to cry.

It was not the response he had been hoping for and he was dismayed.

'I have offended you,' he said. 'I am sorry. Please forget that I asked.'

'Please, wait, Mr. Gavin. I need to ask you one question. Why do you want to marry me?'

Hugh looked at her. How could he tell her that she had invaded his thoughts since she had come to work in his home? That he had struggled to make the decision to leave only because of her? That she meant everything to him? That without her, his future and life in America would be meaningless? He took a deep breath and told her the truth.

'I love you, Miss Harton,' he said.

Abigail wondered what she had done to deserve him. She wanted to say yes, that she would be his wife. But what of her family? Could she make this decision easily? Could she leave her home and her family forever for a man she hardly knew? But was this not what she wanted after all, an adventure in an unknown land?

He moved close to her and took her hand. 'Please, take time to consider it.'

Her mind raced. She could be his wife. Her brother-in-law would finance the household. No one would know her past in

America, only her husband and he said that he loved her. She looked down as his fingers enfolded her own.

'Will you think about it?' he asked.

'I do not need to think about it. I will marry you, Mr. Gavin.'

He could not believe what he heard. It was more than he had hoped for. He had been certain that she would reject him. He laughed and took her in his arms.

'Are you sure?'

'I have long envied you. If I had been born a man, I believe I would be much like you. I have always wanted to see the world and I am very happy to see it with you.'

'Do you think you can love me, Miss Harton?'

'I already do,' she said.

He kissed her softly. 'I will take care of you.'

'We will take care of each other,' she said.

They kissed again until she pulled away.

'I had best get home. I will come back to talk to your father tomorrow morning.'

'I will see you then.'

They walked out into the hall together.

'Be gentle with your mother. I fear she does not like me much.'

When Abigail smiled, he hesitated at the door, then kissed her one last time.

'Goodnight, Mr. Gavin,' she said and stepped away from him and closed the door.

Hugh couldn't believe that his whole life had turned around. He walked to the corner of Francis Street and did not care to go home. The door to St. Patrick's Cathedral was open and he went inside. The nave was lit by candlelight and the ceilings rose so high that when he looked above, he felt dizzy. He prayed that her father would give his permission for the marriage. He had given himself a month to prepare for the journey, which would now entail bringing a wife. With the sale of his loom to Mr. Long, he could afford better accommodation on board. And Abigail. He could call her Abigail now. They would have a good life in America. And children.

He left the cathedral and walked home. It was raining, though that did not quicken his step. He imagined the happy future he would have with Miss Harton. She would be Abigail Gavin soon. How it made his heart feel to say that name.

When he arrived back home in Coles Alley, he smiled at his sister as they ate supper together. He would tell her of his good fortune in the morning.

When Sarah and Henry left to go back to their lodgings, Abigail went straight to her bedroom to calm herself before facing her parents. It would be best to tell them tonight. Her mother would not appreciate the surprise of Mr. Gavin calling again in the morning, and she wanted her to be civil to him.

She looked around the only bedroom she had ever known. Her narrow bed was situated beside the window. It would be dismantled so that Henry and Sarah could move in. There was room enough for a cot for the child Sarah would bring into the world. All was changing around her. She knew she was doing the right thing. The lid to her trunk was open. She would easily fit all of her clothes inside it. She would take her bluebird dress of course. It would be her wedding dress. What else would she take to America? Could she take a small embroidery frame with her? How long would she be on the ship? And where would she lie with her husband? She sat down on her bed and knew that she would miss her parents, but there was another life waiting for her across an ocean.

First, she must be married. Her father would understand and her mother would reconcile to it eventually. She brushed out her hair before she went down the stairs to her parents' bedroom. The door creaked as she opened it.

'My dear, there you are,' her father said. 'I hope you enjoyed a good evening.'

'Yes, I did, Father.' She sat on the bed beside her mother.

'You seem happy again, daughter.' Margaret brushed a strand of hair away from her daughter's face as she used to do when Abigail was a child.

'Did you like Mr. Gavin, Father?' Abigail asked.

'Very much so. He is indeed as fine as you painted him to be. It is a shame that he leaves for America. I am sorry that I will not see him again.'

It would be hard to leave them behind, but she had her own life to make. They would be safe when Sarah and Henry moved in.

'Abigail, this business will soon be behind us,' Margaret said and kissed her daughter. 'Now get to bed and we can talk more in the morning.'

'Mama, Papa, I have news,' she said.

'Yes?' her father said.

Both of her parents looked at her in anticipation.

'Mr. Gavin has proposed to me this evening. I have said yes. He will ask your permission in the morning, Father.'

At first her parents stared at her in astonishment, then they cried and held her close.

'Abigail, I had not thought you would find such a man,' her father said.

'Do you love him, Abigail?' her mother asked.

'Yes, I do, Mama,' she said. 'Are you not happy for me?'

'I know Mr. Gavin is a good man, Abigail. I only cry because he will take you away from us.'

CHAPTER 51

Brigid was up before dawn. She would make fish pie with oysters for the celebrations. It was Abigail's favourite. She liked the quietness of the streets at this hour. Beggars were still huddled in alleys trying to sleep though some merchants were already about, on their way to the Customs House no doubt. She heard a baby crying. Its mother sat on a doorstep and put the baby's mouth to her breast, her other babes snuggling beside her for warmth. For an instance she met the woman's eyes and looked away again.

Brigid reminded herself that she was one of the lucky ones as she walked over the bridge to the fishmonger stalls.

She concentrated on her immediate task. Cod would make a fine pie for the wedding meal. At the nearest fish stall, the young fishmonger looked her over. She asked what was on offer.

'Well, I'm on offer myself if you're interested, miss,' he said, winking at her.

'It is only the fish that I'm interested in, sir,' she said. She did not dare look him in the eye. She should have gone further down the road to her usual fishmonger.

'How many people do you intend to feed?' the young man asked.

She could hear the laughter in his voice and tried not to smile herself.

'It is for a wedding feast today. Three will be enough.'

'I hope you will be tasting some of it yourself,' he said.

'How much for the cod?' She really didn't have time for this nonsense. Abigail was getting married at ten o'clock and she had too much to do to be dillydallying with this boy.

'Well, since it's for a wedding, and if you promise to buy your fish from me in future, I'll let you have it for a good price. I'll even throw in a quart of oysters for free. What do you say?'

He told Brigid the price. She had expected to pay twice as much for the cod alone.

'I hope you're giving me fresh cod. I can't have my mistress's daughter sick on her wedding day.'

'It's today's catch. Fresh in off the boat this morning. I'm giving you a good price because I'd like if you'd buy from me every week.'

Brigid looked at the young fishmonger. She couldn't tell if he was being sincere. She watched as he wrapped the fish and oysters for her and liked the look of him.

'What is your name?' she asked.

'It is Niall Ryan, miss. May I ask yours?'

'My name is Brigid Reilly.'

'Well, I hope to see you next week, Brigid.'

'Miss Reilly to you, sir.'

'Miss Reilly it is so.' He bowed in adieu. She was a pretty thing, he thought, and he sincerely hoped that she would come back.

She tried to stop smiling when she got back across the river. Her basket seemed lighter. Despite herself, she was still grinning by the time she reached Pluncot Street. Back in the kitchen she unwrapped the fish and checked it again. The cod was very fresh, as were the oysters. She saw that the fishmonger had given her some anchovies too. She thought about his clear blue eyes, all the while chastising herself for daydreaming. She was being ridiculous. There was a fish pie to cook. Mrs. Harton had spared no expense. Brigid added salt and lemon juice to a pot of water. There were sweet herbs and pickled capers in the larder. She added them to the pot. Nutmeg and a few barberries went in too. When the pot was simmering, she busied herself filleting the fish, removing as many bones as she could find. Her stomach rumbled when she put the fish whole into the pot of warm water. If some cod's head was left over, she would save it for her own supper. It was one of her favourites. The sauce was next to be made, with wine, butter and eggs. She remembered to save some of the capers to serve with it later. She made a start on the pastry. By the time it was ready, the fish would be cooked. It was all going well.

The fires had already been lit in Abigail's and the mistress's bedrooms before she had left for the fishmonger's. All she had to do was light the fire in the dining room and the whole house would be warm by the time the wedding party returned. In the dining room Miss Abigail had already set out the place settings. All was ready.

When she went up to her room in the attic to change into her best dress, she could hear Miss Abigail moving about. On her way back downstairs, she knocked on her door.

'Is there anything I can get you, miss?'

Miss Abigail was very pale. Brigid thought again how lucky she was to have a place with the Hartons. She couldn't fathom how she would feel if she had to leave Ireland for good on a ship bound halfway around the world. Miss Abigail would be gone in a month, probably forever. She remembered the fishmonger. He would never leave Ireland. That made her smile again.

'Could you bring me up some sweet wine? My mother will dress my hair and I thought we could drink it here.'

'Yes, miss,' Brigid said and hesitated. 'I wish you luck today.'

'Thank you, Brigid.'

Abigail had been awake for hours. She had breakfasted in the kitchen when Brigid had gone out and had brought her parents their breakfast in bed. They were busy dressing in their finest clothes now, so she had some time to think.

She looked around her room. It was her last refuge before her world changed forever. She took in her surroundings. This was the last time she would sit on this bed. Tonight, she would lie with Mr. Gavin in Coles Alley. And next month that they would be on a ship bound for Boston. It was as if it was happening to someone else and not to her. She closed her eyes and breathed deeply. She wouldn't think of that now. Her mother would be here soon to help her dress her hair for the wedding. These were the last moments she would spend in her childhood room. She had to treasure every second.

Downstairs, in the kitchen Brigid poured two small glasses of wine and went back up to Abigail's room, thinking that she would fry the oysters in wine with some butter the moment the wedding party arrived home.

Abigail wore the blue poplin dress on her wedding day. It was the dress she loved best. Her brother Benjamin had loved the silver vines with the bluebirds embroidered on the poplin. To him, they had been the lovers from the fairytale, the Prince and Princess in their avian form. In a way Benjamin would be at the ceremony with them because of it. She brushed her hair and bound up soft curls on her head. Her mother had already helped her into her stays and gown. Mrs. Smyth, the apothecary's wife, had sent her primroses from her garden to put in her hair.

She trusted that she and Hugh would have a good life together, though her union would cost her dearly. She would never see her parents after she sailed, or Sarah and Henry, nor their unborn child. All the ribbons that tied her to her family were gradually unravelling.

Hugh stood at the altar waiting for Abigail Harton to become his wife. Her sister had arranged flowers on the altar for the ceremony.

When the Vicar announced the bride's arrival, he turned to face the altar. He couldn't believe that Abigail would be his from today. He hoped that she would find a way to love him as he did her. He looked back as she made her way up the aisle. In his eyes, she was truly the loveliest woman he had ever seen, inside and out.

Abigail tried to focus on his face so that she would not cry. Dean Swift seemed a long way away as she walked up the nave of the cathedral with her father. He was recovered well and steadied her as she approached the altar. She tried to concentrate on her part in the ceremony.

When the Dean announced that they were man and wife, her mother started to cry. She turned back to look at her parents and a sadness overwhelmed her. She hoped this wasn't the last image of them that she would carry with her across the sea.

Perhaps she would return to Dublin someday if she and her husband made their fortune. She thanked God her parents had Sarah and Henry to take care of them. There would be a small child in the house and they would find joy there. She would write to them and only give them good news from her new home, no matter how lonely she felt.

When the ceremony was over, Hugh took her hand and together they walked out of the cathedral into spring sunshine. Then the wedding party made their way back to the Harton household and enjoyed the feast that Brigid had prepared.

Abigail could barely eat her food as she sat next to Hugh. He was her husband but it didn't seem real yet.

After they had finished their meal, the party made their way into the drawing room. Abigail looked at all of her family before her and wondered if leaving them all would be too hard to bear. She would miss everyone very much, most especially her parents. She spent another several happy hours reminiscing with her mother and father and Sarah, all the while wishing that Benjamin was with them.

When she was ready to leave, she nodded to Hugh.

There was much laughter in the room until they were finally

allowed to go on their way. Sarah hugged Abigail before she let her go.

'I am sorry that you will not get to meet your niece or nephew,' she said.

'I'm sorry too,' Abigail said.

'I have something for you,' Sarah said and went down into their father's office. Abigail followed her downstairs. When Sarah emerged back into the hall, she pressed the book of fairy tales into her sister's hands. 'I want you to have them to remember us by.'

'But they are for you, Sarah, and the baby.' Abigail tried to give the book back to her sister.

'They were always yours, Abigail. It is right that you should have them.'

Hugh stepped outside to wait for his wife to say goodbye to Sarah. His sister had left the Harton household earlier with Mr. Long. They had stood as bridesmaid and groomsman and Mary had been honoured by the gesture. He looked back at his new wife at the door of Pluncot Street. He couldn't quite believe that Abigail Harton belonged to him. She was his responsibility and he would keep her safe. No harm would come to her while she was in his care, he would make sure of it. He hoped that would be the case for the rest of his life.

He waited on the street as Abigail walked down the steps from the house and held her hand as they made their way towards Francis Street.

'Let's take a walk down to the river,' he said, and Abigail nodded. He could see tears in her eyes. He hoped that they were for her parents and not because of the new life she was about to start with him.

'I am sorry to leave them all behind,' she said.

'I know, Abigail.' He hugged her close to him. 'But you will not be alone.'

They spent an hour walking, to say goodbye to the city they would soon leave forever.

When they reached the house on Coles Alley, Hugh took her in his arms and carried her across the threshold. Mr. Long, Mary and Michael were at the hall door to welcome them. Mary poured four glasses of wine and they toasted the union again.

They sat and talked and Mr. Long stayed with them for another while. Mary eventually gave him a look to go and he bid them adieu.

When she had cleared the table, she promised the new couple that she would make a hearty breakfast in the morning, before leaving them to go to bed.

Now it was just Abigail and Hugh in the kitchen. He dampened down the fire and took her hand in his.

'We must get some rest,' he said.

She rose and went to sleep with her husband for the first time.

In the morning Miss Gavin and the boy sat and ate breakfast with the new couple. She noticed how they touched hands as they sat side by side. How they stole small glances at each other. She looked away and tried to concentrate on her porridge.

'When I am older, might I go to Virginia too? I would work for you of course,' young Michael said.

'You will be welcome, Michael, when you have finished your apprenticeship with Mr. Long.' He tousled the boy's hair.

'You could come too, Miss Gavin,' Michael said.

'Hush now, boy. I'll not be travelling past Dublin again, never mind across an ocean. If you are to join my brother, you'd best be planning on going without me.'

'Never mind my sister, Michael. She will likely join us but only when I have made my fortune.'

The boy laughed.

'Well, I hope it keeps fine for you,' Mary said.

CHAPTER 52

When at last the day came to sail, Hugh and Abigail rose early. They would call into Pluncot Street before boarding the *Charlotte*, bound for Boston. Abigail's hands were shaking as she packed the last of her belongings into her trunk.

They ate in silence until they heard the rumble of a cart outside.

'There's Mr. Long in the yard. You'd best make a start now,' Mary said.

Hugh said goodbye to his sister and the boy in the yard, hugging them both tightly together.

Mr. Long helped load their two trunks on his cart.

'Mary,' Abigail said, 'I never told you how much I appreciated your help last year. I will be forever grateful and will make it my duty to keep your brother happy.'

'I know you will, Abigail. So long as you love him, that is all that he needs.' She kissed the young woman goodbye. She looked at Daniel Long and was happy that she had accepted his proposal.

'Goodbye, sister,' Abigail said before turning away.

Mary watched as her brother helped his new wife onto the cart. Daniel was already seated, ready to drive.

'Be safe now,' she said and watched as they left Coles Alley for the last time.

In Pluncot Street, her mother and Sarah found it hard to let her go. Abigail kissed her father goodbye for the last time. His sickness had made him seem older and she would cry on the ocean many times, remembering his face.

'I will write every month,' she said as she walked out into the street.

There she hugged her parents and Brigid and Sarah and Henry goodbye again. She would not cry in front of them. It was best that her mother and father think her strong. Both would worry less that way when she was gone.

'You will write to let us know when you safely reach Boston and when you have settled in Virginia,' her mother said.

'Yes, Mama. Rest assured, I will tell you all of my news.' Abigail gave her mother another kiss goodbye.

Hugh could not remember his own parents well. They had died when he had turned six. He could not imagine how she must feel. It would not be the same as leaving his sister Mary behind. His wife most probably would never see her family again.

He shook Dr. Harton's hand and bade Mrs. Harton farewell and helped Abigail back onto the cart before climbing on himself.

'I will keep her safe,' he said and waved them goodbye.

Mr. Long delivered the newlyweds to the quayside in plenty of time. He helped load the trunks onto the ship, bid them goodbye and hoped that he might see them again in this lifetime.

As dawn broke, the *Charlotte* set sail and made her way out of Dublin port and out into the Irish sea.

Hugh and Abigail stood side by side on deck.

'We will have a good life, just you wait and see, Abigail,' he said.

It was cold on deck and he drew her closer to him, pulling his cloak around her to keep her warm. She encircled her arms around him and looked out onto the open water, wondering what lay ahead for them both.

Life was a funny thing, she thought. She should have been afraid but found for the first time in her life she was not. As they lost sight of land, she was excited for her future. For her life with Hugh Gavin. If chance had differed, she might have been Mrs. William Monroe instead. She shivered thinking about it and felt her husband hold her tighter. She looked into his honest face and knew that she had lost her heart to him forever.

CHAPTER 53

Radburn opened the letter from Alden's secretary in London. It informed him that his master's son had died in London of the smallpox. The child had not reached his first birthday. Radburn was instructed to burn the boy's belongings. His master and mistress would not return to Dublin. The secretary Mr. French added that the castle would be sold at the Duke's convenience and that he would be informed of the new owner in due course.

Radburn was sorry that the boy had died, though he was pleased that his master would not return. He had kept the servants away from the north-west tower room on the third floor, telling everyone that the key had been lost. He had let the girl die in the secret room. She may have survived for few days but what else could he have done? Thankfully, the smell had started to fade. It would be safest to leave her body there until he considered what to do with it.

He had feigned illness that morning, declining to go to service. When all was quiet, he stepped into the room, opened the priest's hiding hole in the corner and went inside. The smell was still quite bad in the enclosed space. He hadn't noticed the fine metal threads in her dress before. They were probably worth retrieving, though that was too macabre, even for him. He turned his gaze from her ghastly face and staring eyes but couldn't resist the impulse to look. It was only then that he noticed her earrings with their large jewels. He reached out but stayed his hand. The girl's death could easily be blamed on him. He would hang for it. He was not going to take that chance. It was best to leave well enough alone.

Mrs. Goulding, the dead girl's mother, had been to visit the castle several times since the ball, looking for her daughter. When she told him Dr. Monroe had disappeared too, he said he had seen her with the upstart that night – no doubt she had run off with him and it was best to forget about her. But the woman didn't want to forget. She kept sending letters to the Duchess addressed to the castle. He acknowledged them though he never sent them on to London. God was smiling on him, especially as the Aldens would not be returning.

In the meantime, he thought that he might marry. Mrs. Wright was a scrawny thing, but he could abide that. It would further tighten his control over the staff who tended to meander in the castle when the family was not at home. If Mrs. Wright was willing, he would have her.

He turned the key in the lock for the last time and put it back in the spine of his daybook. He left the tower room, locked the door and took the key with him. He would keep the door locked for as long as he could. Back in his office, he secured the book under the floorboards.

Once he had hidden the book, he left the castle to see his cousin in town, a carpenter. He would commission him to remove the loose panel and its hidden mechanism and replace it with solid timber, making the wainscotting a solid floor-to-ceiling barrier between the room and the priest's hole. If anyone asked, he would say that the repairs had been ordered by Alden himself. When a new owner was found, they need never know of the secret room behind the wainscotting where he hoped the girl would sit for all eternity.

He had tried to find the stone that had fallen from her ring, but it must have fallen through the floorboards, for he couldn't find it. Like the earrings, it would be risky to have it on his person anyway or attempt to sell it.

As Radburn walked through the castle grounds on his way to the city, he glanced up and thought someone was watching him from the tower-room window. He dismissed the movement as the sun glanced off the glass and didn't give the matter another thought.

CHAPTER 54

Dublin, Present Day

I had a week left in Dublin and had already booked my tickets home. Aunt Jeannie had deteriorated further and I was anxious to show her the Professor's research on Hugh Gavin and his sister Mary before she got any worse.

I called to the Professor's office after lunch and I was glad he was there. I would miss him.

'There you are, Lucy. How was your morning?'

'It was good. I bought an extra suitcase.'

The Professor laughed.

'Well, you'll be delighted to know that I've made some progress while you were out shopping. The Duchess of Alden's letters came out of storage yesterday.'

'Really? Have you read them already? What did they say?'

'I've only read a few. I found several to the Duchess from a Mrs. Goulding.'

'Who was she?'

'She and her husband were landowners in Galway. It seems her daughter, Elizabeth Goulding, attended the Boden Castle Ball in December 1719 and never returned home. Her mother believed she had eloped with a lover but she doesn't name him. I'll read the rest of the letters this evening to see if there's any other mention of him. Mrs. Goulding tells the Duchess that she has exhausted all her acquaintances in Dublin looking for her daughter, including the dressmaker, a Miss Mary Gavin of Coles Alley, Dublin, who delivered a dress of emerald damask to Elizabeth the day she disappeared. In the letters, Mrs. Goulding appeals to the Duchess for the Duke's intervention in the matter.'

'So that was the connection with the castle? So much for my family having blue blood. I was hoping the Miss Gavin had married into the aristocracy, so that we could at least claim a tenuous connection. Aunt Jeannie is going to be seriously disappointed.' I smiled and took out a journal to make some notes.

'I'm afraid it does seem that you come from peasant stock after all, Miss Young.'

I laughed with him and told him that he was probably no better than me.

'It's interesting though … you'll be interested to know that Mrs. Goulding also mentions a Miss Abigail Harton in her letters. It looks like she worked as an embroideress for Mary Gavin.'

I remembered something and took out my laptop. I opened the *Charlotte*'s manifest file from 1720 with a list of the passenger names.

'See where the *Charlotte*'s manifest lists Hugh Gavin's wife's name. Could that be an 'A'? Could this Abigail have become Hugh Gavin's wife or am I grasping at straws?'

'She could have. And here's another link – Mrs. Goulding mentions that Miss Harton was the daughter of a Dr. John Harton …' He raised an eyebrow at me.

'The same Dr. Harton who saved the Duchess and her baby son earlier the previous year?'

'Yes, indeed.' The Professor grinned. 'Aunt Jeannie was getting close. This is the Alden connection she was hoping for with your family.'

I thought of Jeannie and wished that she could be here with me.

'You can read the rest of the Goulding letters for yourself, Lucy. I'll take you over to the Long Room archive this afternoon.'

'What about Abigail Harton? Is there a way to find out more about her too?'

'There is another avenue we can try.' The Professor smiled. 'Leave it with me.'

We went over to the Long Room Library, running over the cobbles in the rain. As I walked up the stairs, I wondered if the Duchess of Alden had ever responded to Mrs. Goulding's letters, and asked the Professor.

'Unfortunately, we have no record of them if she did,' he said.

While I waited for the Goulding letters to be brought out, I took out my laptop again and searched on the internet for Abigail Harton's name. As I expected, there weren't any references to that name from that time.

Who was she? And where had she lived in Dublin?

The Professor brought the letters down to my desk and we looked through them together. The writing was clear but looked hurried. I couldn't imagine how Mrs. Goulding must have felt when she wrote them. To lose her sixteen-year-old daughter and not to know what had happened to her didn't bear thinking about. As I read on, it was evident that Mrs. Goulding was convinced that the Duke of Alden had helped the lover – a Dr. William Monroe.

'Alden and Monroe may have been friends,' the Professor said.

'How could that be when Monroe was a lowly doctor?'

'He was an associate of Dr. Harton who had saved Alden's wife. Maybe Alden felt obliged to help him.'

'I read that Alden was a scoundrel and not likely to be obliged to anyone.'

'There were not many doctors who could save the life of a wife and child then. It could be that in this instance his feelings were an exception to the rule.'

'Maybe you're right.'

I searched the internet to see if I could find a reference to doctors in Dublin who had practised in 1719. On the results page, I found a link to Marsh's Library which had been founded in 1701. It was situated beside St. Patrick's Cathedral where Jonathan Swift had been Dean at that time. The library had existed when Doctors Harton and Monroe had practised in Dublin and it had a repository of medical texts and pamphlets from the 17th and 18th centuries. I checked my watch. It had already closed for the day. I would have to wait until tomorrow to visit, to see if I could find a reference for Abigail's father Dr. John Harton there.

After reading Mrs. Goulding's letters in the library, I left the Professor and went back to the hotel. I decided to leave my research for the evening and have an early night.

It was almost time to go back to my real life across the ocean. I needed to plan for the future. First, I would visit my Aunt Jeannie to let her know what the Professor and I had discovered about Hugh Gavin. Then I would go home to Los Angeles and visit my mother and sister. I hadn't seen them since my cancelled wedding. I felt the pain of it surfacing again but I had to face it. My fiancé had slept with someone else. It was that simple. We were both lawyers in the same firm and I didn't know if I could go back to work there with him. I would figure it out when I got home. This trip had been a welcome diversion but it wasn't real life. There were other jobs, and hopefully another person that I could start to build a life with. I just had to have the courage to go out and find whoever that was. When Aunt Jeannie had suggested that I take a break and go to Ireland to trace our Irish family ancestors I had jumped at the chance. Now it was time to face reality.

My cell phone rang. It was the Professor.

'Hi Lucy, I'm sorry to disturb you.'

'Not at all. I was just thinking of asking if you'd like to meet for dinner.'

'I'd like that,' he said.

'Are you still at the office?'

'Yes. I'll walk over and pick you up at your hotel in twenty minutes. Is that OK?'

'Sure. I'll wait for you in the bar.'

'Great. I was calling you with an update actually. I found a newspaper announcement from November 1719. It mentions Dr. Harton. It's bad news, I'm afraid.'

'Oh no. What did you find?'

'A death in the family – a young boy – and I don't think Abigail Harton could have been Hugh Gavin's wife.'

'Why not?'

'I'll fill you in at dinner, OK?'

'OK. See you then.' I took a quick shower to freshen up and was down waiting in the bar before the Professor arrived.

'There you are,' he said and came over to my table, reaching over to kiss me on the cheek.

I gulped my wine as he took out a photocopy and handed it to me. I tried to focus on the page in front of me. It was from a very old newspaper called *Thomas Humes – The Dublin Courant*.

I read: **October 23rd, 1719: Master Benjamin Harton, Aged 9 years. Buried at St. Patrick's Cathedral, son of Dr. John Harton of Pluncot Street and John's Lane Free Hospital.**

'He must have been Abigail Harton's little brother,' I said.

'Yes. Poor little mite. There's another mention of Dr. Harton in a later edition. Here it is …' He handed me another photocopy, again from the *Dublin Courant*.

November 17th, 1719: Dr. and Mrs. Harton of Pluncot Street announce the engagement of their daughter Miss Abigail

Harton to Dr. William Monroe, of John's Lane Free Hospital.

'So she wasn't Hugh Gavin's wife ... I'm so disappointed. I was really hoping that we'd solved that piece of the puzzle.'

'We may never know who he married.'

'It mentions a free hospital? What does that mean?'

'Dublin was an advanced centre for medicine in the early 18th Century if you can believe it. The Rotunda Hospital in Dublin City is said to be one of the first maternity hospitals in Europe.'

'That's amazing. So Abigail's father was a doctor and a philanthropist?'

'Yes, and by the looks of it so was Abigail's husband Dr. Monroe.'

'I wonder why Mrs. Goulding mentioned Abigail in her letters to the Duchess.'

'Her daughter Elizabeth and Abigail may have become friends.'

'But wait a minute. Wasn't Dr. Monroe the name of Elizabeth's supposed lover?' I asked and my stomach rumbled.

He laughed. 'You're really hungry. Do you want to eat here?'

'That would be great.'

He called over the waiter and we placed our order.

'I'll miss our research when I get back home,' I said.

'Perhaps we can stay in touch?'

'I'd like that,' I said. 'Besides, we haven't solved the mystery yet.'

He laughed and I sipped a glass of the water that had been brought to the table.

'You were talking about Dr. Monroe and Elizabeth ...'

'Yes. Elizabeth's parents would have expected her to marry someone from the gentry, and medics were considered tradesmen in their day. So of course she would have to elope. But how can that be when Dr. Monroe was Abigail Harton's fiancé at the time?'

'Perhaps Dr. Monroe acted as a decoy, and Elizabeth had another lover? Maybe that's why her mother and father couldn't track her down.'

'It's puzzling all right.'

Our dinner arrived at the table. The food was delicious. I reached for my glass of wine as did the Professor. Our hands touched accidently. He looked over and I held his gaze for a second too long. We ate in silence for a minute while I pretended to read the ancient newspaper.

'Frank has invited us out to Boden Castle tomorrow,' the Professor said. 'They've opened up some old tunnels in the basement that I'd like to see. We could take another look around the castle too, if you like? We might even find what the castle's account-book key opened if we're lucky. Though I expect whatever it may have been is no longer there.'

'I'd love to go,' I said and felt like a kid in a playground.

'Great, I'll bring the key with me.'

The Professor went on to tell me about his research. And eventually I found myself telling him about the reason that had first prompted my travel to Dublin on Aunt Jeannine's behalf and of how my mom had wanted me to marry my fiancé despite his affair.

'I almost got married myself once.' He smiled though it didn't quite reach his eyes.

'Were you together long?'

'Seven years. Doesn't seem so long now, though it did at the time. Ann and I bought the house where I live, you know … Thinking about it, I should have known it wouldn't work. We were completely different people. She was Italian and wanted to live in Rome and be with her family. I wanted to research and continue my career here. We thought we could compromise. Go to Italy in the summer and live in Dublin during the academic year. It all sounded perfect on paper, but in the end it didn't work. So, I bought out her half of the house and we agreed to go our separate ways.'

'I'm sorry,' I said.

'It was no-one's fault really. We parted friends two years ago, but still stay in touch. She invited me to her wedding next month, to an Italian banker would you believe.'

'Are you going to go?'

'I might . . . if I had someone new to bring along.'

'Well, I might be available,' I said and smiled.

When he looked up at me, I laughed and took my last sip of wine. 'It's getting late. Should we get the check?'

'I'll get this,' he said and called the waiter. 'I'll miss you, Lucy.'

'And I you.'

The waiter came over and the Professor paid the bill, giving the young man a handsome tip.

'I'll pick you up in the morning at ten and we'll go straight to the castle. How does that sound?'

'I'll be waiting outside for you,' I said.

He got up and we hugged an awkward goodbye.

'Is there any way to find out who Hugh's wife might have been before I leave?'

'I'll ask Gráinne to take another look in the morning. But I can't promise you anything.'

'See you tomorrow then.'

I watched him leave the bar and wondered what he would do when he got home. More study, I supposed. Then I remembered the key from the old accounts book. I hoped I'd get a chance to see which lock it opened at the castle.

On the drive out to Boden the next day, the Professor was quiet. The traffic was heavy and when we at last arrived there were only a few parking slots left in the castle's car park.

Walking up to the castle, I glanced up at the north-west flanker tower. There was no-one at the window on the third floor.

Frank was waiting in the entrance hall and greeted us when we stepped inside.

'Are you all right, Frank?' the Professor asked when the guide dropped a large jangle of keys on the floor.

'Don't mind me. We had a call this morning from the President's office. He was to visit this afternoon but had to move his schedule up and now we are expecting him within the hour. There's still a lot of preparation to do.'

'We can come back tomorrow, if that suits better,' I said.

'Not at all. I can't stay with you long though. Come on, no time to waste. Follow me.'

The keys Frank held were much bigger than the one I'd found in the spine of the castle book. Perhaps the key didn't open a door after all, though it was large enough? Could it have been for a strongbox of some kind instead?

'I saw our ghost Isobel yesterday, Lucy,' Frank said.

'Not the ghost story again,' the Professor said. 'You're losing the run of yourself altogether, Frank. You'll be seeing the Virgin Mary next.'

'Leave him be, Professor. Ignore him, Frank. I believe you,' I said, trying to hide a smile.

'I'm used to him, Lucy, don't worry about it.'

We followed Frank down to the basement where an old entrance way had been found.

'Mind yourselves in there. There's not a lot to see, I'm afraid.'

The basement felt cold and damp.

'I hope we don't bump into Isobel's ghost down here,' I said.

The Professor was peering through the passageway off the basement that led down to more tunnels.

'There's no evidence that she ever existed, so I think we'll be pretty safe,' the Professor said. 'The Earl had two daughters and neither of them were named Isobel. The ghost story was just a Victorian marketing ruse to get people out from Dublin for the castle tours.'

'Oh, I didn't know they did that kind of thing back then,' I said. Maybe the person I'd seen in the tower on my first trip out had just been a shadow from the sun, or a figment of my imagination.

'Watch your step here, Lucy.'

'Is it safe to go on?'

'Let me see first.'

The Professor shone the flashlight on his iPhone up towards the roof and then back down to the ground.

'It seems safe enough,' he said.

We walked on for about twenty feet through darkened cobwebbed tunnels.

'What's at the other end?' I asked.

'I think this one goes under the main road and comes out at the Church in the village. It' a little way yet, Lucy. Be careful where you step.'

After another ten feet, I tripped and fell against a medieval door. The large ring handle was rusted and appeared not to have been opened for a long time.

'Do you think we should turn back?' I felt a shiver run down my spine.

'Maybe it's open,' the Professor said. He pulled at the handle and it came off in his hand. Then the door opened as if someone on the other side was welcoming us in. I moved as close to the Professor as I could.

'I think we should go back,' I said.

The Professor wasn't listening to me and carried on through to the other side. I had left my phone at the hotel and with no light I was forced to follow him. I held on to his arm and we walked a little further on rough ground. My spidey-sense told me that we were circling back. After another five minutes a second door brought us back into the basement of the castle, albeit on the other side. The floor was oozing dampness from the recent rains and I could hear footsteps above.

'This will bring us back up to the old Victorian kitchen,' the Professor said, and closed the door behind us.

'That was very creepy,' I said, glad to be back on solid ground.

'I hope you're not referring to me?' he said, and I laughed.

'Obviously not, Professor.'

'That door over there leads to the flanker tower on the west.' He pushed opened a small door and stooped to go through. I felt like Alice in Wonderland for a moment until I realised that we were back in the tower that was being renovated. We were in the tower that Frank and I thought the ghost Isobel was haunting.

'We can get out to the main hall from here,' the Professor said.

'Wait. I want to have a look.'

I took the flashlight from his hand and directed the beam up towards the damaged corner of the room. There was no first-floor ceiling because of the staircase leading up to the second floor in this tower, but the second-floor ceiling had fallen away in the corner and the floorboards in the room above had been exposed. At the edge, a floorboard had been removed and I could see into the base of the third-floor tower room. Then I noticed it. A small door behind the wood panelling up there.

'What do you see?' the Professor asked.

'Maybe it's nothing ... look ..."

The Professor followed me over to the other side of the staircase.

'In the room above, do you see a small door in the wall?'

'I'm not sure. We'll have to go up there to check it out.'

'OK,' I said and wondered if it could be the door that the mystery key opened?

'There you are. I thought I'd lost you both,' Frank called out as we emerged into the second-floor anteroom.

'We got lost in the tunnels and somehow ended back in here,' I said.

'Not to worry, though I'm going to have to ask you both to leave soon. The President will be here in less than half an hour. You're very welcome to come back tomorrow.'

'Of course, Frank,' the Professor said. 'We'll get out of your way. Thanks for letting us explore the tunnels. We appreciate it.'

'Shouldn't we tell him about the hidden door?' I asked.

'He probably already knows about it, Lucy. And besides, he's got a lot on his mind today. We can talk to him in the morning.'

'What about the key?'

The Professor smiled. 'Here, you take it for safe keeping until tomorrow.'

I took the key from the Professor and slipped it into my pocket.

He dropped me back to the hotel and we agreed to meet up the next morning at ten o'clock. The Professor had a meeting in the afternoon so I decided to have lunch in the hotel. As I was walking past the check-in desk, a receptionist called me over. There was a parcel delivery from California for me. The address was in my sister Becca's handwriting.

I went up to my room and took a quick shower. Then I ordered room service and took the brown-paper box tied up with string to the bed. I wondered why Becca had sent it to me. It wasn't even close to my birthday. When I removed the paper, there was a wooden box made of walnut inside. It looked very old. The hinges and clasp hadn't been cleaned or polished for a long time. There was a note with it.

Hi Lucy, thought you'd be interested in this. Cousin Emma in Baltimore sent it by Fedex today. She had been helping Aunt Jeannie with her research. Hope it helps you find what you're looking for, Love Becca x

I opened the clasp at the front of the box and found an assortment of little tools and cloth inside. It seemed to be an elaborate sewing kit of some kind. There was a small scissors that folded. Pieces of red and blue thread were wrapped around what looked like white bone or ivory. There were two bobbins and three spools of various colour threads on top of a small faded pink pin cushion. A small wooden egg-shaped object was nestled in the corner of the box and inside it held three different sized needles that looked so fragile I was afraid to handle them. There was even a tool with a slim wooden handle that looked like a Lilliputian whaling hook. Underneath the tools lay a piece of blue cloth with two beautiful bluebirds turned towards each other on a small branch embroidered with silver thread. A neat row of pins pierced the cloth. It was a very old embroidery tool set. On the lid of the box, the initials *A.H.* had been engraved.

Could A.H. stand for Abigail Harton?

The base of the drawer in the box seemed high and I wondered if it had a hidden drawer. I'd seen the type on *Antiques Roadshow* before. I felt inside the lid and gently turned the box upside down. There was a metal spring device there and I pressed it. A little drawer opened. Unfortunately, there was no hidden treasure inside, just an old piece of paper. I took it out gently and unfolded the yellow parchment. It was a letter, in copperplate script.

I brought the letter to the light and carefully read it.

30th June 1772

My dearest Lorna,

I give your grandmother Abigail's embroidery box to you on the occasion of your marriage. Promise to pass it to one of your own daughters when it is time. You were a child when my mother Abigail was taken from us. She loved you dearly and made me make the same promise that I ask of you today.

The cloth inside is from a piece of her wedding dress when she was married to your grandfather Hugh Gavin in Dublin, Ireland, all of those years ago. Mama told me that she had embroidered the bluebirds on the dress herself from a fairytale that she used to read to her brother Benjamin before he died. When the dress was too old to wear, she kept a piece as a reminder of Benjamin and a memory of her wedding day at St. Patrick's Cathedral.

I wish you every happiness in your new home with Jonathan and hope that you will live as fulfilled a life as I have had with your father.

Your loving mother,

Henriette

Rochester County, New York

The sentiment in the letter was so tender that I brushed tears aside. This was proof that Abigail Harton had married Hugh Gavin. Finally, Aunt Jeannie would have a happy ending. Miss Elizabeth Goulding may have eloped with Dr. Monroe after all. It must have been a scandal in its day. Abigail, though, had found happiness with her husband, Hugh. I folded the letter and put the contents of the box back inside for safekeeping, touching the initials A.H. on the sewing-box lid as I closed it shut. I would cherish it forever.

To think that I held Abigail Harton's sewing box in my hands at that very moment was incredible and that I was now in the city where she had first used it three hundred years before. How Aunt Jeannine would love to hear the whole story.

I had only a few days left in Dublin and would miss it and my visits with the Professor too. It was strange how a person I hardly knew could spark something new inside.

After a restless night, the next morning I received a text from the Professor asking me to meet him at the café in the National Library for breakfast. I got out of the bed and made my way there as fast as I could, taking the sewing box with me.

'You look a little tired this morning,' the Professor said when I arrived.

'I've been tossing and turning all night.' I took the box out of my bag. 'Look what I received in the post yesterday from my sister.'

The Professor watched as I showed him the initials A.H. on the outside.

'*A.H.* Could it be Abigail Harton's embroidery box?' he asked.

'It is. I can't believe it myself. Abigail married Hugh Gavin after all. Look what was inside ...'

I opened the box and gave him Henriette's letter to read.

'It's beautiful,' he said. 'What a wonderful thing to have. You certainly come from a very special family, Lucy.'

'I am so proud to have Abigail and Henriette as my ancestors.'

I watched as the Professor ran his hand over the initials of the box.

'So Abigail was inspired by a fairy tale to create the bluebird design,' he said.

'Yes. I would love to find out if we still have that book in our family.'

'If anyone will know, it'll be your Aunt Jeannie.'

'I wonder how Abigail felt, though, when her fiancé Dr. Monroe seduced the young Miss Elizabeth Goulding and left her in the lurch.'

'We don't know that happened, Lucy. Anything could have happened to Elizabeth. Though as Mrs. Goulding pleads with the Duchess for help to find Monroe in her letters, it's probably what happened.'

'I wonder if Mrs. Goulding ever located her daughter.'

'We probably will never know.'

'It must have been devasting for Elizabeth's mother and father. She must have really been in love with this Dr. Monroe, and he with her, to run away like that,' I said. 'Allegedly.'

'And Abigail Harton was jilted.'

'What a scoundrel,' I said, thinking of my own ex-fiancé.

'I have one other piece of evidence that you should see before you leave, Lucy. I was looking for references to dressmakers online and found a link for a dressmaker's account book dating from 1717 to 1719 in Dublin. When I clicked the link, guess who I found it belonged to?'

'Miss Mary Gavin.'

'Precisely. It's a great find even if I do say so myself.'

I smiled at his enthusiasm which matched mine. 'It is indeed, Professor. Where is the book now?'

'Right here in the National Library, upstairs in the reading room and waiting for us. When you finish your breakfast, I'll show it to you.'

I took a bite of my pastry and one last gulp of my coffee and said I was ready to go. After I had checked in my bag at security, I followed him upstairs and sat down at an empty desk. The Professor went to the small anteroom and came out with two pairs of white gloves, which we both put on before opening the three-hundred-year-old book. The cover was made of vellum and must have cost Mary Gavin a pretty penny. The Professor looked through the pages.

'Look, Lucy, it's almost the last entry. See there, a payment to Abigail Harton.'

'It says she paid Abigail for embroidery on a green silk gown with bluebirds on gold and silver vines for a Miss Elizabeth Goulding. It's the same pattern on the piece of cloth in Abigail's sewing box, the piece of cloth from her wedding dress.'

'And look here,' the Professor said as he turned back the pages to a previous entry, 'it seems Abigail sold an original bluebird pattern to Hugh Gavin earlier in the year. That was unusual for a woman to do in those days.'

I sat back in my seat and tried to take it all in.

'Abigail Harton had known Elizabeth, the girl who had absconded with her fiancé after the Boden Ball,' I said. 'How must she have felt about that? Utterly devasted probably.'

'I can only imagine, poor girl,' the Professor said. 'The book definitely belongs to our Mary Gavin. It ties in to our earlier research. It's the same Mary Gavin who went to Belfast and gives you a direct connection between Hugh Gavin, Abigail Harton and Elizabeth, who were all connected to Boden Castle in some way. That must have been where your family's story originated – the scandal of Elizabeth Goulding and Dr. William Monroe eloping together the night of the Boden Castle Ball. I hope your Aunt Jeannie will be satisfied with what you've discovered.'

'I couldn't have made the connections without you,' I said and hugged him.

'Then we'll have to celebrate,' he said, and we stood apart again. 'How about tonight?'

He laughed and said yes, and that he would book the restaurant later.

'I've had an idea,' he said. 'Now that we know that Abigail was married at St. Patrick's Cathedral, why don't we search their registers for Baptisms, Marriages & Burials. If my memory serves me correctly, there were records published in 1907 that cover the period from 1677 to 1800. The original records are held in the Representative Church Body Library in Braemor Park which is close enough to Boden Castle. We could stop off there on the way. We might find an entry for her wedding to Hugh Gavin. It had to have taken place after the announcement of her engagement in the *Dublin Courant* in 1719 and before she and Hugh Gavin left on the *Charlotte* for Boson in 1720. Would you like to go now? We can call Frank and delay our meeting at the castle until this afternoon.'

'That would be great, Professor.'

We drove to the library in Braemor Park and had to buzz at the main door to gain entry. The Professor had to take a call outside so gave me his card. I went upstairs to the reception desk. A young man was sitting at the desk.

'Can I help you?' he asked.

'I'd like to look at the marriage records for St. Patrick's Cathedral if that's possible. I'm trying to figure out about a love story from the early 1700s.'

The librarian looked at his watch and I looked at mine. I realised the library was about to close for lunch.

'I'm sorry, I could come back at another time,' I said.

'No, it's all right. My lunch can wait. If we have a love story to unravel, then we'd better get started. Tell me more.'

I smiled and gave him the details of Abigail Harton and Hugh Gavin. I told him that if they had married the wedding would have taken place between November 1719 and the date the ship the *Charlotte* left Dublin for America in 1720.

'Well, those records are not on the shelves. If you wait here, I'll bring them out to you,' he said, and then disappeared through the side door.

'Thanks so much,' I called out after him but he had gone.

As I waited the Professor came up the stairs to join me.

'Any luck?' he asked.

'Maybe. We'll have to wait and find out.'

The librarian reappeared. 'Hi Professor, it's good to see you again,' he said with a smile.

'Hi, Paul,' the Professor said. 'Did Lucy introduce herself? No? Well, this is Lucy Young, all the way from California.'

'Good to meet you, Lucy.'

'Likewise.'

'Come with me into the reading room. You'll need to be careful. The paper is fragile.'

At the desk, the librarian opened the protective box that held the register. I carefully opened the book and searched through the records from October 1719 onwards, turning each page, hoping to find Abigail's name. It was there, towards the start of the entries.

29th March 1720, Hugh Gavin of the Liberties and Abigail Harton of St. Nicholas Wthout were joynd together in Holy Matrimony.

That was all it said.

It was a wonderful moment.

I took a photo of the page and sent it to my sister Becca in California.

'I'm glad you were able to find the record you were looking for,' the librarian said.

'Thank you,' I said. 'It's been quite a journey to find Hugh Gavin and Miss Abigail Harton, I can tell you.'

'I'm delighted to have helped solve the mystery,' the librarian said.

'Enjoy your lunch,' I said with a smile.

'I will.'

Outside, we stood and looked at each other.

'What now?' the Professor asked. 'Do you want to get lunch before we go to the castle?'

'We can have lunch in the visitor's café there. I can't wait any longer to see what's behind the panelling in that tower room.'

'Let's go then,' the Professor said and we made our way back to his car.

As we walked, I wondered what had been on Abigail's mind when she had married Hugh that day. Had she been in love with him? Had he loved her too? I guessed I would never really know.

CHAPTER 55

The key that I had found in the spine of the castle accounts book had been burning a hole in my pocket since the day before when the Professor had handed it to me. I probably wouldn't be visiting Dublin again any time soon so I had to discover its purpose now.

When we arrived, the Professor quickly checked his email in the car.

'Good news, Lucy. The university's conservation team were able to restore the spine of the castle accounts book. I thought you'd like to know before you leave.'

'That's such a relief, Professor. Thanks for letting me know.'

'Let's go see if we can find the door the key opens. Though with renovations over the centuries, it may be no longer there.'

Frank met us at the main entrance of the castle.

After we had shown him the key, we told him of a possible door behind the panelling in the north-west tower room on the third floor. He was as intrigued as we were, and the three of us set off up the servants' staircase to the main room on that level. We walked down a narrow corridor and came to the tower-room door. Frank opened it just as a beam of light shone in from the tower window, making large moving shapes on the wall. I had to force myself to go inside.

The day had become overcast and the light in the room dimmed as a result.

I went across to the loose panelling to see if I could move it out far enough out to find a lock in the hidden door behind it. But when I got close, the wooden panelling came loose of its own accord and fell to the floor, barely missing my head. I covered my mouth and nose from the dust until it settled.

'Are you all right?' the Professor asked, pulling me towards him.

'I'm OK,' I said though I was more than a little shaken.

'There's the door, Lucy, and it has a keyhole. You've come this far. You'll have to open it.'

I stepped up to the door, careful to avoid the gap in the floor, and put the key into the lock. It turned as easily as if it had been oiled that morning.

The door opened and I peered inside, trying to make out the shapes there.

The Professor shone his phone's flashlight in the tiny room and my heart leapt as I saw a figure sitting in the enclosed space.

'Oh my God,' Frank whispered. 'It's Isobel.'

'I can't believe it,' the Professor said and stepped inside.

I was so scared I couldn't speak.

Then I forced myself to go in too.

Frank stayed in the doorway.

The Professor shone his flashlight on the dress. It wasn't medieval. It was an 18th century court dress. The room smelled of dust and decay.

It was clear she had been there for a very long time. She was sitting on a wooden chair.

'It looks like she died from a head wound. Her skull looks fractured,' the Professor said. He was shining a torch at the back of her head.

'It's so awful,' Frank said.

Her face was no longer there. Her hands were merely bones. I could see a gold ring around her finger with empty prongs that held no stone. What had she felt in those last moments? Who had locked her away? Had someone murdered her?

The dress was made of emerald silk with bluebirds on gold and silver branches on the breast. It was the same pattern as Abigail Harton's wedding dress. In fact, the pattern was almost identical.

This poor girl had to be Miss Elizabeth Goulding. She had never eloped with Dr. Monroe. Instead she had been left to die inside the castle's walls, hidden for almost three centuries, her spirit forced to wander the castle alone.

'We had best leave her be. With human remains we need to contact the police as a formality,' the Professor said and held my hand as we left the room.

'She can be laid to rest at last, the poor soul,' Frank said as he turned the key in the hidden door.

I thought about Elizabeth and Abigail as I flew back home. The papers in Dublin had made a sensation of the girl in the emerald dress, and it had gotten news coverage on all of the national channels by the time I left.

I looked across to the window where the Professor slept. He had wanted to be with me when I told Aunt Jeannie the news first-hand. After that we planned to visit my family in California. When the summer was over the Professor would have to return home. I guessed I would be visiting Dublin on a regular basis after that.

I sat back in my seat and ordered a glass of wine. The future looked bright and I smiled, thinking of how Hugh Gavin and Abigail Harton must have felt three hundred years ago when they made their first voyage to America.

THE END

BIBLIOGRAPHY

Journals

Baudis, Macushla. "Smoaking hot with fashion from Paris': The Consumption of French Fashion in Eighteenth-Century Ireland'. *The Costume Journal* Volume 48, Issue 2, pp. 141-159. Edinburgh, 2014.

Lee, Gerard A. 'The Dublin of Jonathan Swift', *Dublin Historical Record* Volume XXI, pp 30-45. Dublin, 1967.

Books

Alexander, Hannah. *A Book of Cookery for Dressing of Several Dishes of Meat and Making of Several Sauces and Seasoning for Meat or Fowl,* edited by Deirdre Nuttall. Cathair na Mart, Co. Mhaigh Eo, Éire: Evertype, 2014.

Barnard, Toby. *Making the Grand Figure: Lives and Possessions in Ireland 1641-1770.* New Haven and London: Yale University Press, 2004.

Blackett-Ord, Mark. *Hell-Fire Duke.* Windsor Forest, Berkshire: Kensal Press, 1982.

Burns, Kieran. *Number Twenty-Nine: A Guide to an Exhibition of Home Life in Dublin 1790-1820.* Dublin: National Museum of Ireland, 2002.

Clarke, Norma. *Queen of the Wits: A Life of Laetitia Pilkington.* London: Faber & Faber, 2008.

Coakley, Davis. *Irish Masters of Medicine.* Dublin: Townhouse, 1992.

Craig, Maurice. *Dublin 1660-1860: The Shaping of a City.* Dublin: Liberties Press, 2007.

Dunlevy, Mairead. *Pomp and Poverty: A History of Silk in Ireland.* New Haven and London: Yale University Press, 2011.

Glendinning, Victoria. *Jonathan Swift.* London: Hutchinson, 1998.

Hart, A. and North, S. *Seventeenth and Eighteenth-Century Fashion in Detail.* London: V&A Publishing, 2009.

Maxwell, Constantia. *Dublin under the Georges.* London: G.G. Harrap, 1936.

Melville, Lewis. *The Life and Writings of Philip Duke of Wharton.* Edinburgh: John Lane/Bodley Head, 1913.

Marsh, Gail. *18th Century Embroidery Techniques.* Lewes, East Sussex: GMC Publications, 2006.

Olsen, Kirsten. *Daily Life in 18th Century England.* Westport Connecticut and London: Greenwood, 1999.

Robbins, Joseph. *Champagne and Buckles: The Viceregal Court at Dublin Castle 1700-1922*. Dublin: The Lilliput Press Ltd, 2001.

Swift, Jonathan. *Directions to Servants.* London: Hesperus Press; New Ed edition, 2003.

Vickery, Amanda. *The Gentleman's Daughter: Women's Lives in Georgian England.* New Haven and London: Yale University Press, 1998.

Waugh, Norah. *Corsets and Crinolines.* New York: HarperCollins Distribution Services; New impression edition, 1970.

Worsley, Lucy. *Courtiers: The Secret History of the Georgian Court.* London: Yale University Press, 2010.

Maps

Lennon, Colm. *Irish Historic Towns Atlas No.19. Dublin Part II, 1610 to 1756.* Map. Dublin: Royal Irish Academy, 2008.